D0521302

FATALE

WITHDRAWN

ED BRUBAKER SEAN PHILLIPS

FATALE

BOOK FIVE

CURSE THE DEMON

By ED BRUBAKER and SEAN PHILLIPS

Colors by Elizabeth Breitweiser

MEDIA INQUIRIES SHOULD BE DIRECTED TO UTA - Agents Julien Thuan and Geoff Morley

IMAGE COMICS, INC.
Robert Kirkman - chief operating officer
Erik Larsen - chief financial officer
Todd McFarlane - president
Marc Silvestri - chief executive officer
Jim Valentino - vice-president

Eric Stephenson - publisher
Ron Richards - director of business development
Jennifer de Guzman - director of trade book sales
Kat Salazar - director of pr & marketing
Corey Murphy - director of retail sales
Jeremy Sullivan - director of digital sales
Emilio Bautista - sales assistant
Branwyn Bigglestone - senior accounts manager
Emily Miller - accounts manager
Jessica Ambriz - administrative assistant
Tyler Shainline - events coordinator
David Brothers - content manager
Jonathan Chan - production manager
Drew Gill - art director
Meredith Wallace - print manager
Monica Garcia - senior production artist
Jenna Savage - production artist
Addison Duke - production artist
Tricia Ramos - production assistant
www.imagecomics.com

FATALE, BOOK FIVE: CURSE THE DEMON. First printing. September 2014. ISBN: 978-1-63215-007-3. Published by Image Comics, Inc. Office of publication: 2001 Center Street, 6th Floor, Berkeley, CA, 94704.
Copyright © 2014 Basement Gang, Inc. All rights reserved. FATALE™ (including all prominent characters featured herein), their logos and all character likenesses are trademarks of Basement Gang, Inc., unless otherwise noted. Image Comics® is a trademark of Image Comics, Inc. All rights reserved. Contains material originally published in magazine form as FATALE #20-24. No part of this publication may be reproduced or transmitted, in any form or by any means (except for short excerpts for review purposes) without the express written permission of Basement Gang, Inc. and Image Comics, Inc. All names, characters, events and locale in this publication are entirely fictional. Any resemblance to actual persons (living or dead), events or places, without satiric intent, is coincidental. Printed in the U.S.A. For information regarding the CPSIA on this printed material call: 203-595-3636 and provide reference #RICH-583752.

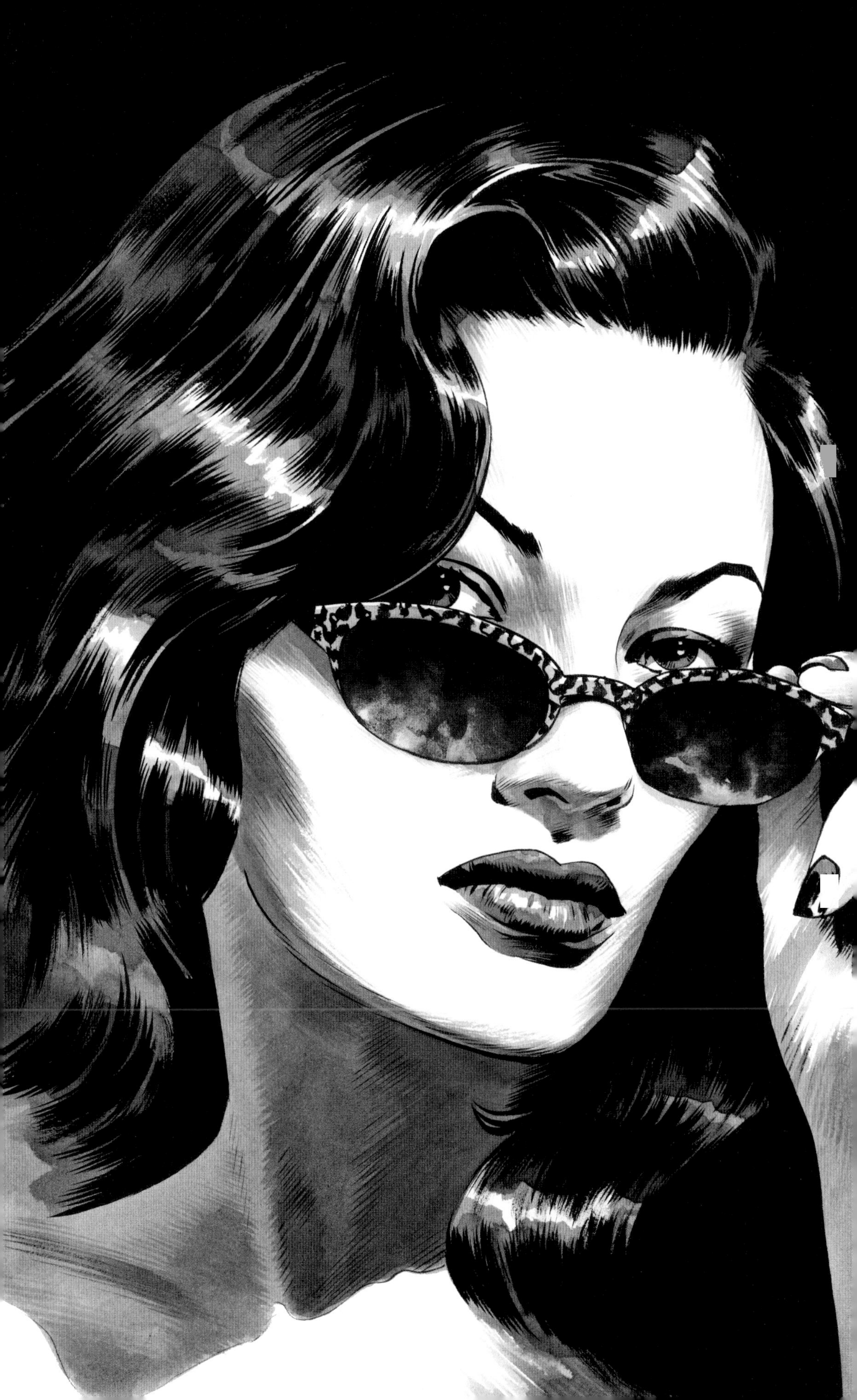

Chapter One

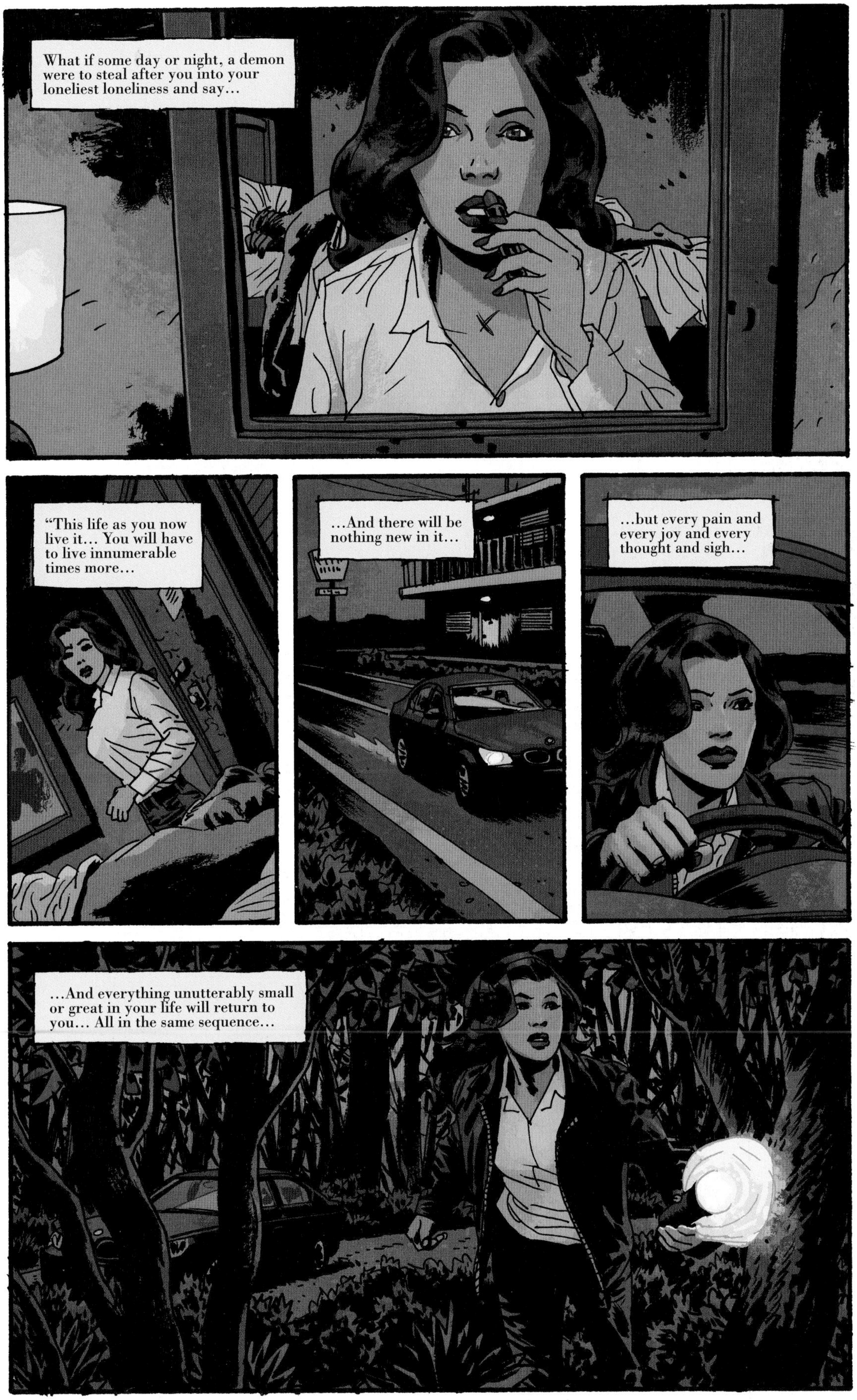
What if some day or night, a demon were to steal after you into your loneliest loneliness and say...
"This life as you now live it... You will have to live innumerable times more...
...And there will be nothing new in it...
...but every pain and every joy and every thought and sigh...
...And everything unutterably small or great in your life will return to you... All in the same sequence...

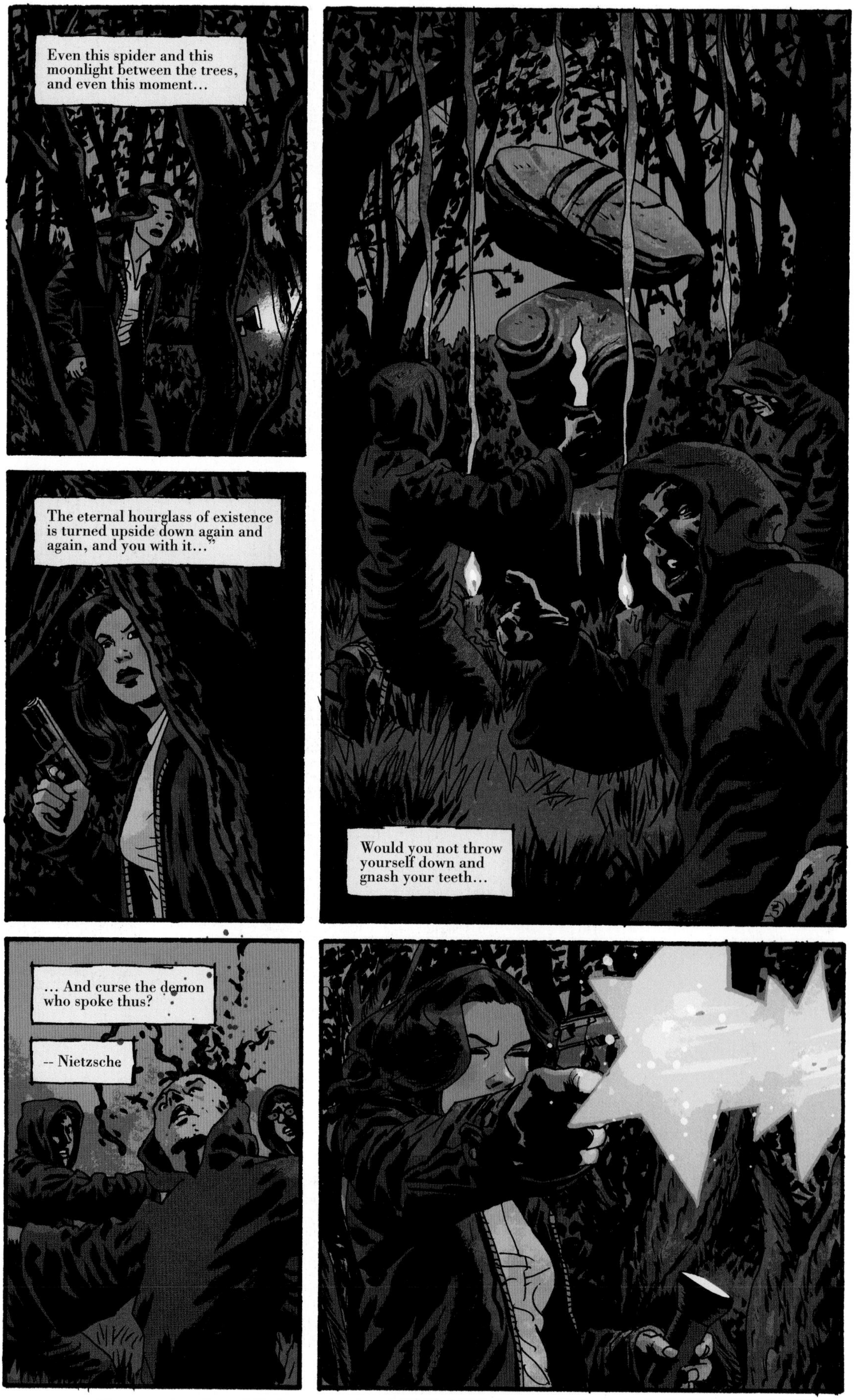
Even this spider and this moonlight between the trees, and even this moment…
The eternal hourglass of existence is turned upside down again and again, and you with it…"
Would you not throw yourself down and gnash your teeth…
… And curse the demon who spoke thus?
-- Nietzsche

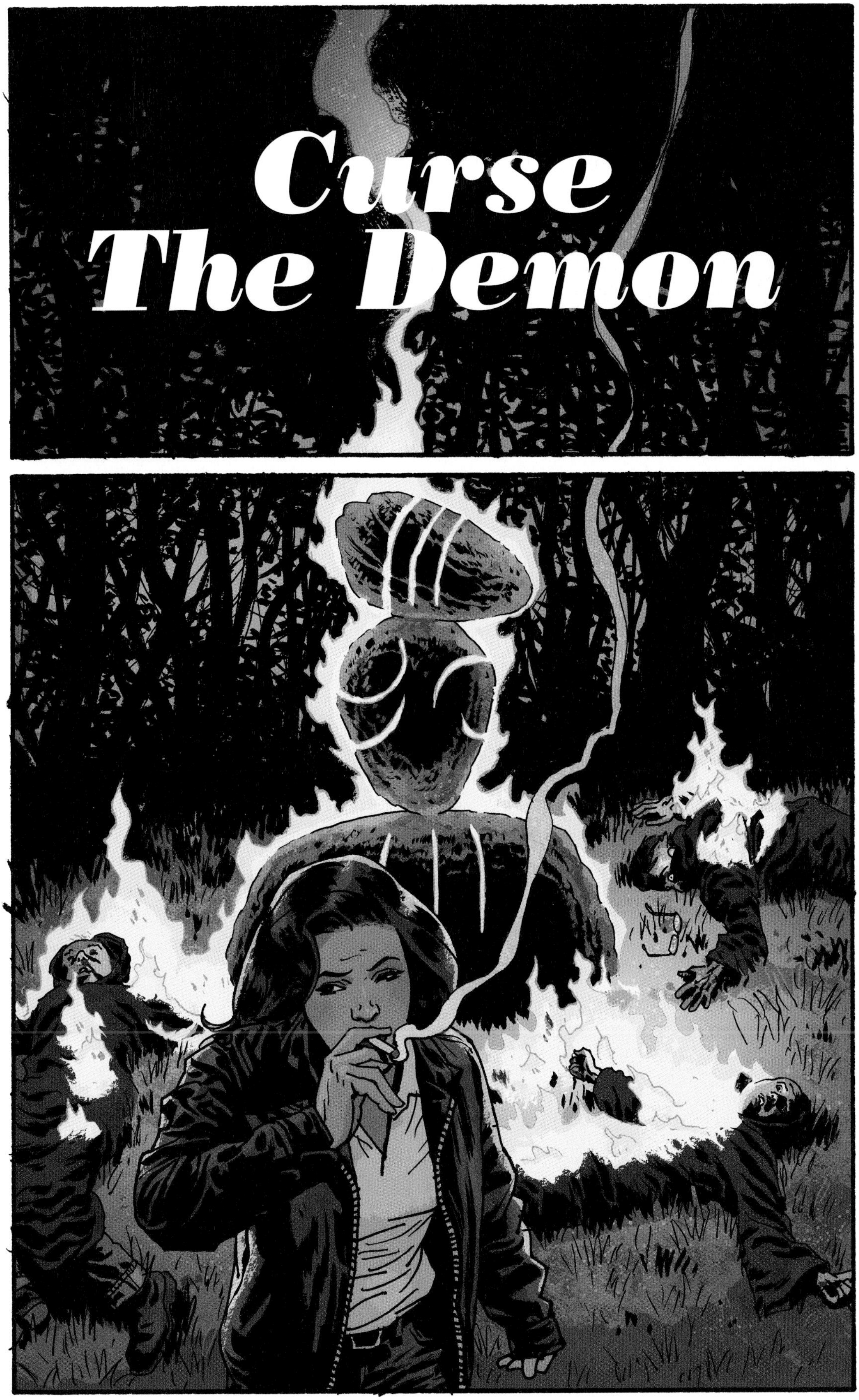
Curse
The Demon

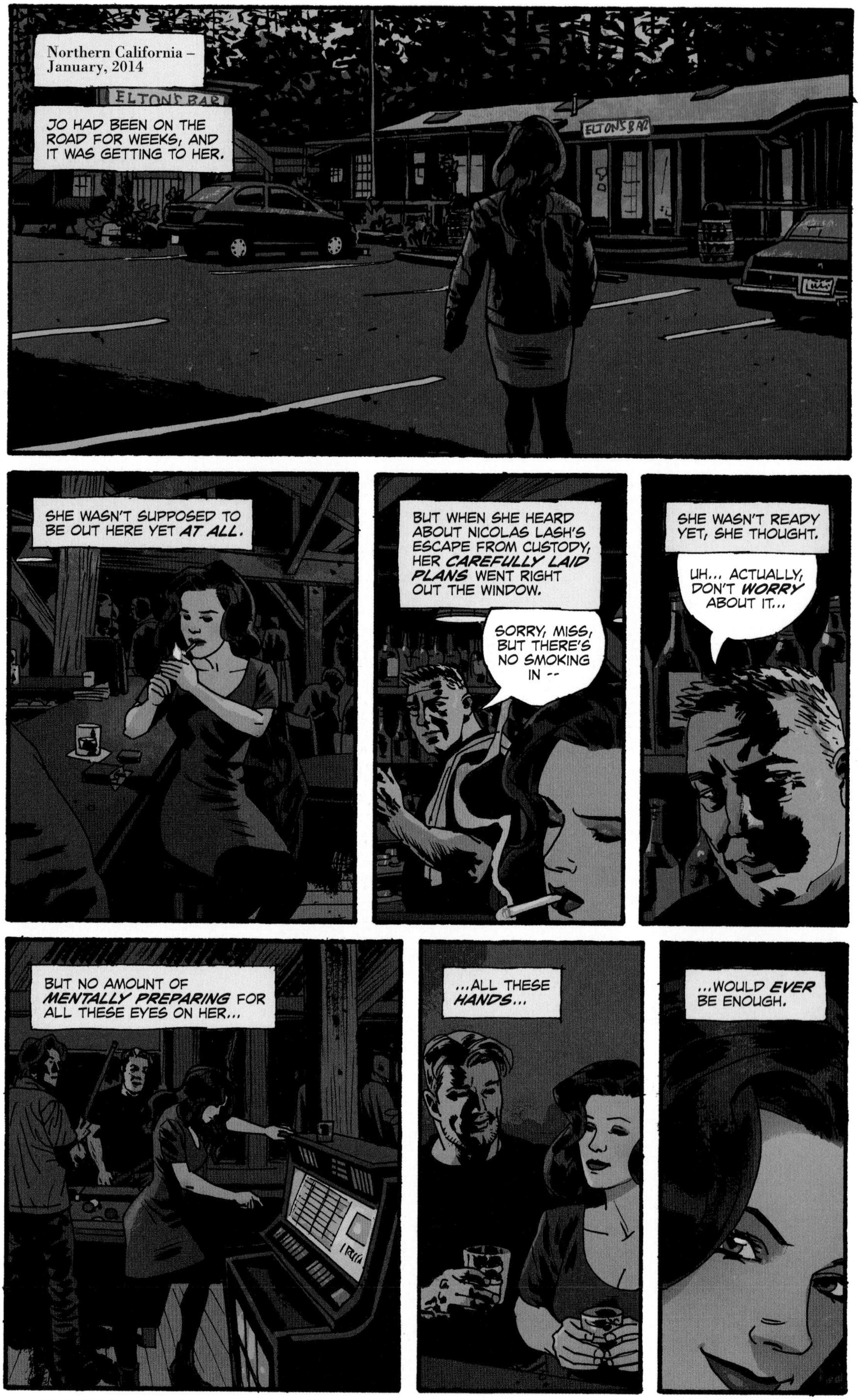

Northern California – January, 2014
ELTON'S BAR
JO HAD BEEN ON THE ROAD FOR WEEKS, AND IT WAS GETTING TO HER.
ELTON'S BAR
SHE WASN'T SUPPOSED TO BE OUT HERE YET AT ALL.
BUT WHEN SHE HEARD ABOUT NICOLAS LASH'S ESCAPE FROM CUSTODY, HER CAREFULLY LAID PLANS WENT RIGHT OUT THE WINDOW.
SORRY, MISS, BUT THERE'S NO SMOKING IN --
SHE WASN'T READY YET, SHE THOUGHT.
UH... ACTUALLY, DON'T WORRY ABOUT IT...
BUT NO AMOUNT OF MENTALLY PREPARING FOR ALL THESE EYES ON HER...
...ALL THESE HANDS...
...WOULD EVER BE ENOUGH.

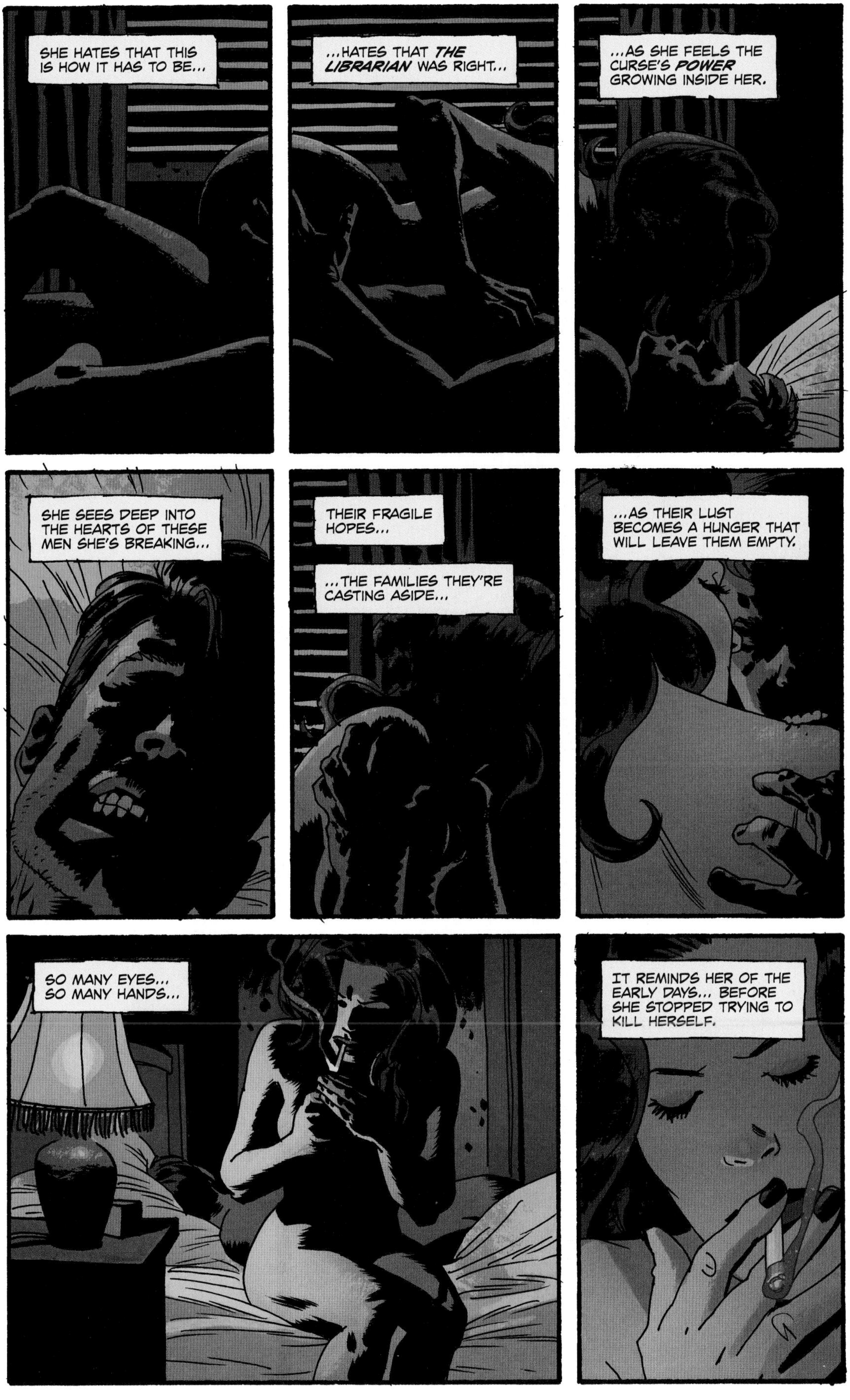
SHE HATES THAT THIS IS HOW IT HAS TO BE...
...HATES THAT *THE LIBRARIAN* WAS RIGHT...
...AS SHE FEELS THE CURSE'S *POWER* GROWING INSIDE HER.
SHE SEES DEEP INTO THE HEARTS OF THESE MEN SHE'S BREAKING...
THEIR FRAGILE HOPES...
...THE FAMILIES THEY'RE CASTING ASIDE...
...AS THEIR LUST BECOMES A HUNGER THAT WILL LEAVE THEM EMPTY.
SO MANY EYES... SO MANY HANDS...
IT REMINDS HER OF THE EARLY DAYS... BEFORE SHE STOPPED TRYING TO KILL HERSELF.

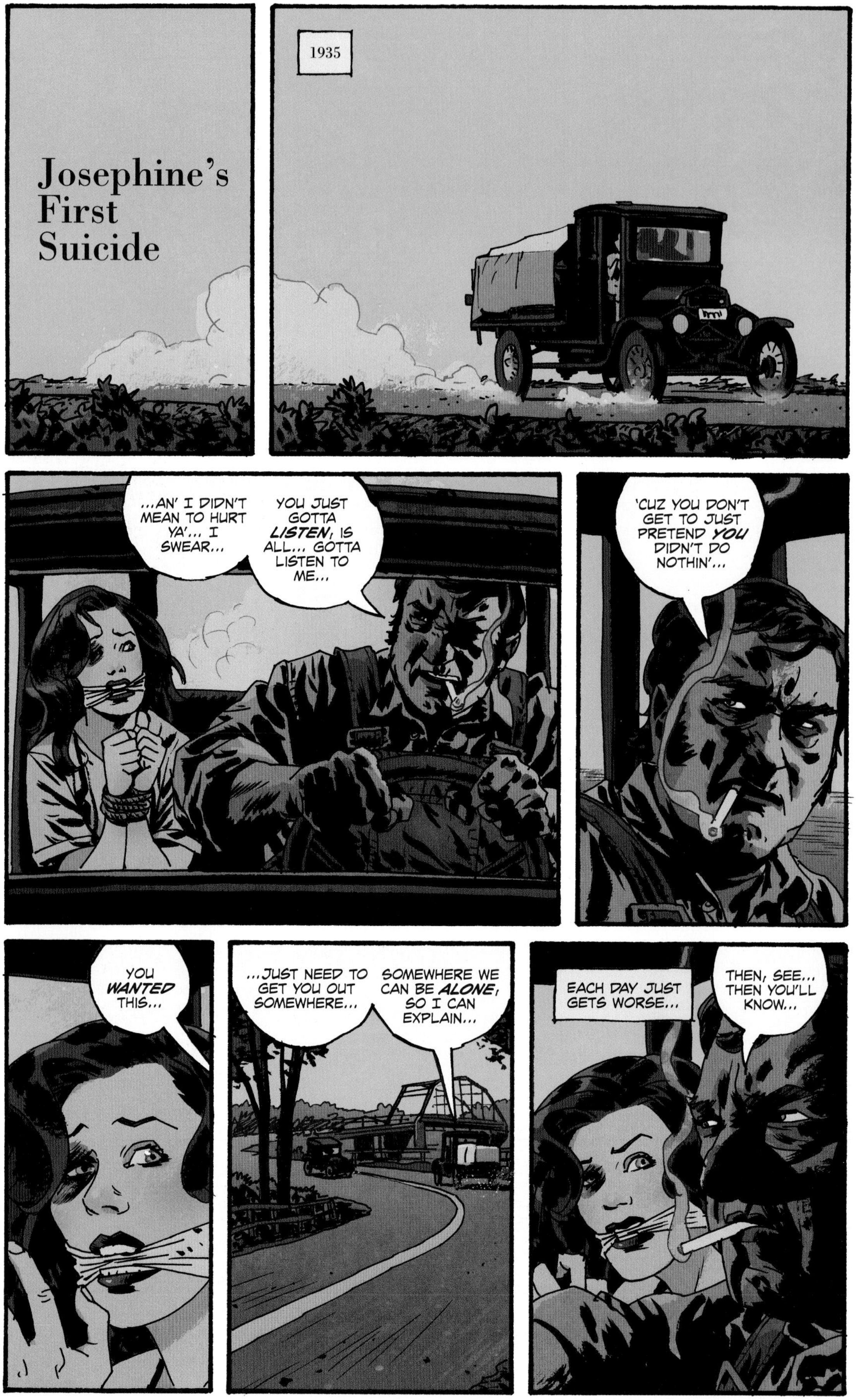
Josephine's First Suicide
1935
...AN' I DIDN'T MEAN TO HURT YA'... I SWEAR...
YOU JUST GOTTA LISTEN, IS ALL... GOTTA LISTEN TO ME...
'CUZ YOU DON'T GET TO JUST PRETEND YOU DIDN'T DO NOTHIN'...
YOU WANTED THIS...
...JUST NEED TO GET YOU OUT SOMEWHERE...
SOMEWHERE WE CAN BE ALONE, SO I CAN EXPLAIN...
EACH DAY JUST GETS WORSE...
THEN, SEE... THEN YOU'LL KNOW...

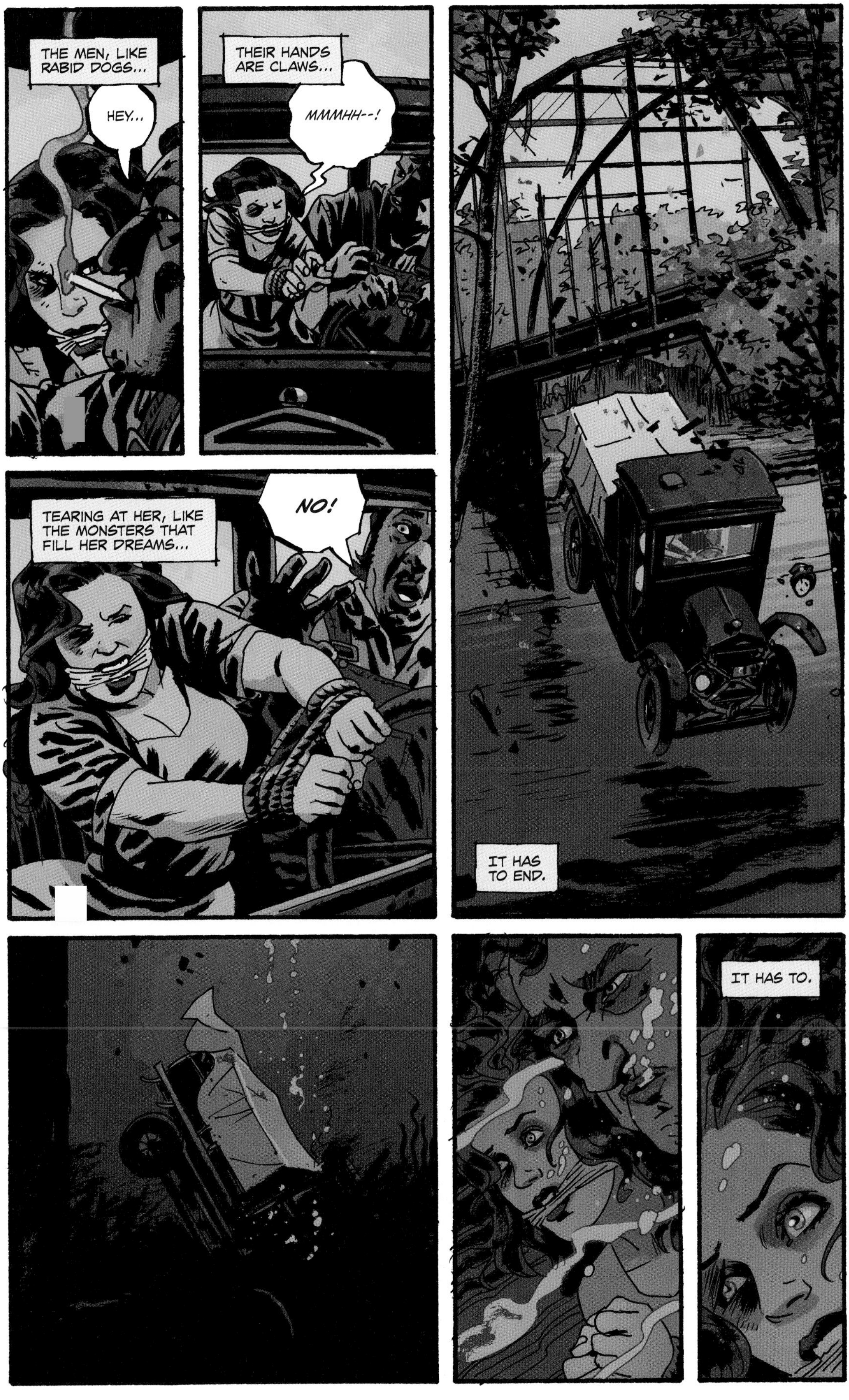
THE MEN, LIKE RABID DOGS...
HEY...
THEIR HANDS ARE CLAWS...
MMMHH--!
TEARING AT HER, LIKE THE MONSTERS THAT FILL HER DREAMS...
NO!
IT HAS TO END.
IT HAS TO.

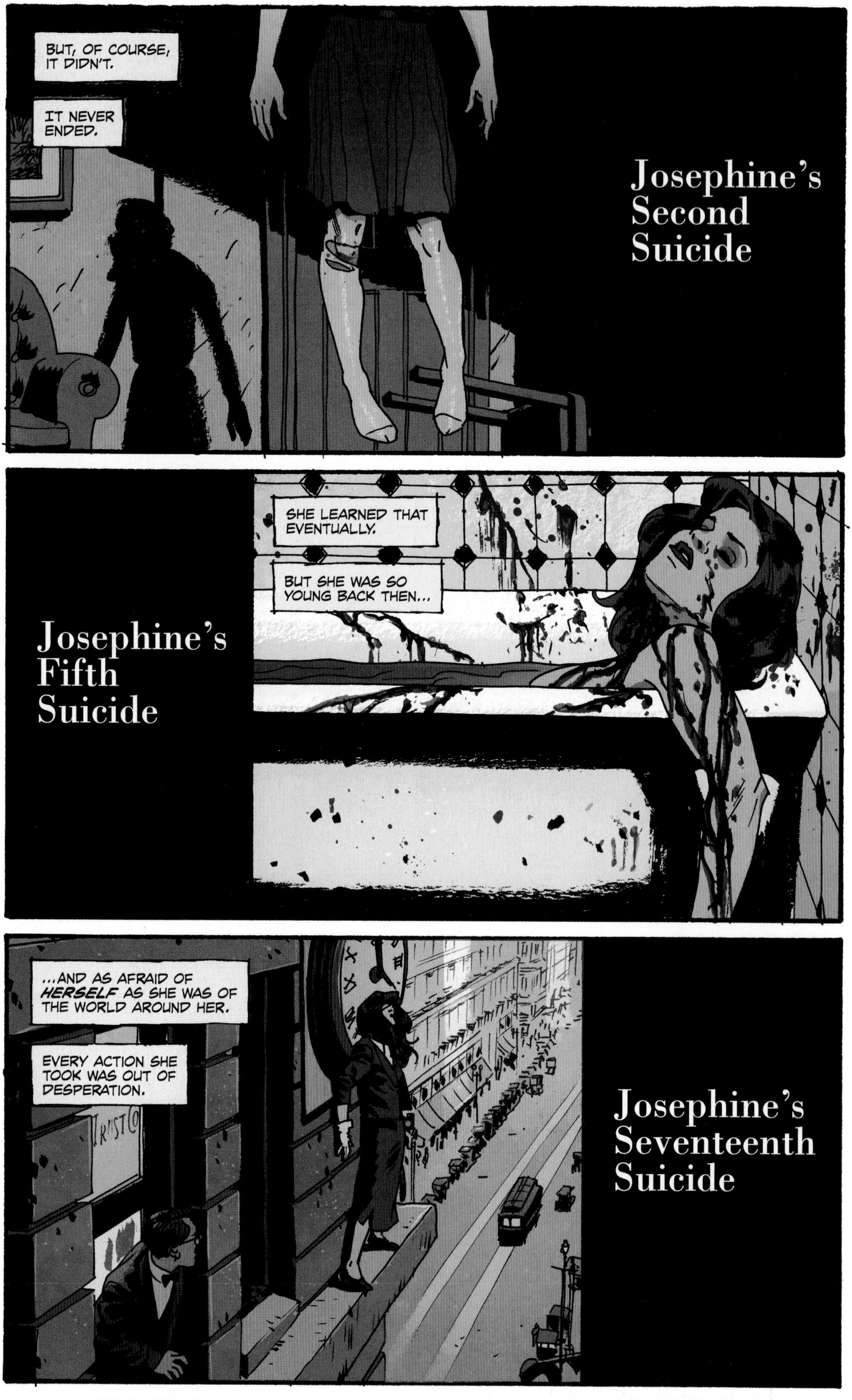
BUT, OF COURSE, IT DIDN'T.
IT NEVER ENDED.
Josephine's Second Suicide
Josephine's Fifth Suicide
SHE LEARNED THAT EVENTUALLY.
BUT SHE WAS SO YOUNG BACK THEN...
...AND AS AFRAID OF *HERSELF* AS SHE WAS OF THE WORLD AROUND HER.
EVERY ACTION SHE TOOK WAS OUT OF DESPERATION.
Josephine's Seventeenth Suicide

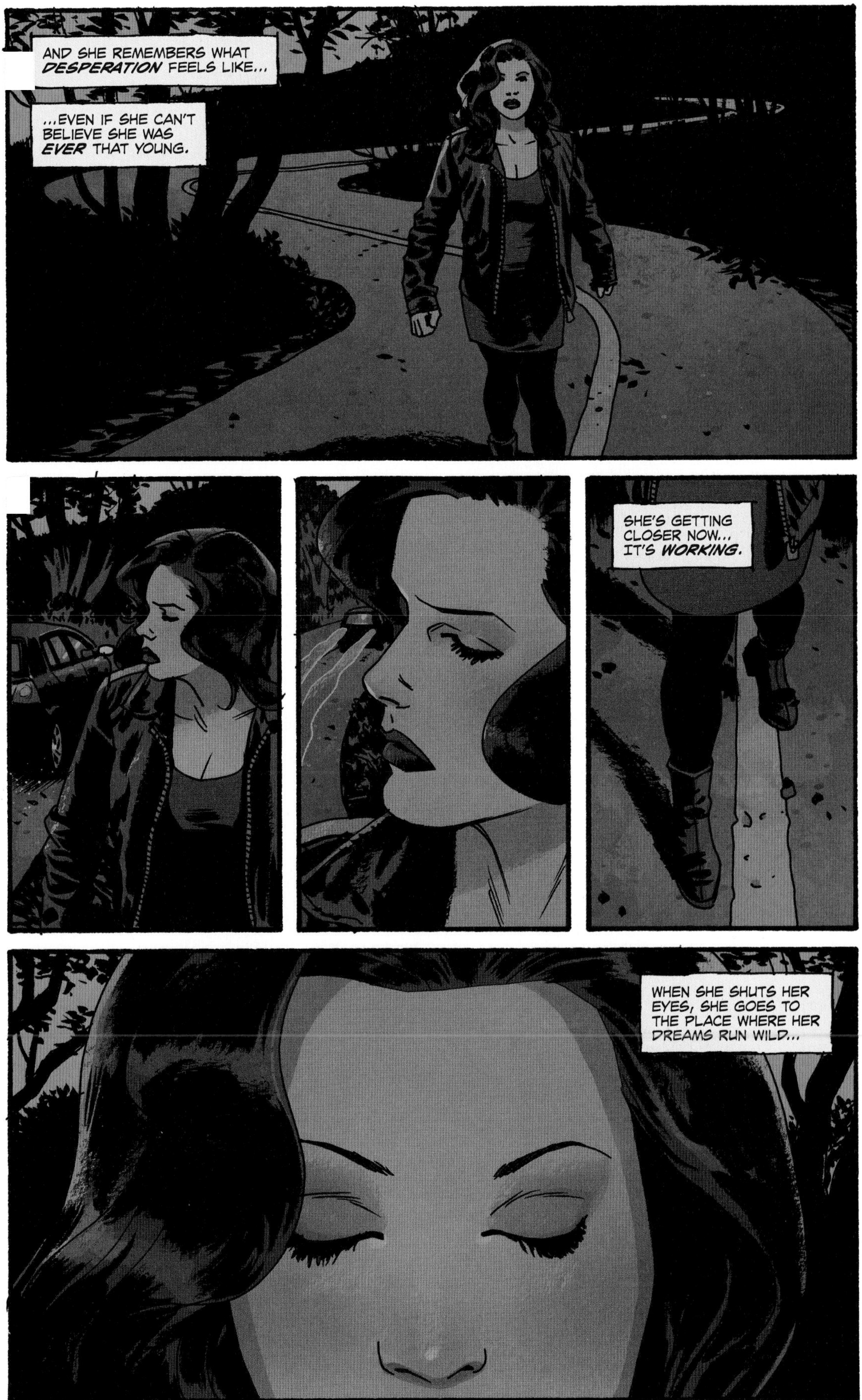
AND SHE REMEMBERS WHAT *DESPERATION* FEELS LIKE...
...EVEN IF SHE CAN'T BELIEVE SHE WAS *EVER* THAT YOUNG.
SHE'S GETTING CLOSER NOW... IT'S *WORKING.*
WHEN SHE SHUTS HER EYES, SHE GOES TO THE PLACE WHERE HER DREAMS RUN WILD...

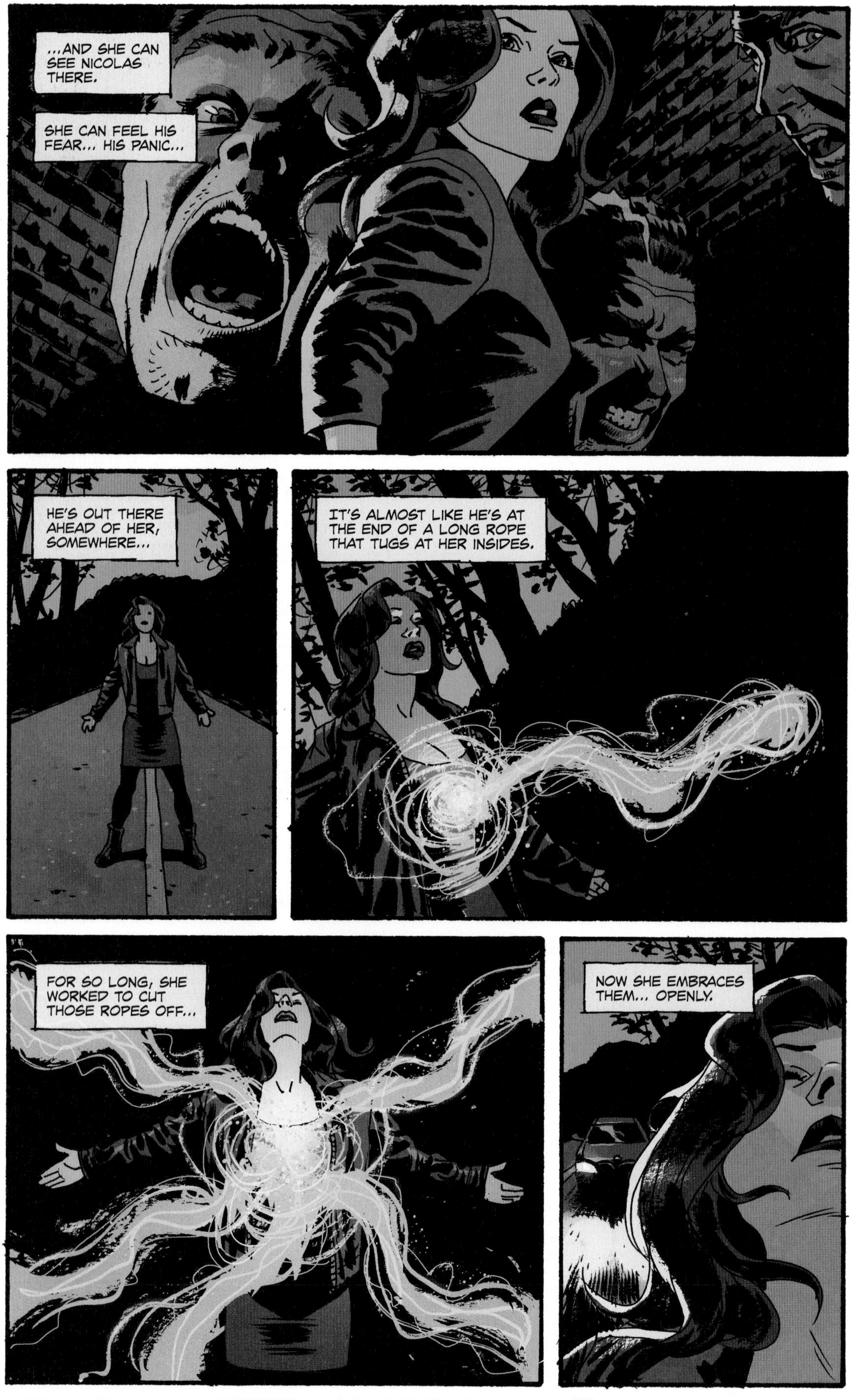
...AND SHE CAN SEE NICOLAS THERE.
SHE CAN FEEL HIS FEAR... HIS PANIC...
HE'S OUT THERE AHEAD OF HER, SOMEWHERE...
IT'S ALMOST LIKE HE'S AT THE END OF A LONG ROPE THAT TUGS AT HER INSIDES.
FOR SO LONG, SHE WORKED TO CUT THOSE ROPES OFF...
NOW SHE EMBRACES THEM... OPENLY.

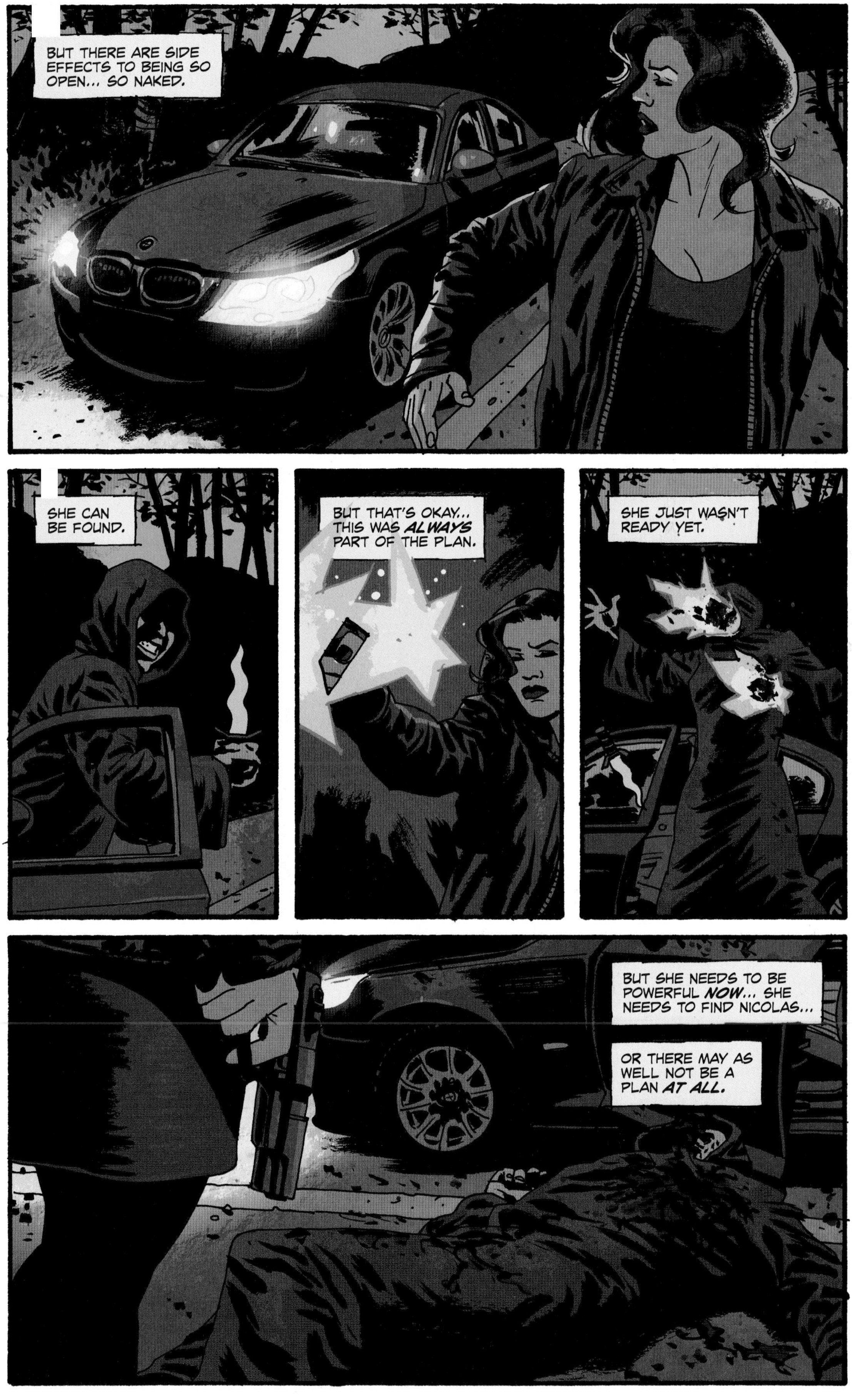
BUT THERE ARE SIDE EFFECTS TO BEING SO OPEN... SO NAKED.
SHE CAN BE FOUND.
BUT THAT'S OKAY... THIS WAS ALWAYS PART OF THE PLAN.
SHE JUST WASN'T READY YET.
BUT SHE NEEDS TO BE POWERFUL NOW... SHE NEEDS TO FIND NICOLAS...
OR THERE MAY AS WELL NOT BE A PLAN AT ALL.

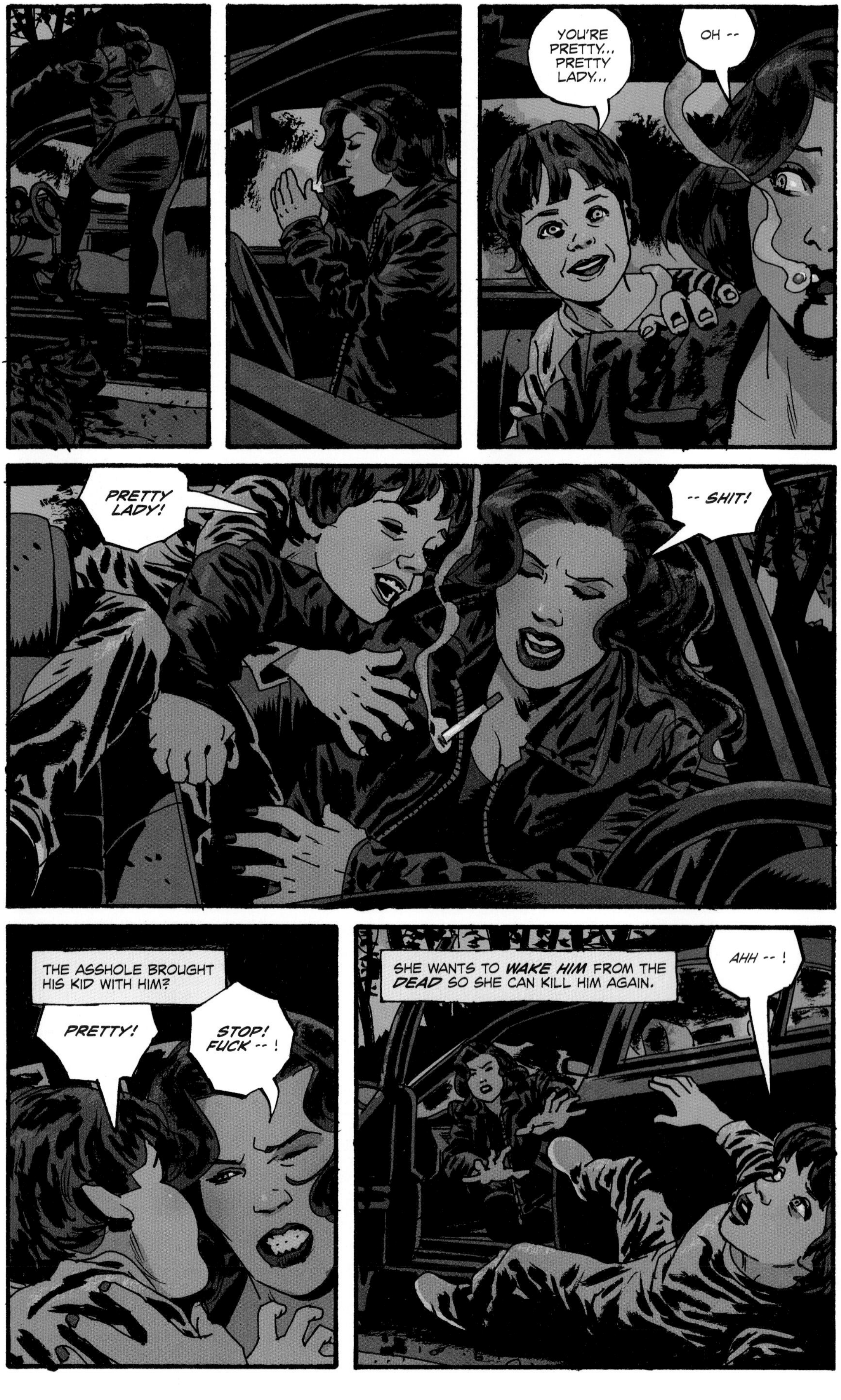
YOU'RE PRETTY... PRETTY LADY...
OH --
PRETTY LADY!
-- SHIT!
THE ASSHOLE BROUGHT HIS KID WITH HIM?
PRETTY!
STOP! FUCK -- !
SHE WANTS TO WAKE HIM FROM THE DEAD SO SHE CAN KILL HIM AGAIN.
AHH -- !

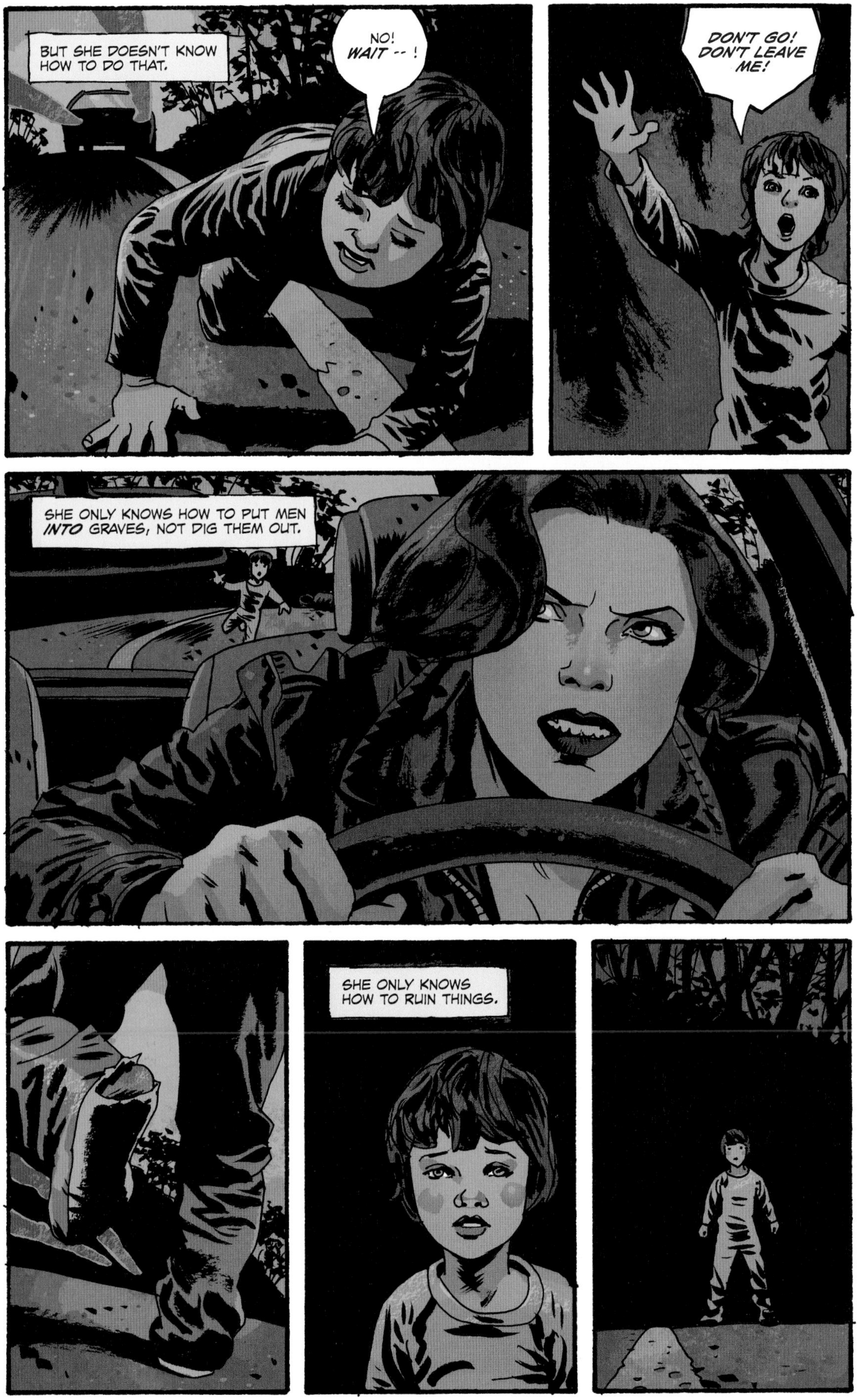
BUT SHE DOESN'T KNOW HOW TO DO THAT.
NO! *WAIT* -- !
DON'T GO! DON'T LEAVE ME!
SHE ONLY KNOWS HOW TO PUT MEN *INTO* GRAVES, NOT DIG THEM OUT.
SHE ONLY KNOWS HOW TO RUIN THINGS.

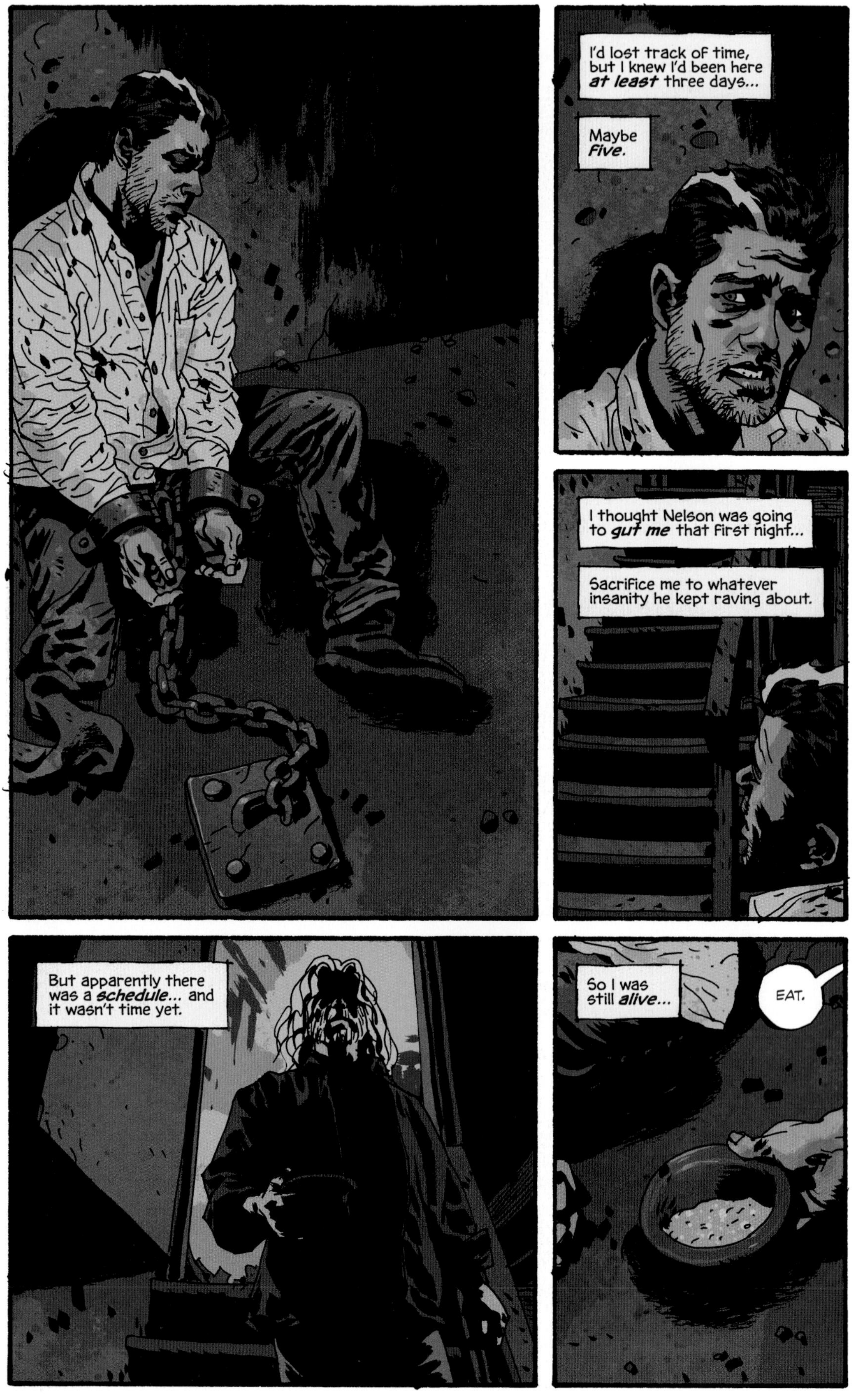
I'd lost track of time, but I knew I'd been here *at least* three days...
Maybe *five*.
I thought Nelson was going to *gut me* that first night...
Sacrifice me to whatever insanity he kept raving about.
But apparently there was a *schedule*... and it wasn't time yet.
So I was still *alive*...
EAT.

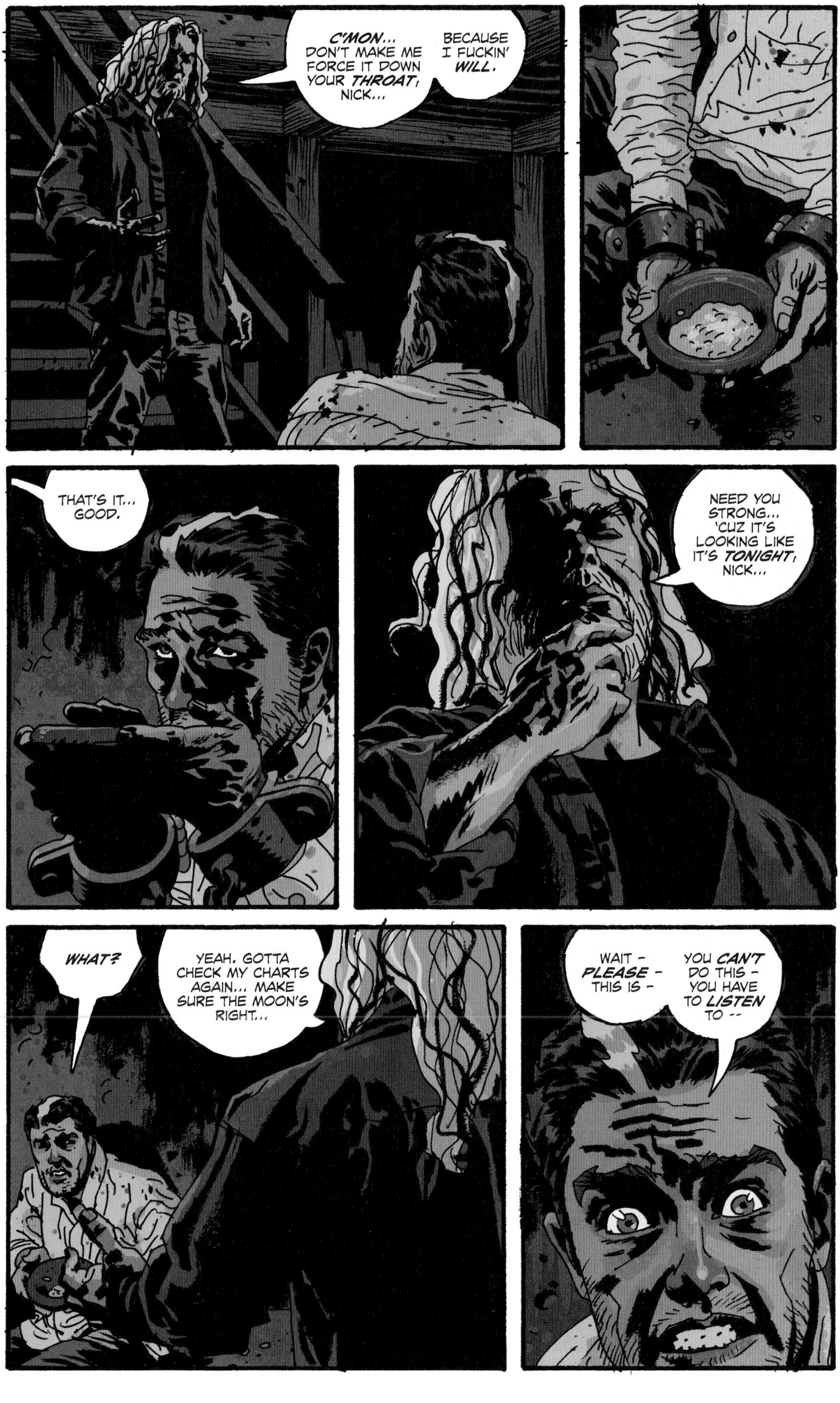
C'MON... DON'T MAKE ME FORCE IT DOWN YOUR THROAT, NICK...
BECAUSE I FUCKIN' WILL.
THAT'S IT... GOOD.
NEED YOU STRONG... 'CUZ IT'S LOOKING LIKE IT'S TONIGHT, NICK...
WHAT?
YEAH. GOTTA CHECK MY CHARTS AGAIN... MAKE SURE THE MOON'S RIGHT...
WAIT - PLEASE - THIS IS -
YOU CAN'T DO THIS - YOU HAVE TO LISTEN TO --

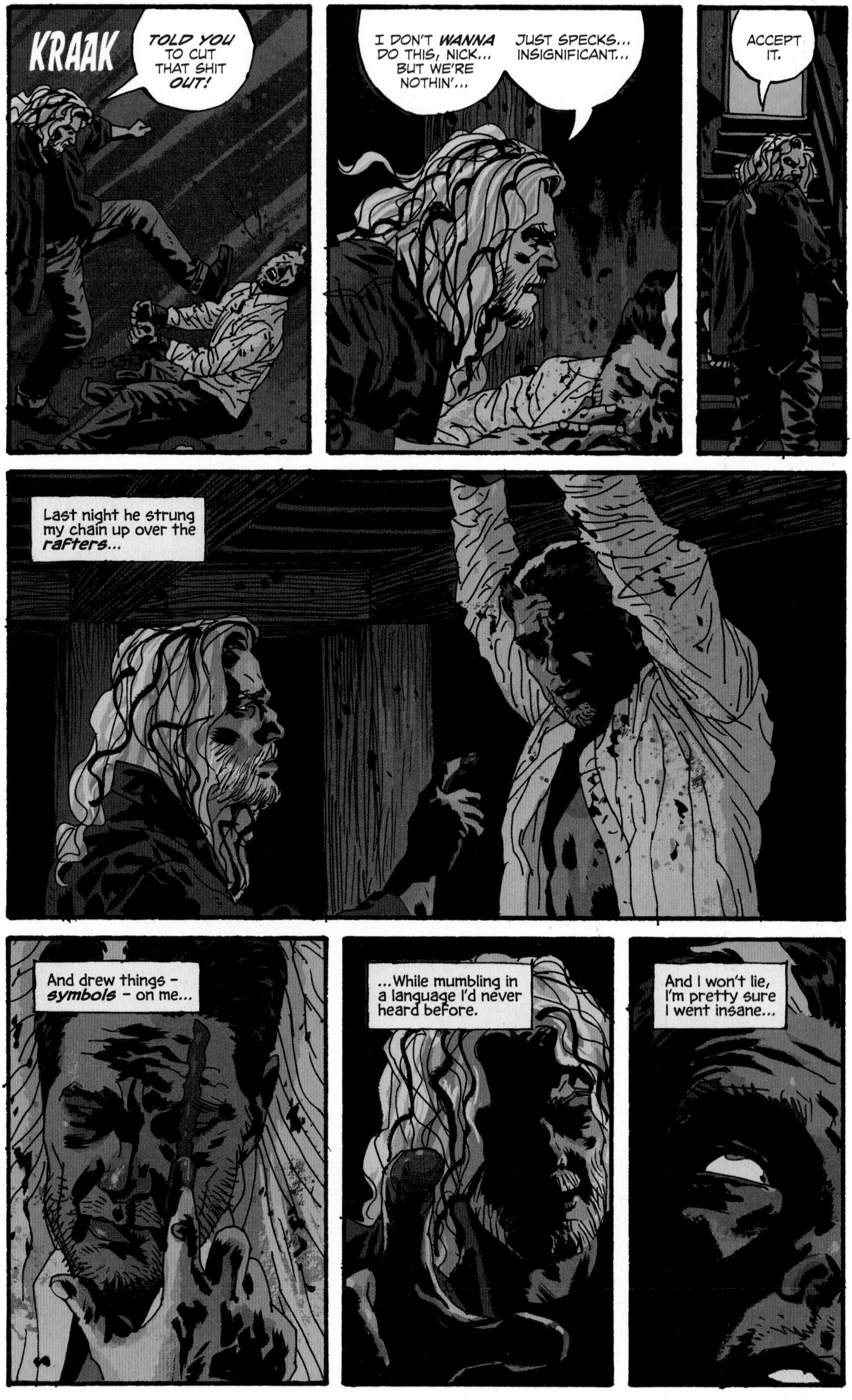

KRAAK
TOLD YOU TO CUT THAT SHIT OUT!
I DON'T WANNA DO THIS, NICK... BUT WE'RE NOTHIN'...
JUST SPECKS... INSIGNIFICANT...
ACCEPT IT.
Last night he strung my chain up over the rafters...
And drew things - symbols - on me...
...While mumbling in a language I'd never heard before.
And I won't lie, I'm pretty sure I went insane...

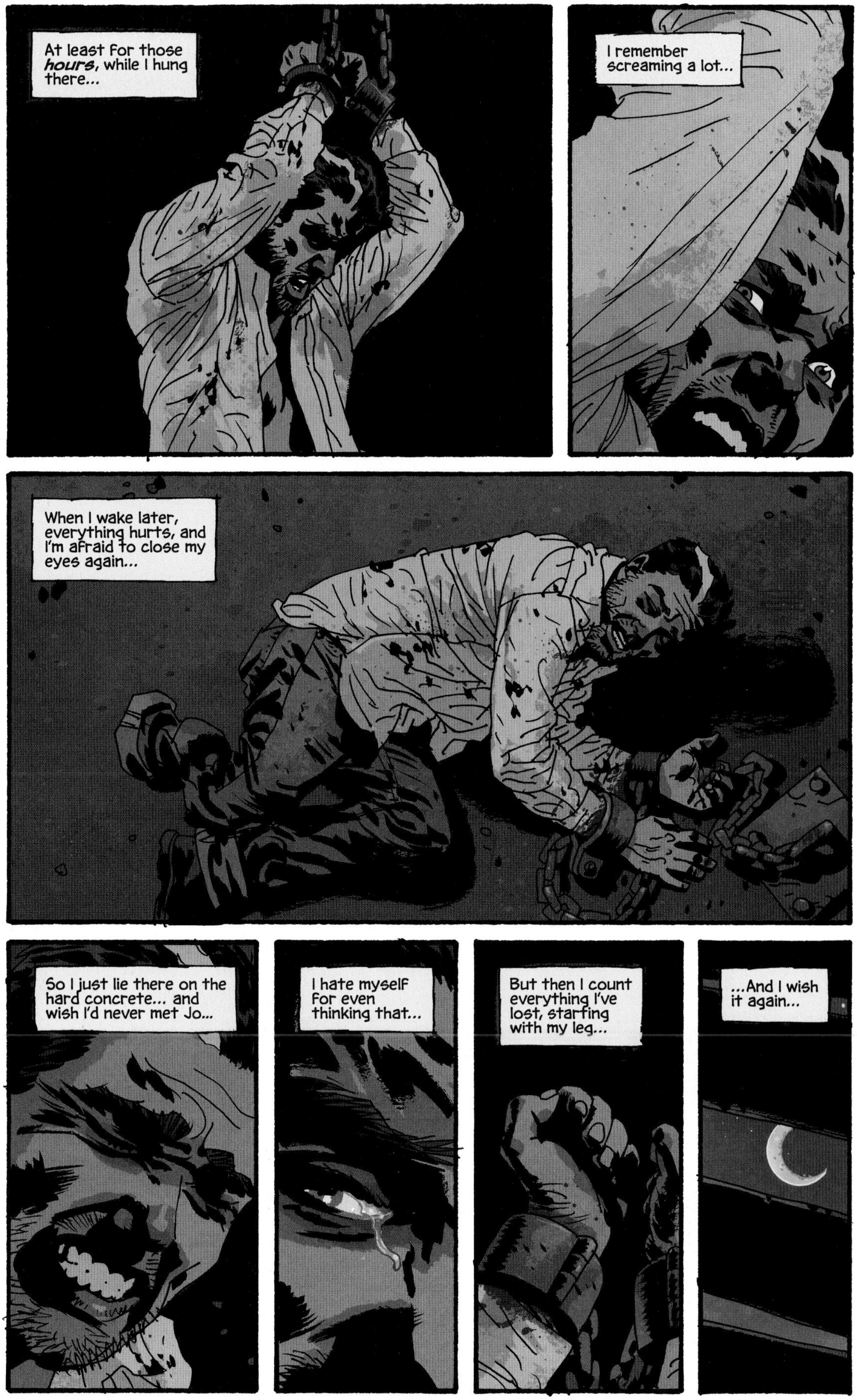
At least for those *hours*, while I hung there...
I remember screaming a lot...
When I wake later, everything hurts, and I'm afraid to close my eyes again...
So I just lie there on the hard concrete... and wish I'd never met Jo...
I hate myself for even thinking that...
But then I count everything I've lost, starting with my leg...
...And I wish it again...

And that's what I'm thinking now, as my mind races, desperate...

Scrambling for one last way out.

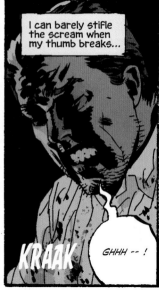

I can barely stifle the scream when my thumb breaks...

KRAAK

GHHH -- !

...But I do.

...C'MON...

FUCK!

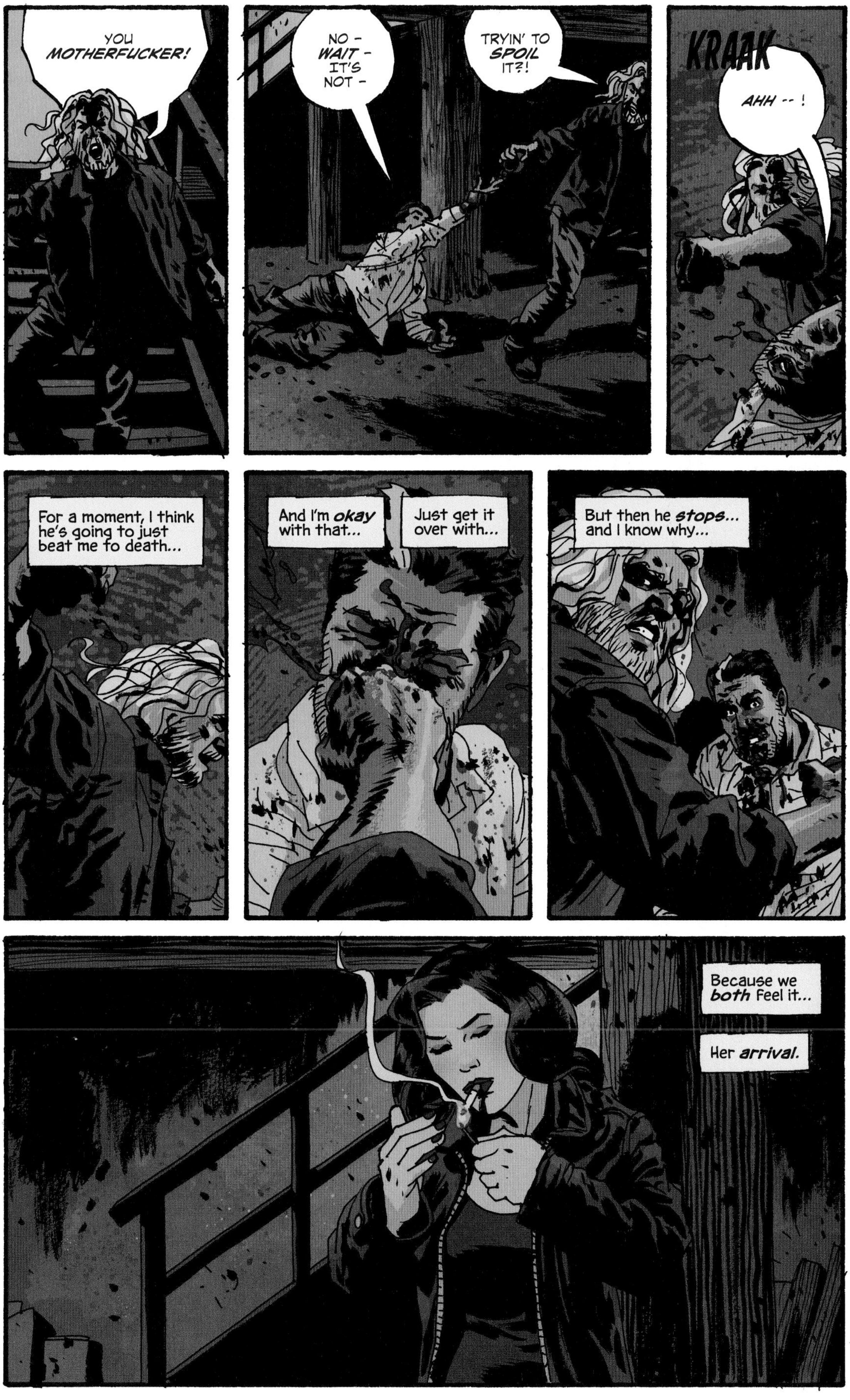

YOU *MOTHERFUCKER!*
NO - *WAIT* - IT'S NOT -
TRYIN' TO *SPOIL* IT?!
KRAAK
AHH -- !
For a moment, I think he's going to just beat me to death...
And I'm *okay* with that...
Just get it over with...
But then he *stops*... and I know why...
Because we *both* feel it...
Her *arrival*.

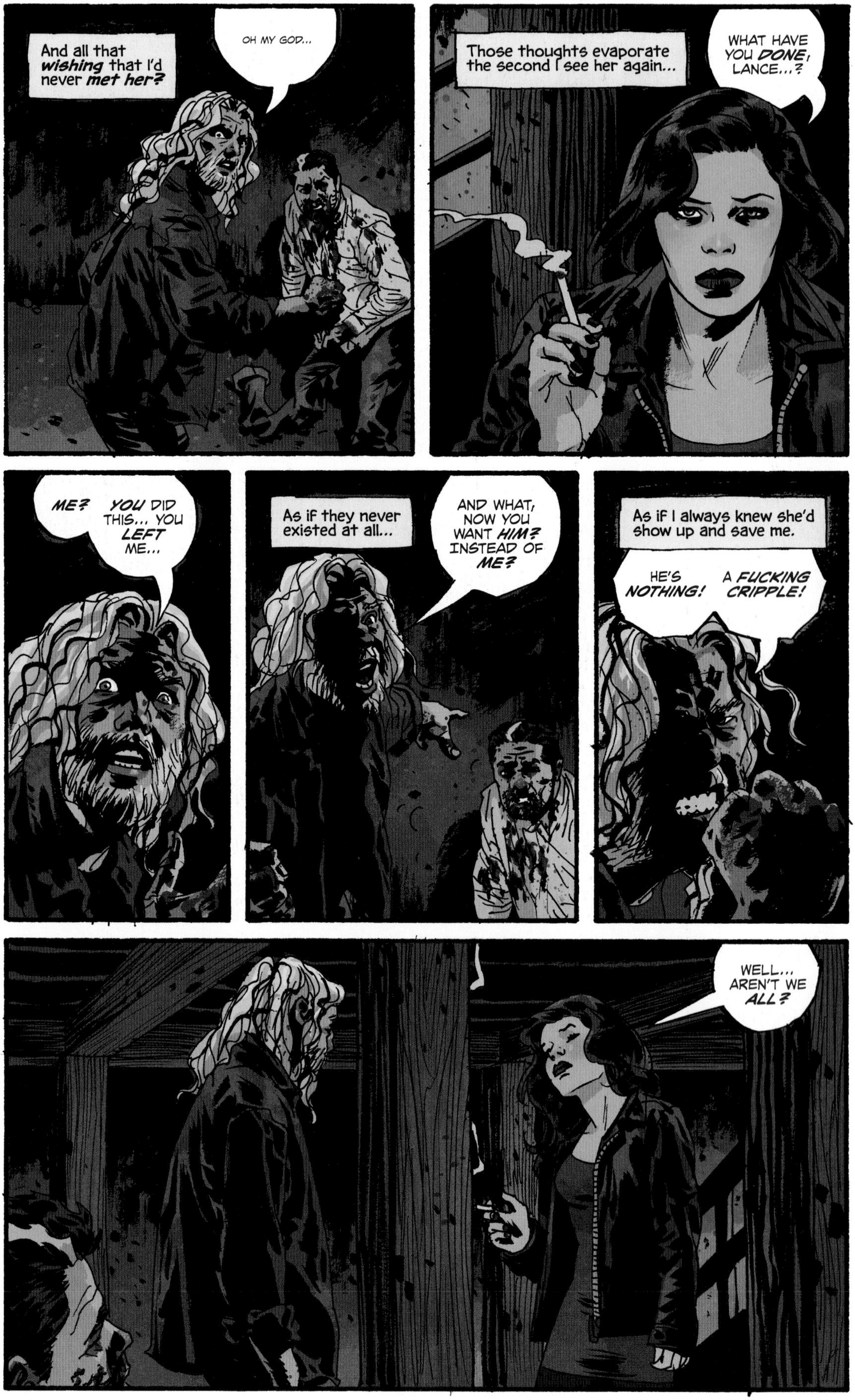

And all that *wishing* that I'd never *met her?*
OH MY GOD...
Those thoughts evaporate the second I see her again...
WHAT HAVE YOU *DONE*, LANCE...?
ME? YOU DID THIS... YOU *LEFT* ME...
As if they never existed at all...
AND WHAT, NOW YOU WANT *HIM?* INSTEAD OF *ME?*
As if I always knew she'd show up and save me.
HE'S *NOTHING!*
A *FUCKING CRIPPLE!*
WELL... AREN'T WE *ALL?*

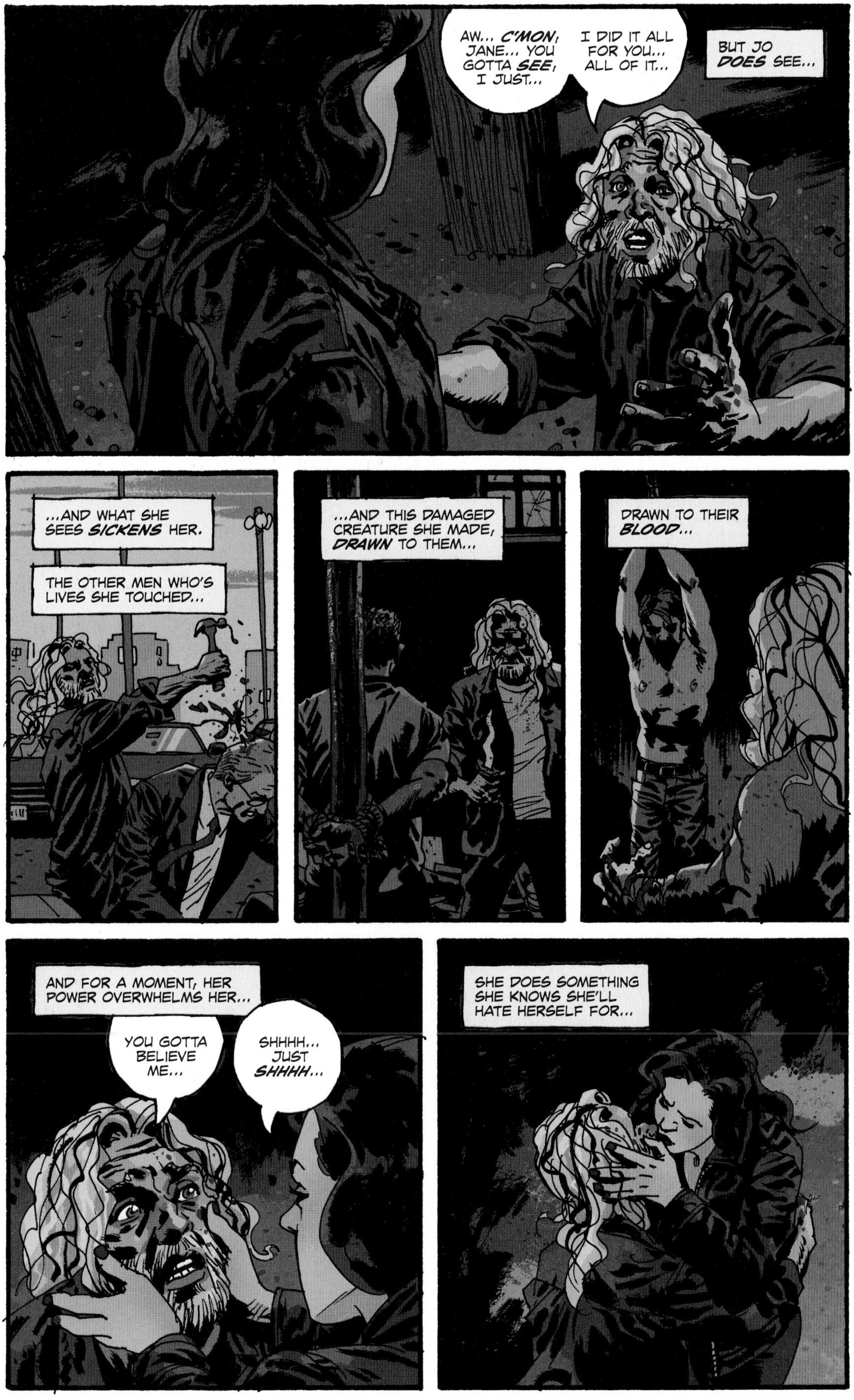
AW... C'MON, JANE... YOU GOTTA SEE, I JUST...
I DID IT ALL FOR YOU... ALL OF IT...
BUT JO DOES SEE...
...AND WHAT SHE SEES SICKENS HER.
THE OTHER MEN WHO'S LIVES SHE TOUCHED...
...AND THIS DAMAGED CREATURE SHE MADE, DRAWN TO THEM...
DRAWN TO THEIR BLOOD...
AND FOR A MOMENT, HER POWER OVERWHELMS HER...
YOU GOTTA BELIEVE ME...
SHHHH... JUST SHHHH...
SHE DOES SOMETHING SHE KNOWS SHE'LL HATE HERSELF FOR...

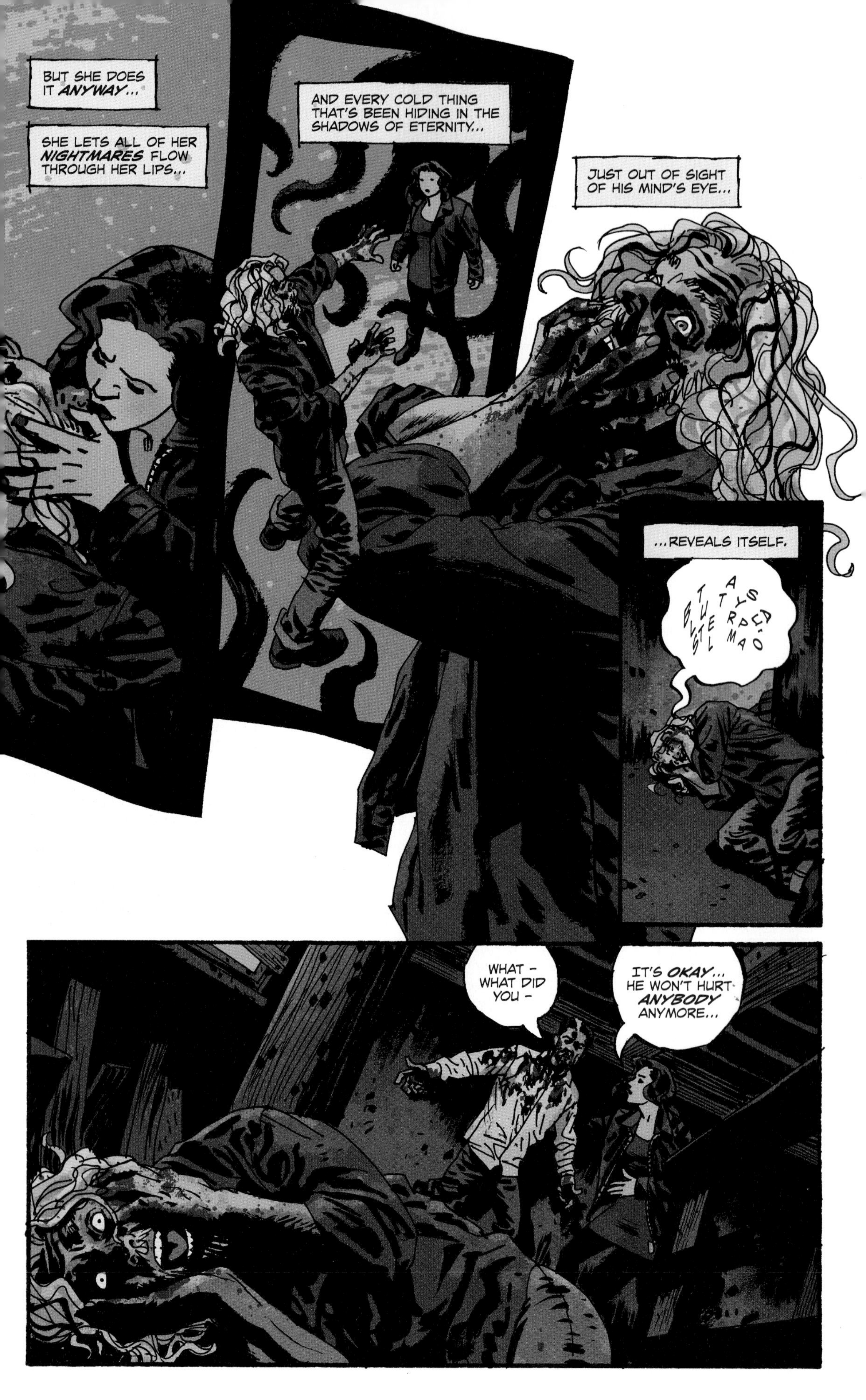
BUT SHE DOES IT *ANYWAY*...
SHE LETS ALL OF HER *NIGHTMARES* FLOW THROUGH HER LIPS...
AND EVERY COLD THING THAT'S BEEN HIDING IN THE SHADOWS OF ETERNITY...
JUST OUT OF SIGHT OF HIS MIND'S EYE...
...REVEALS ITSELF.
WHAT - WHAT DID YOU -
IT'S *OKAY*... HE WON'T HURT *ANYBODY* ANYMORE...

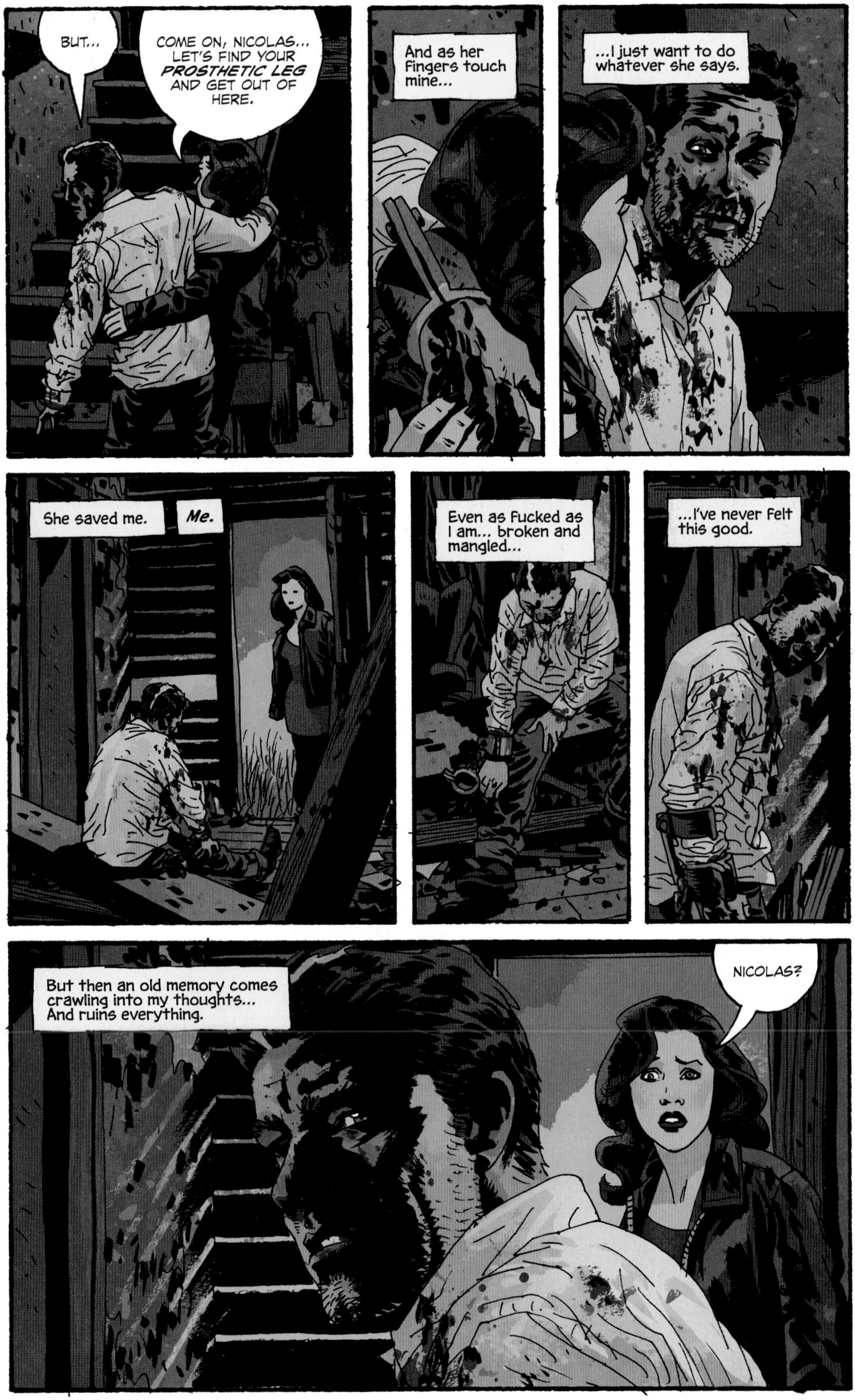
BUT...
COME ON, NICOLAS... LET'S FIND YOUR *PROSTHETIC LEG* AND GET OUT OF HERE.
And as her fingers touch mine...
...I just want to do whatever she says.
She saved me.
Me.
Even as fucked as I am... broken and mangled...
...I've never felt this good.
But then an old memory comes crawling into my thoughts... And ruins everything.
NICOLAS?

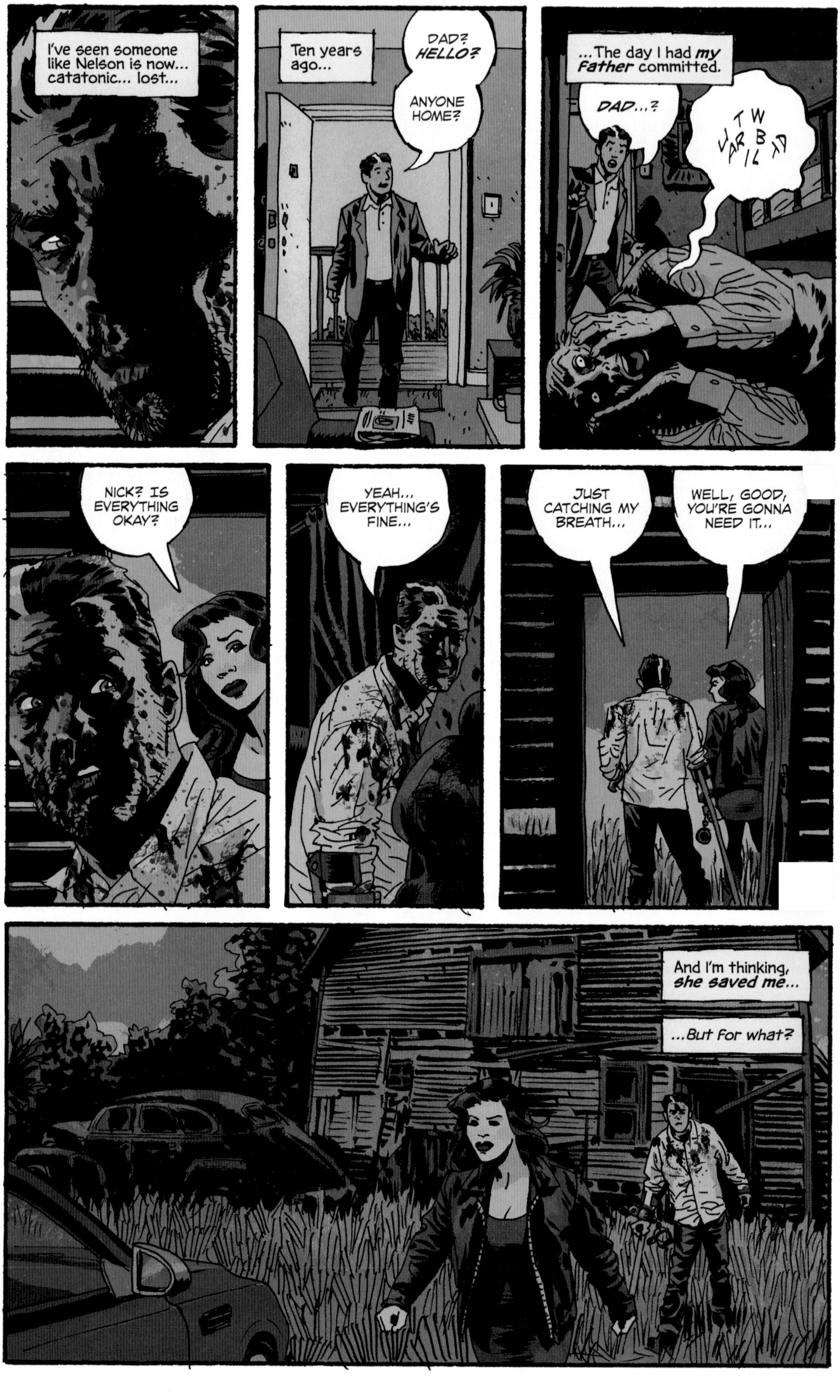
I've seen someone like Nelson is now... catatonic... lost...
Ten years ago...
DAD? HELLO?
ANYONE HOME?
...The day I had my father committed.
DAD...?
NICK? IS EVERYTHING OKAY?
YEAH... EVERYTHING'S FINE...
JUST CATCHING MY BREATH...
WELL, GOOD, YOU'RE GONNA NEED IT...
And I'm thinking, she saved me...
...But for what?

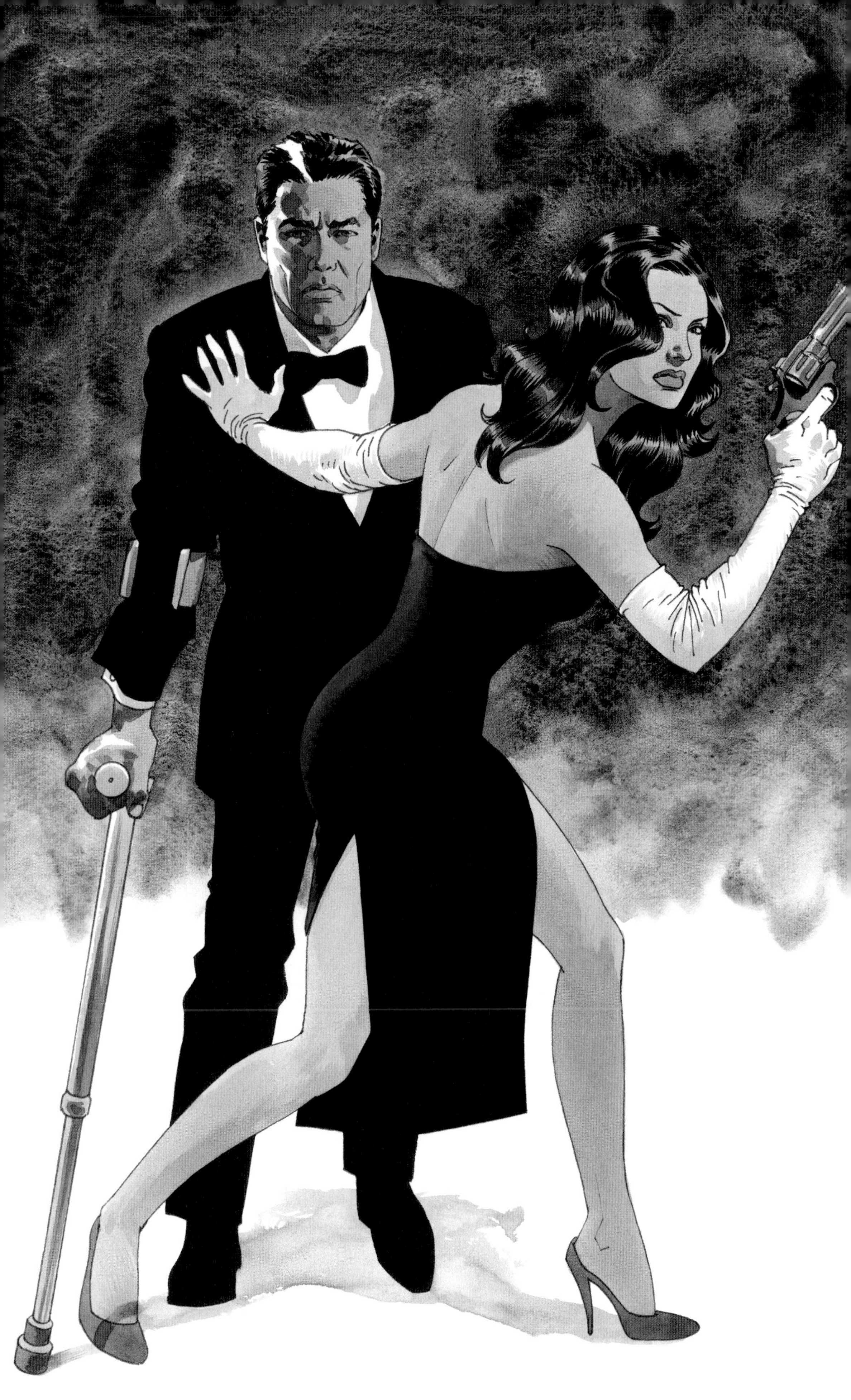

Chapter Two

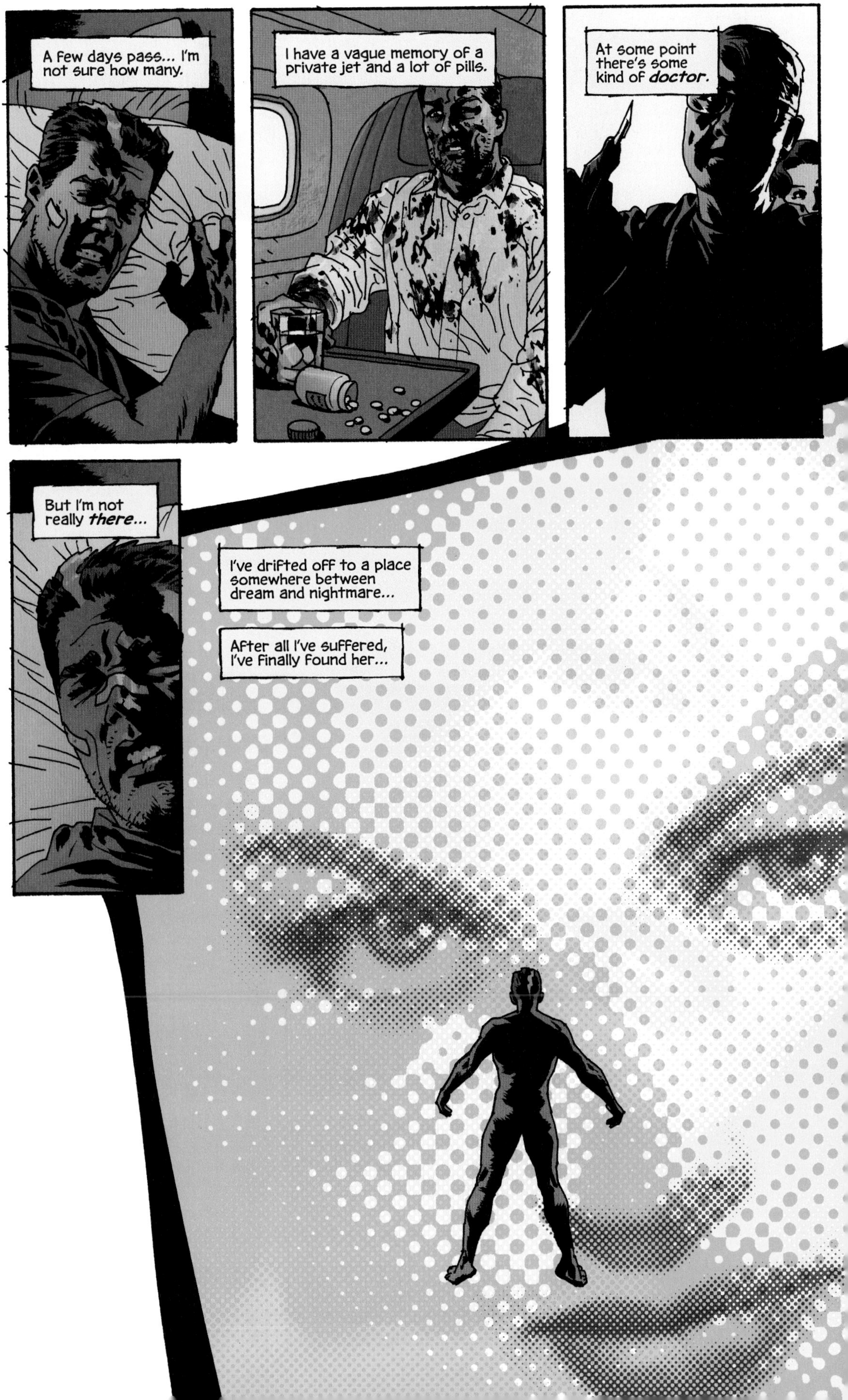
A few days pass... I'm not sure how many.
I have a vague memory of a private jet and a lot of pills.
At some point there's some kind of *doctor*.
But I'm not really *there*...
I've drifted off to a place somewhere between dream and nightmare...
After all I've suffered, I've finally found her...

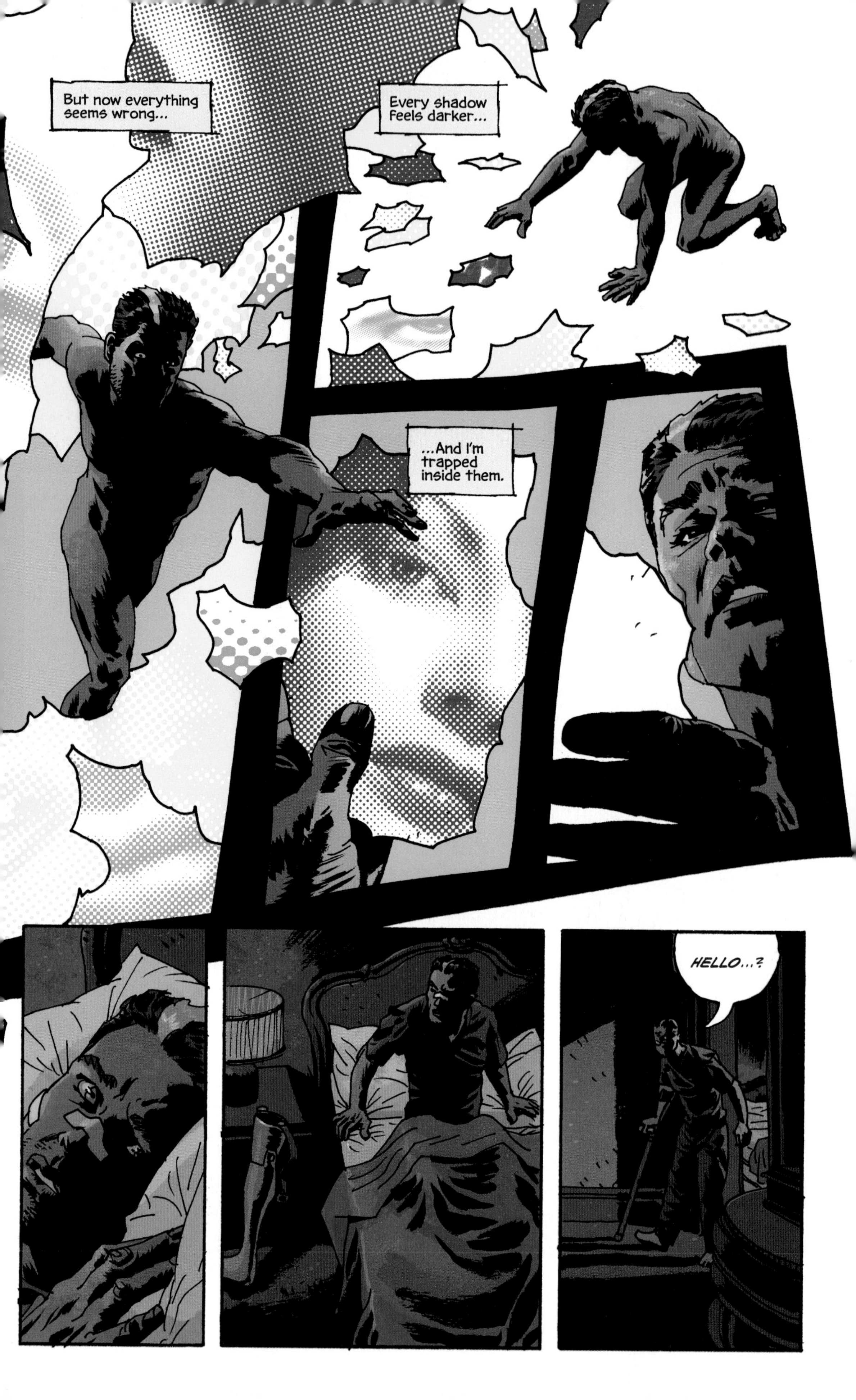
But now everything seems wrong...
Every shadow feels darker...
...And I'm trapped inside them.
HELLO...?

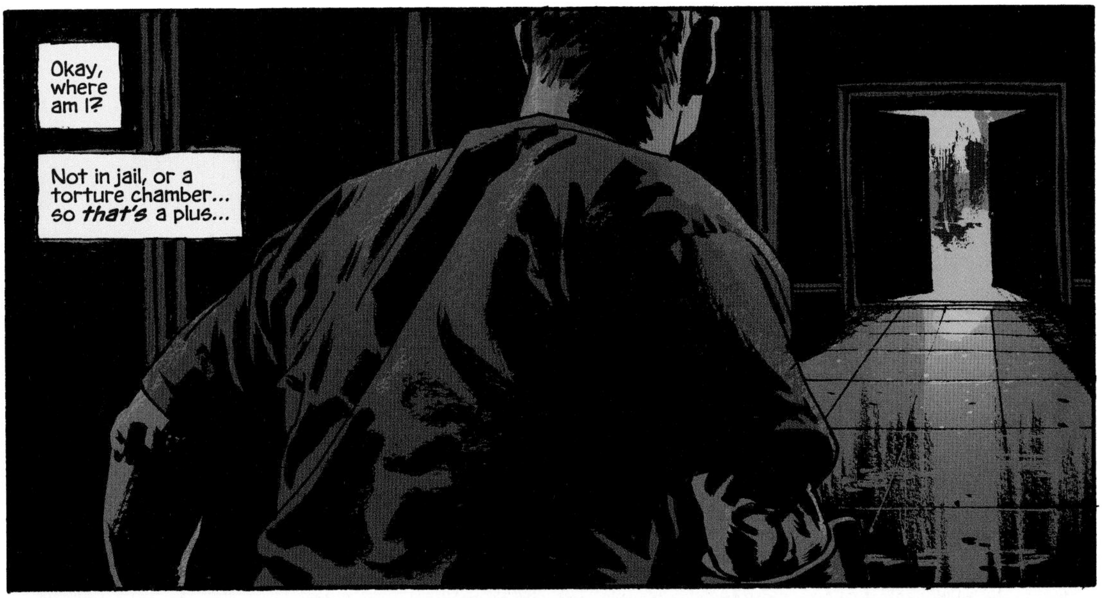
Okay, where am I?
Not in jail, or a torture chamber... so *that's* a plus...

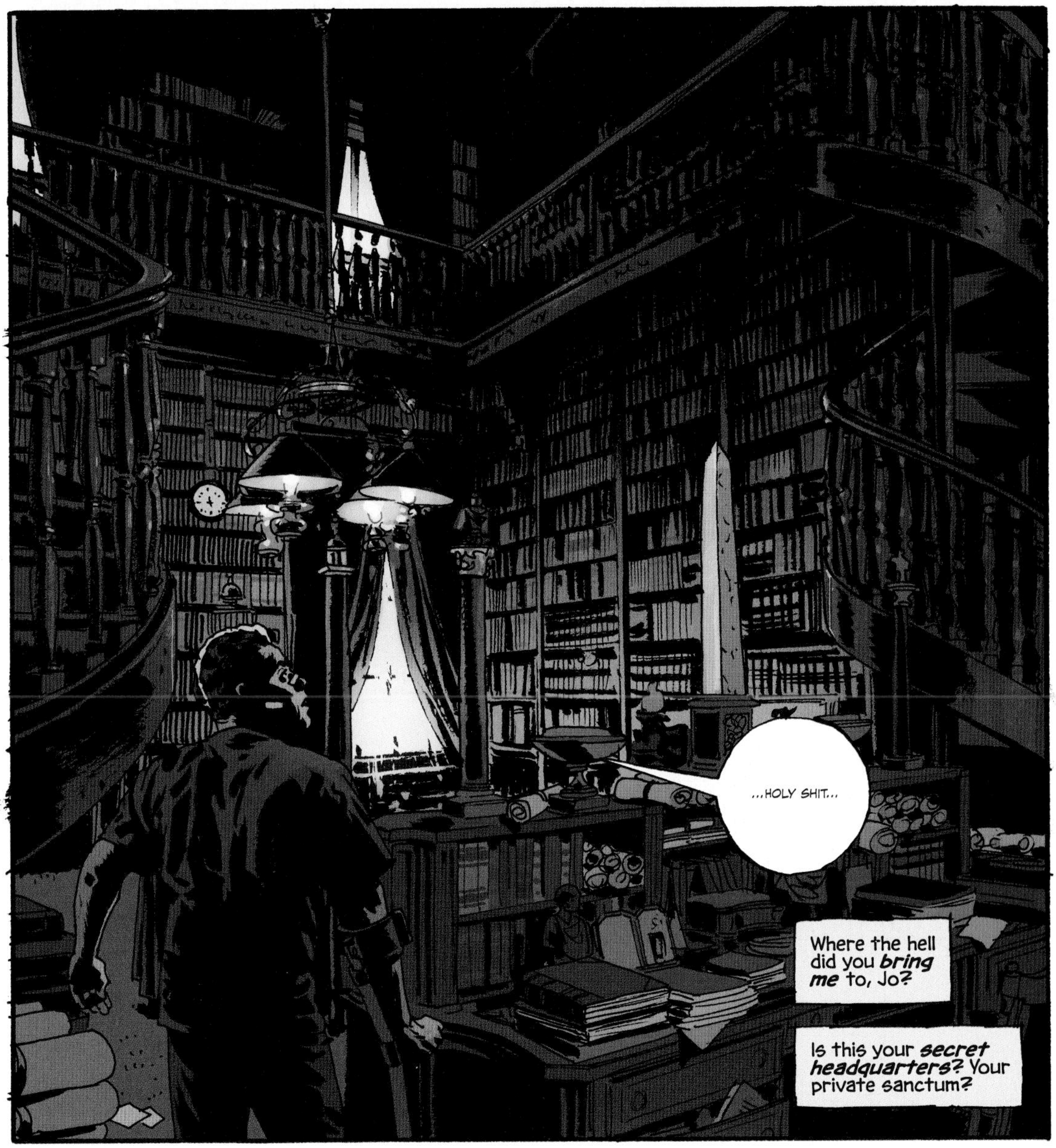
...HOLY SHIT...
Where the hell did you *bring me* to, Jo?
Is this your *secret headquarters?* Your private sanctum?

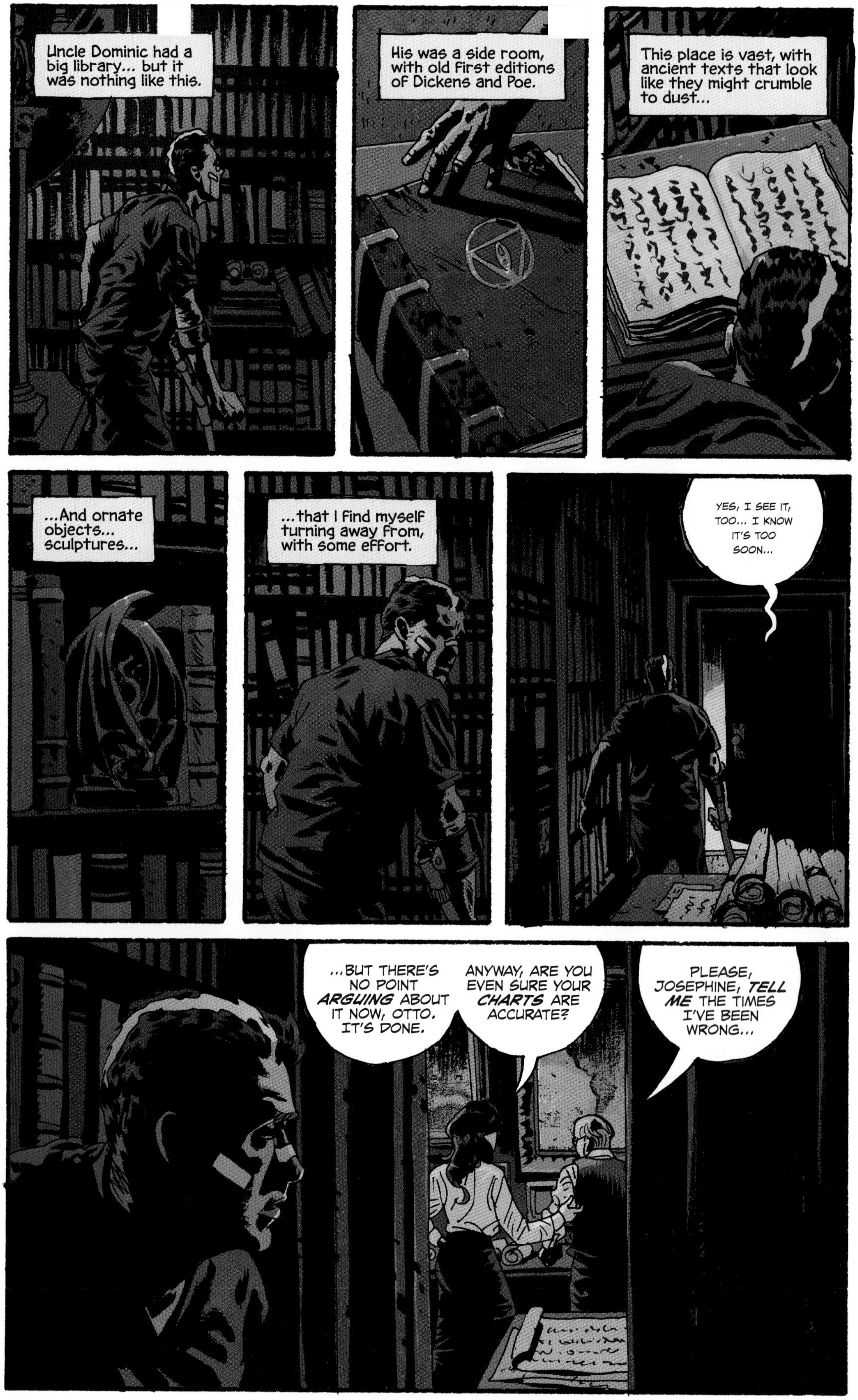
Uncle Dominic had a big library... but it was nothing like this.
His was a side room, with old first editions of Dickens and Poe.
This place is vast, with ancient texts that look like they might crumble to dust...
...And ornate objects... sculptures...
...that I find myself turning away from, with some effort.
YES, I SEE IT, TOO... I KNOW IT'S TOO SOON...
...BUT THERE'S NO POINT ARGUING ABOUT IT NOW, OTTO. IT'S DONE.
ANYWAY, ARE YOU EVEN SURE YOUR CHARTS ARE ACCURATE?
PLEASE, JOSEPHINE, TELL ME THE TIMES I'VE BEEN WRONG...

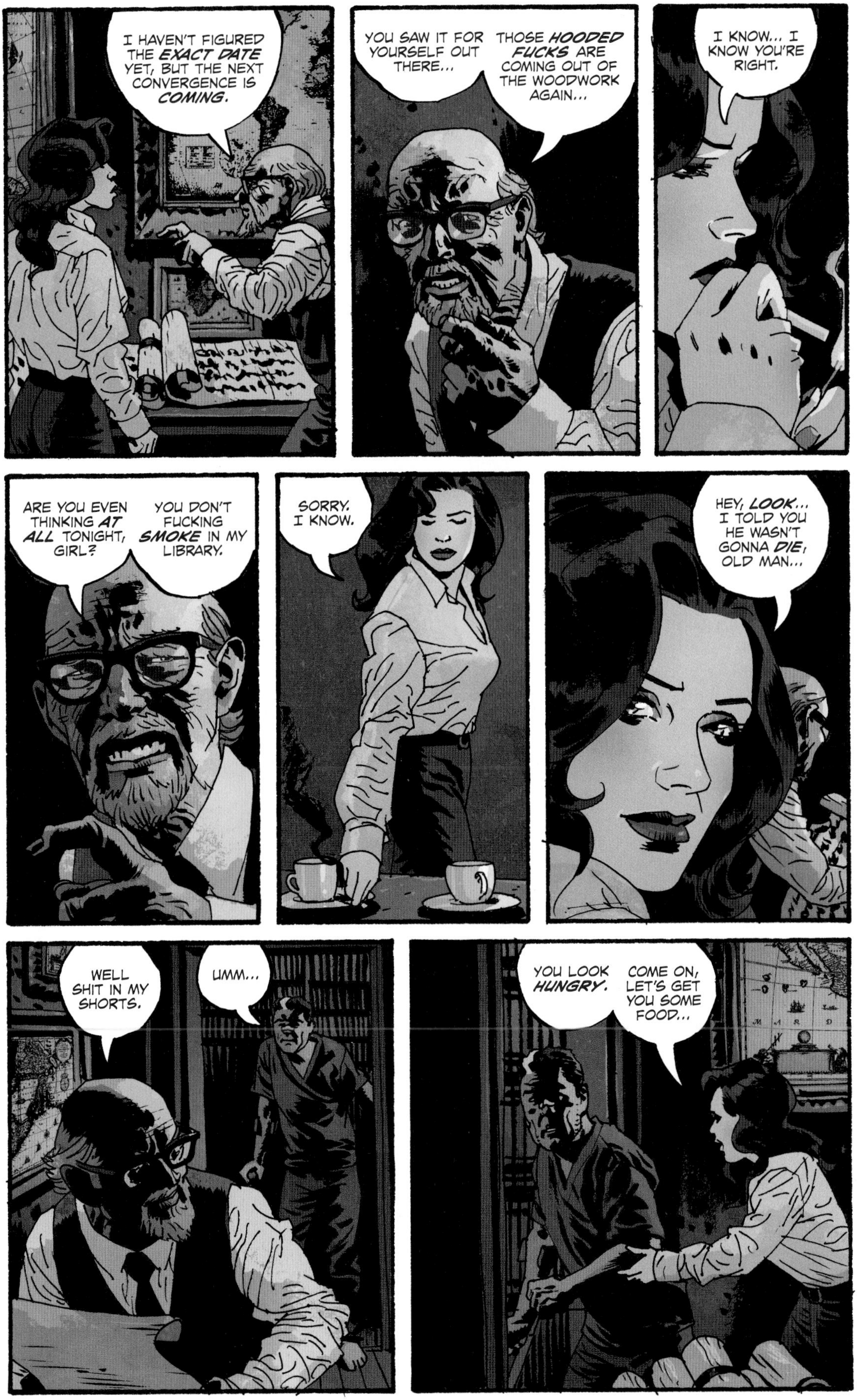
I HAVEN'T FIGURED THE EXACT DATE YET, BUT THE NEXT CONVERGENCE IS COMING.
YOU SAW IT FOR YOURSELF OUT THERE...
THOSE HOODED FUCKS ARE COMING OUT OF THE WOODWORK AGAIN...
I KNOW... I KNOW YOU'RE RIGHT.
ARE YOU EVEN THINKING AT ALL TONIGHT, GIRL?
YOU DON'T FUCKING SMOKE IN MY LIBRARY.
SORRY. I KNOW.
HEY, LOOK... I TOLD YOU HE WASN'T GONNA DIE, OLD MAN...
WELL SHIT IN MY SHORTS.
UMM...
YOU LOOK HUNGRY.
COME ON, LET'S GET YOU SOME FOOD...

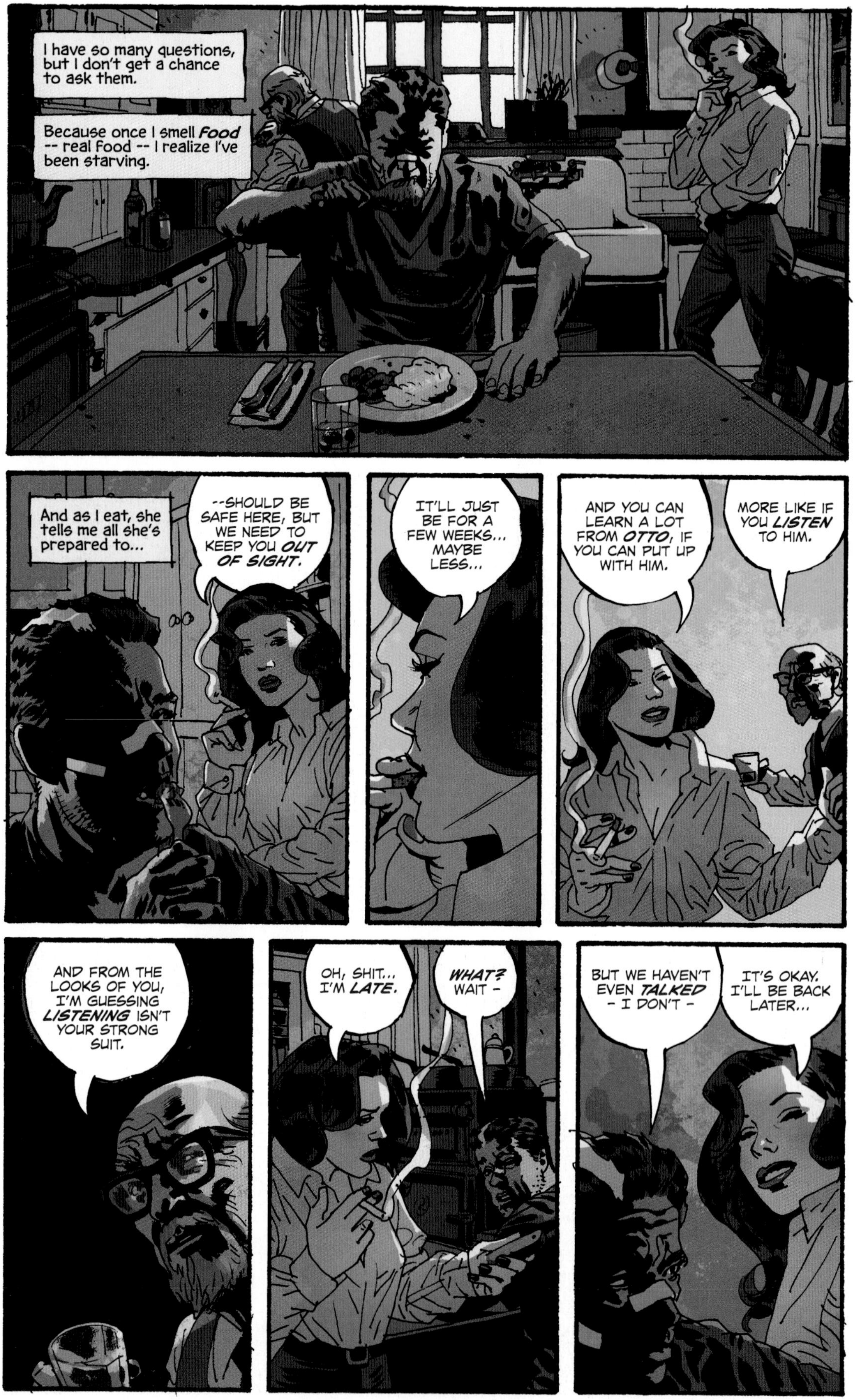

I have so many questions, but I don't get a chance to ask them.
Because once I smell *food* -- real food -- I realize I've been starving.
And as I eat, she tells me all she's prepared to...
--SHOULD BE SAFE HERE, BUT WE NEED TO KEEP YOU *OUT OF SIGHT*.
IT'LL JUST BE FOR A FEW WEEKS... MAYBE LESS...
AND YOU CAN LEARN A LOT FROM *OTTO*, IF YOU CAN PUT UP WITH HIM.
MORE LIKE IF YOU *LISTEN* TO HIM.
AND FROM THE LOOKS OF YOU, I'M GUESSING *LISTENING* ISN'T YOUR STRONG SUIT.
OH, SHIT... I'M *LATE*.
WHAT? WAIT -
BUT WE HAVEN'T EVEN *TALKED* - I DON'T -
IT'S OKAY. I'LL BE BACK LATER...

And just like that, she's gone.

And I fight every urge to chase after her.

Because she as much as told me to stay.

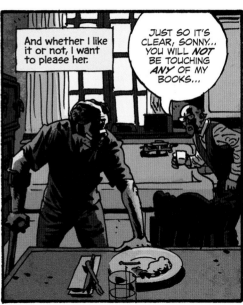

And whether I like it or not, I want to please her.

JUST SO IT'S CLEAR, SONNY... YOU WILL *NOT* BE TOUCHING *ANY* OF MY BOOKS...

OH... *OKAY*... WHEN WILL *SHE* BE BACK?

DON'T YOU WORRY ABOUT HER... MISS JOSEPHINE HAS BIGGER THINGS ON HER MIND THAN YOU.

CHRIST, ALL YOU FUCKIN' *KIDS* THINK THE WHOLE WORLD REVOLVES AROUND YOU...

But she doesn't come back that night...

I watch for her from the window in my room, until my exhaustion drags me away from it.

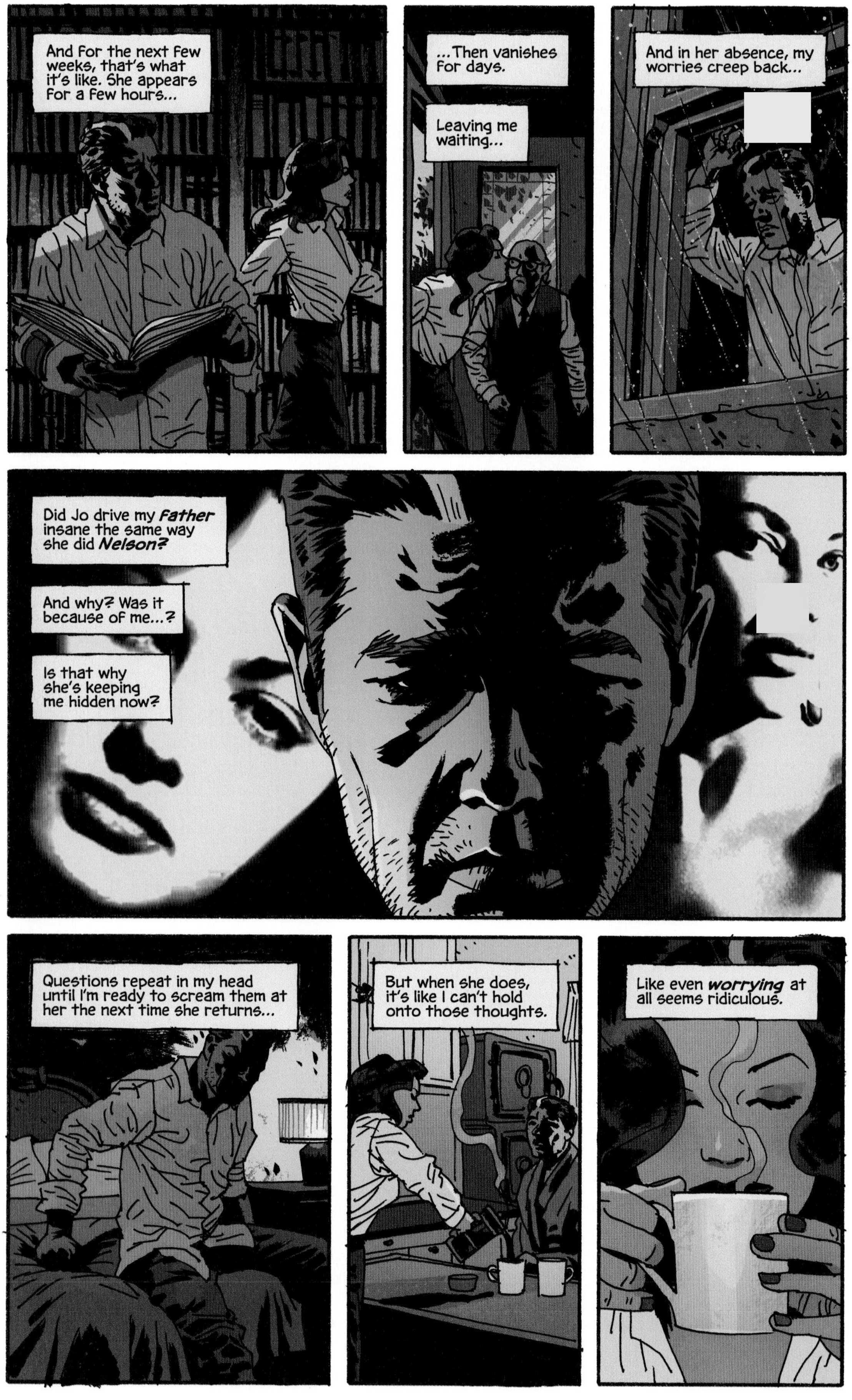
And for the next few weeks, that's what it's like. She appears for a few hours...
...Then vanishes for days.
Leaving me waiting...
And in her absence, my worries creep back...
Did Jo drive my *Father* insane the same way she did *Nelson?*
And why? Was it because of me...?
Is that why she's keeping me hidden now?
Questions repeat in my head until I'm ready to scream them at her the next time she returns...
But when she does, it's like I can't hold onto those thoughts.
Like even ***worrying*** at all seems ridiculous.

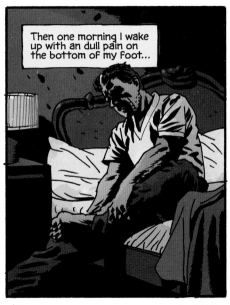

Then one morning I wake up with an dull pain on the bottom of my foot...

...A tattoo.

JUST LEAVE IT BE, KID.

WHAT IS THIS? IS SHE *MARKING* ME?

NO, IDIOT... SHE'S *PROTECTING* YOU.

I GUESS DOING THAT PROTECTS *HER*, TOO, FOR NOW...

BUT STILL...

SHE DOESN'T AFFECT YOU, DOES SHE?

NOT HOW YOU MEAN, *NO*...

AND LOOKIN' AT YOUR MESSED UP HEAD, I'M THANKFUL SHE AND I HAVE ALWAYS BEEN *JUST FRIENDS*.

WHO THE FUCK *ARE YOU*, OLD MAN?

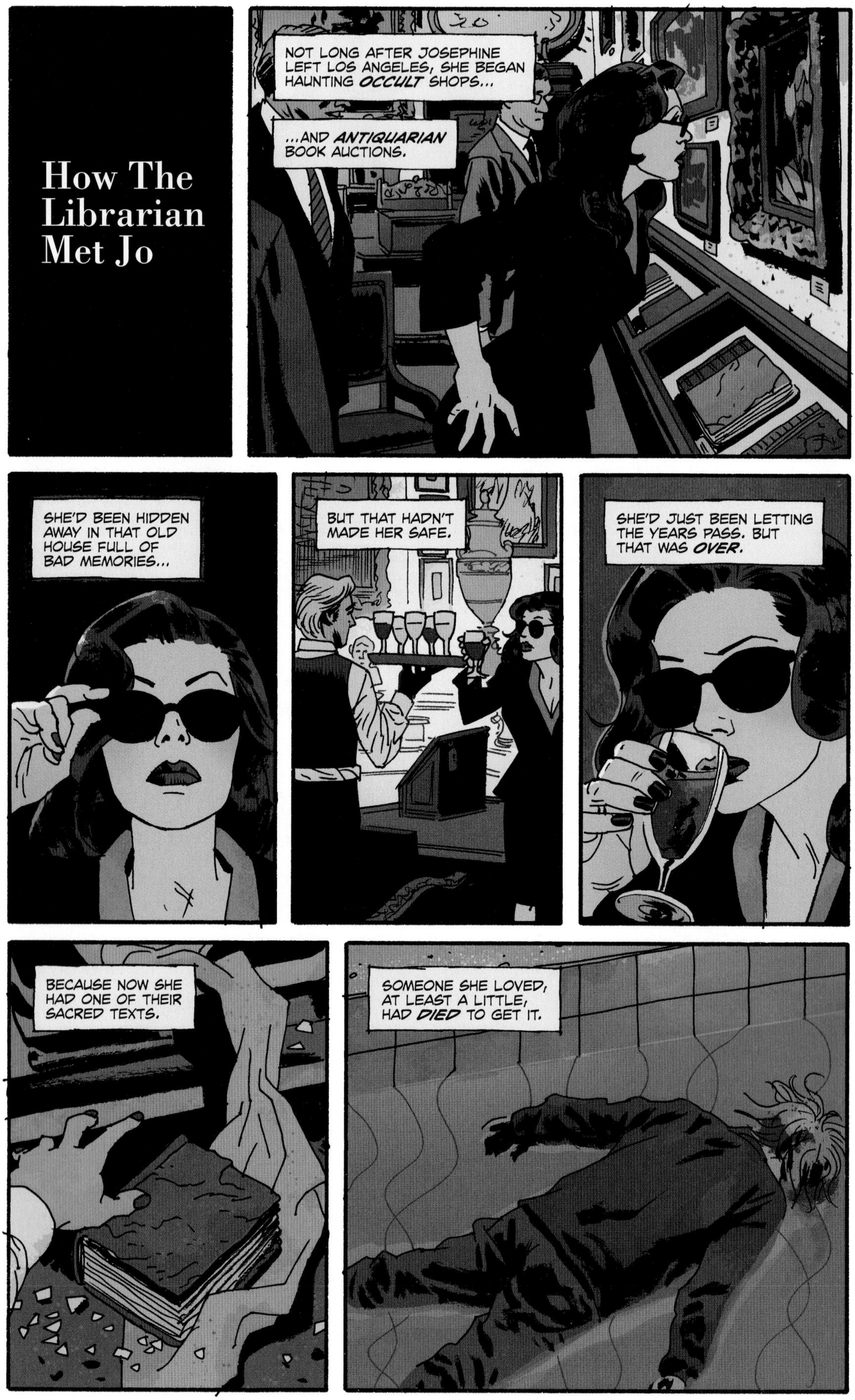
How The Librarian Met Jo
NOT LONG AFTER JOSEPHINE LEFT LOS ANGELES, SHE BEGAN HAUNTING OCCULT SHOPS...
...AND ANTIQUARIAN BOOK AUCTIONS.
SHE'D BEEN HIDDEN AWAY IN THAT OLD HOUSE FULL OF BAD MEMORIES...
BUT THAT HADN'T MADE HER SAFE.
SHE'D JUST BEEN LETTING THE YEARS PASS. BUT THAT WAS OVER.
BECAUSE NOW SHE HAD ONE OF THEIR SACRED TEXTS.
SOMEONE SHE LOVED, AT LEAST A LITTLE, HAD DIED TO GET IT.

SHE KNEW THERE WERE SECRETS IN ITS PAGES... ABOUT *HER*, ABOUT THE CREATURES *HUNTING* HER...

...BUT SHE NEEDED SOMEONE WHO COULD *READ* THE DAMNED THING. SHE SURE AS HELL COULDN'T.

SHE REMEMBERED THE *OLD WOMAN* IN PARIS, WHO'D TAUGHT HER SO MUCH.

MIRELA WAS LONG DEAD, BUT THERE WERE OTHERS LIKE HER.

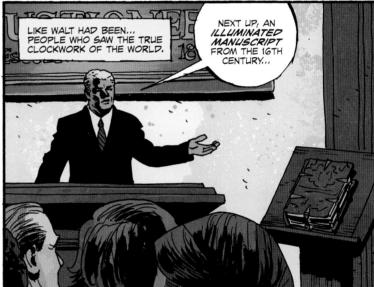

LIKE WALT HAD BEEN... PEOPLE WHO SAW THE TRUE CLOCKWORK OF THE WORLD.

NEXT UP, AN *ILLUMINATED MANUSCRIPT* FROM THE 16TH CENTURY...

IT ONLY TOOK FOUR YEARS TO FIND ONE.

YOU'RE GOING TO BID ON THAT ITEM.

YEAH. I *KNOW* I AM.

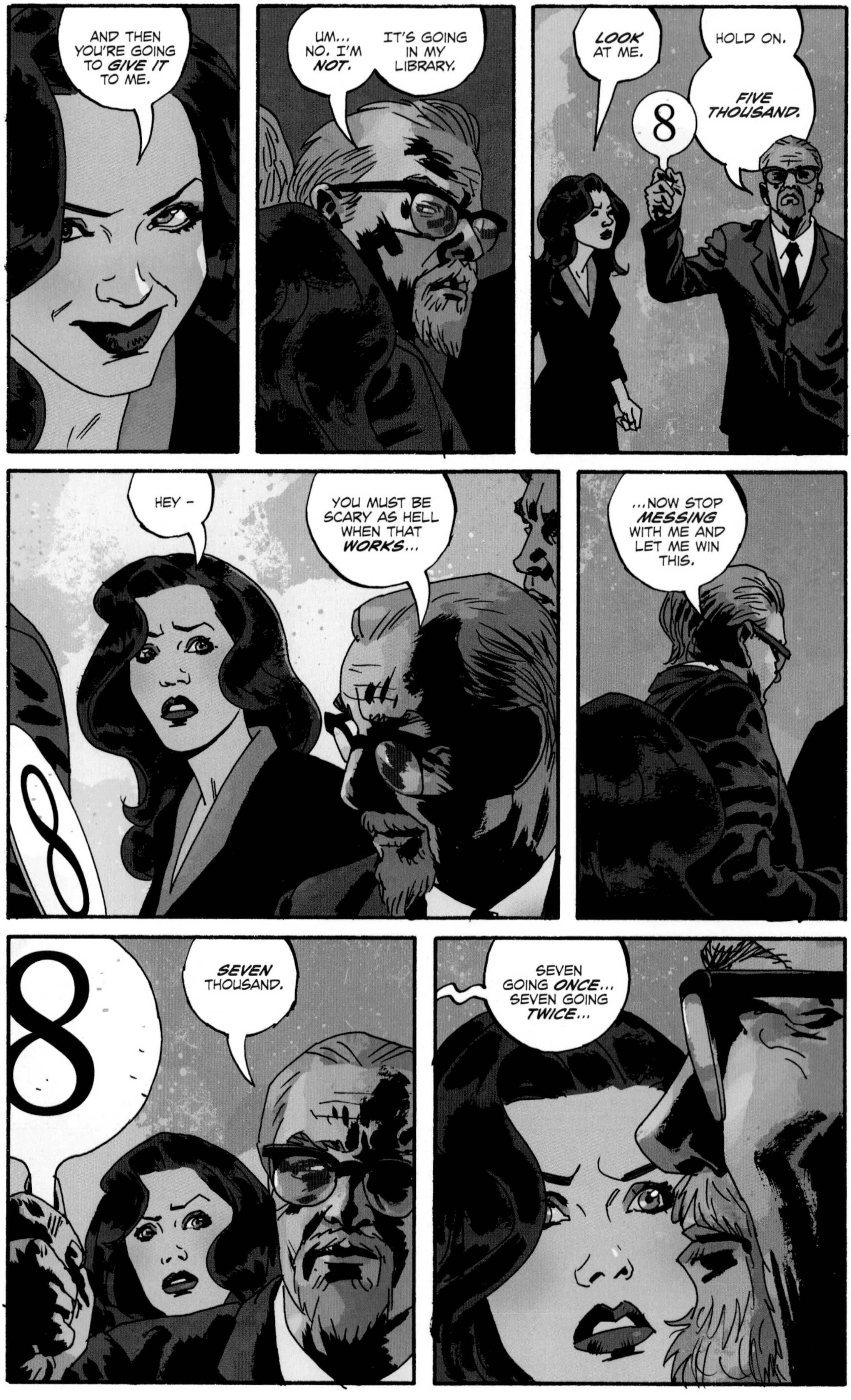
AND THEN YOU'RE GOING TO GIVE IT TO ME.
UM... NO. I'M NOT.
IT'S GOING IN MY LIBRARY.
LOOK AT ME.
HOLD ON.
8
FIVE THOUSAND.
HEY -
YOU MUST BE SCARY AS HELL WHEN THAT WORKS...
8
...NOW STOP MESSING WITH ME AND LET ME WIN THIS.
8
SEVEN THOUSAND.
SEVEN GOING ONCE... SEVEN GOING TWICE...

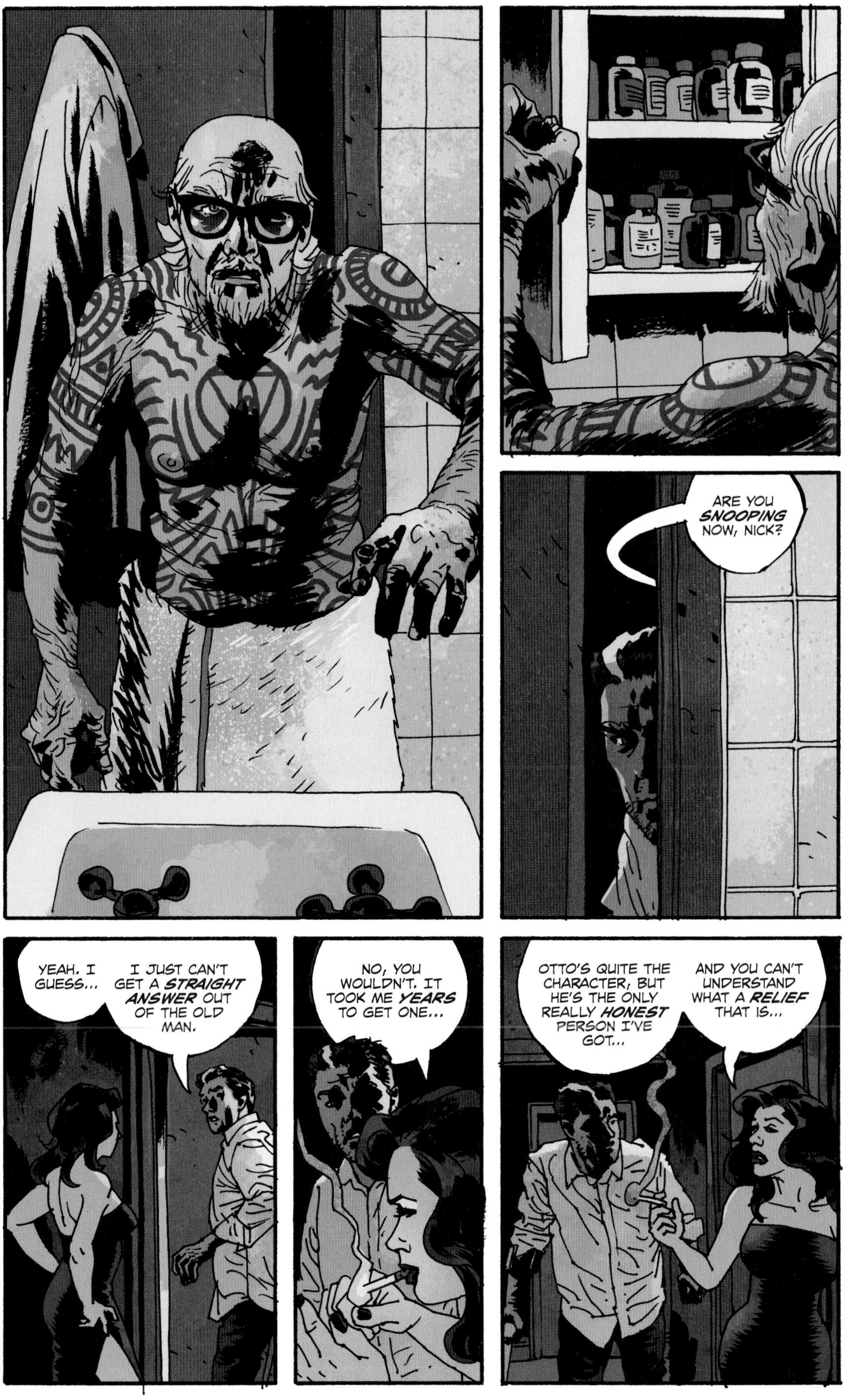

ARE YOU SNOOPING NOW, NICK?
YEAH. I GUESS...
I JUST CAN'T GET A STRAIGHT ANSWER OUT OF THE OLD MAN.
NO, YOU WOULDN'T. IT TOOK ME YEARS TO GET ONE...
OTTO'S QUITE THE CHARACTER, BUT HE'S THE ONLY REALLY HONEST PERSON I'VE GOT...
AND YOU CAN'T UNDERSTAND WHAT A RELIEF THAT IS...

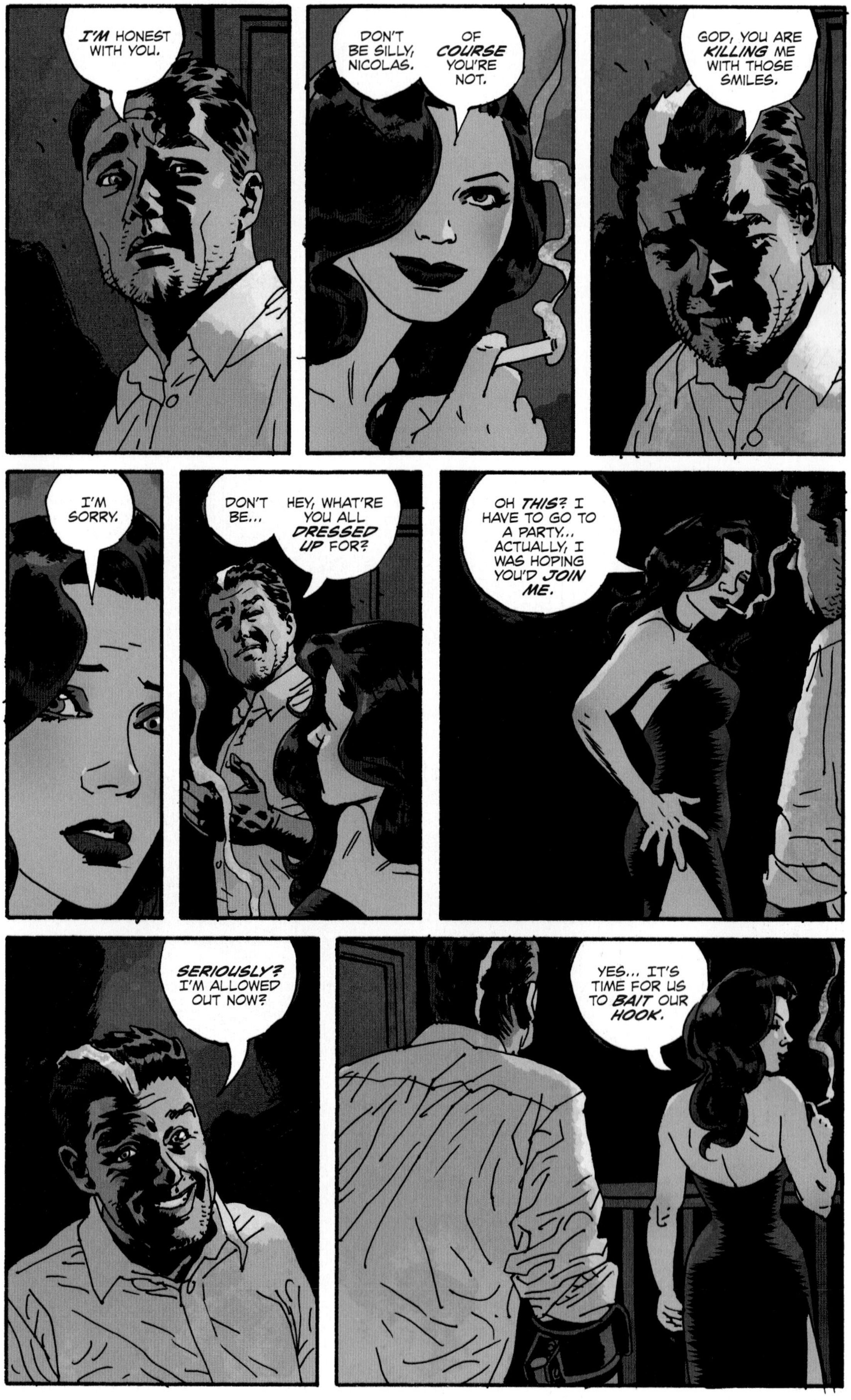
I'M HONEST WITH YOU.
DON'T BE SILLY, NICOLAS.
OF COURSE YOU'RE NOT.
GOD, YOU ARE KILLING ME WITH THOSE SMILES.
I'M SORRY.
DON'T BE...
HEY, WHAT'RE YOU ALL DRESSED UP FOR?
OH THIS? I HAVE TO GO TO A PARTY... ACTUALLY, I WAS HOPING YOU'D JOIN ME.
SERIOUSLY? I'M ALLOWED OUT NOW?
YES... IT'S TIME FOR US TO BAIT OUR HOOK.

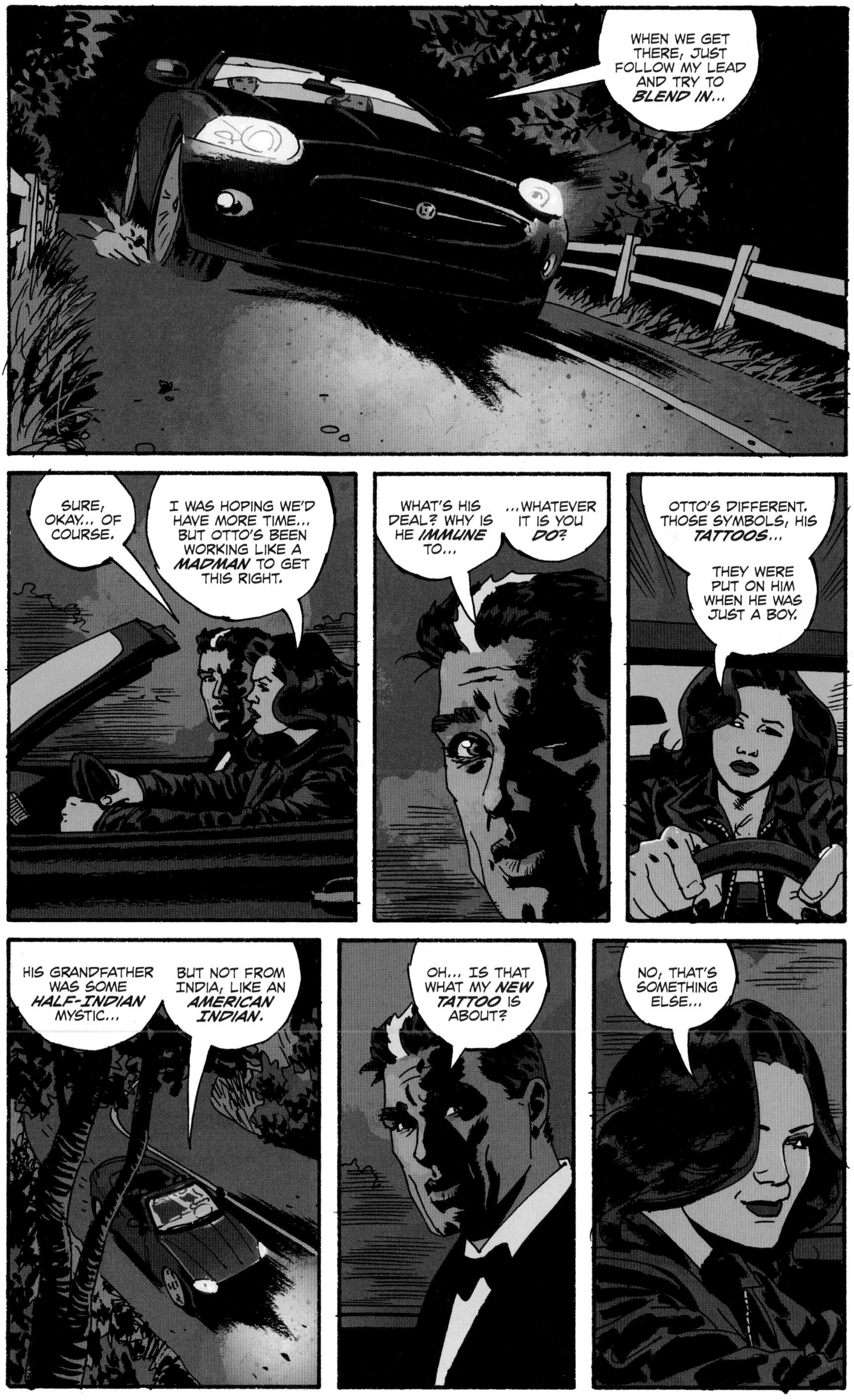
WHEN WE GET THERE, JUST FOLLOW MY LEAD AND TRY TO BLEND IN...
SURE, OKAY... OF COURSE.
I WAS HOPING WE'D HAVE MORE TIME... BUT OTTO'S BEEN WORKING LIKE A MADMAN TO GET THIS RIGHT.
WHAT'S HIS DEAL? WHY IS HE IMMUNE TO...
...WHATEVER IT IS YOU DO?
OTTO'S DIFFERENT. THOSE SYMBOLS, HIS TATTOOS...
THEY WERE PUT ON HIM WHEN HE WAS JUST A BOY.
HIS GRANDFATHER WAS SOME HALF-INDIAN MYSTIC...
BUT NOT FROM INDIA, LIKE AN AMERICAN INDIAN.
OH... IS THAT WHAT MY NEW TATTOO IS ABOUT?
NO, THAT'S SOMETHING ELSE...

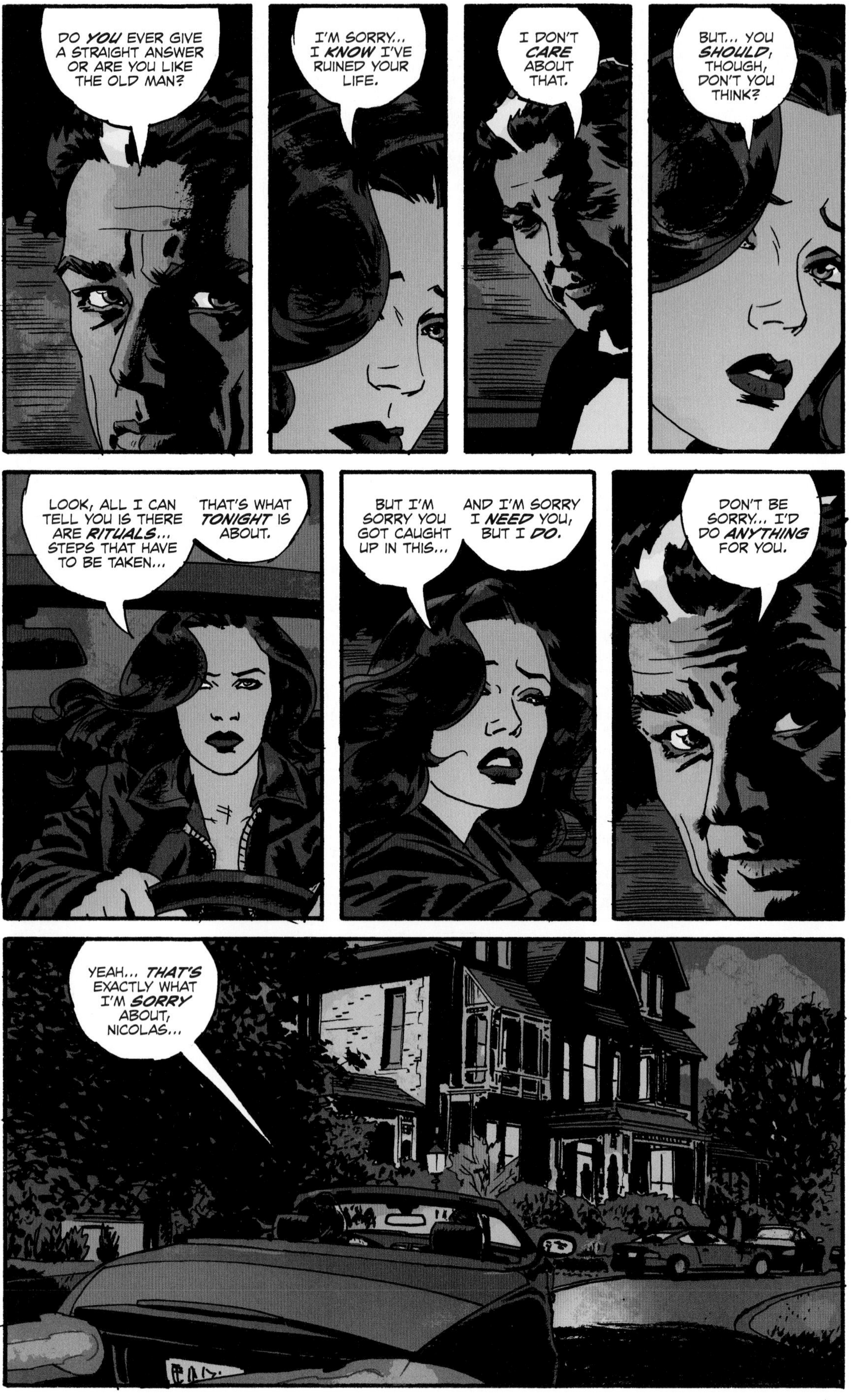
DO YOU EVER GIVE A STRAIGHT ANSWER OR ARE YOU LIKE THE OLD MAN?
I'M SORRY... I KNOW I'VE RUINED YOUR LIFE.
I DON'T CARE ABOUT THAT.
BUT... YOU SHOULD, THOUGH, DON'T YOU THINK?
LOOK, ALL I CAN TELL YOU IS THERE ARE RITUALS... STEPS THAT HAVE TO BE TAKEN...
THAT'S WHAT TONIGHT IS ABOUT.
BUT I'M SORRY YOU GOT CAUGHT UP IN THIS...
AND I'M SORRY I NEED YOU, BUT I DO.
DON'T BE SORRY... I'D DO ANYTHING FOR YOU.
YEAH... THAT'S EXACTLY WHAT I'M SORRY ABOUT, NICOLAS...

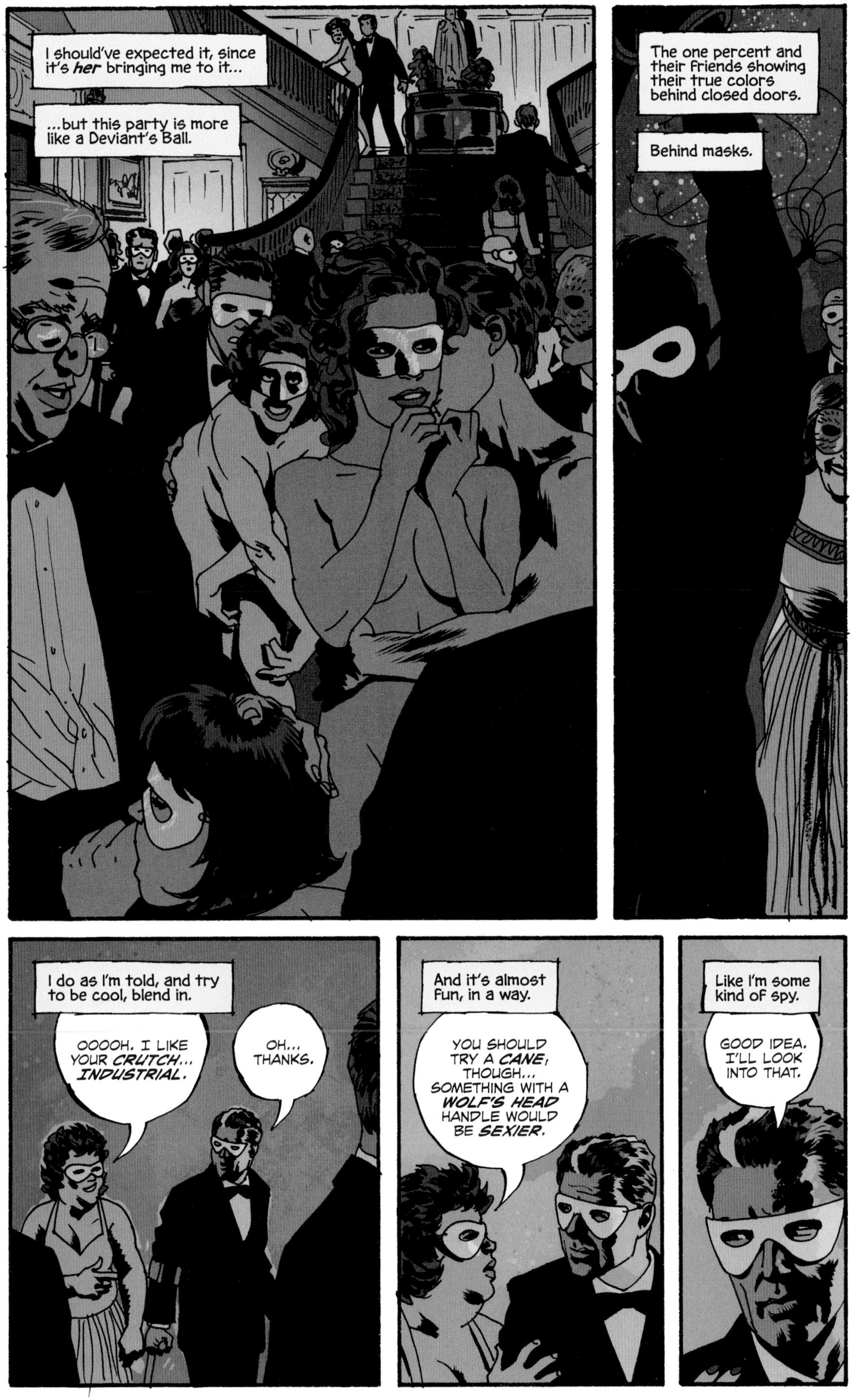
I should've expected it, since it's *her* bringing me to it...
...but this party is more like a Deviant's Ball.
The one percent and their friends showing their true colors behind closed doors.
Behind masks.
I do as I'm told, and try to be cool, blend in.
OOOOH. I LIKE YOUR *CRUTCH*... *INDUSTRIAL.*
OH... THANKS.
And it's almost fun, in a way.
YOU SHOULD TRY A *CANE*, THOUGH... SOMETHING WITH A *WOLF'S HEAD* HANDLE WOULD BE *SEXIER.*
Like I'm some kind of spy.
GOOD IDEA. I'LL LOOK INTO THAT.

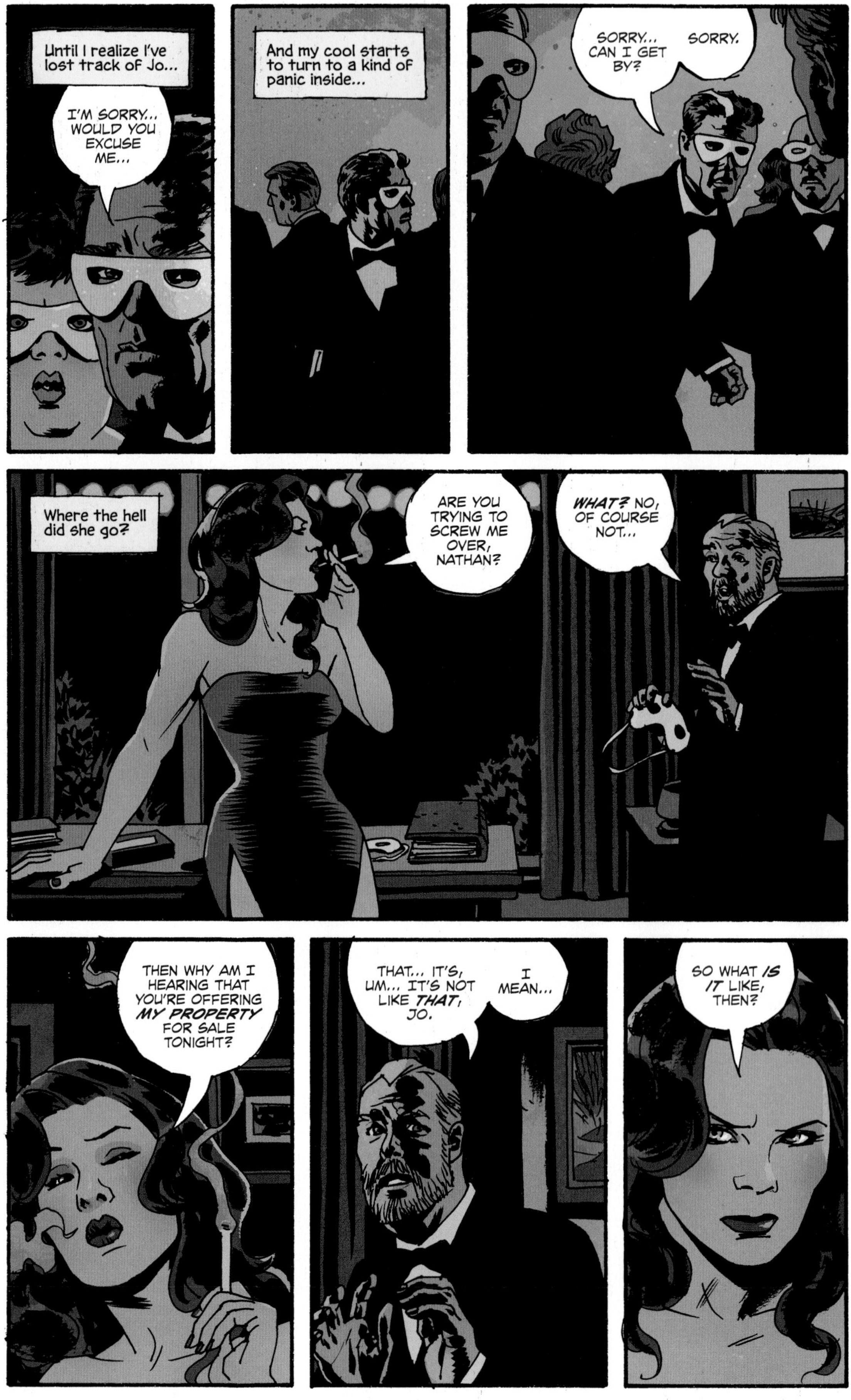

Until I realize I've lost track of Jo...
I'M SORRY... WOULD YOU EXCUSE ME...
And my cool starts to turn to a kind of panic inside...
SORRY... CAN I GET BY?
SORRY.
Where the hell did she go?
ARE YOU TRYING TO SCREW ME OVER, NATHAN?
WHAT? NO, OF COURSE NOT...
THEN WHY AM I HEARING THAT YOU'RE OFFERING MY PROPERTY FOR SALE TONIGHT?
THAT... IT'S, UM... IT'S NOT LIKE THAT, JO.
I MEAN...
SO WHAT IS IT LIKE, THEN?

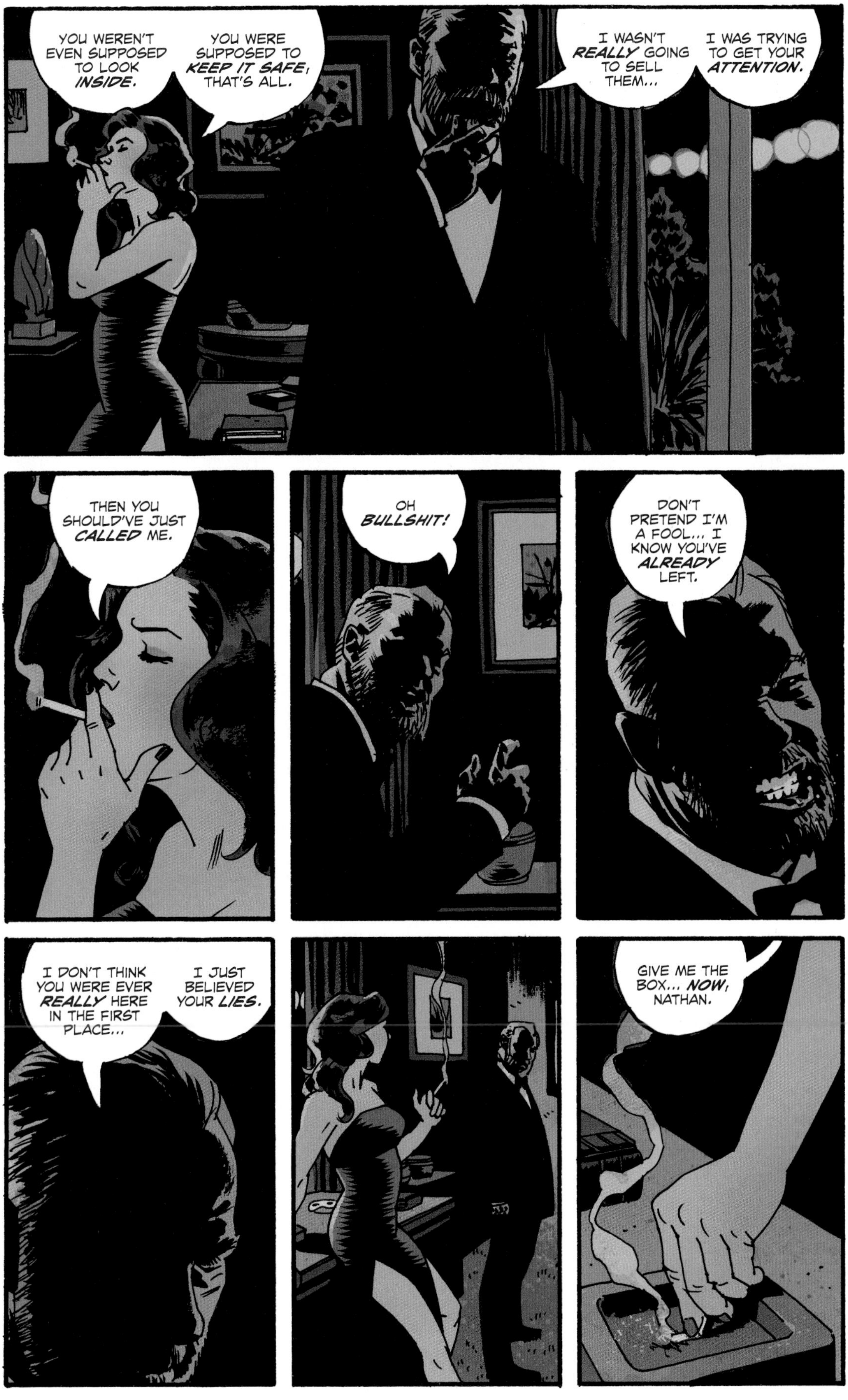

YOU WEREN'T EVEN SUPPOSED TO LOOK INSIDE.
YOU WERE SUPPOSED TO KEEP IT SAFE, THAT'S ALL.
I WASN'T REALLY GOING TO SELL THEM...
I WAS TRYING TO GET YOUR ATTENTION.
THEN YOU SHOULD'VE JUST CALLED ME.
OH BULLSHIT!
DON'T PRETEND I'M A FOOL... I KNOW YOU'VE ALREADY LEFT.
I DON'T THINK YOU WERE EVER REALLY HERE IN THE FIRST PLACE...
I JUST BELIEVED YOUR LIES.
GIVE ME THE BOX... NOW, NATHAN.

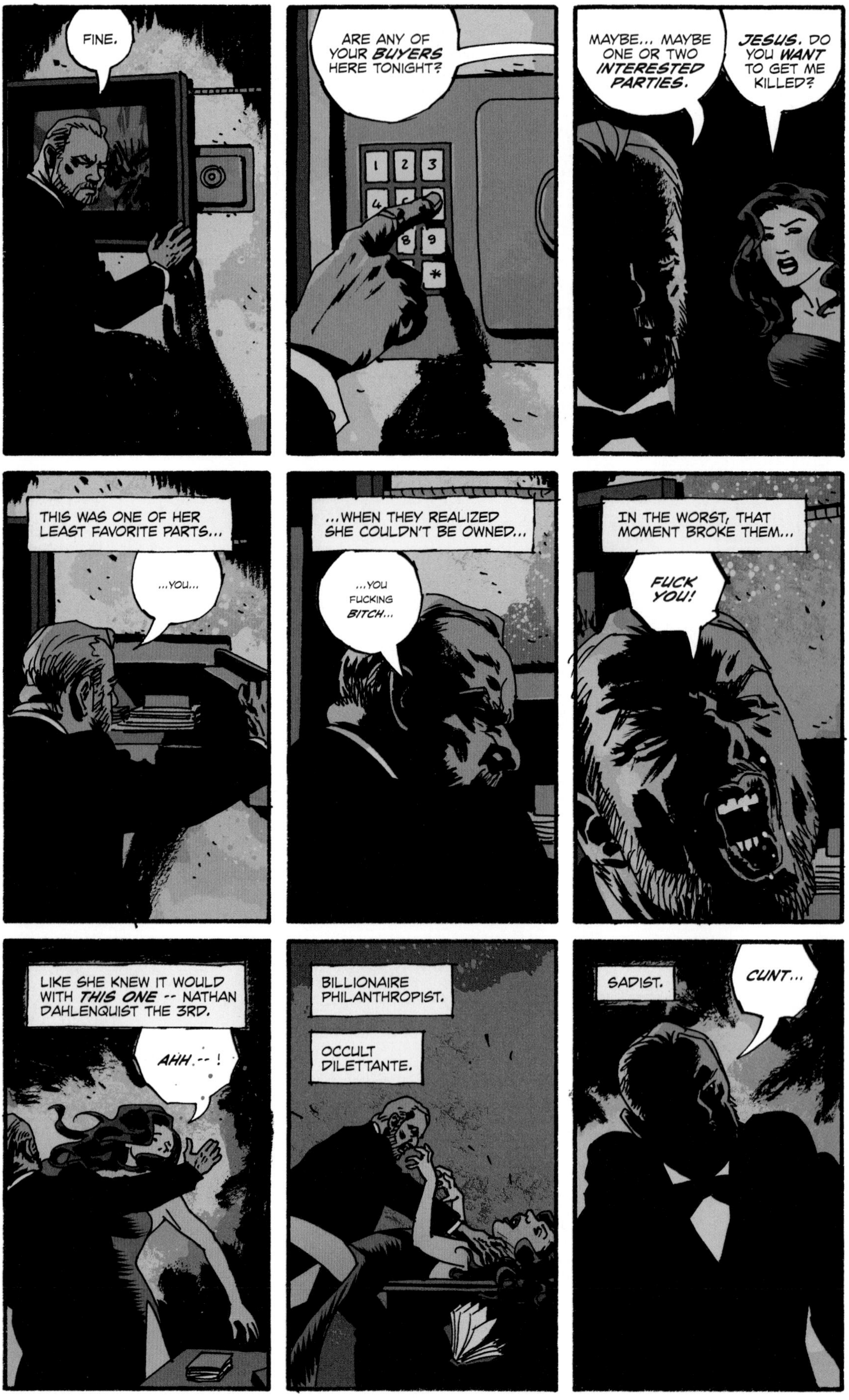
FINE.
ARE ANY OF YOUR BUYERS HERE TONIGHT?
MAYBE... MAYBE ONE OR TWO INTERESTED PARTIES.
JESUS. DO YOU WANT TO GET ME KILLED?
THIS WAS ONE OF HER LEAST FAVORITE PARTS...
...YOU...
...WHEN THEY REALIZED SHE COULDN'T BE OWNED...
...YOU FUCKING BITCH...
IN THE WORST, THAT MOMENT BROKE THEM...
FUCK YOU!
LIKE SHE KNEW IT WOULD WITH THIS ONE -- NATHAN DAHLENQUIST THE 3RD.
AHH -- !
BILLIONAIRE PHILANTHROPIST.
OCCULT DILETTANTE.
SADIST.
CUNT...

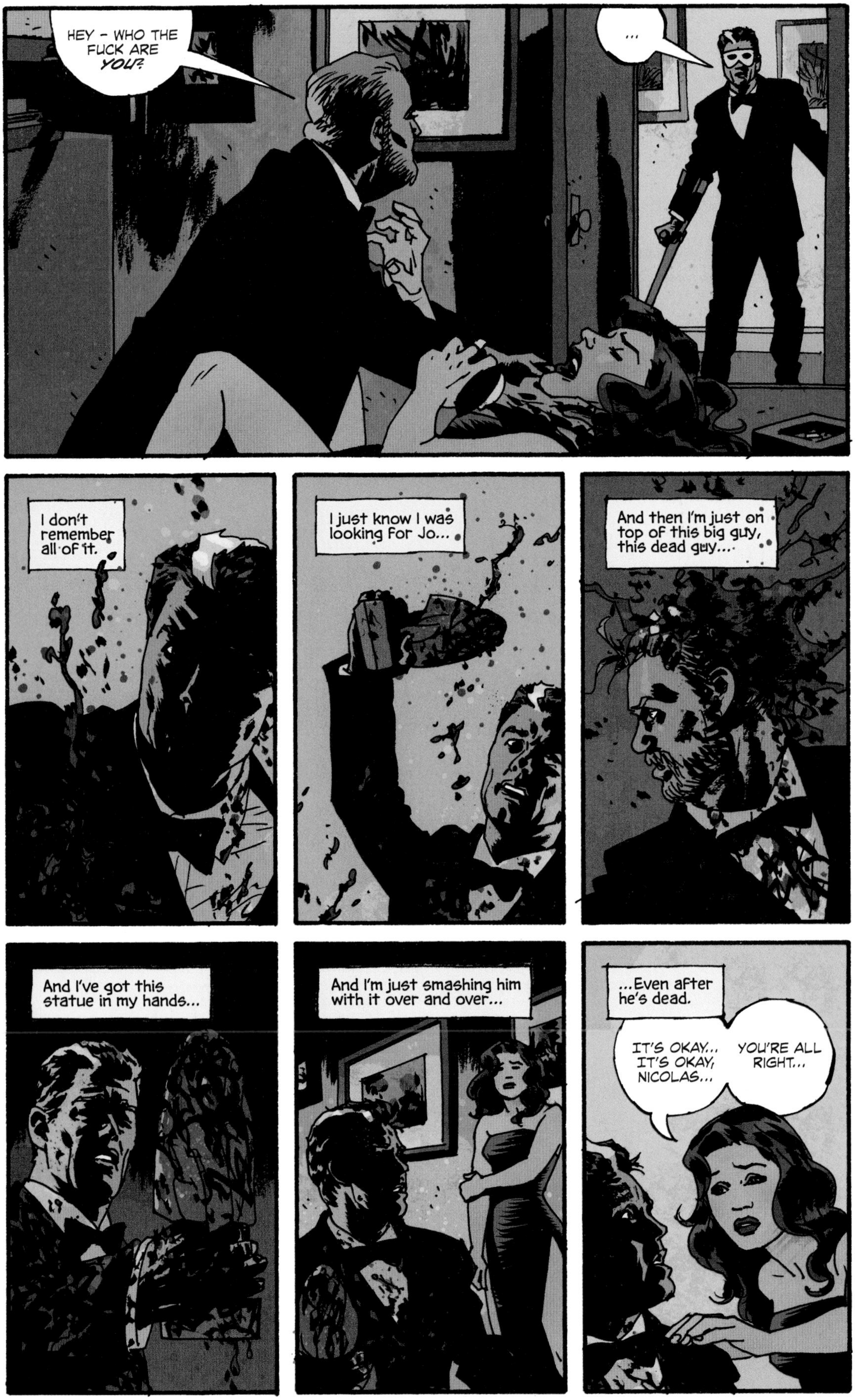
HEY - WHO THE FUCK ARE YOU?
...
I don't remember all of it.
I just know I was looking for Jo...
And then I'm just on top of this big guy, this dead guy...
And I've got this statue in my hands...
And I'm just smashing him with it over and over...
...Even after he's dead.
IT'S OKAY... IT'S OKAY, NICOLAS...
YOU'RE ALL RIGHT...

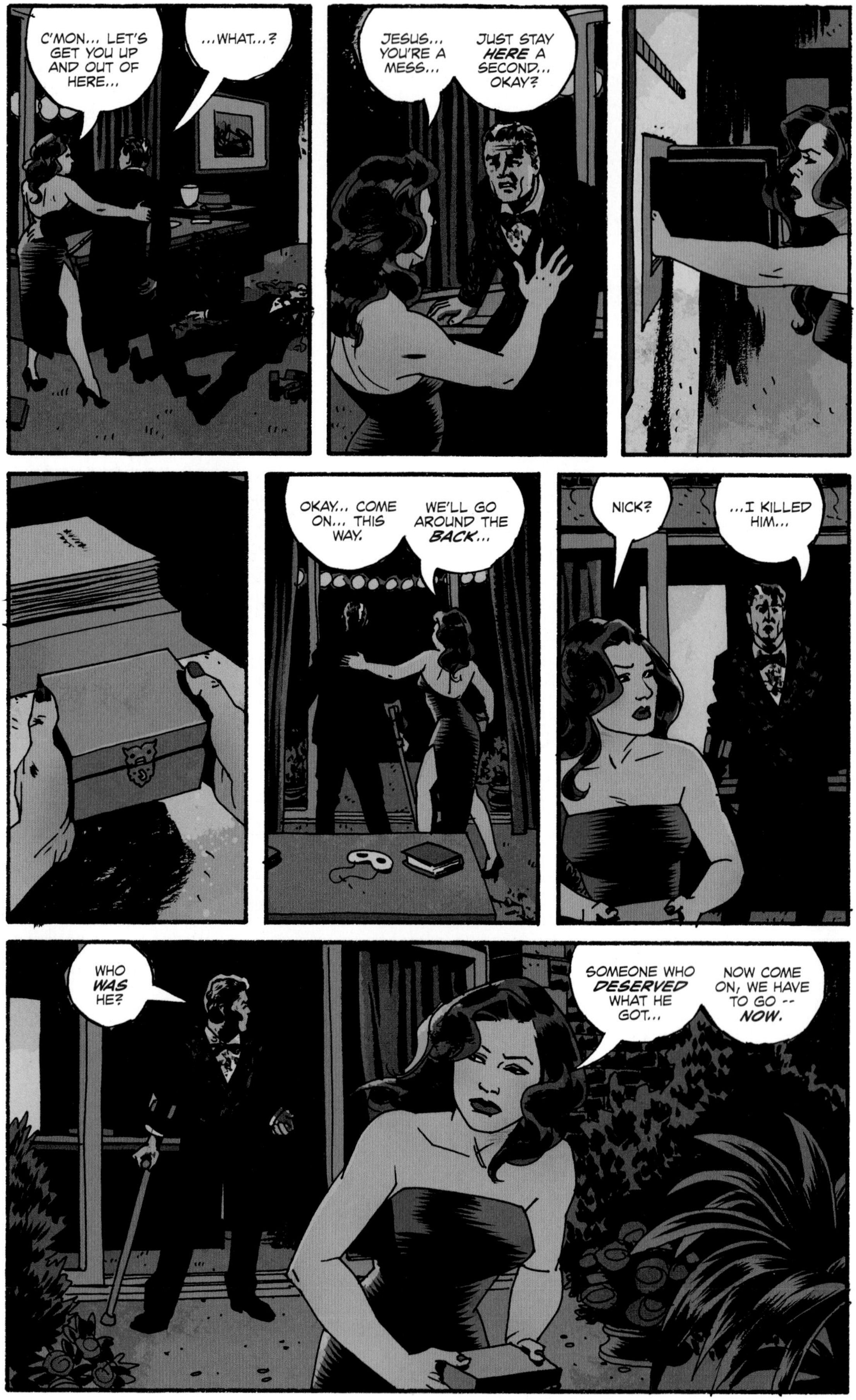
C'MON... LET'S GET YOU UP AND OUT OF HERE...
...WHAT...?
JESUS... YOU'RE A MESS...
JUST STAY HERE A SECOND... OKAY?
OKAY... COME ON... THIS WAY.
WE'LL GO AROUND THE BACK...
NICK?
...I KILLED HIM...
WHO WAS HE?
SOMEONE WHO DESERVED WHAT HE GOT...
NOW COME ON, WE HAVE TO GO -- NOW.

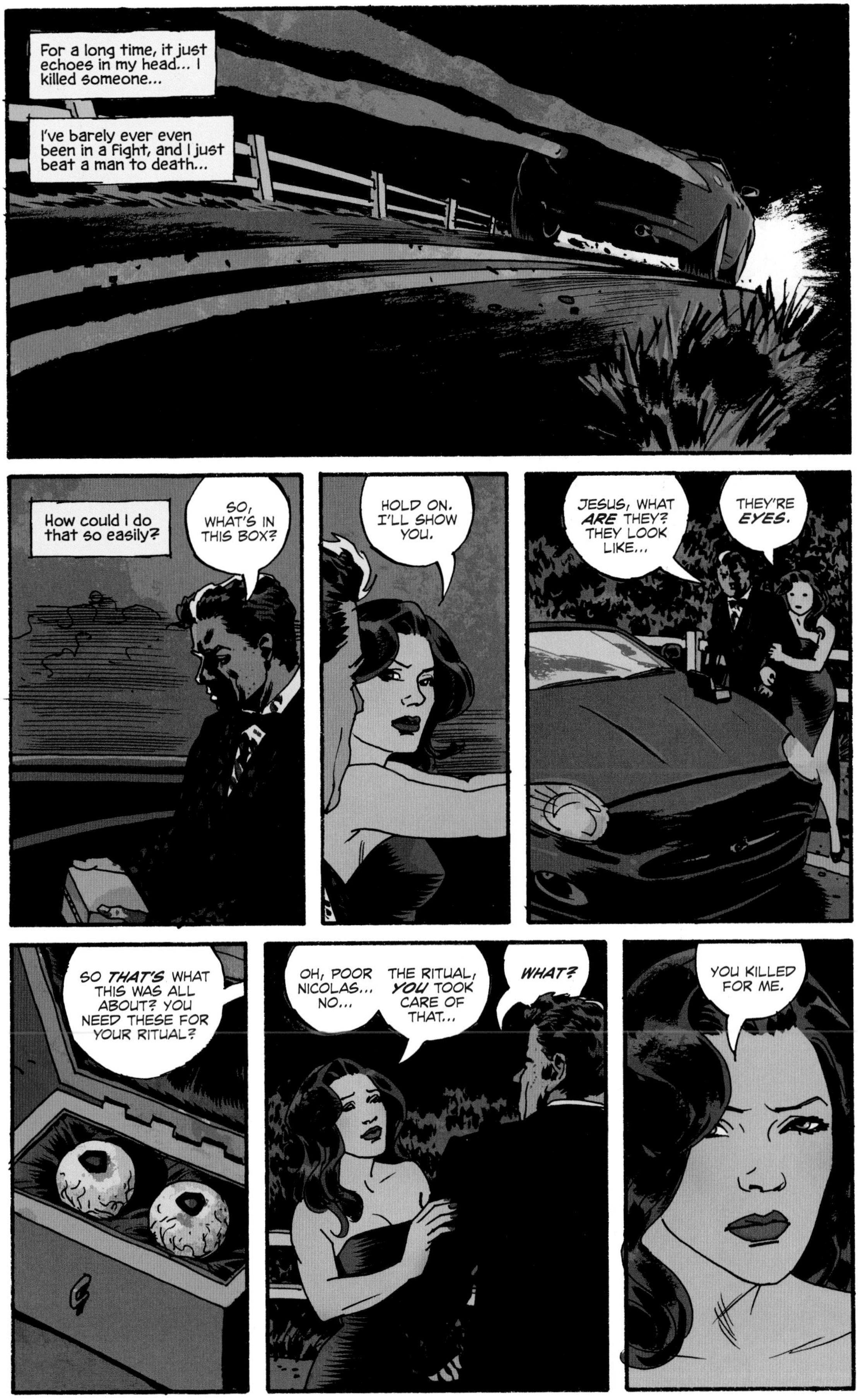
For a long time, it just echoes in my head... I killed someone...
I've barely ever even been in a fight, and I just beat a man to death...
How could I do that so easily?
SO, WHAT'S IN THIS BOX?
HOLD ON. I'LL SHOW YOU.
JESUS, WHAT *ARE* THEY? THEY LOOK LIKE...
THEY'RE *EYES.*
SO *THAT'S* WHAT THIS WAS ALL ABOUT? YOU NEED THESE FOR YOUR RITUAL?
OH, POOR NICOLAS... NO...
THE RITUAL, *YOU* TOOK CARE OF THAT...
WHAT?
YOU KILLED FOR ME.

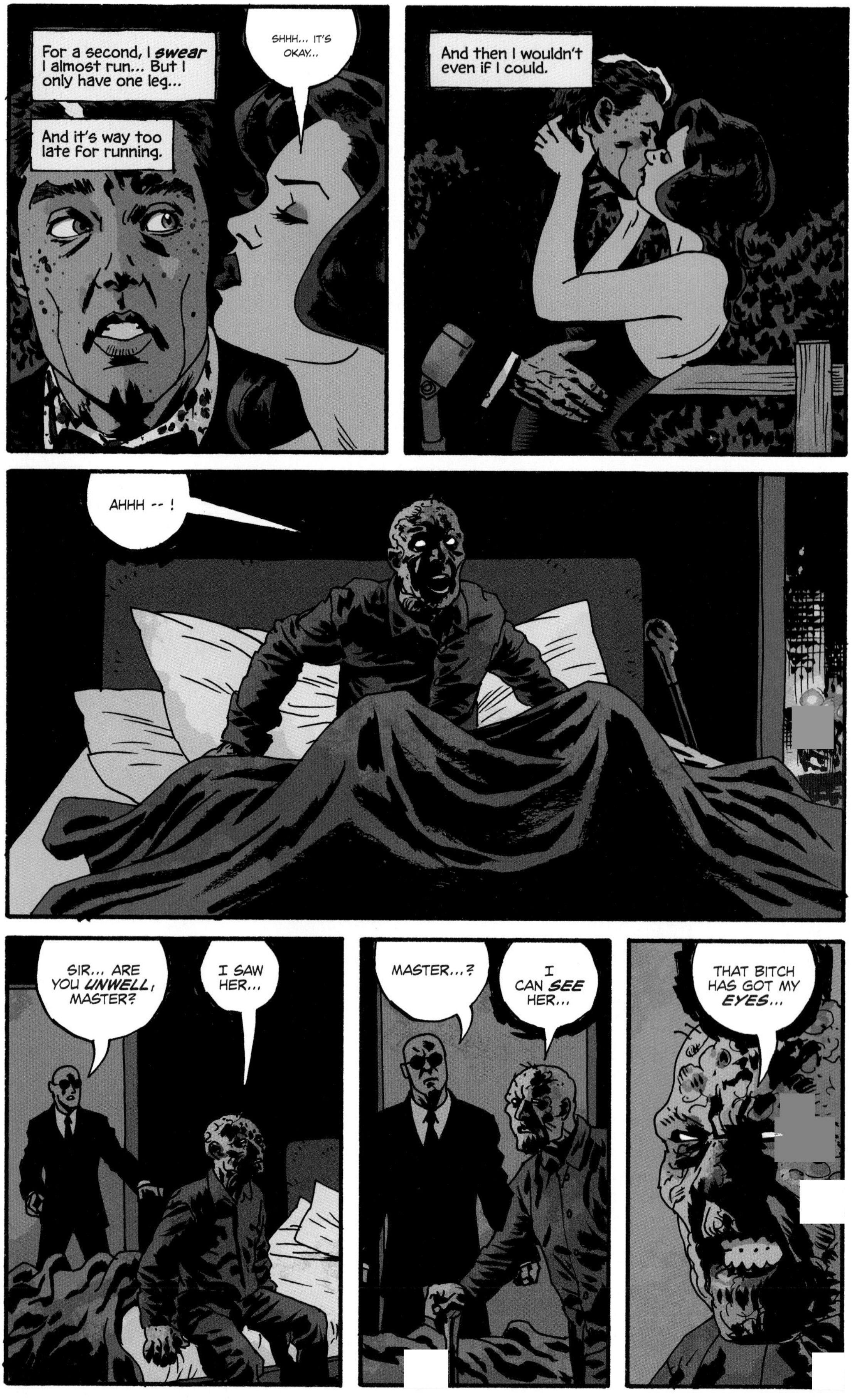
For a second, I *swear* I almost run... But I only have one leg...
SHHH... IT'S OKAY...
And it's way too late for running.
And then I wouldn't even if I could.
AHHH -- !
SIR... ARE YOU *UNWELL*, MASTER?
I SAW HER...
MASTER...?
I CAN *SEE* HER...
THAT BITCH HAS GOT MY *EYES*...

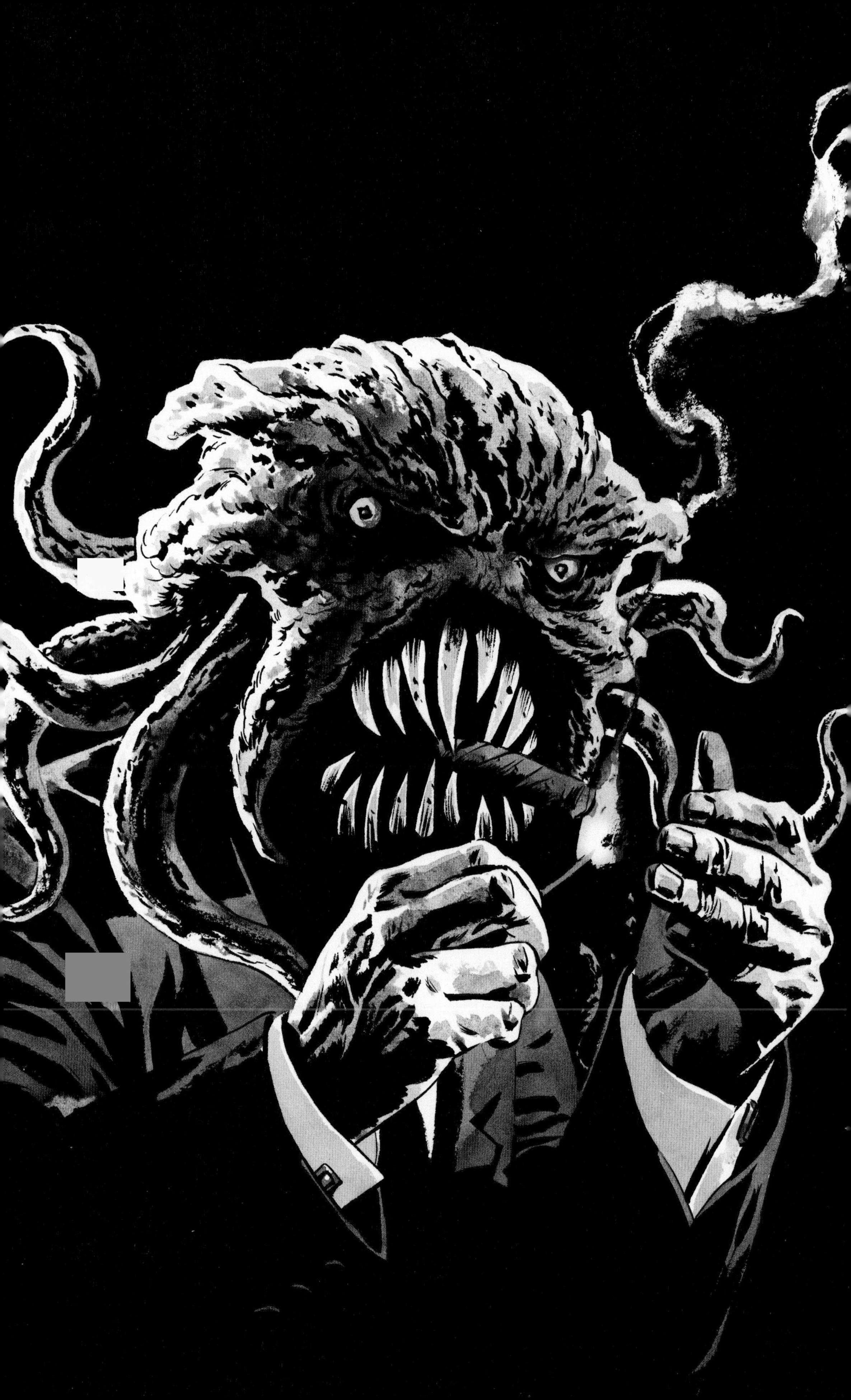

Chapter Three

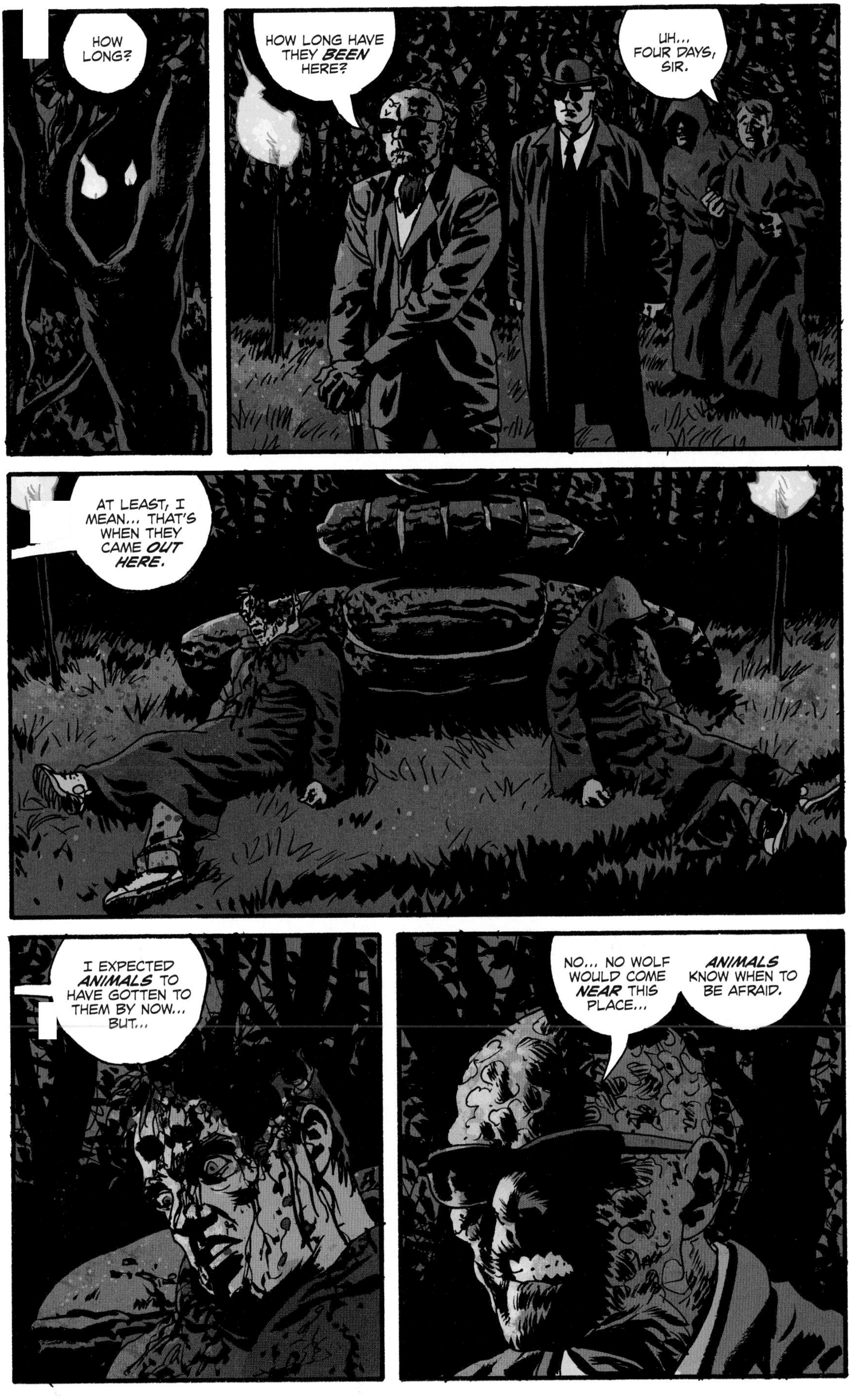
HOW LONG?
HOW LONG HAVE THEY BEEN HERE?
UH... FOUR DAYS, SIR.
AT LEAST, I MEAN... THAT'S WHEN THEY CAME OUT HERE.
I EXPECTED ANIMALS TO HAVE GOTTEN TO THEM BY NOW... BUT...
NO... NO WOLF WOULD COME NEAR THIS PLACE...
ANIMALS KNOW WHEN TO BE AFRAID.

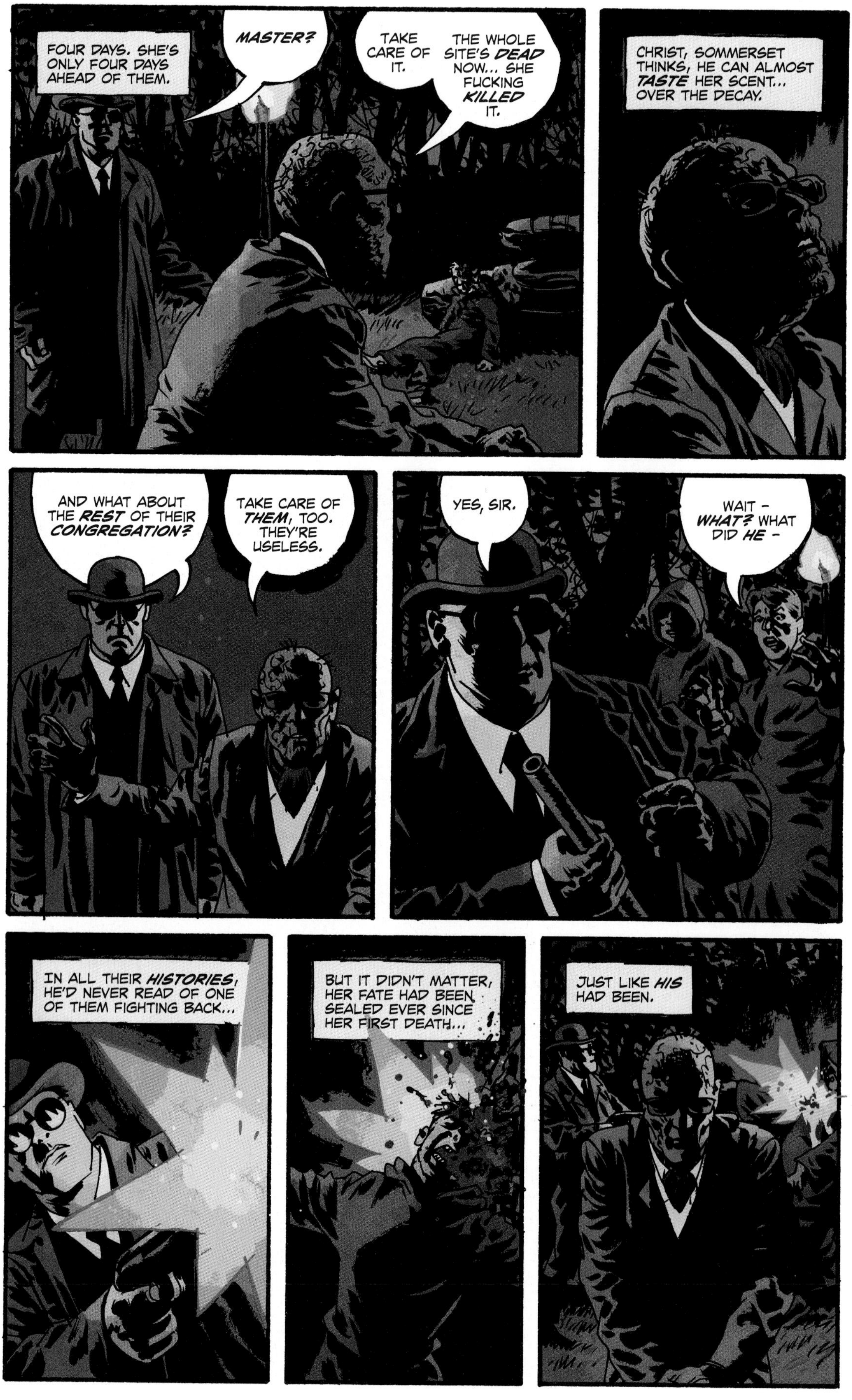

FOUR DAYS. SHE'S ONLY FOUR DAYS AHEAD OF THEM.
MASTER?
TAKE CARE OF IT.
THE WHOLE SITE'S DEAD NOW... SHE FUCKING KILLED IT.
CHRIST, SOMMERSET THINKS, HE CAN ALMOST TASTE HER SCENT... OVER THE DECAY.
AND WHAT ABOUT THE REST OF THEIR CONGREGATION?
TAKE CARE OF THEM, TOO. THEY'RE USELESS.
YES, SIR.
WAIT - WHAT? WHAT DID HE -
IN ALL THEIR HISTORIES, HE'D NEVER READ OF ONE OF THEM FIGHTING BACK...
BUT IT DIDN'T MATTER, HER FATE HAD BEEN SEALED EVER SINCE HER FIRST DEATH...
JUST LIKE HIS HAD BEEN.

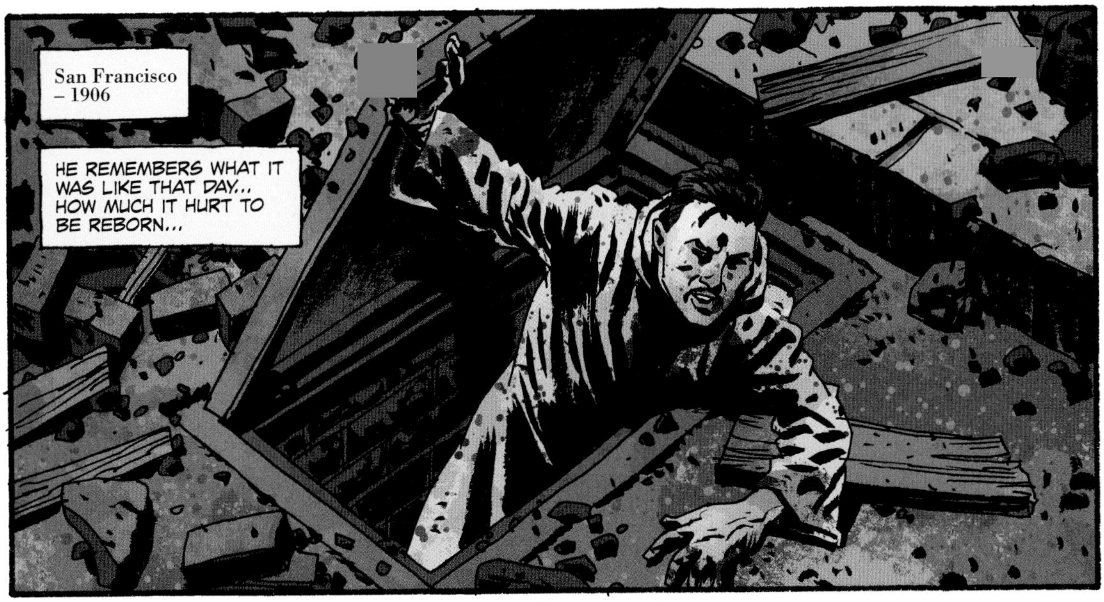
San Francisco – 1906
HE REMEMBERS WHAT IT WAS LIKE THAT DAY... HOW MUCH IT HURT TO BE REBORN...

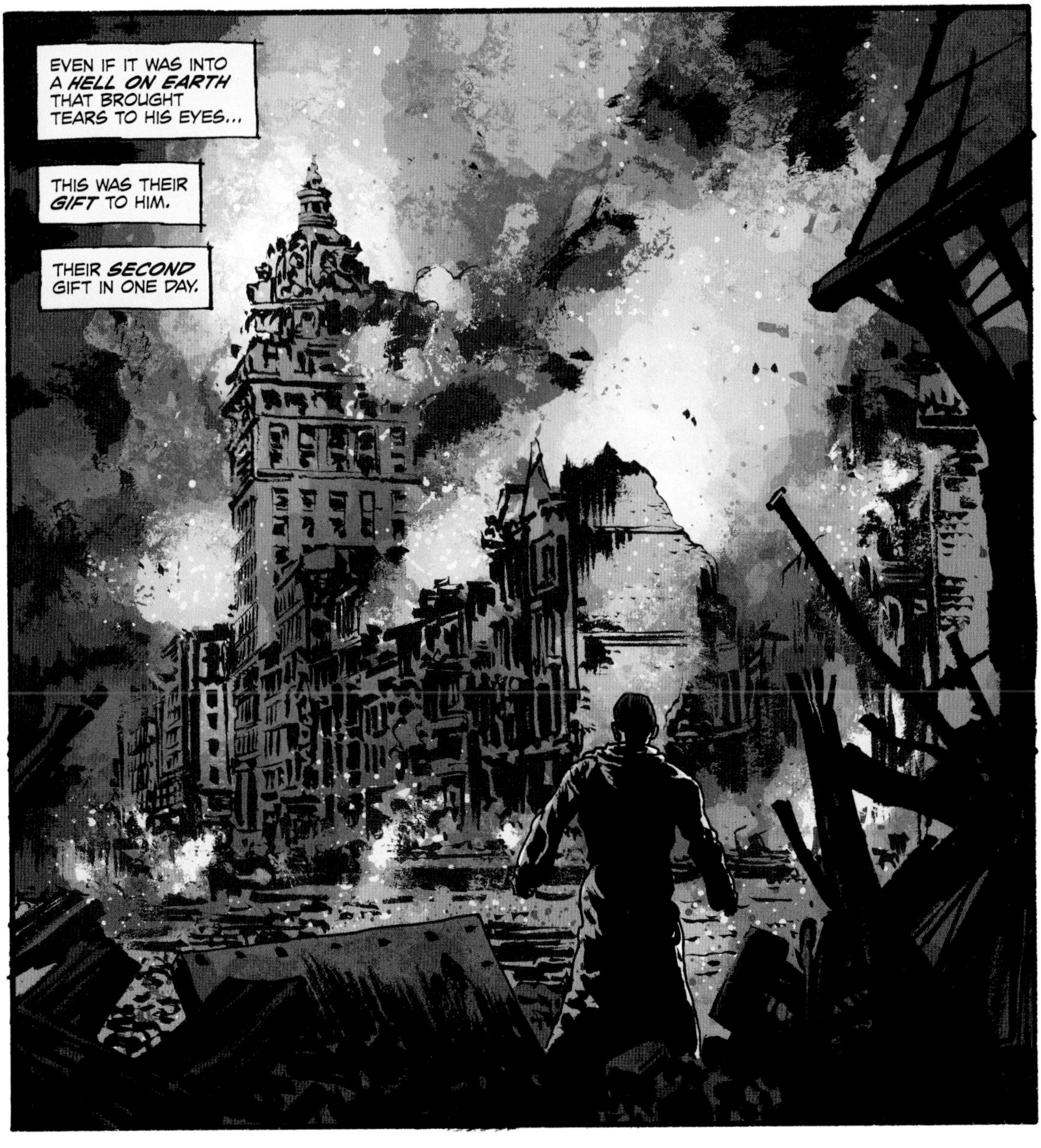
EVEN IF IT WAS INTO A HELL ON EARTH THAT BROUGHT TEARS TO HIS EYES...
THIS WAS THEIR GIFT TO HIM.
THEIR SECOND GIFT IN ONE DAY.

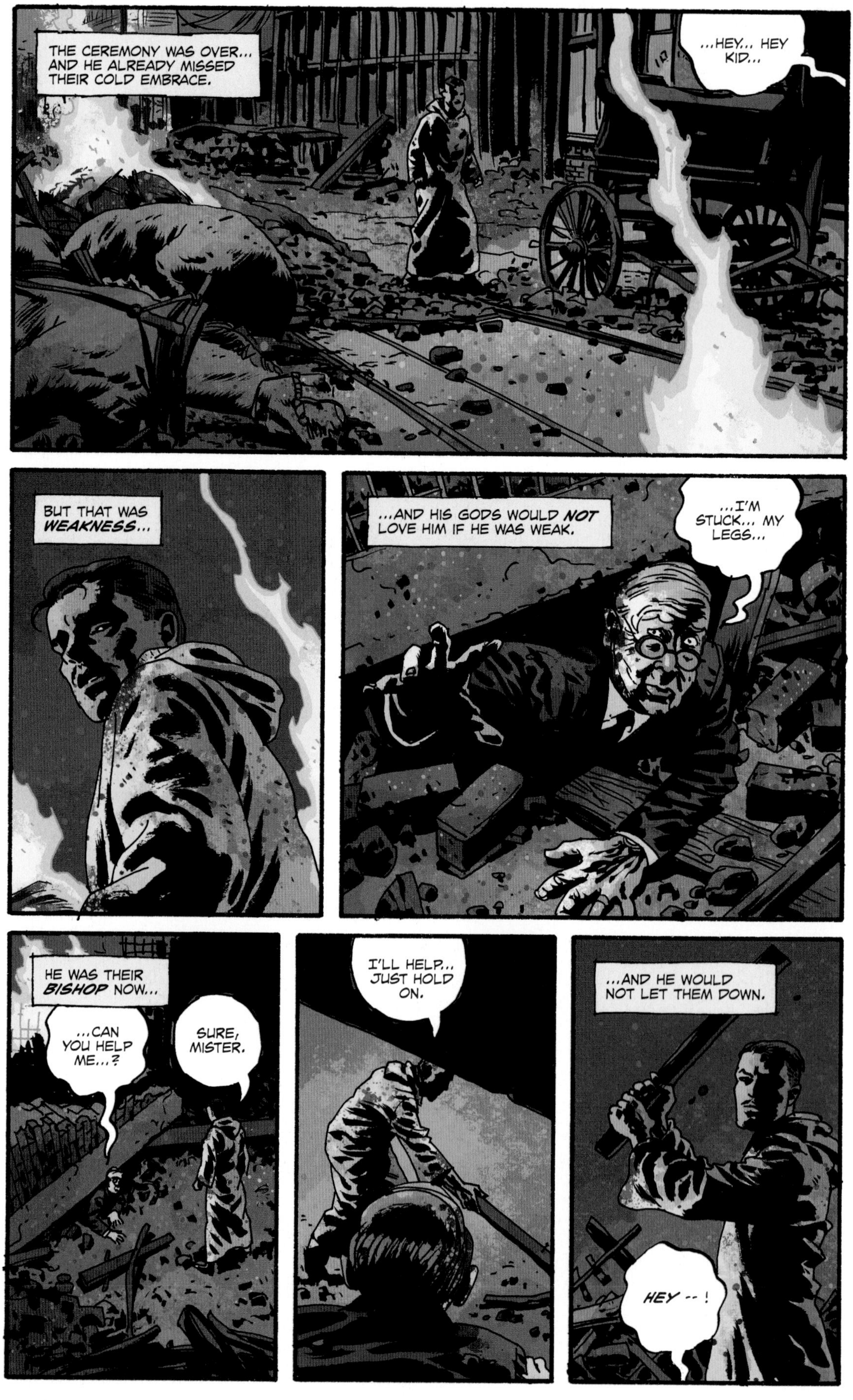
THE CEREMONY WAS OVER... AND HE ALREADY MISSED THEIR COLD EMBRACE.
...HEY... HEY KID...
BUT THAT WAS WEAKNESS...
...AND HIS GODS WOULD NOT LOVE HIM IF HE WAS WEAK.
...I'M STUCK... MY LEGS...
HE WAS THEIR BISHOP NOW...
...CAN YOU HELP ME...?
SURE, MISTER.
I'LL HELP... JUST HOLD ON.
...AND HE WOULD NOT LET THEM DOWN.
HEY -- !

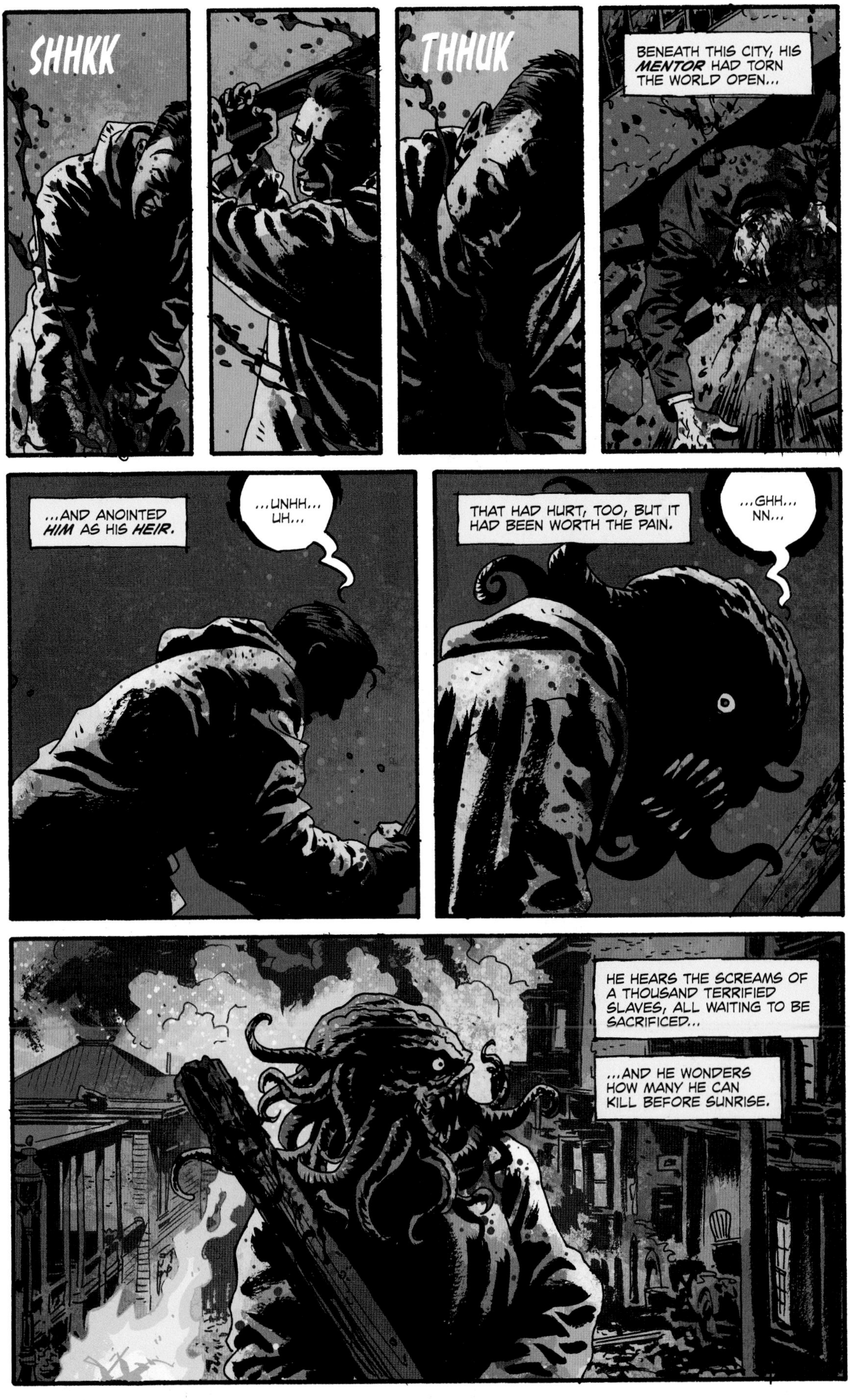
SHHKK
THHUK
BENEATH THIS CITY, HIS MENTOR HAD TORN THE WORLD OPEN...
...AND ANOINTED HIM AS HIS HEIR.
...UNHH... UH...
THAT HAD HURT, TOO, BUT IT HAD BEEN WORTH THE PAIN.
...GHH... NN...
HE HEARS THE SCREAMS OF A THOUSAND TERRIFIED SLAVES, ALL WAITING TO BE SACRIFICED...
...AND HE WONDERS HOW MANY HE CAN KILL BEFORE SUNRISE.

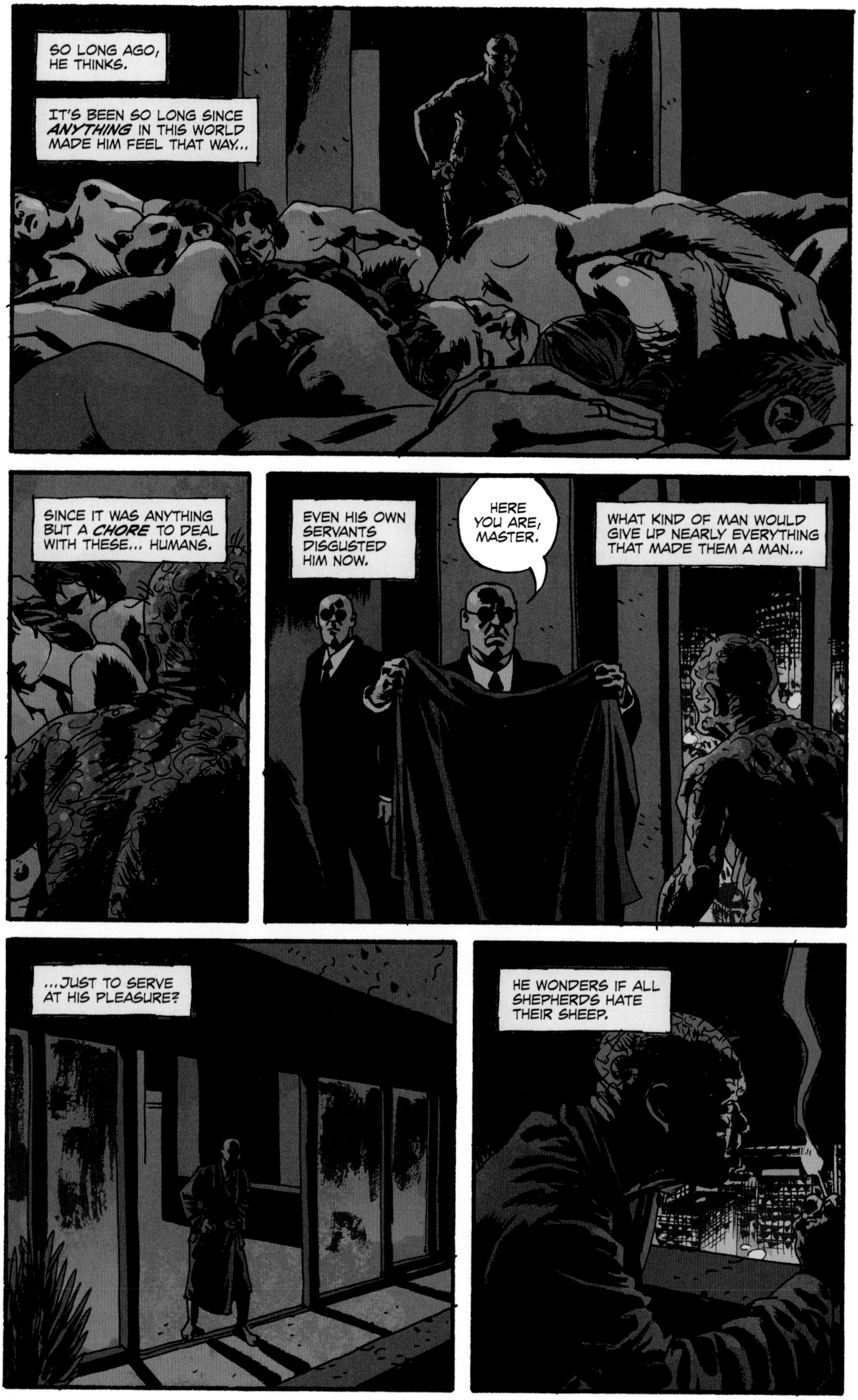
SO LONG AGO, HE THINKS.
IT'S BEEN SO LONG SINCE ANYTHING IN THIS WORLD MADE HIM FEEL THAT WAY...
SINCE IT WAS ANYTHING BUT A CHORE TO DEAL WITH THESE... HUMANS.
EVEN HIS OWN SERVANTS DISGUSTED HIM NOW.
HERE YOU ARE, MASTER.
WHAT KIND OF MAN WOULD GIVE UP NEARLY EVERYTHING THAT MADE THEM A MAN...
...JUST TO SERVE AT HIS PLEASURE?
HE WONDERS IF ALL SHEPHERDS HATE THEIR SHEEP.

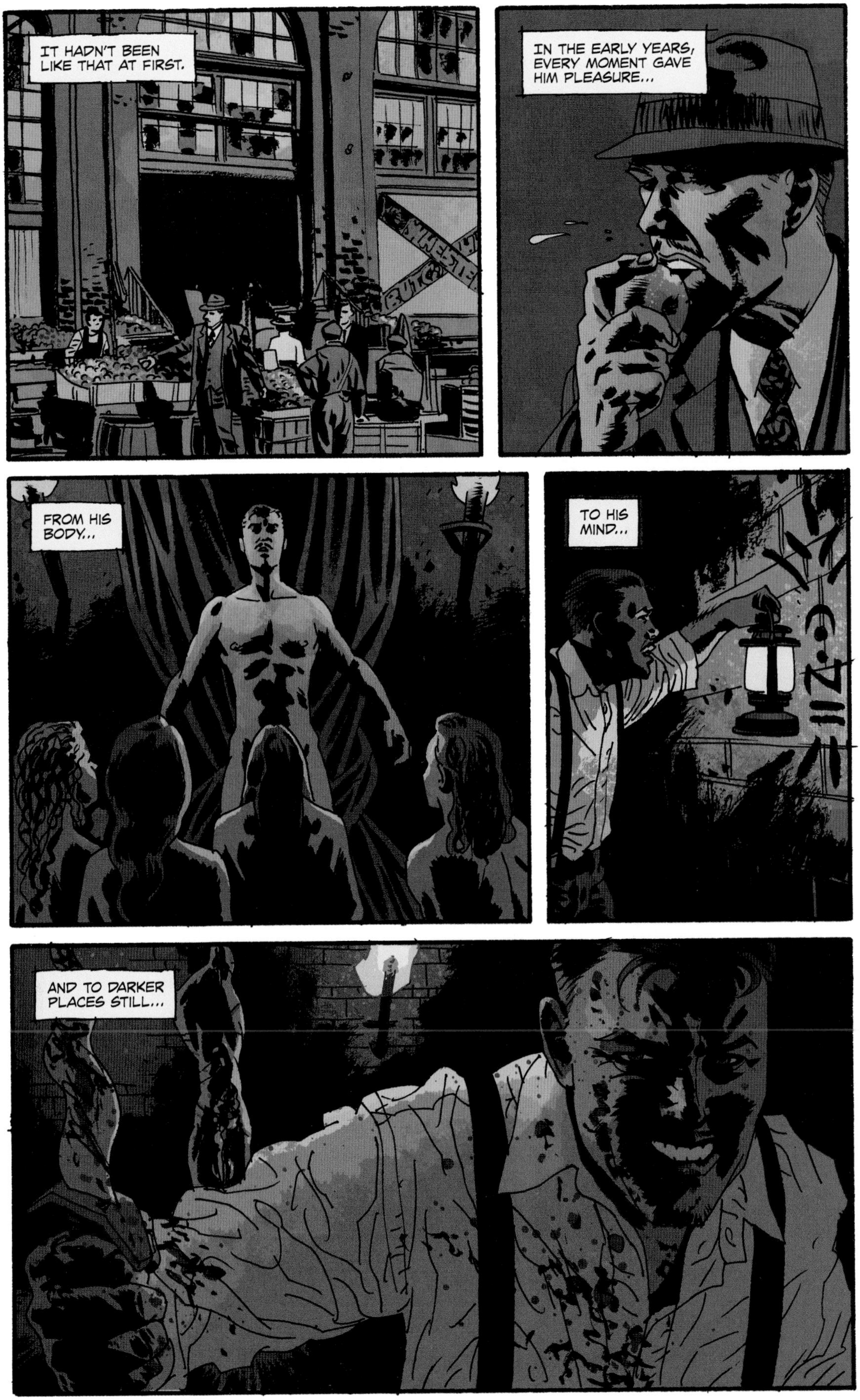
IT HADN'T BEEN LIKE THAT AT FIRST.
IN THE EARLY YEARS, EVERY MOMENT GAVE HIM PLEASURE...
FROM HIS BODY...
TO HIS MIND...
AND TO DARKER PLACES STILL...

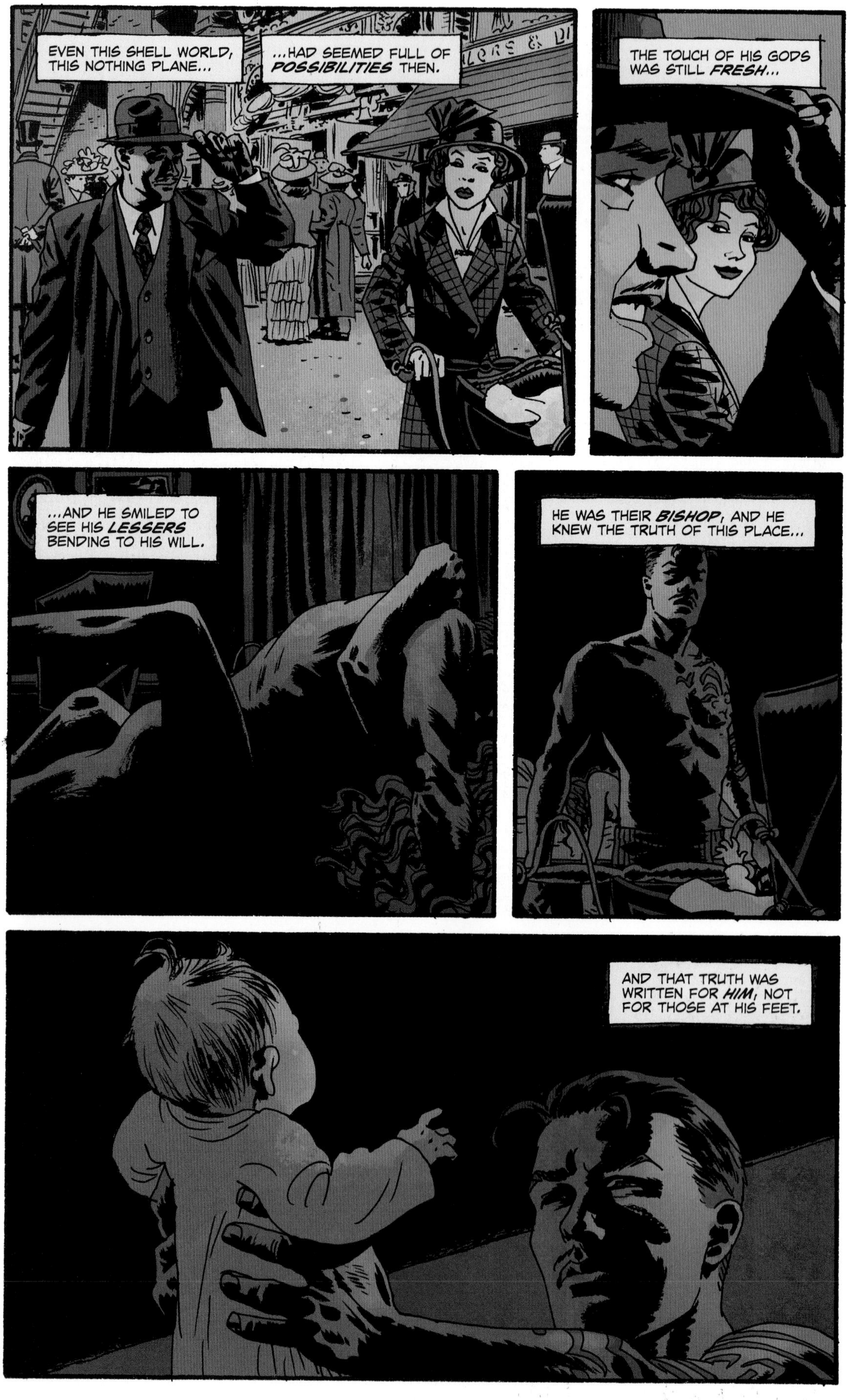
EVEN THIS SHELL WORLD, THIS NOTHING PLANE...
...HAD SEEMED FULL OF *POSSIBILITIES* THEN.
THE TOUCH OF HIS GODS WAS STILL *FRESH*...
...AND HE SMILED TO SEE HIS *LESSERS* BENDING TO HIS WILL.
HE WAS THEIR *BISHOP*, AND HE KNEW THE TRUTH OF THIS PLACE...
AND THAT TRUTH WAS WRITTEN FOR *HIM*, NOT FOR THOSE AT HIS FEET.

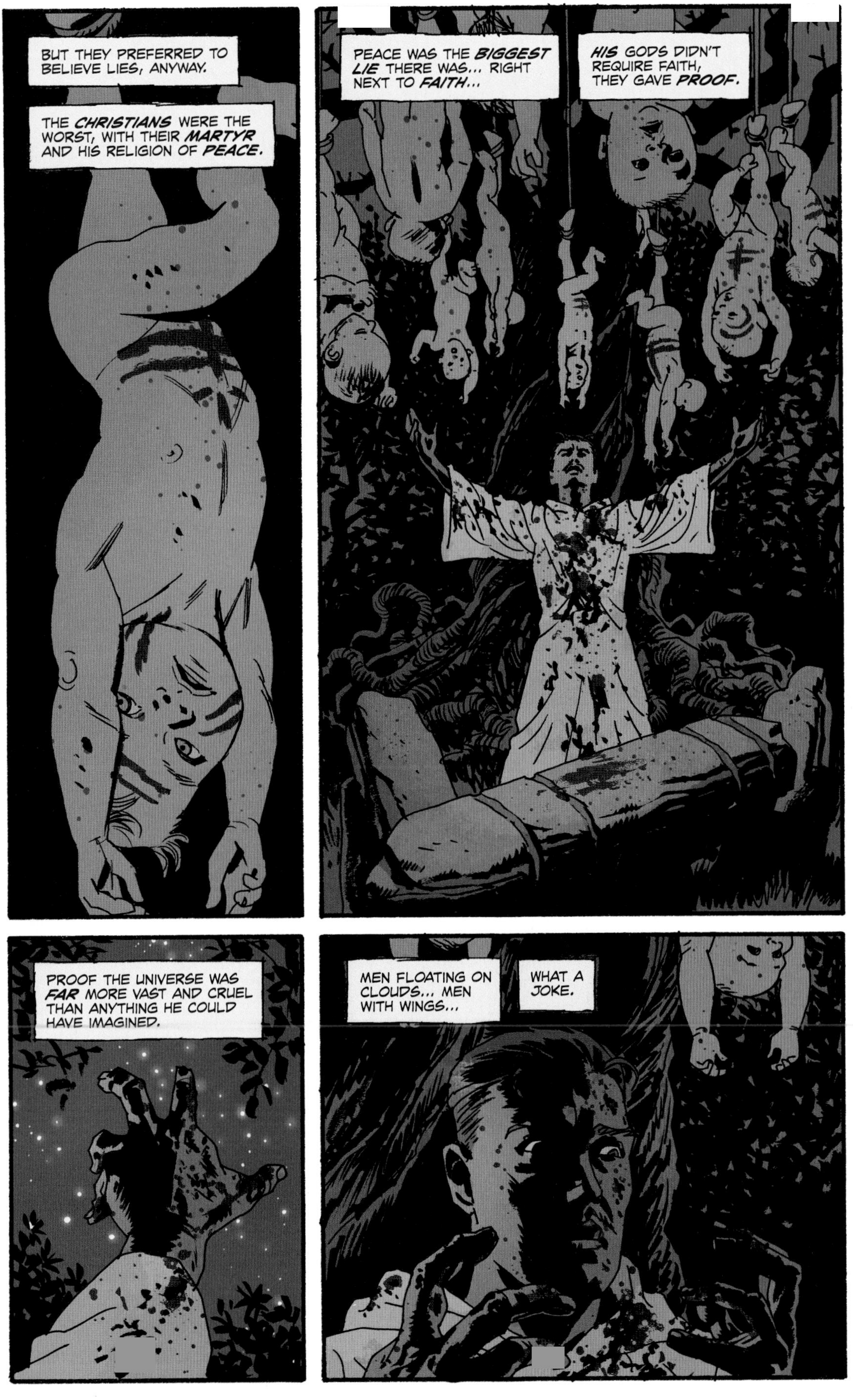
BUT THEY PREFERRED TO BELIEVE LIES, ANYWAY.
THE CHRISTIANS WERE THE WORST, WITH THEIR MARTYR AND HIS RELIGION OF PEACE.
PEACE WAS THE BIGGEST LIE THERE WAS... RIGHT NEXT TO FAITH...
HIS GODS DIDN'T REQUIRE FAITH, THEY GAVE PROOF.
PROOF THE UNIVERSE WAS FAR MORE VAST AND CRUEL THAN ANYTHING HE COULD HAVE IMAGINED.
MEN FLOATING ON CLOUDS... MEN WITH WINGS...
WHAT A JOKE.

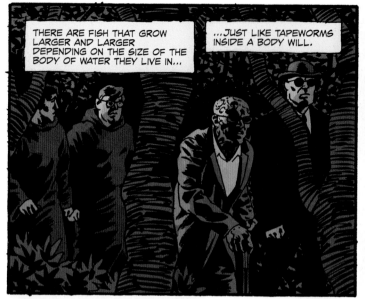

THERE ARE FISH THAT GROW LARGER AND LARGER DEPENDING ON THE SIZE OF THE BODY OF WATER THEY LIVE IN...

...JUST LIKE TAPEWORMS INSIDE A BODY WILL.

THAT WAS HOW *TRUE GODS* WERE, THEY GREW TO FILL EVERY CORNER...

...TO BLOCK OUT ALL SOURCES OF LIGHT...

BISHOP? *SIR*...? IS THERE SOMETHING WE CAN DO TO --

SHUT UP.

I NEED TO HEAR THE TREE.

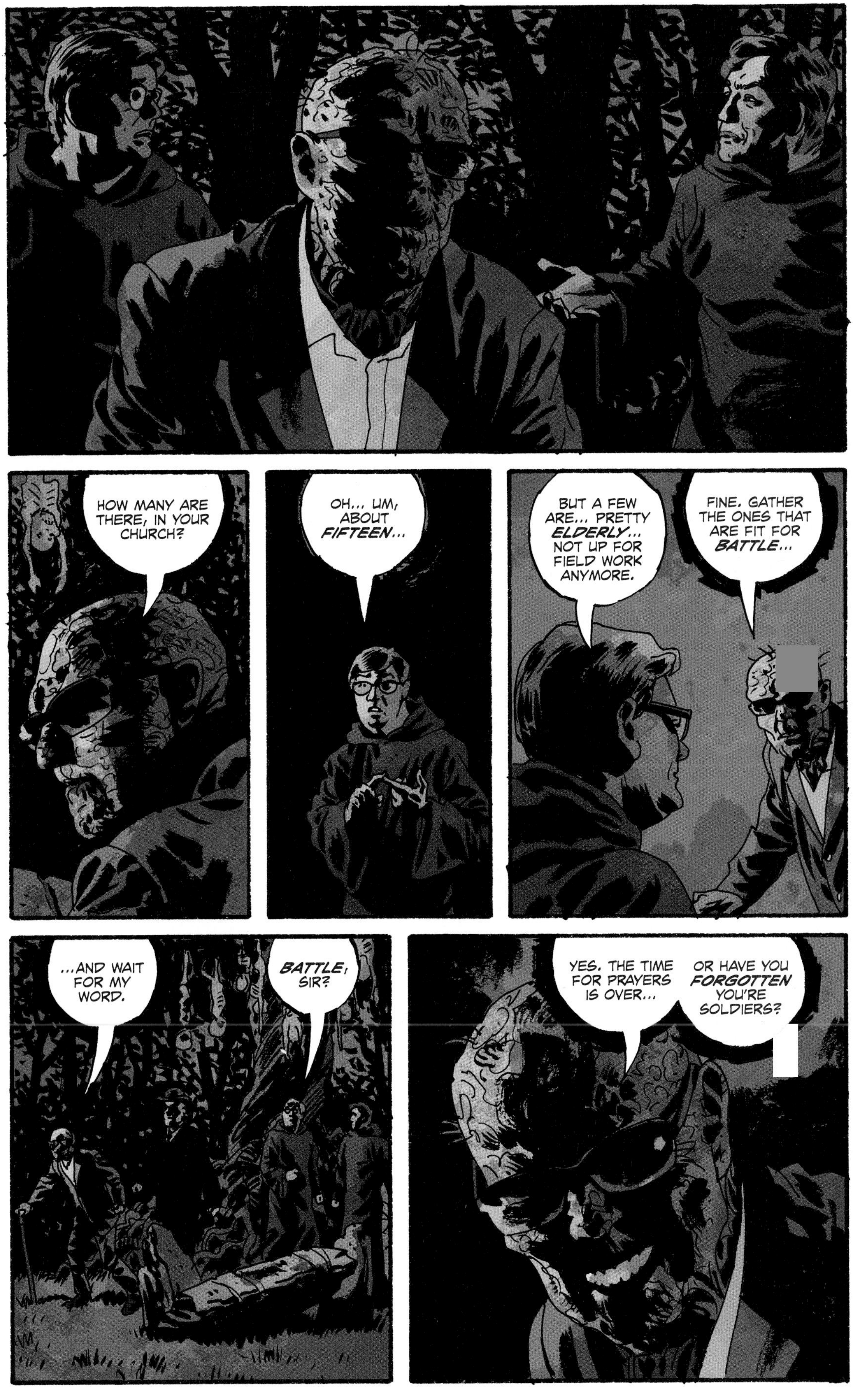
HOW MANY ARE THERE, IN YOUR CHURCH?
OH... UM, ABOUT *FIFTEEN*...
BUT A FEW ARE... PRETTY *ELDERLY*... NOT UP FOR FIELD WORK ANYMORE.
FINE. GATHER THE ONES THAT ARE FIT FOR *BATTLE*...
...AND WAIT FOR MY WORD.
BATTLE, SIR?
YES. THE TIME FOR PRAYERS IS OVER...
OR HAVE YOU *FORGOTTEN* YOU'RE SOLDIERS?

ALL HIS LIFE HE'D KNOWN IT, BUT IT WASN'T UNTIL THE *FIRST WORLD WAR* THAT HE SAW THE TRUTH FOR HIMSELF...

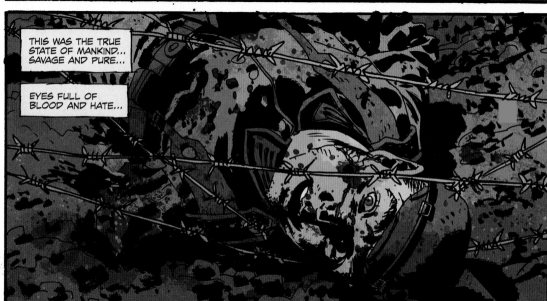

THIS WAS THE TRUE STATE OF MANKIND... SAVAGE AND PURE...

EYES FULL OF BLOOD AND HATE...

EVEN THOSE *TOO WEAK* TO SEE THE WORLD AS HE AND HIS KIND DID COULD KILL THEIR ENEMIES WITH THEIR OWN HANDS...

LIKE THEIR PRIMITIVE ANCESTORS HAD...

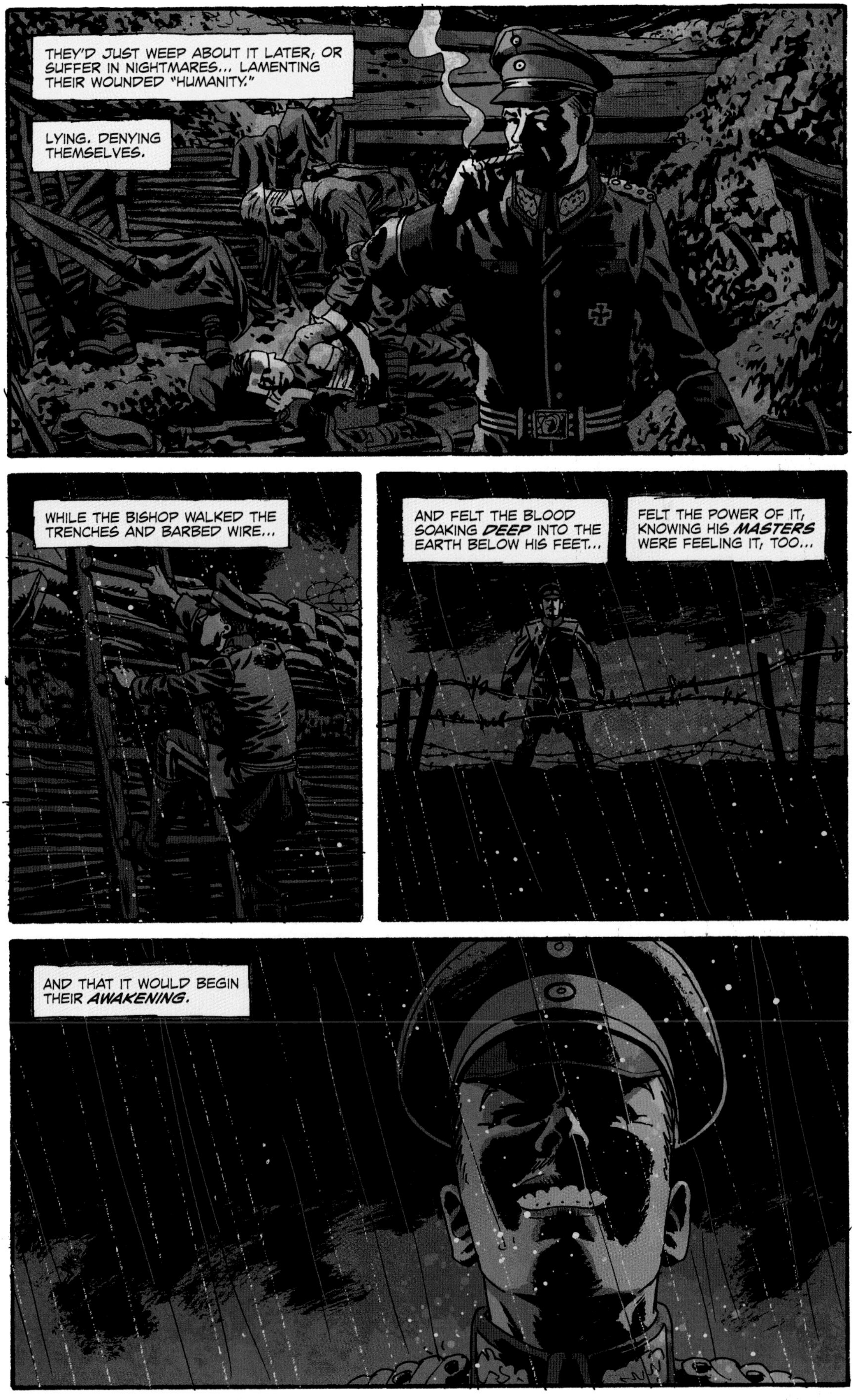
THEY'D JUST WEEP ABOUT IT LATER, OR SUFFER IN NIGHTMARES... LAMENTING THEIR WOUNDED "HUMANITY."
LYING. DENYING THEMSELVES.
WHILE THE BISHOP WALKED THE TRENCHES AND BARBED WIRE...
AND FELT THE BLOOD SOAKING DEEP INTO THE EARTH BELOW HIS FEET...
FELT THE POWER OF IT, KNOWING HIS MASTERS WERE FEELING IT, TOO...
AND THAT IT WOULD BEGIN THEIR AWAKENING.

HE LAUGHED INSIDE ON THOSE NIGHTS, WATCHING PRIESTS AND SOLDIERS *PRAYING* OVER THEIR DEAD COMRADES...

SAYING THEY'D GONE TO *A BETTER PLACE*...

BECAUSE HE KNEW THERE WAS NO BETTER PLACE...

NOT THE WAY *THEY* MEANT...

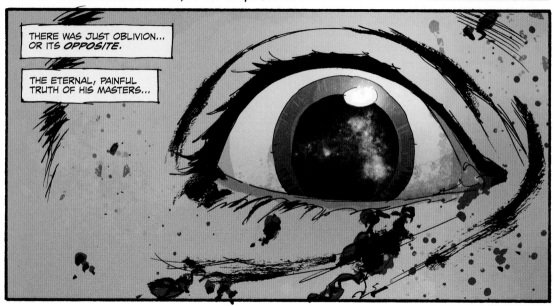

THERE WAS JUST OBLIVION... OR ITS *OPPOSITE*.

THE ETERNAL, PAINFUL TRUTH OF HIS MASTERS...

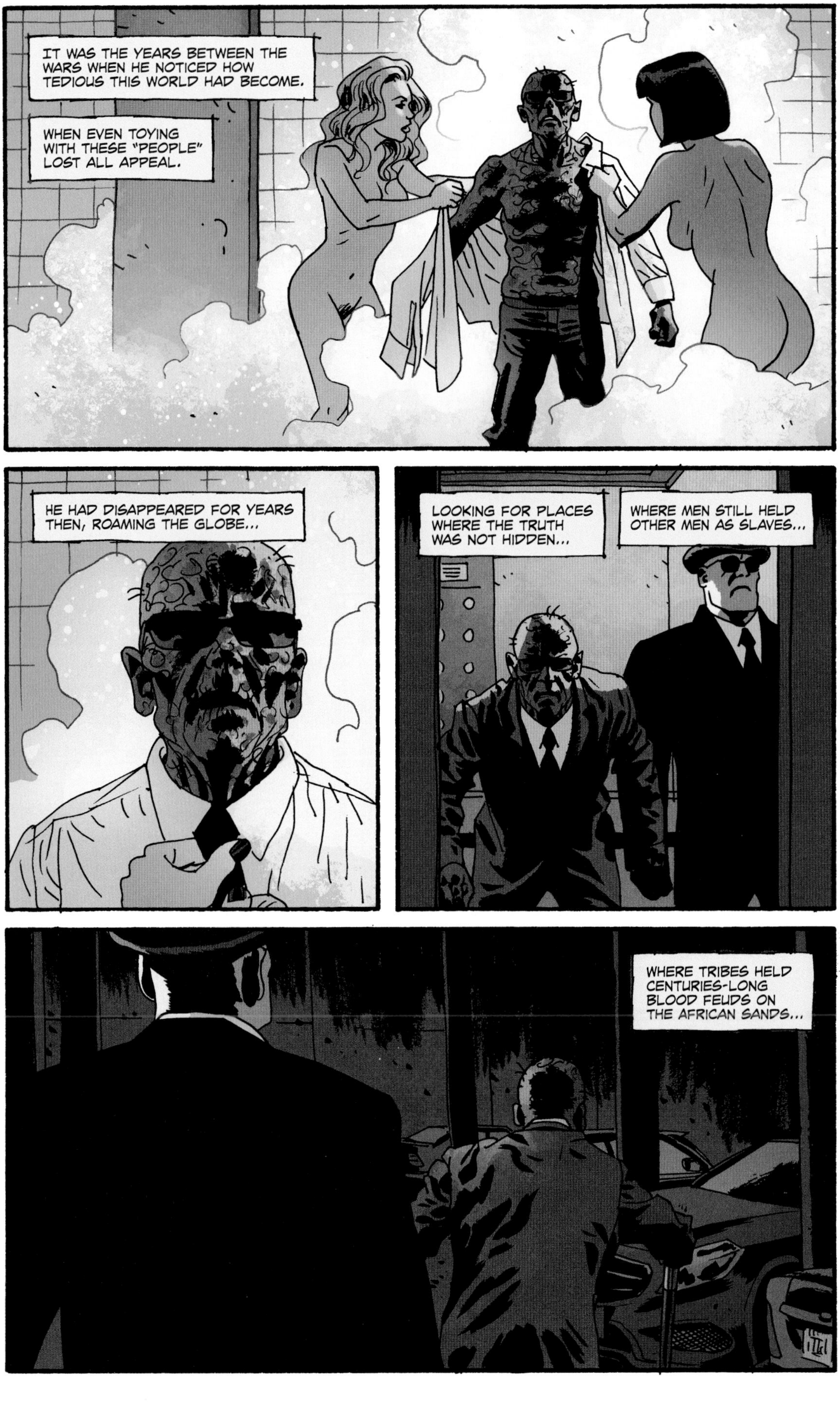
IT WAS THE YEARS BETWEEN THE WARS WHEN HE NOTICED HOW TEDIOUS THIS WORLD HAD BECOME.
WHEN EVEN TOYING WITH THESE "PEOPLE" LOST ALL APPEAL.
HE HAD DISAPPEARED FOR YEARS THEN, ROAMING THE GLOBE...
LOOKING FOR PLACES WHERE THE TRUTH WAS NOT HIDDEN...
WHERE MEN STILL HELD OTHER MEN AS SLAVES...
WHERE TRIBES HELD CENTURIES-LONG BLOOD FEUDS ON THE AFRICAN SANDS...

BUT NO MATTER WHERE HE WENT, THE *WEARINESS* GREW INSIDE HIM.

HE WAS *READY* FOR IT TO BE OVER...

HIS TIME IN THIS PLACE.

AND AS THE NEXT *GREAT WAR* CREPT ACROSS EUROPE, HIS PRIESTS BEGAN TELLING HIM OF THE SIGNS, AND THE ALIGNMENT OF THE STARS...

BLOOD RAINS IN SOUTH AMERICAN JUNGLES...

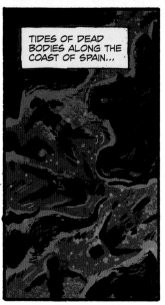

TIDES OF DEAD BODIES ALONG THE COAST OF SPAIN...

THE WINDOW FOR HIS FINAL COMMUNION WAS OPENING...

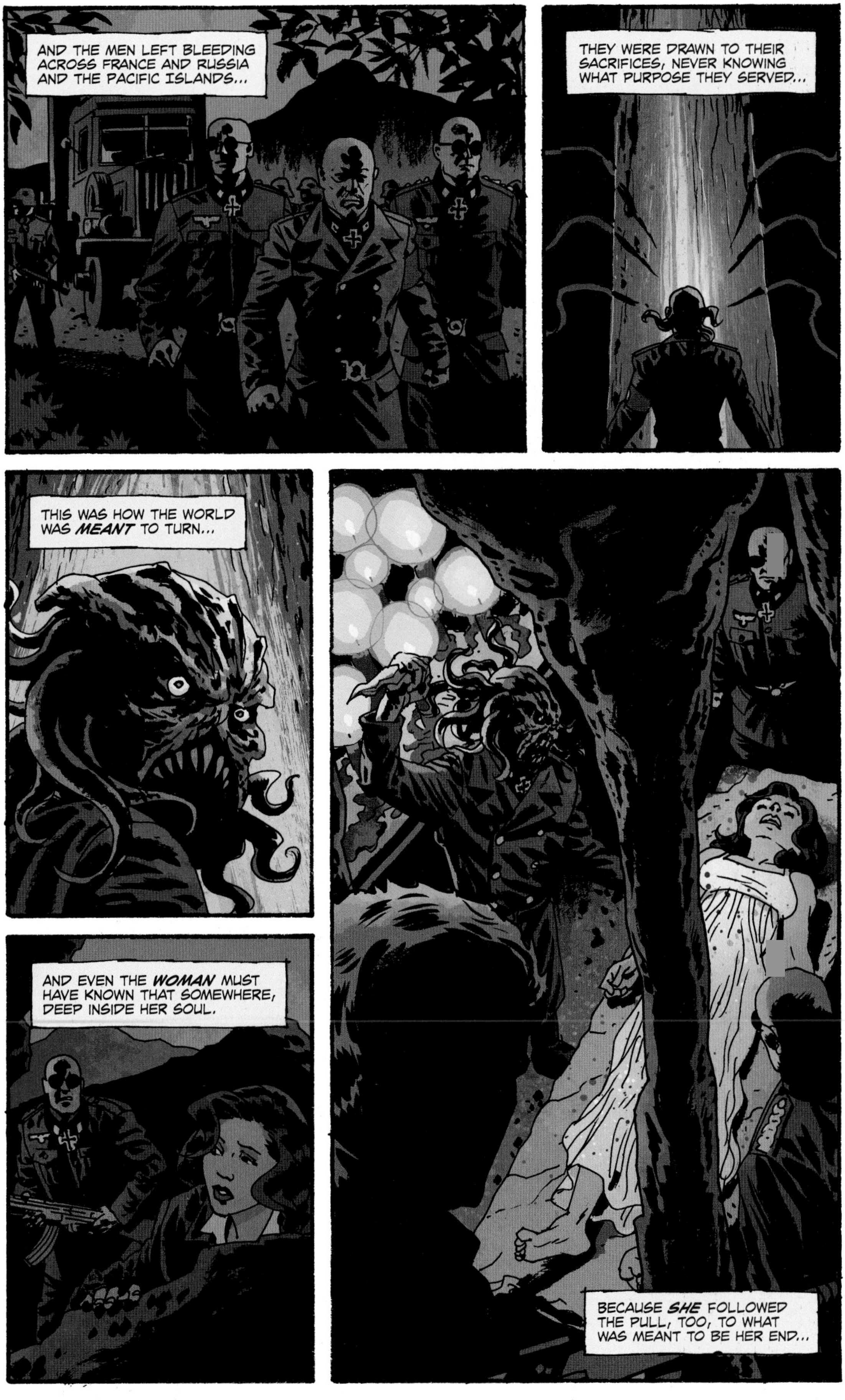
AND THE MEN LEFT BLEEDING ACROSS FRANCE AND RUSSIA AND THE PACIFIC ISLANDS...
THEY WERE DRAWN TO THEIR SACRIFICES, NEVER KNOWING WHAT PURPOSE THEY SERVED...
THIS WAS HOW THE WORLD WAS MEANT TO TURN...
AND EVEN THE WOMAN MUST HAVE KNOWN THAT SOMEWHERE, DEEP INSIDE HER SOUL.
BECAUSE SHE FOLLOWED THE PULL, TOO, TO WHAT WAS MEANT TO BE HER END...

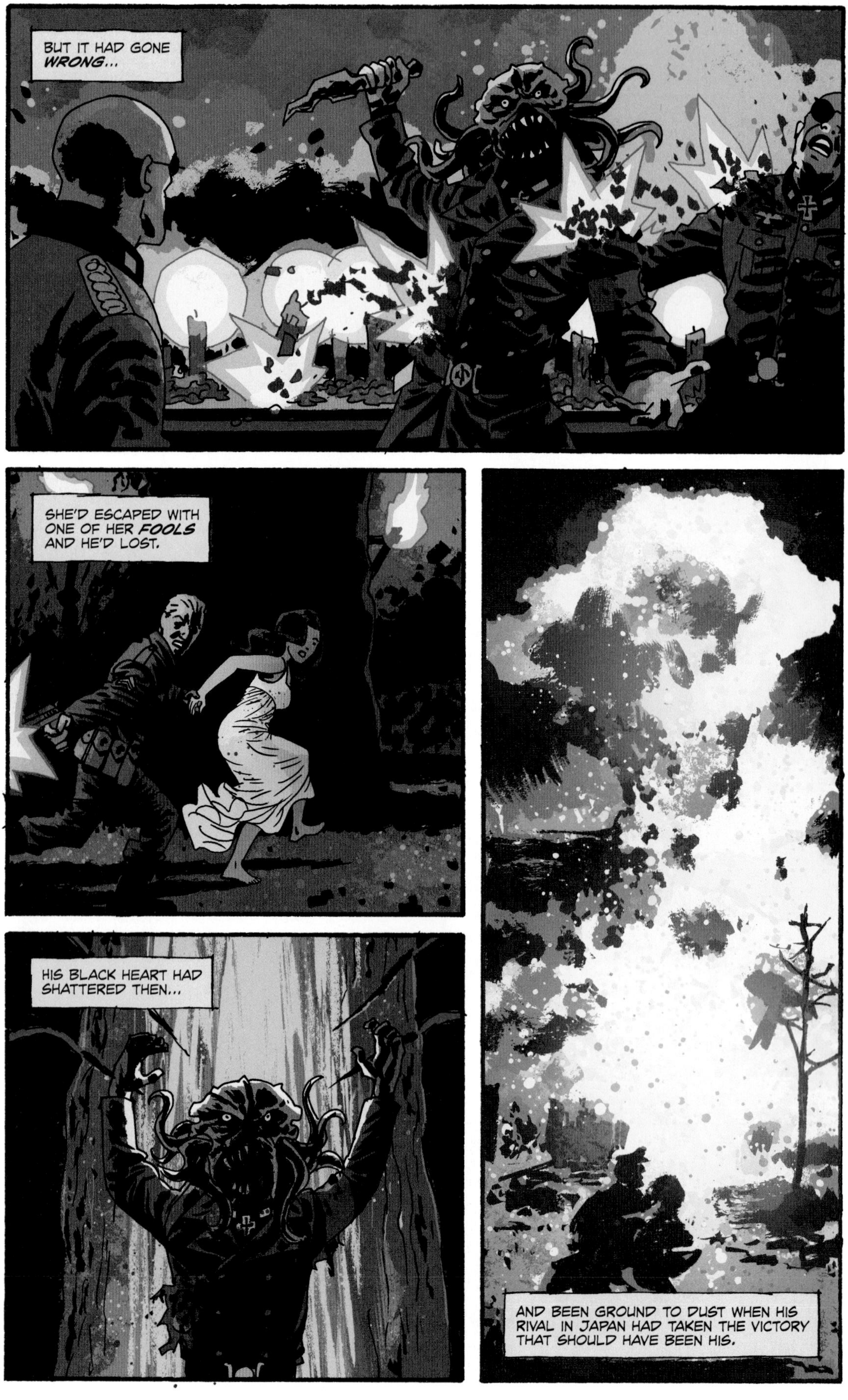
BUT IT HAD GONE *WRONG*...
SHE'D ESCAPED WITH ONE OF HER *FOOLS* AND HE'D LOST.
HIS BLACK HEART HAD SHATTERED THEN...
AND BEEN GROUND TO DUST WHEN HIS RIVAL IN JAPAN HAD TAKEN THE VICTORY THAT SHOULD HAVE BEEN HIS.

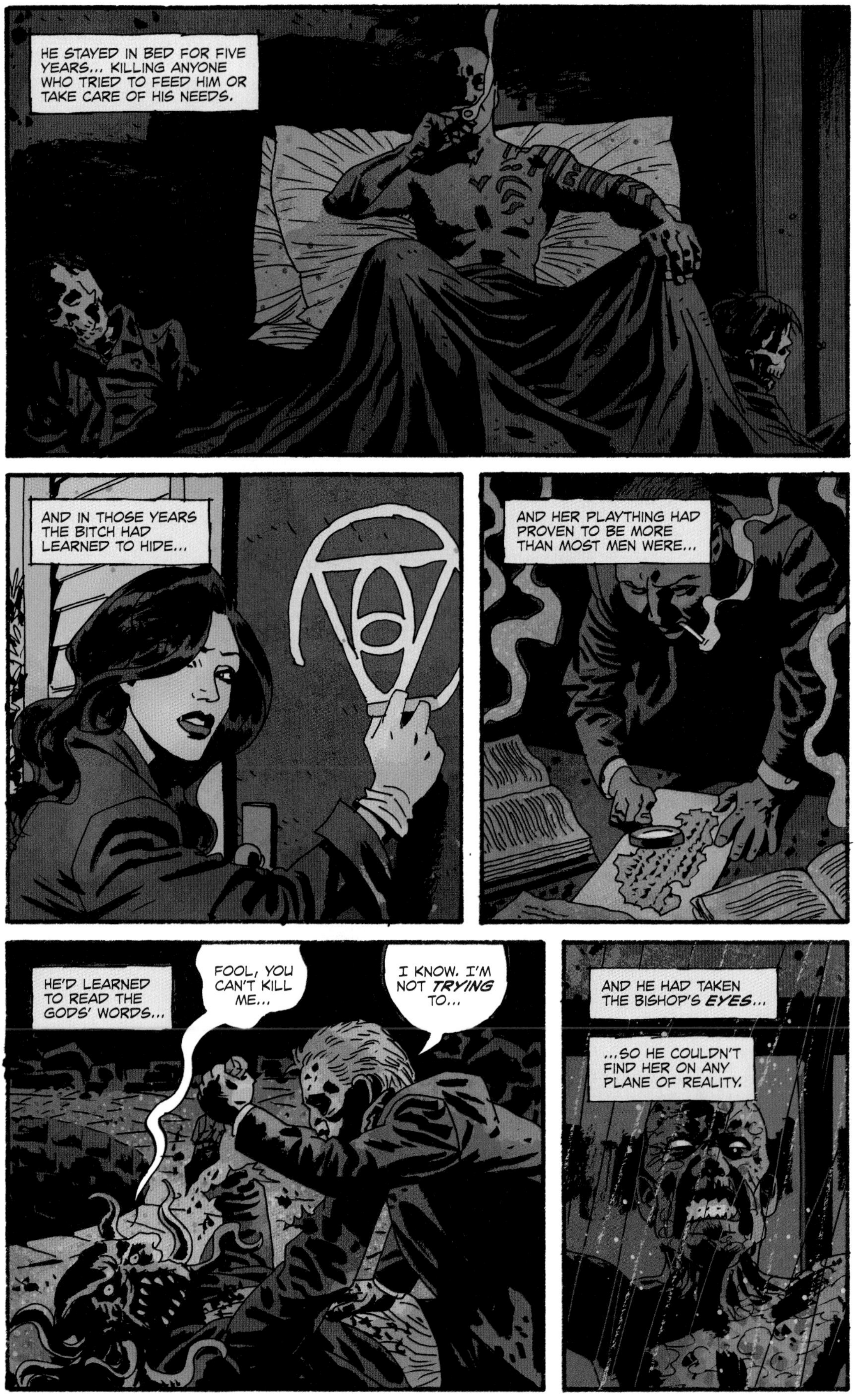
HE STAYED IN BED FOR FIVE YEARS... KILLING ANYONE WHO TRIED TO FEED HIM OR TAKE CARE OF HIS NEEDS.
AND IN THOSE YEARS THE BITCH HAD LEARNED TO HIDE...
AND HER PLAYTHING HAD PROVEN TO BE MORE THAN MOST MEN WERE...
HE'D LEARNED TO READ THE GODS' WORDS...
FOOL, YOU CAN'T KILL ME...
I KNOW. I'M NOT TRYING TO...
AND HE HAD TAKEN THE BISHOP'S EYES...
...SO HE COULDN'T FIND HER ON ANY PLANE OF REALITY.

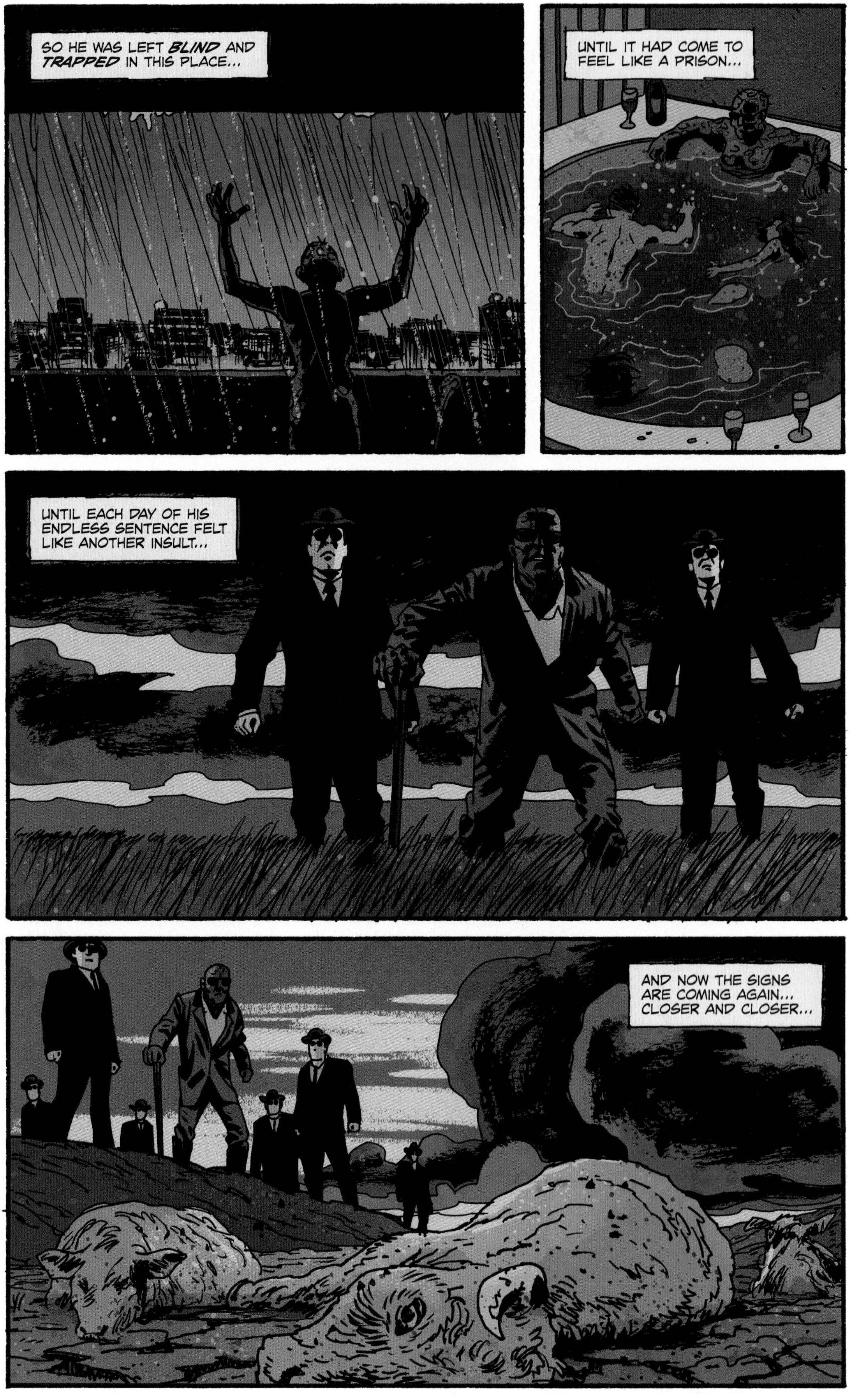
SO HE WAS LEFT BLIND AND TRAPPED IN THIS PLACE...
UNTIL IT HAD COME TO FEEL LIKE A PRISON...
UNTIL EACH DAY OF HIS ENDLESS SENTENCE FELT LIKE ANOTHER INSULT...
AND NOW THE SIGNS ARE COMING AGAIN... CLOSER AND CLOSER...

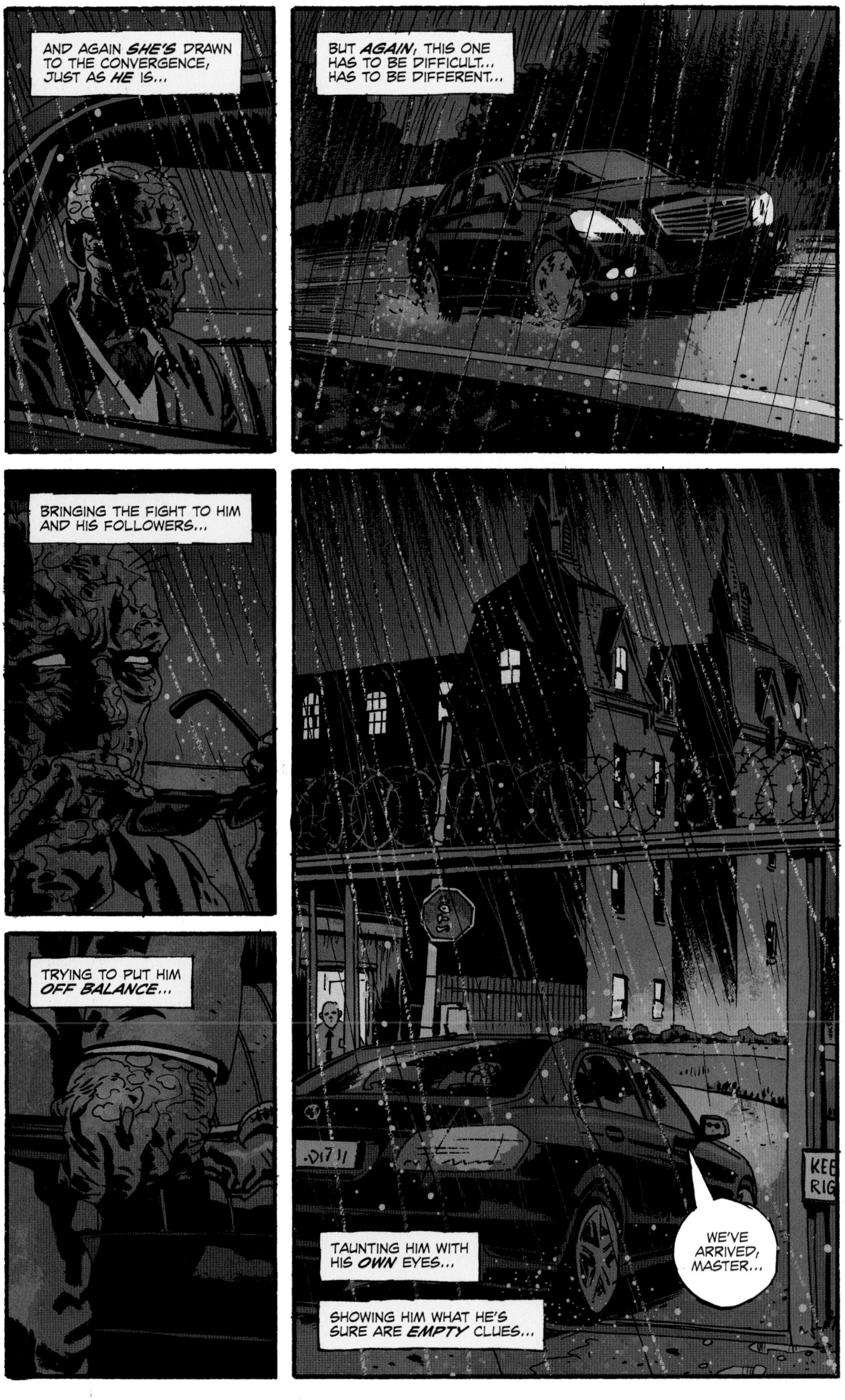
AND AGAIN SHE'S DRAWN TO THE CONVERGENCE, JUST AS HE IS...
BUT AGAIN, THIS ONE HAS TO BE DIFFICULT... HAS TO BE DIFFERENT...
BRINGING THE FIGHT TO HIM AND HIS FOLLOWERS...
TRYING TO PUT HIM OFF BALANCE...
TAUNTING HIM WITH HIS OWN EYES...
SHOWING HIM WHAT HE'S SURE ARE EMPTY CLUES...
WE'VE ARRIVED, MASTER...

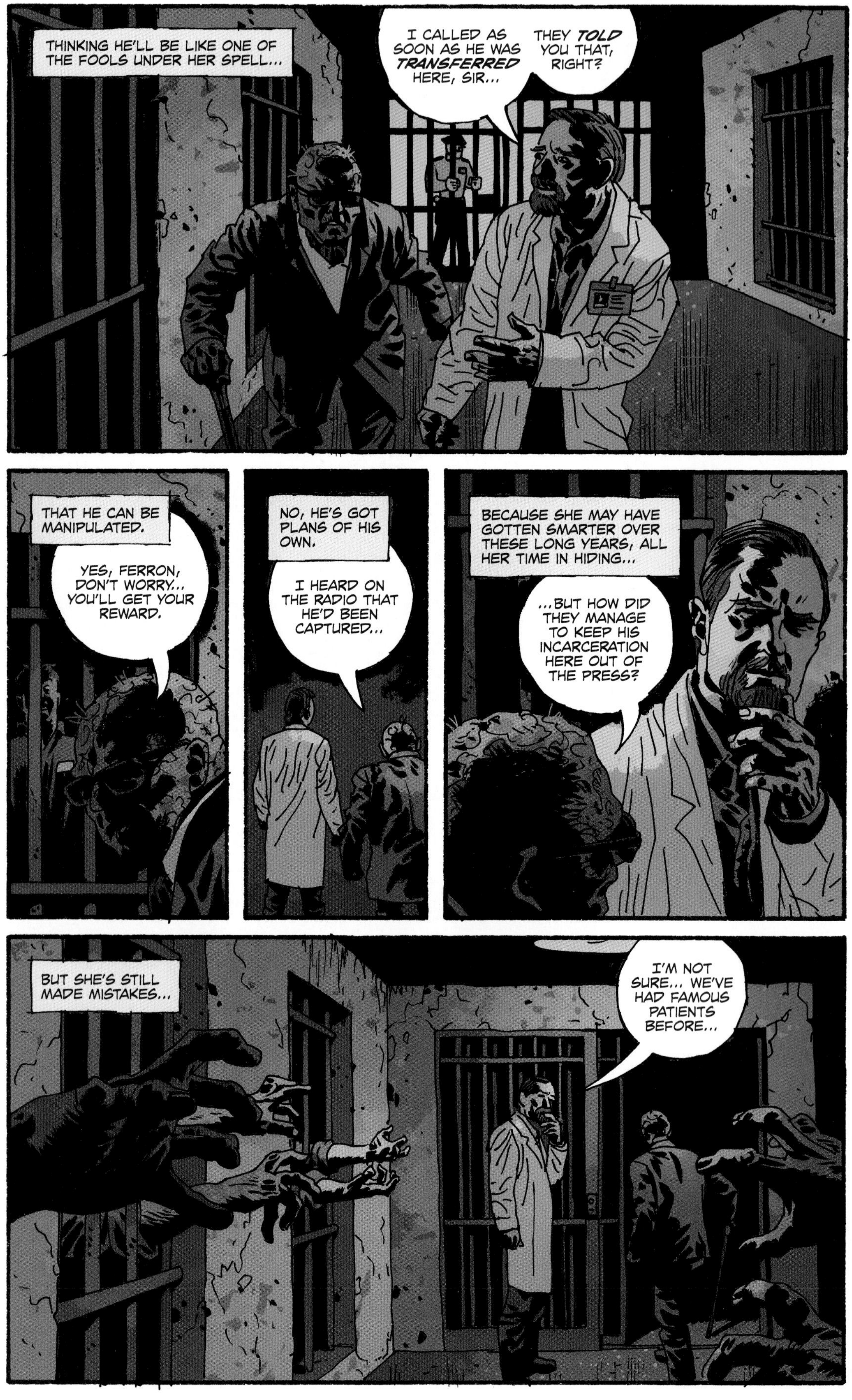
THINKING HE'LL BE LIKE ONE OF THE FOOLS UNDER HER SPELL...
I CALLED AS SOON AS HE WAS *TRANSFERRED* HERE, SIR...
THEY *TOLD* YOU THAT, RIGHT?
THAT HE CAN BE MANIPULATED.
YES, FERRON, DON'T WORRY... YOU'LL GET YOUR REWARD.
NO, HE'S GOT PLANS OF HIS OWN.
I HEARD ON THE RADIO THAT HE'D BEEN CAPTURED...
BECAUSE SHE MAY HAVE GOTTEN SMARTER OVER THESE LONG YEARS, ALL HER TIME IN HIDING...
...BUT HOW DID THEY MANAGE TO KEEP HIS INCARCERATION HERE OUT OF THE PRESS?
BUT SHE'S STILL MADE MISTAKES...
I'M NOT SURE... WE'VE HAD FAMOUS PATIENTS BEFORE...

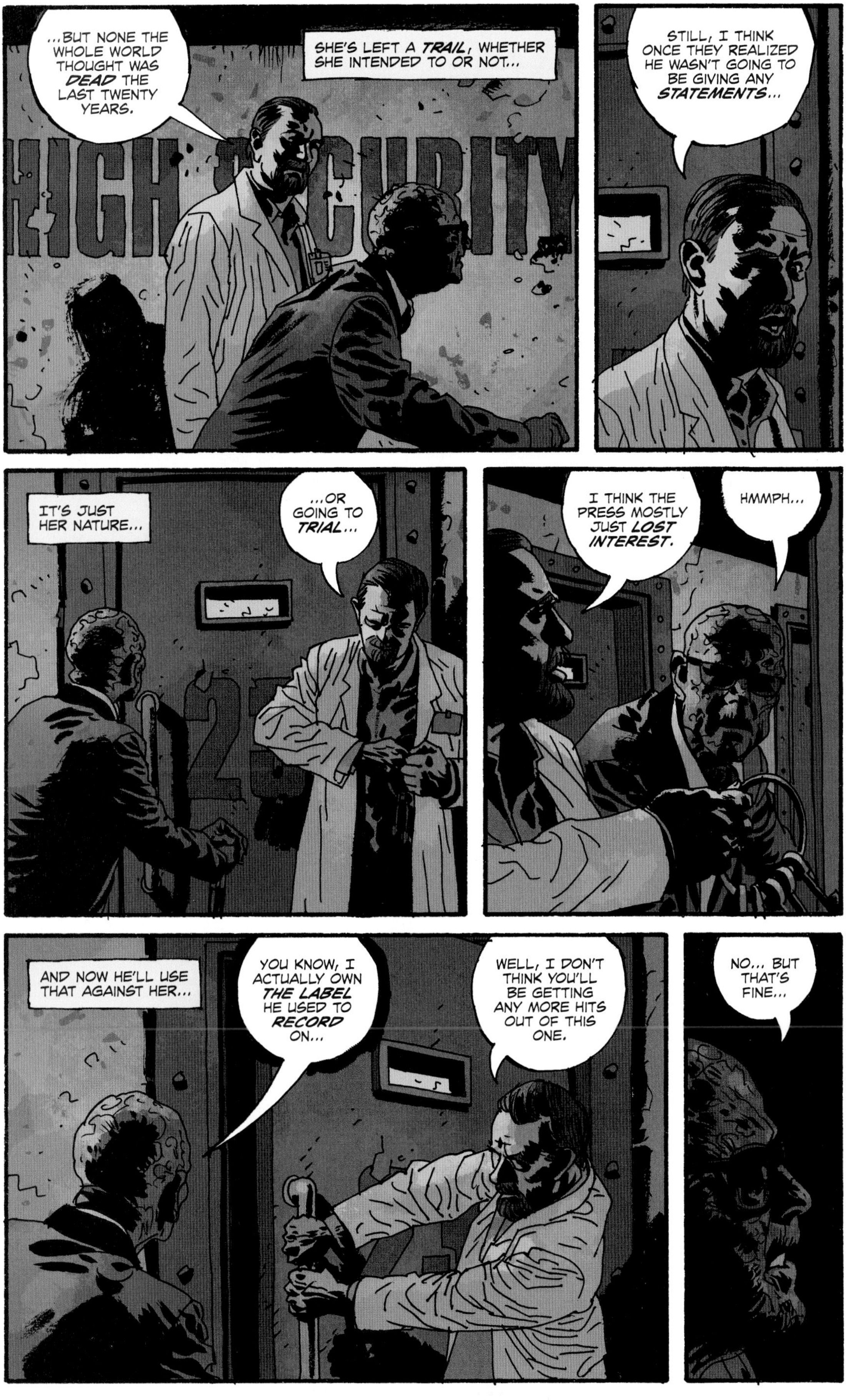
...BUT NONE THE WHOLE WORLD THOUGHT WAS DEAD THE LAST TWENTY YEARS.
SHE'S LEFT A TRAIL, WHETHER SHE INTENDED TO OR NOT...
HIGH SECURITY
STILL, I THINK ONCE THEY REALIZED HE WASN'T GOING TO BE GIVING ANY STATEMENTS...
IT'S JUST HER NATURE...
...OR GOING TO TRIAL...
I THINK THE PRESS MOSTLY JUST LOST INTEREST.
HMMPH...
AND NOW HE'LL USE THAT AGAINST HER...
YOU KNOW, I ACTUALLY OWN THE LABEL HE USED TO RECORD ON...
WELL, I DON'T THINK YOU'LL BE GETTING ANY MORE HITS OUT OF THIS ONE.
NO... BUT THAT'S FINE...

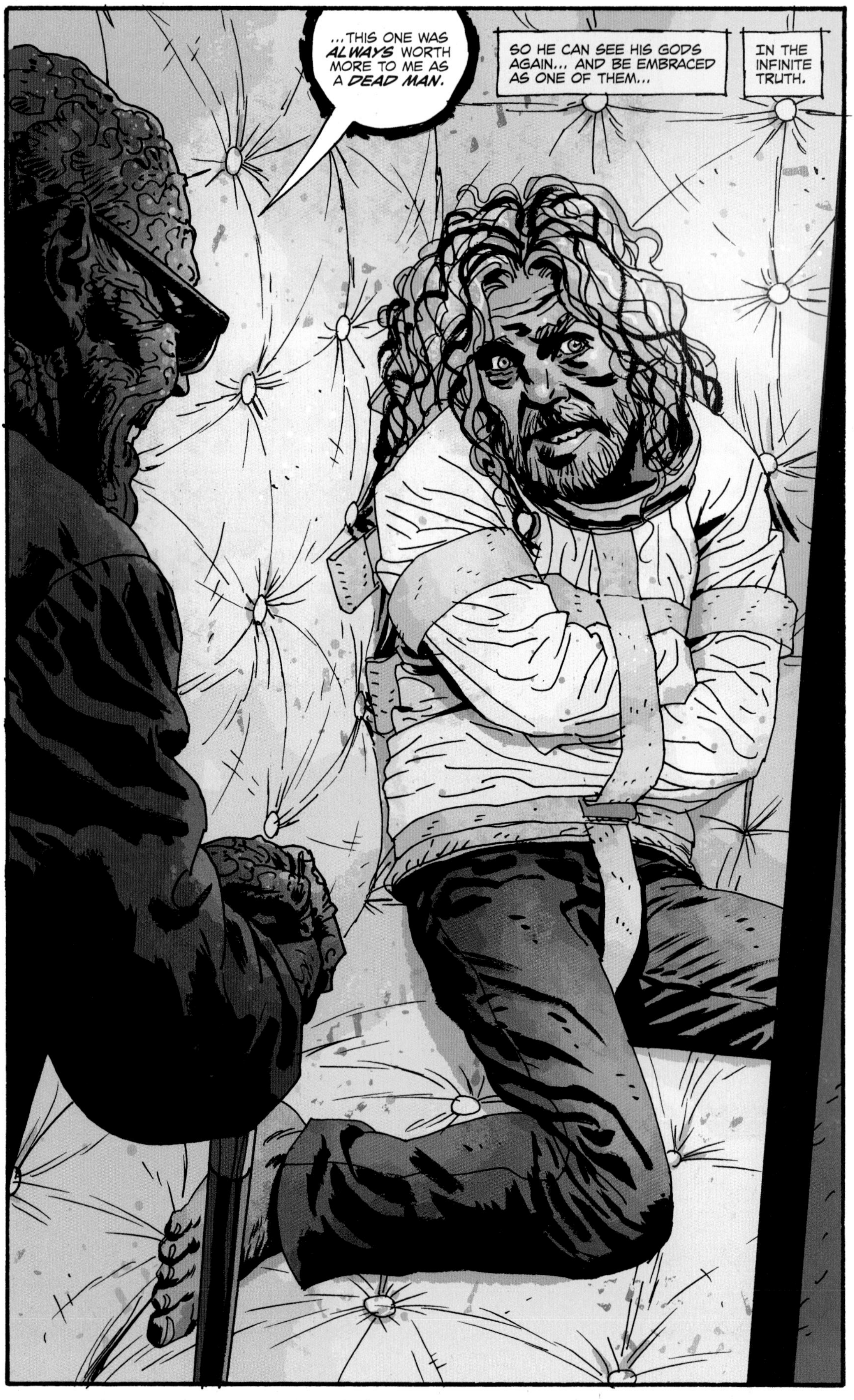
...THIS ONE WAS ALWAYS WORTH MORE TO ME AS A DEAD MAN.
SO HE CAN SEE HIS GODS AGAIN... AND BE EMBRACED AS ONE OF THEM...
IN THE INFINITE TRUTH.

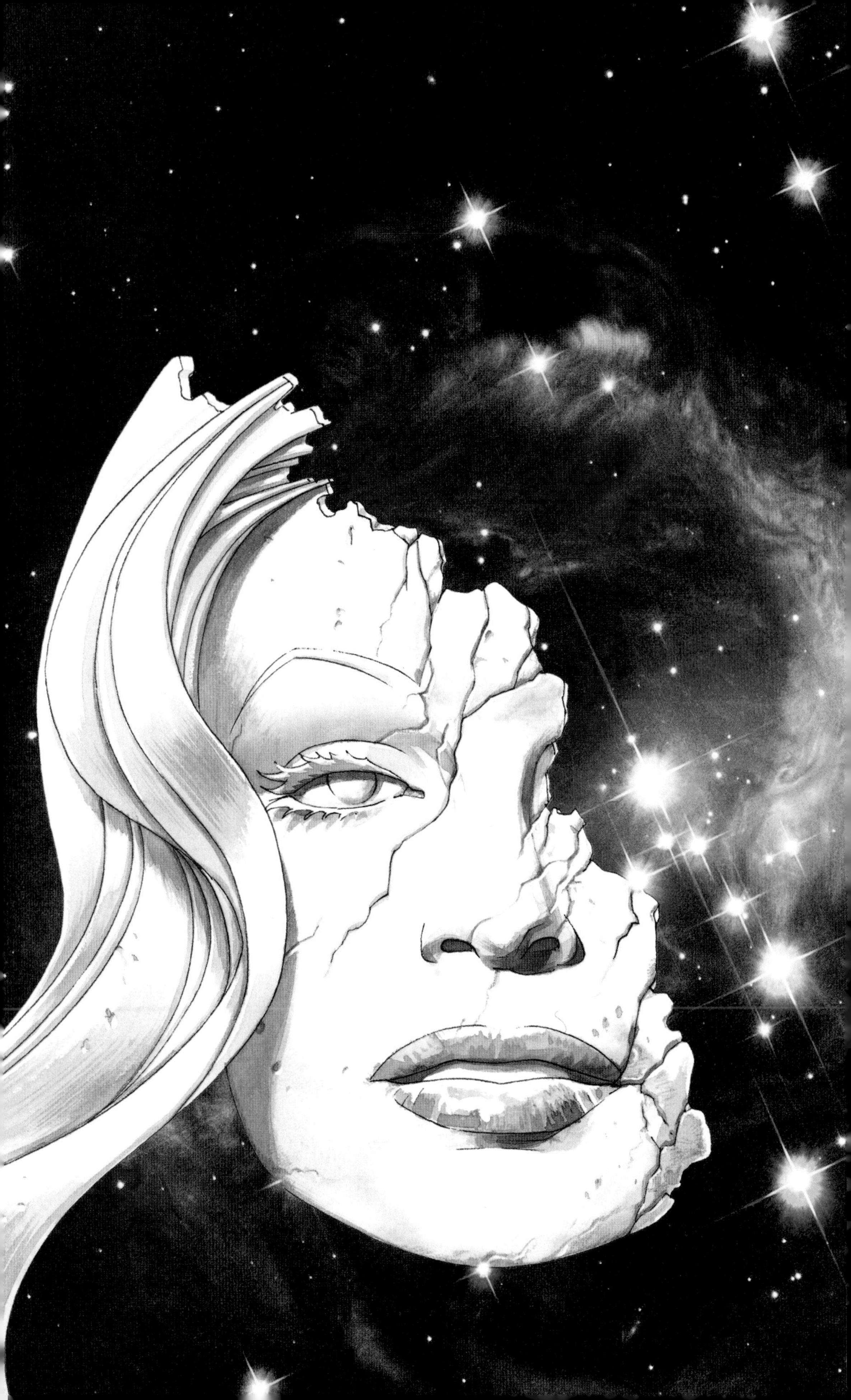

Chapter Four

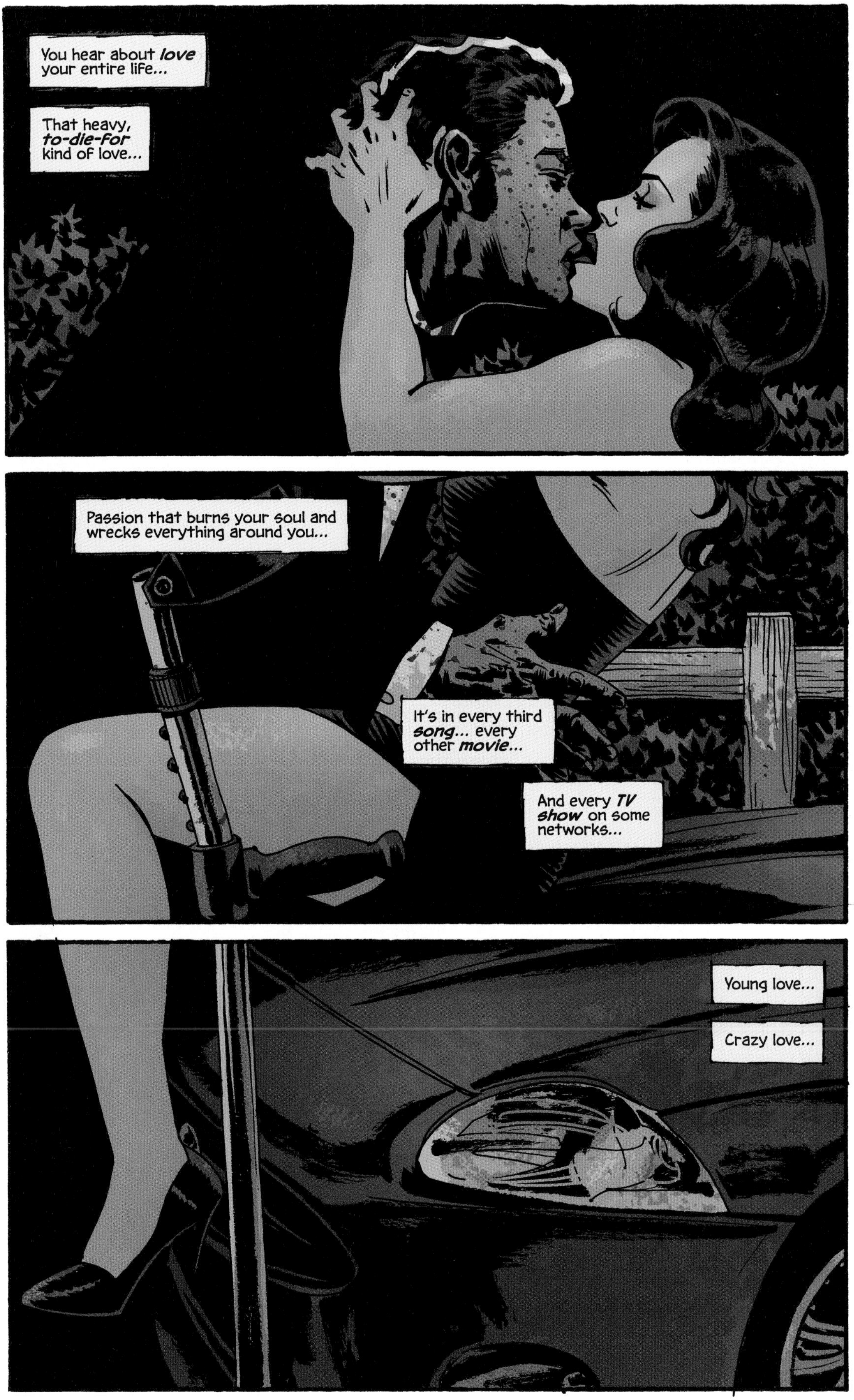

You hear about *love* your entire life...
That heavy, ***to-die-for*** kind of love...
Passion that burns your soul and wrecks everything around you...
It's in every third ***song***... every other ***movie***...
And every ***TV show*** on some networks...
Young love...
Crazy love...

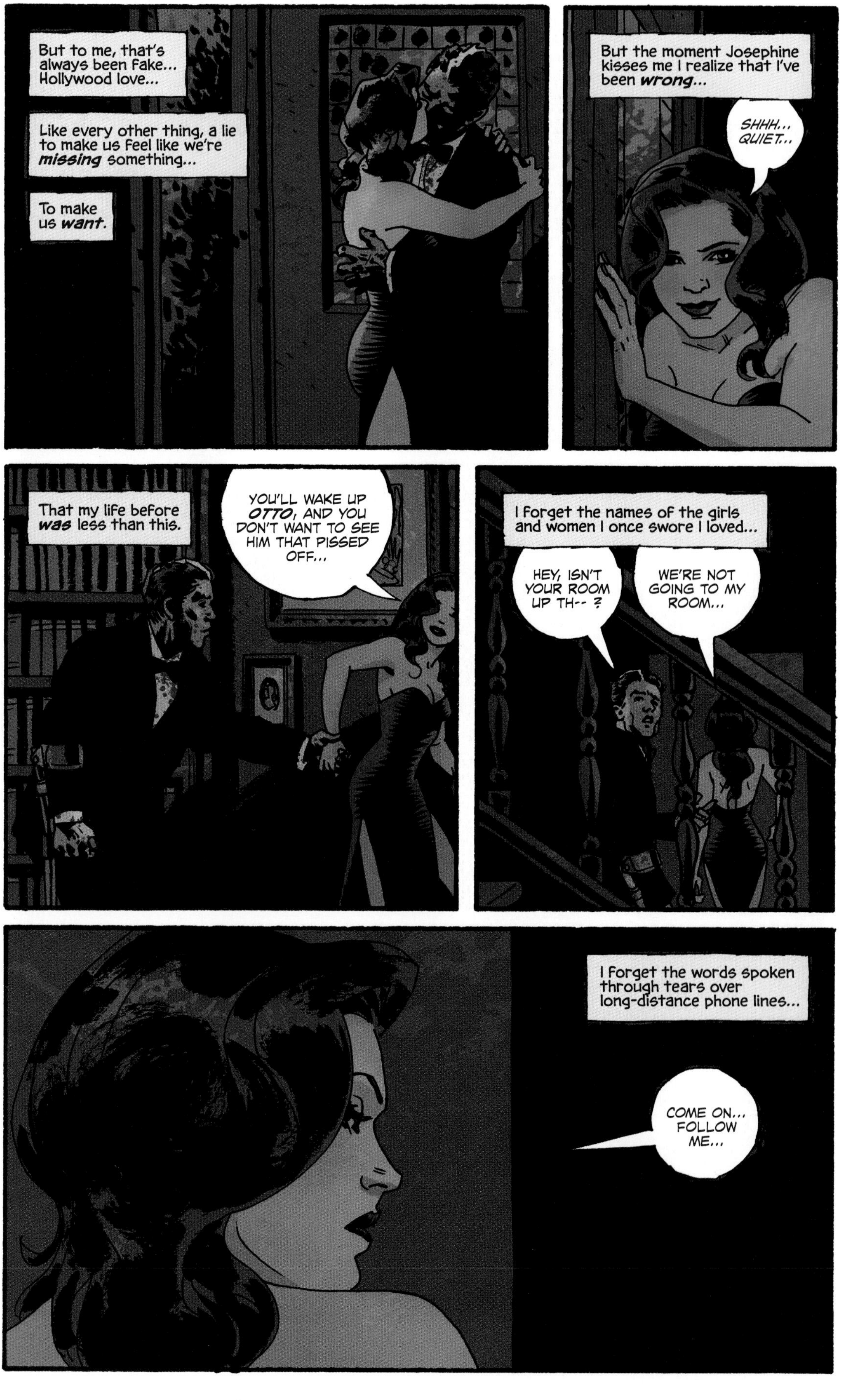
But to me, that's always been fake... Hollywood love...
Like every other thing, a lie to make us feel like we're *missing* something...
To make us *want*.
But the moment Josephine kisses me I realize that I've been *wrong*...
SHHH... QUIET...
That my life before *was* less than this.
YOU'LL WAKE UP *OTTO*, AND YOU DON'T WANT TO SEE HIM THAT PISSED OFF...
I forget the names of the girls and women I once swore I loved...
HEY, ISN'T YOUR ROOM UP TH-- ?
WE'RE NOT GOING TO MY ROOM...
I forget the words spoken through tears over long-distance phone lines...
COME ON... FOLLOW ME...

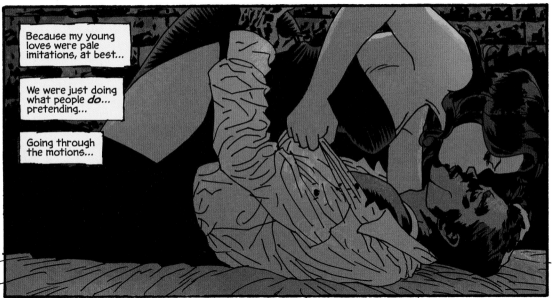

Because my young loves were pale imitations, at best...

We were just doing what people *do*... pretending...

Going through the motions...

Like it was all some *ancient ritual* we didn't know the origin of...

But now I know.

I'M SORRY ABOUT THIS...

I MUTILATED YOU...

IT WASN'T *YOU* IN THAT PLANE...

BUT EITHER WAY, IT'S OKAY...

IT WAS WORTH IT.

It was so worth it.

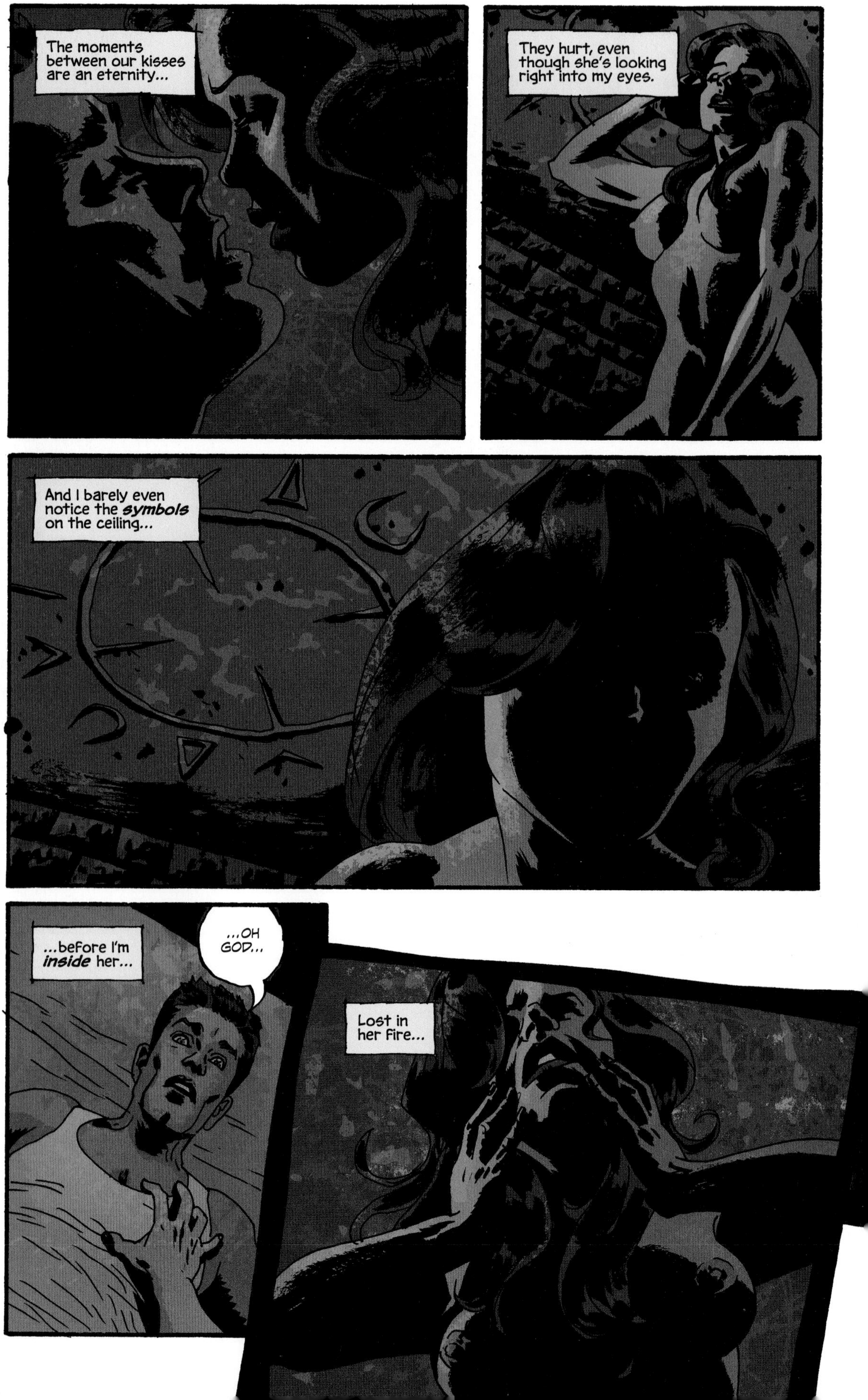
The moments between our kisses are an eternity...
They hurt, even though she's looking right into my eyes.
And I barely even notice the *symbols* on the ceiling...
...before I'm *inside* her...
...OH GOD...
Lost in her fire...

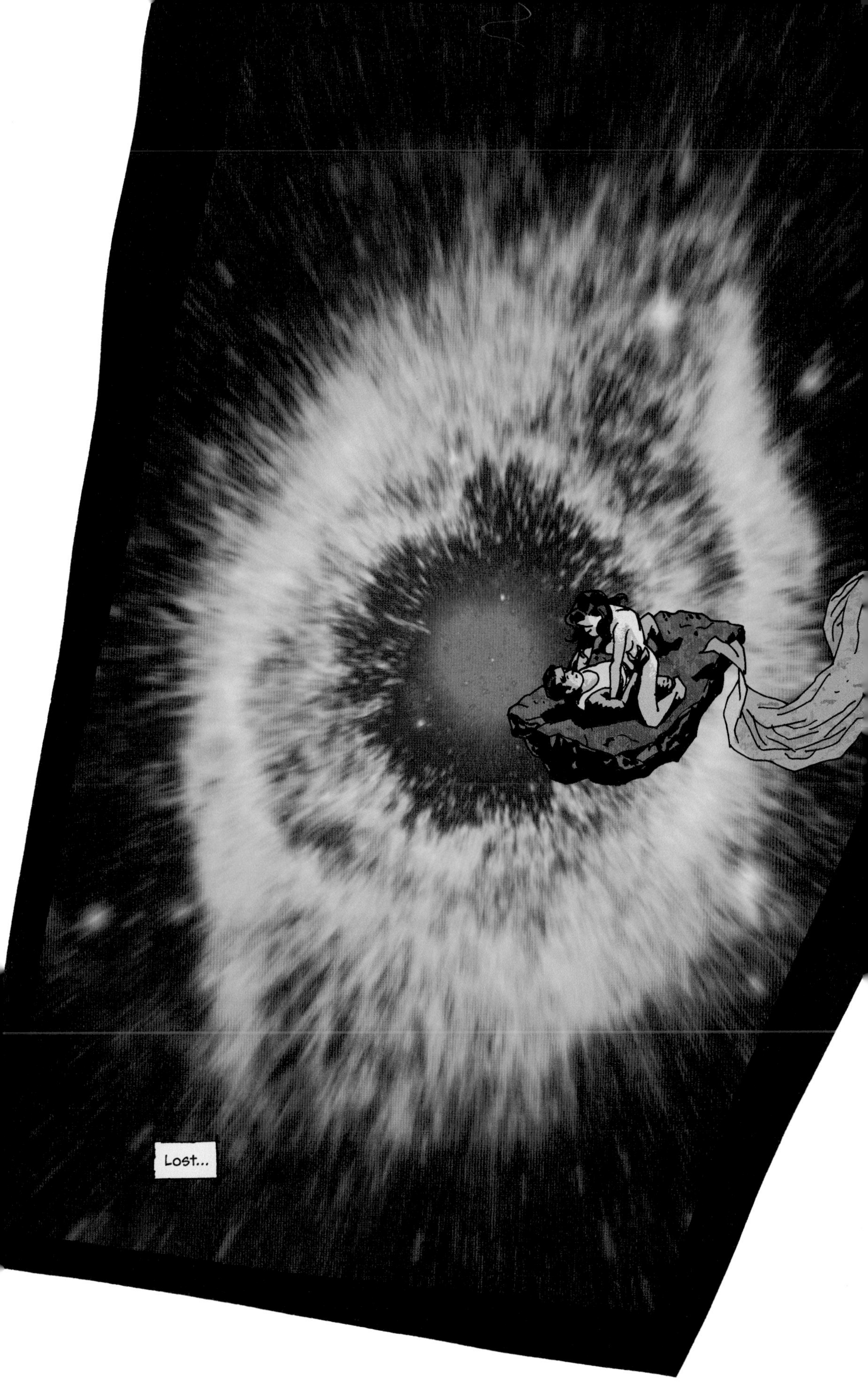
Lost...

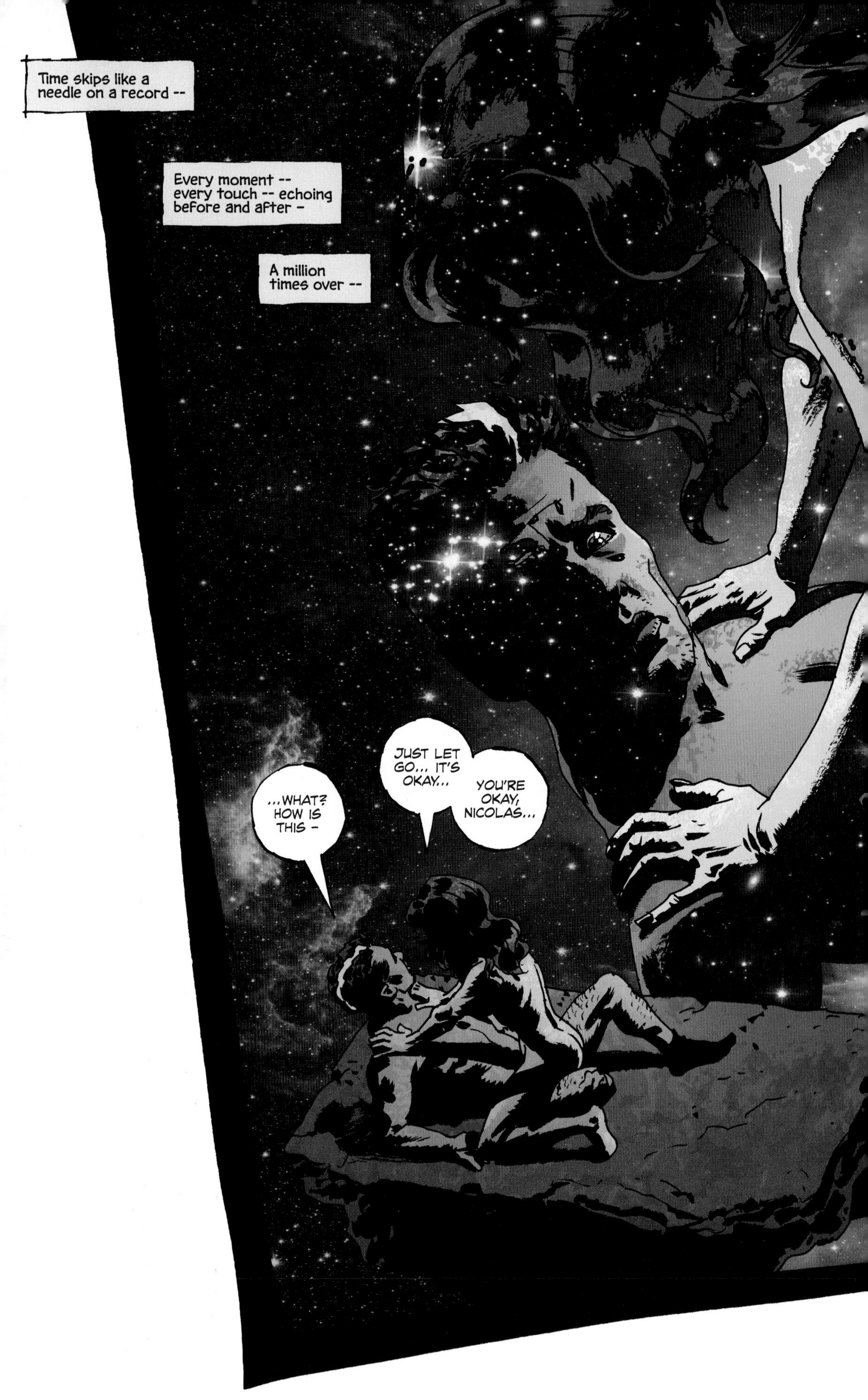
Time skips like a needle on a record --
Every moment -- every touch -- echoing before and after -
A million times over --
...WHAT? HOW IS THIS -
JUST LET GO... IT'S OKAY...
YOU'RE OKAY, NICOLAS...

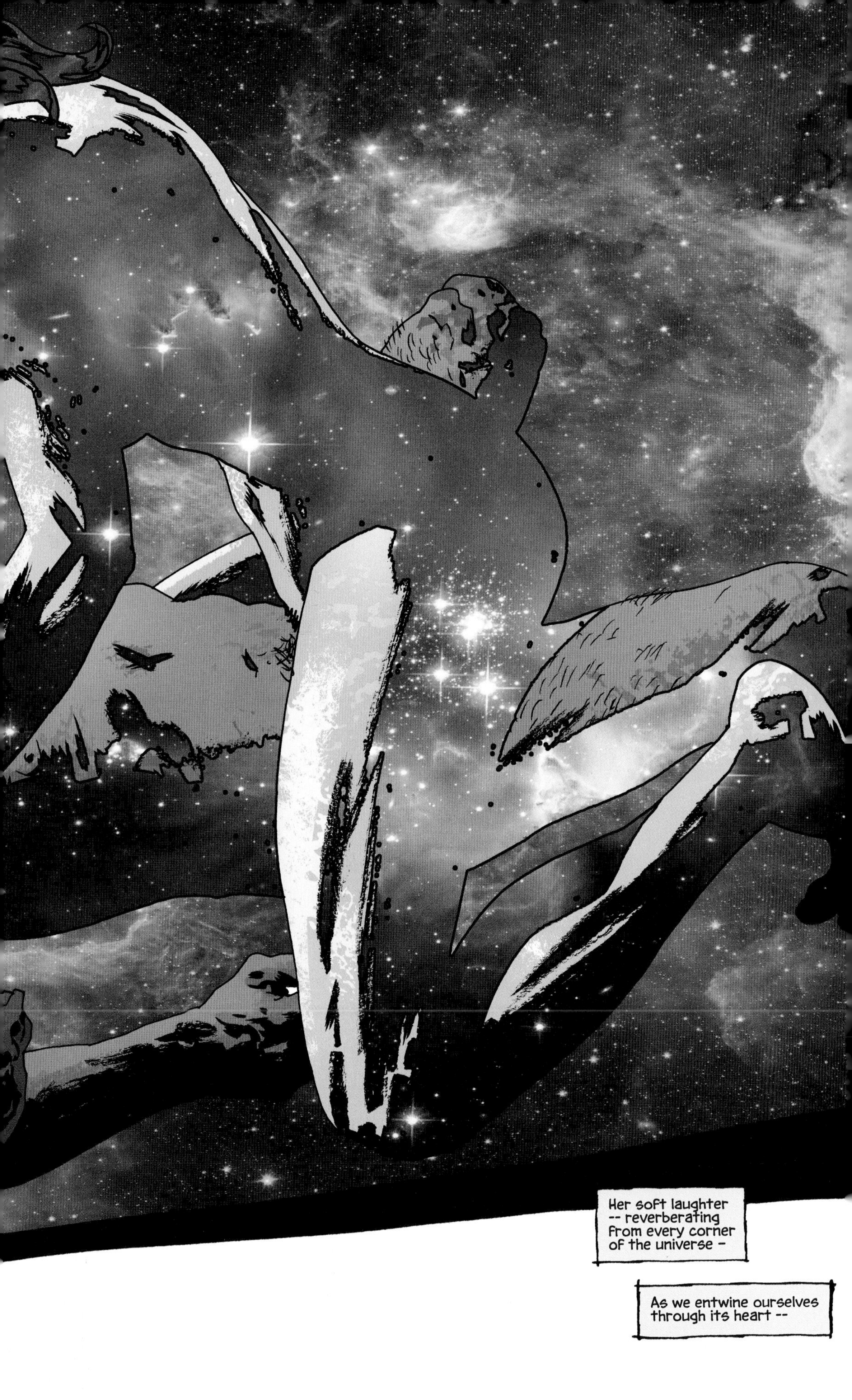
Her soft laughter -- reverberating from every corner of the universe –
As we entwine ourselves through its heart --

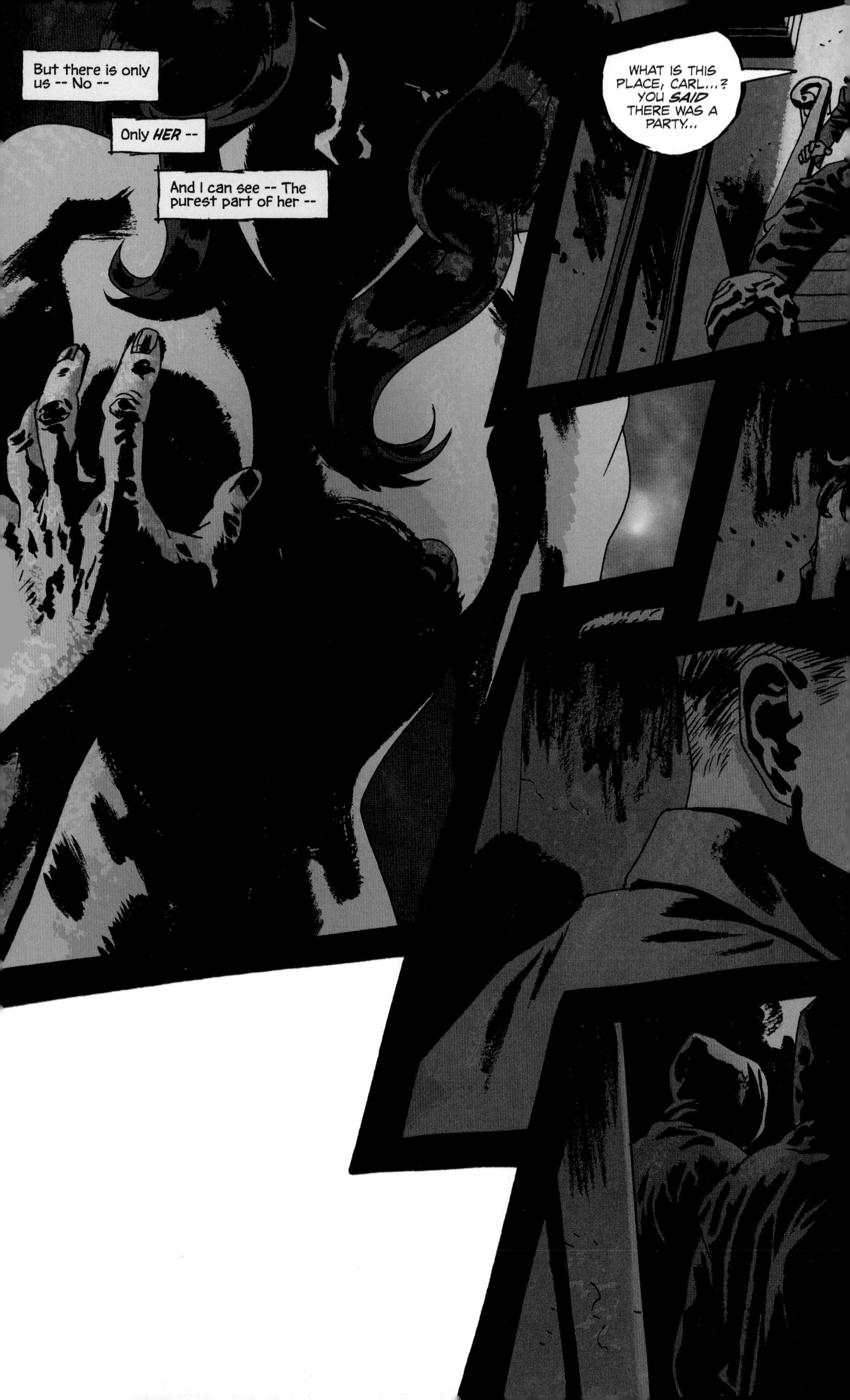

But there is only us -- No --
Only HER --
And I can see -- The purest part of her --
WHAT IS THIS PLACE, CARL...? YOU SAID THERE WAS A PARTY...

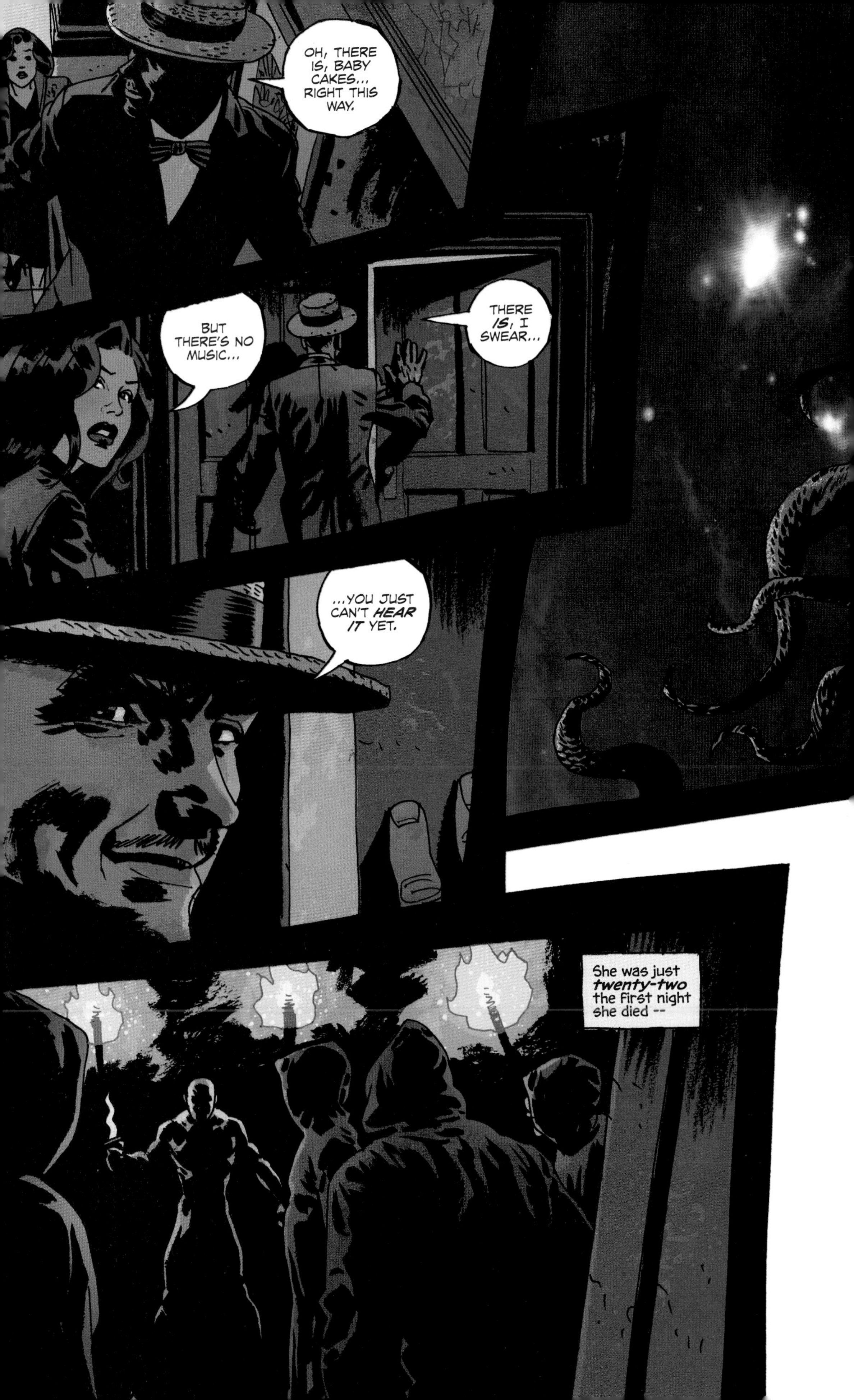
OH, THERE IS, BABY CAKES... RIGHT THIS WAY.
BUT THERE'S NO MUSIC...
THERE *IS*, I SWEAR...
...YOU JUST CAN'T *HEAR IT* YET.
She was just *twenty-two* the first night she died --

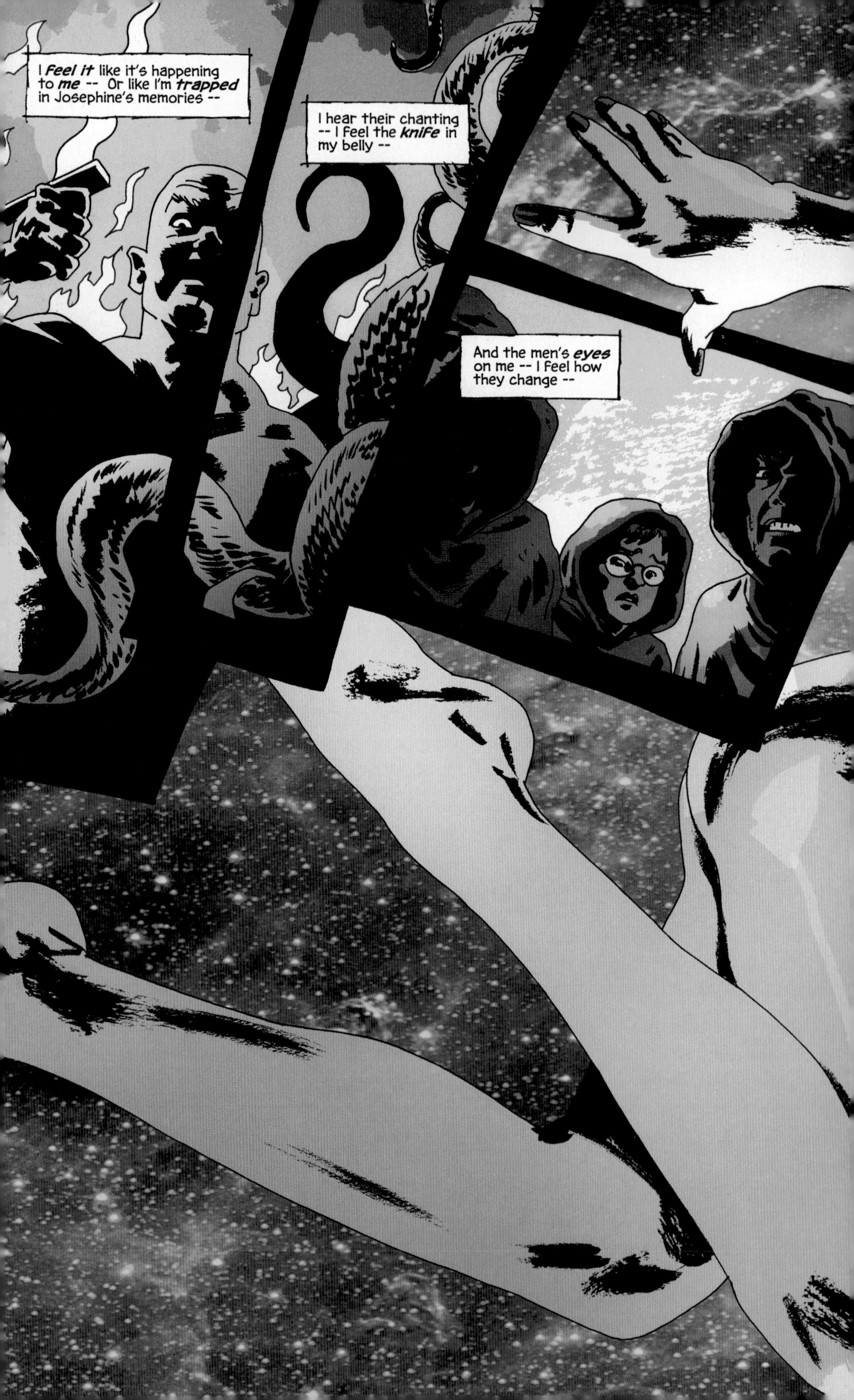
I *feel it* like it's happening to *me* -- Or like I'm *trapped* in Josephine's memories --
I hear their chanting -- I feel the *knife* in my belly --
And the men's *eyes* on me -- I feel how they change --

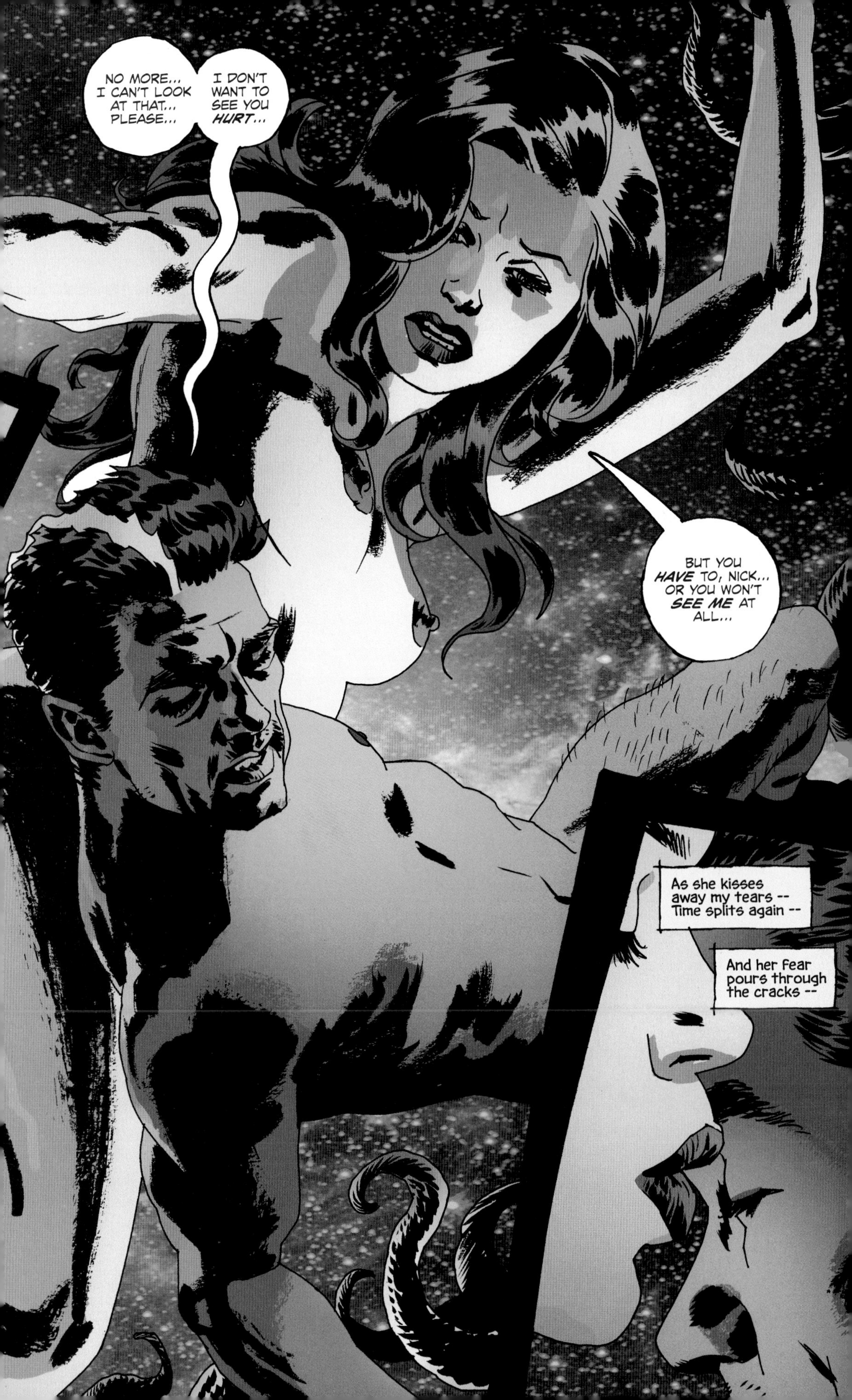
NO MORE... I CAN'T LOOK AT THAT... PLEASE...
I DON'T WANT TO SEE YOU *HURT*...
BUT YOU *HAVE* TO, NICK... OR YOU WON'T *SEE ME* AT ALL...
As she kisses away my tears -- Time splits again --
And her fear pours through the cracks --

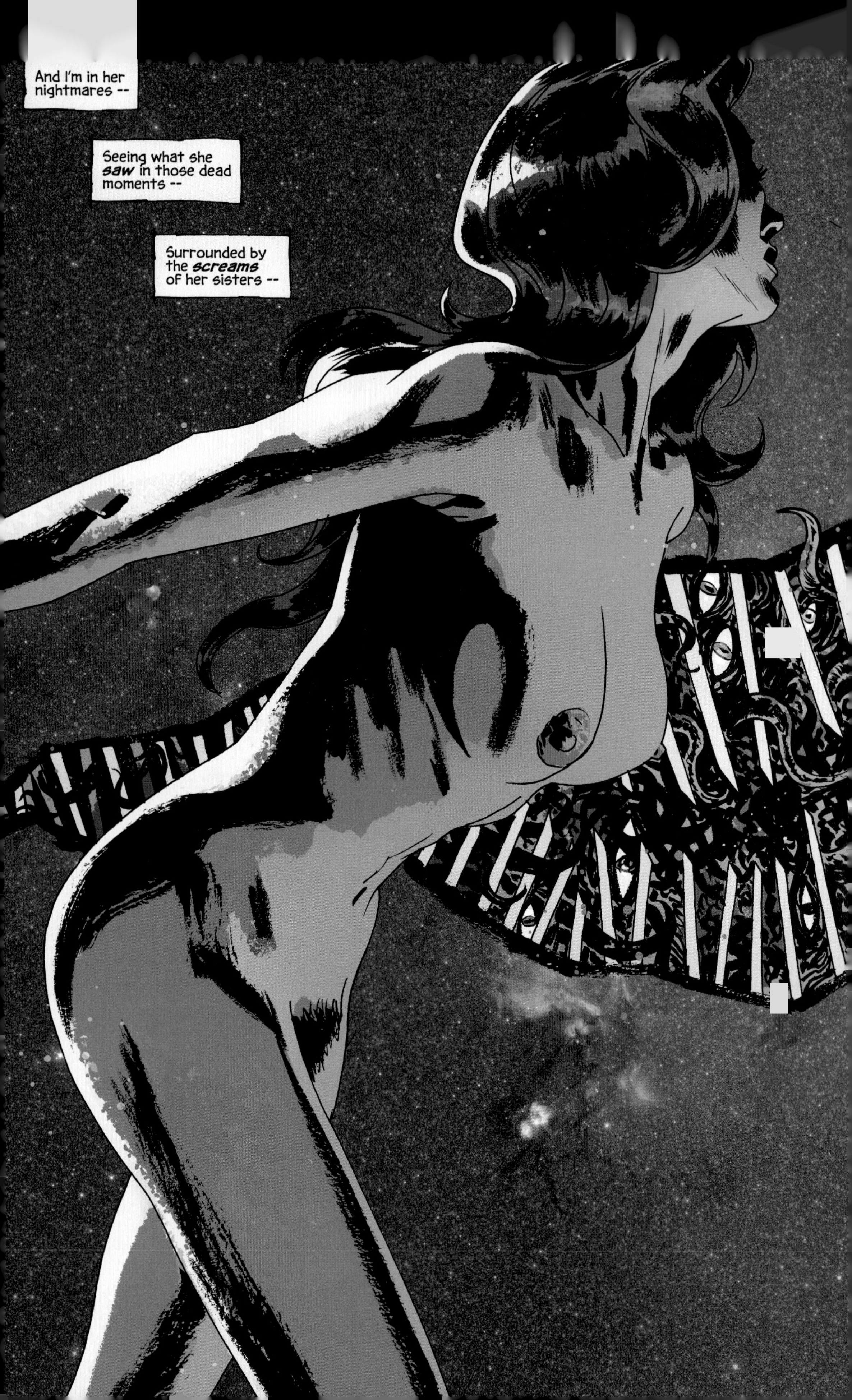
And I'm in her nightmares --
Seeing what she saw in those dead moments --
Surrounded by the screams of her sisters --

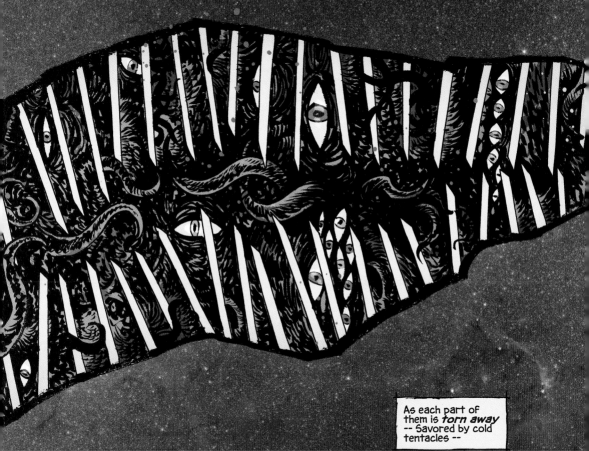

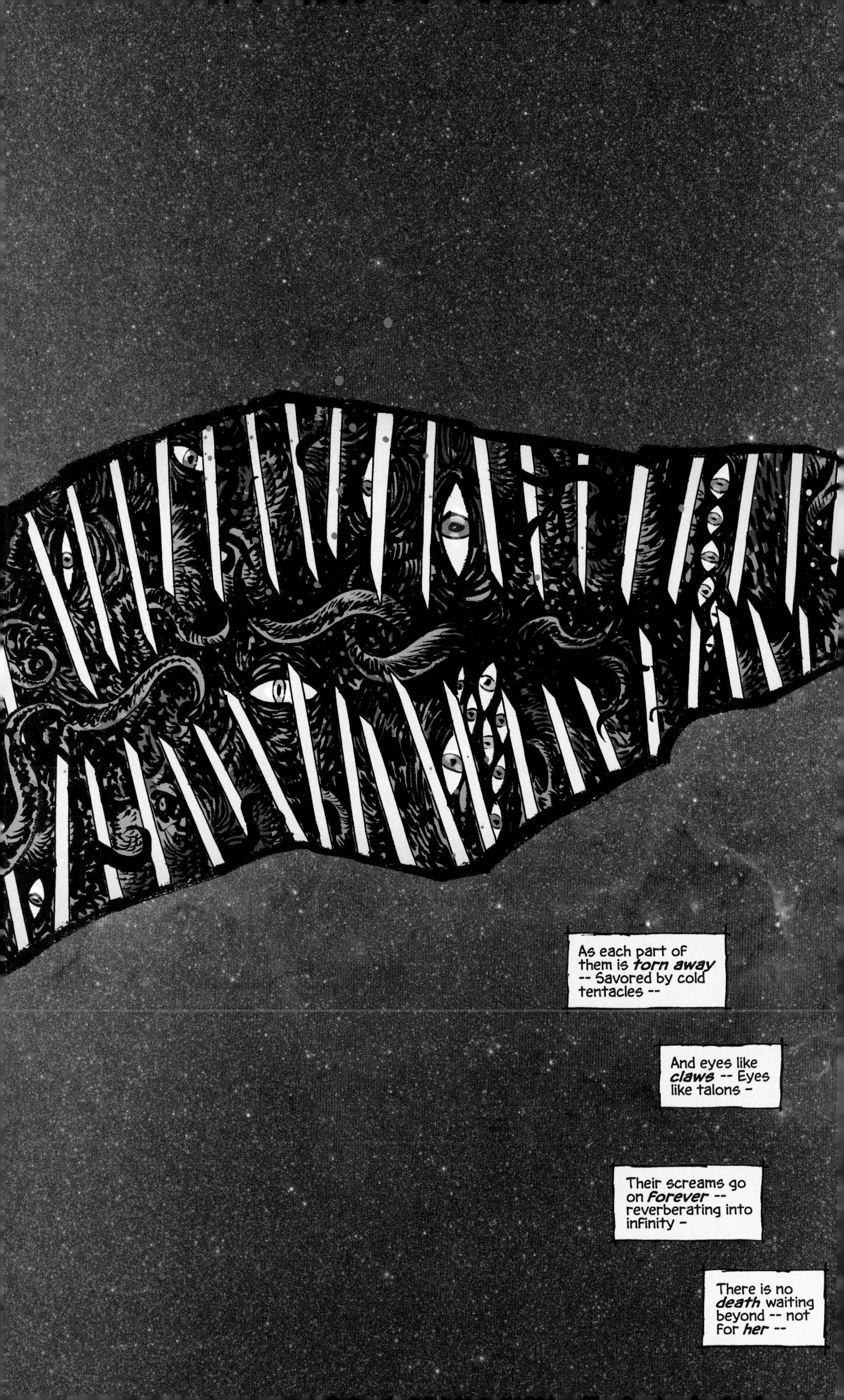

As each part of them is *torn away* -- Savored by cold tentacles --

And eyes like *claws* -- Eyes like talons --

Their screams go on *forever* -- reverberating into infinity --

There is no *death* waiting beyond -- not for *her* --

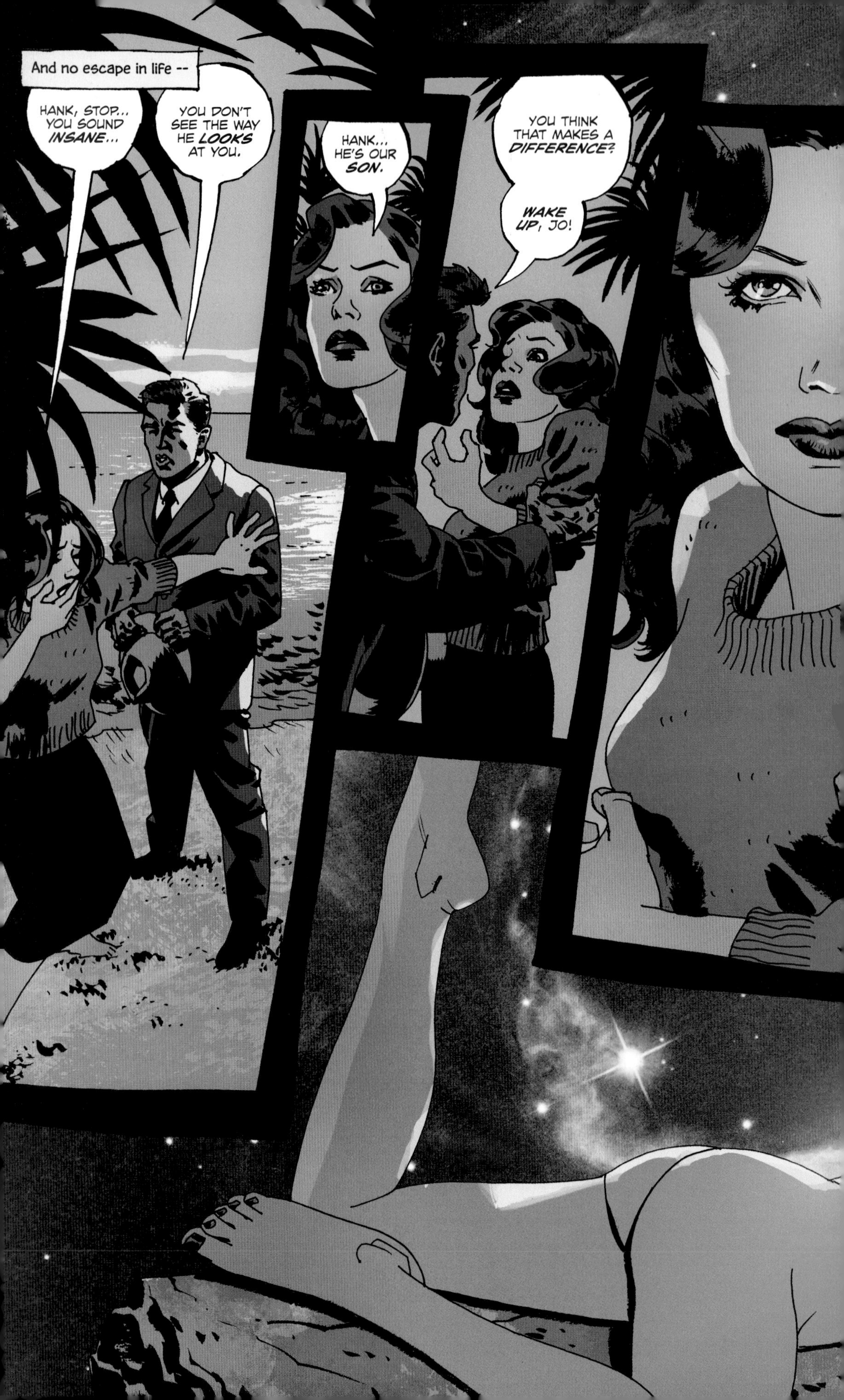

And no escape in life --
HANK, STOP... YOU SOUND INSANE...
YOU DON'T SEE THE WAY HE LOOKS AT YOU.
HANK... HE'S OUR SON.
YOU THINK THAT MAKES A DIFFERENCE?
WAKE UP, JO!

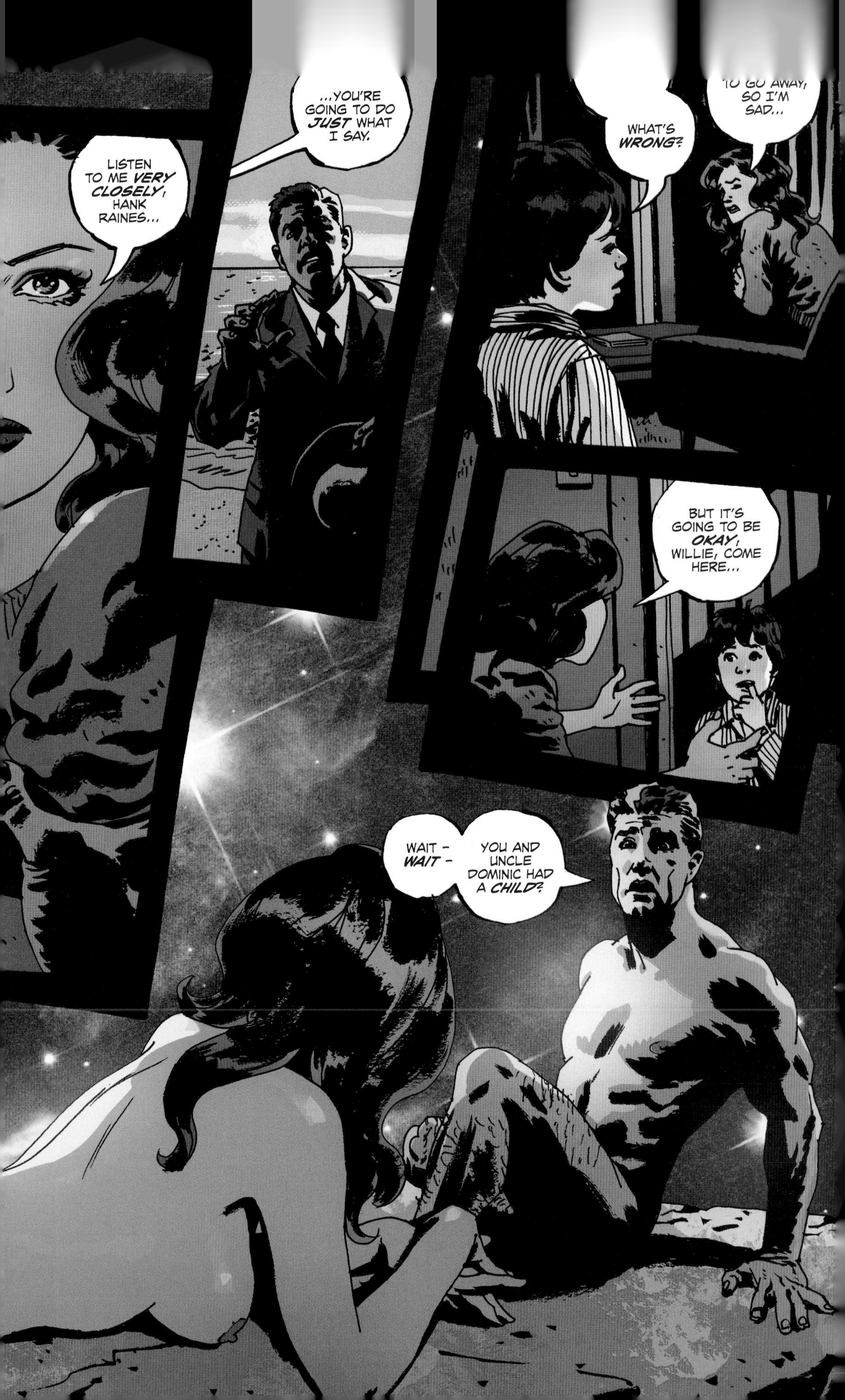
LISTEN TO ME VERY CLOSELY, HANK RAINES...
...YOU'RE GOING TO DO JUST WHAT I SAY.
WHAT'S WRONG?
TO GO AWAY, SO I'M SAD...
BUT IT'S GOING TO BE OKAY, WILLIE, COME HERE...
WAIT - WAIT -
YOU AND UNCLE DOMINIC HAD A CHILD?

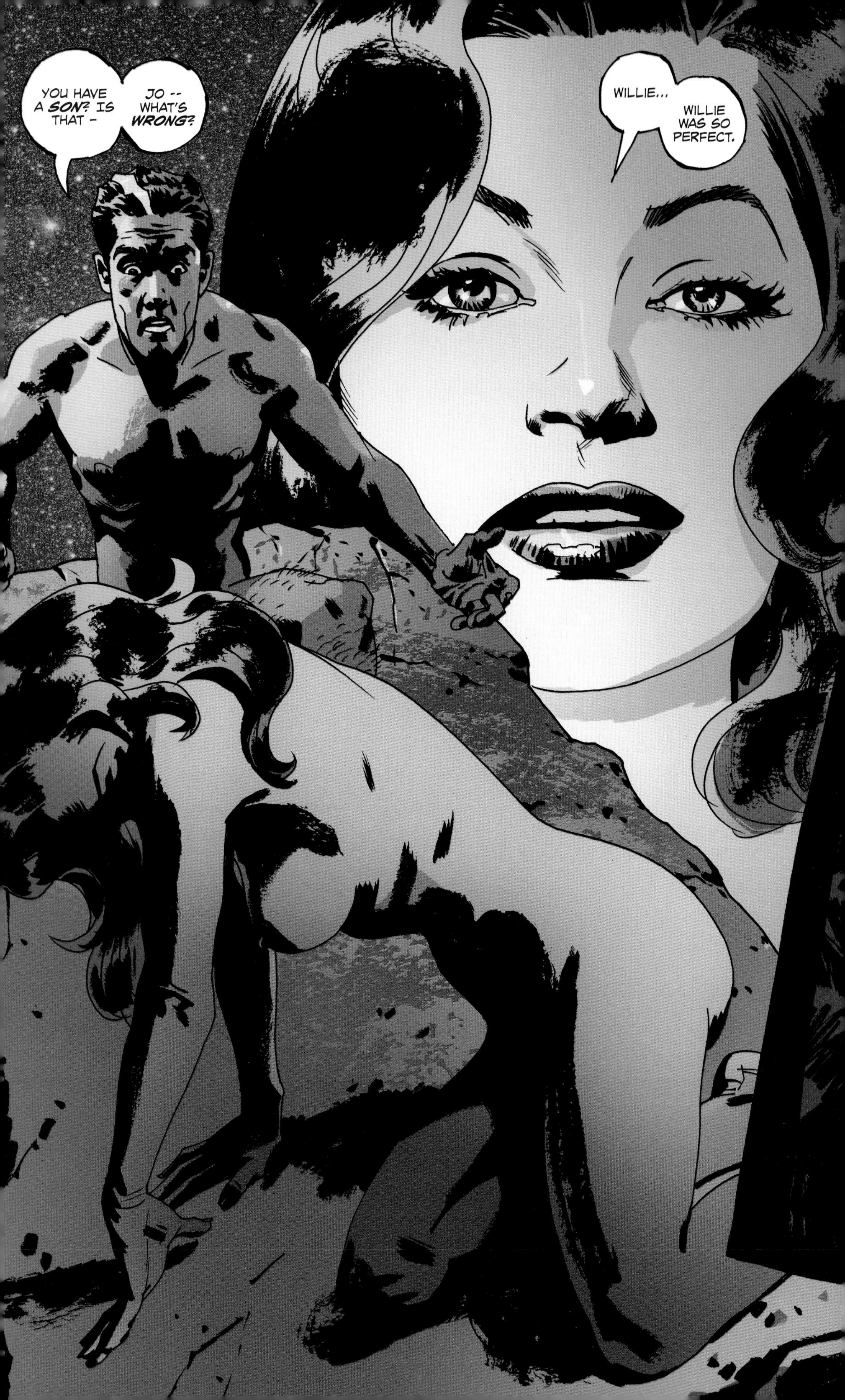
YOU HAVE A SON? IS THAT -
JO -- WHAT'S WRONG?
WILLIE...
WILLIE WAS SO PERFECT.

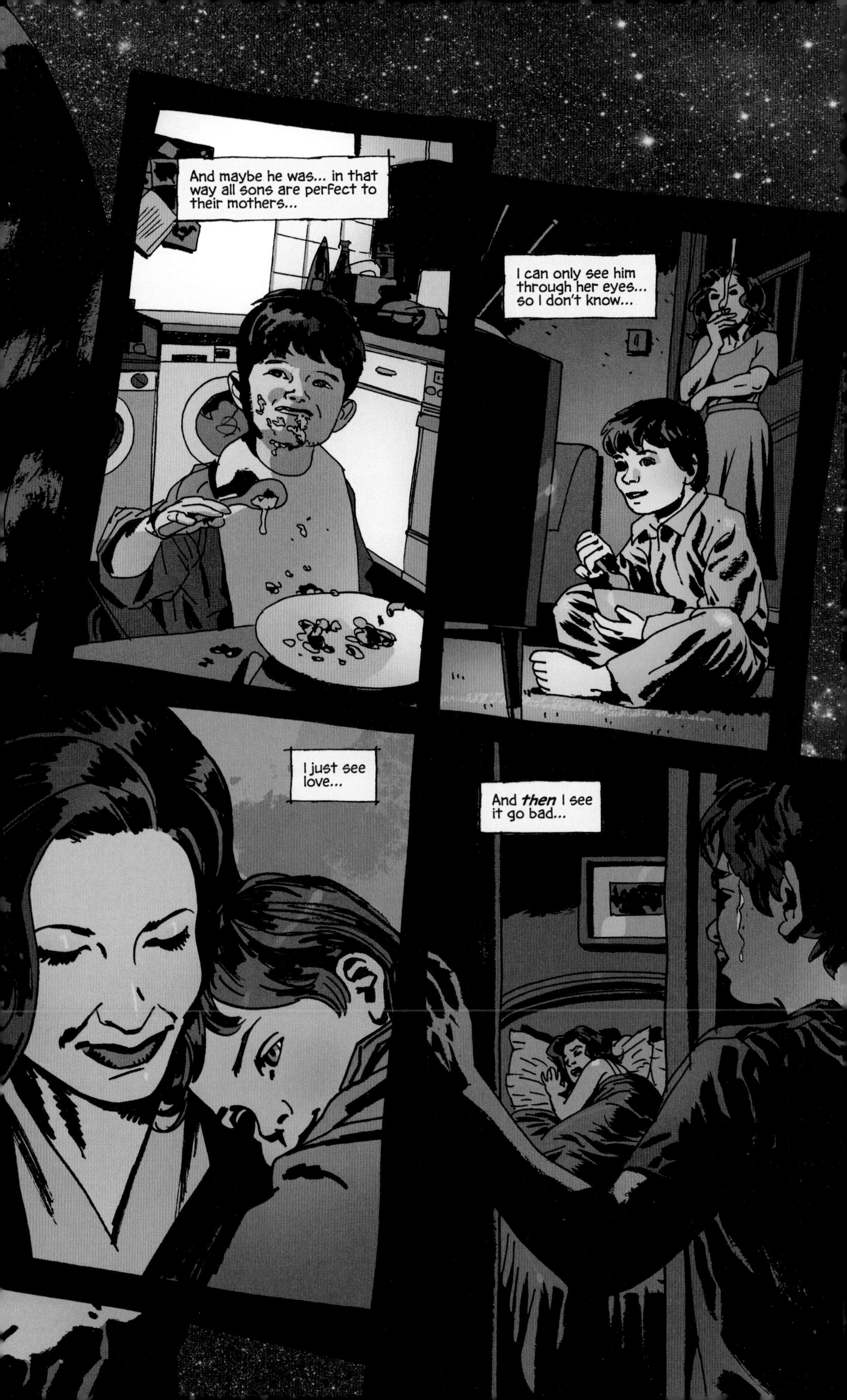
And maybe he was... in that way all sons are perfect to their mothers...
I can only see him through her eyes... so I don't know...
I just see love...
And *then* I see it go bad...

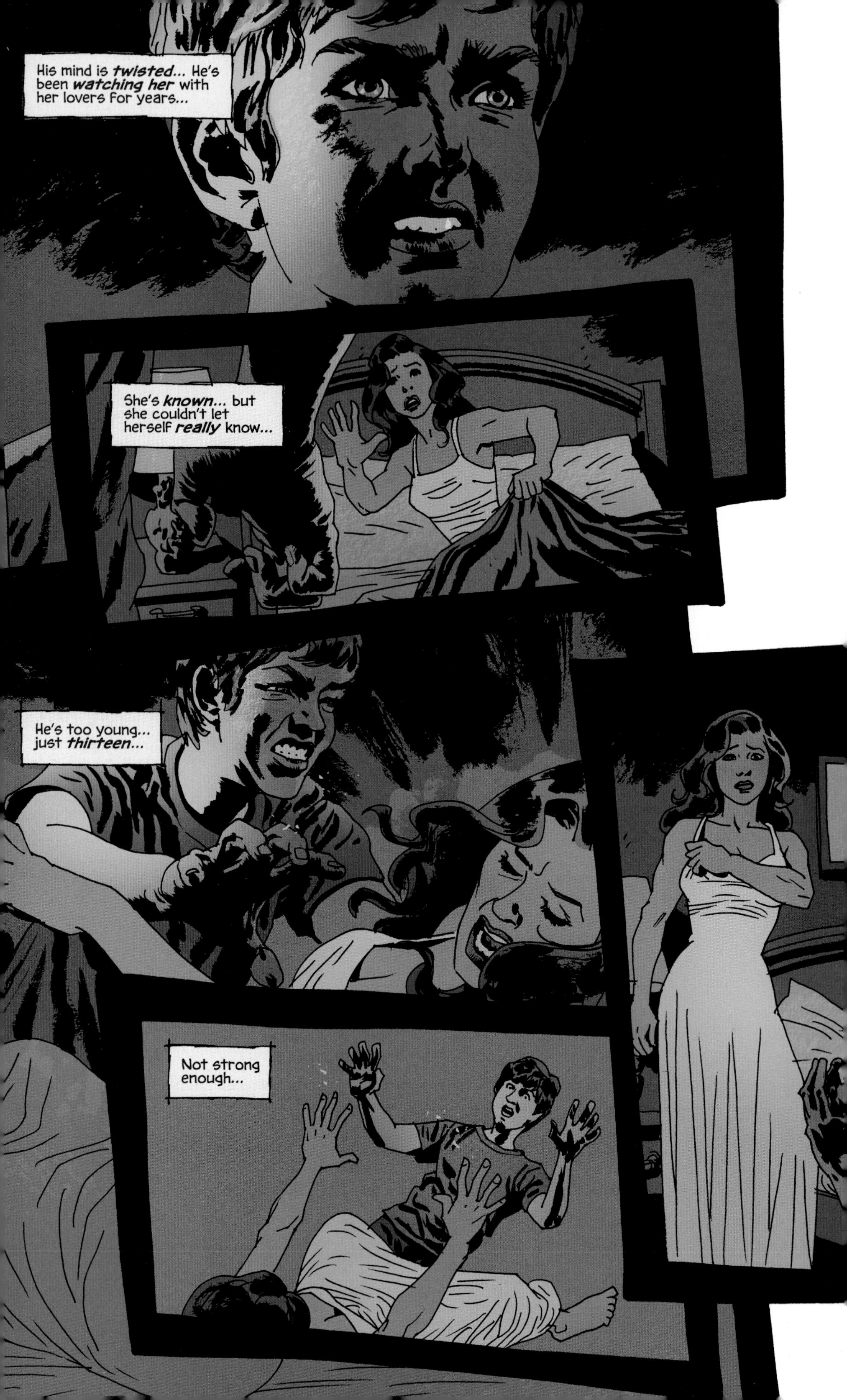
His mind is twisted... He's been watching her with her lovers for years...
She's known... but she couldn't let herself really know...
He's too young... just thirteen...
Not strong enough...

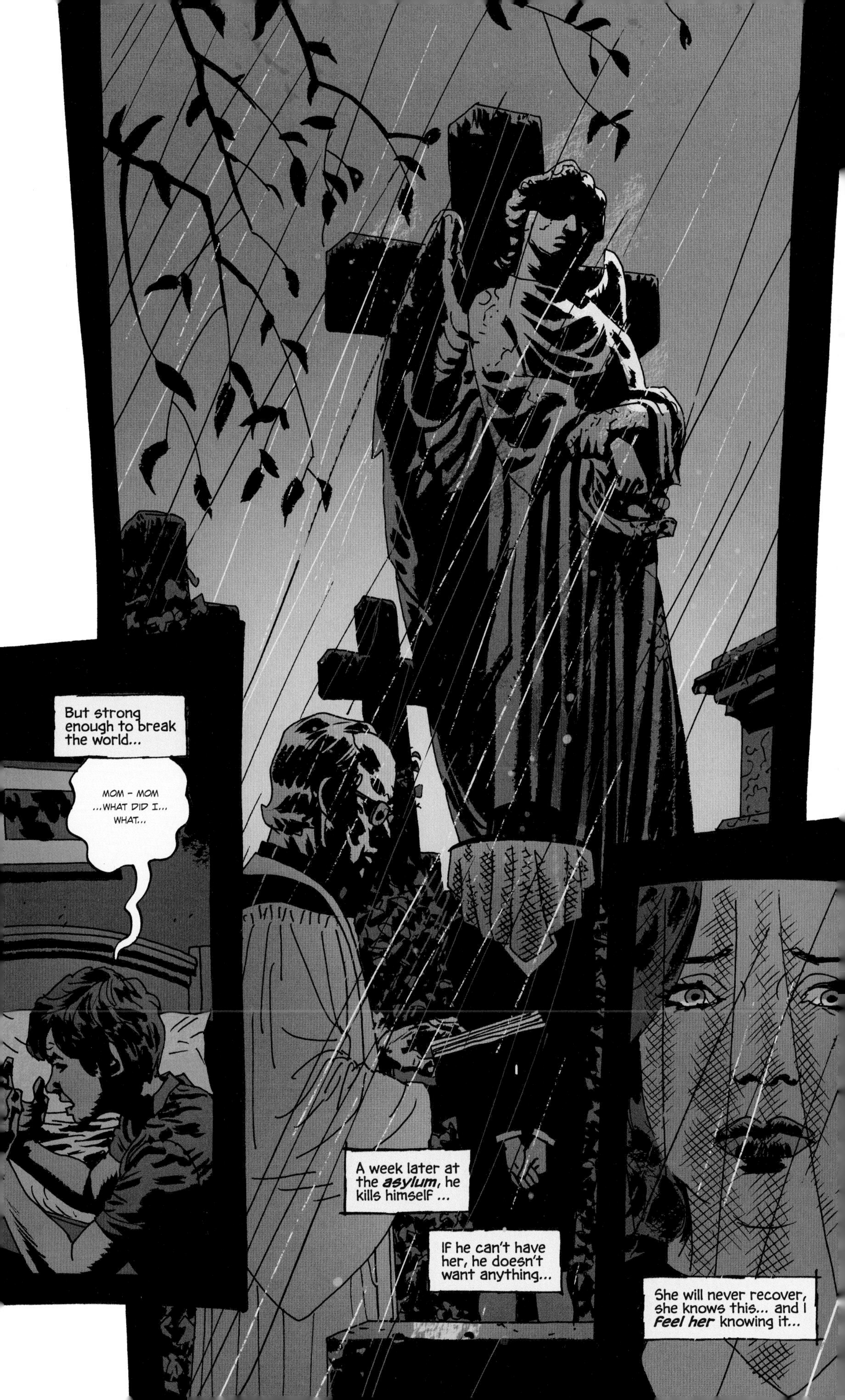
But strong enough to break the world...
MOM - MOM ...WHAT DID I... WHAT...
A week later at the *asylum*, he kills himself ...
If he can't have her, he doesn't want anything...
She will never recover, she knows this... and I *feel her* knowing it...

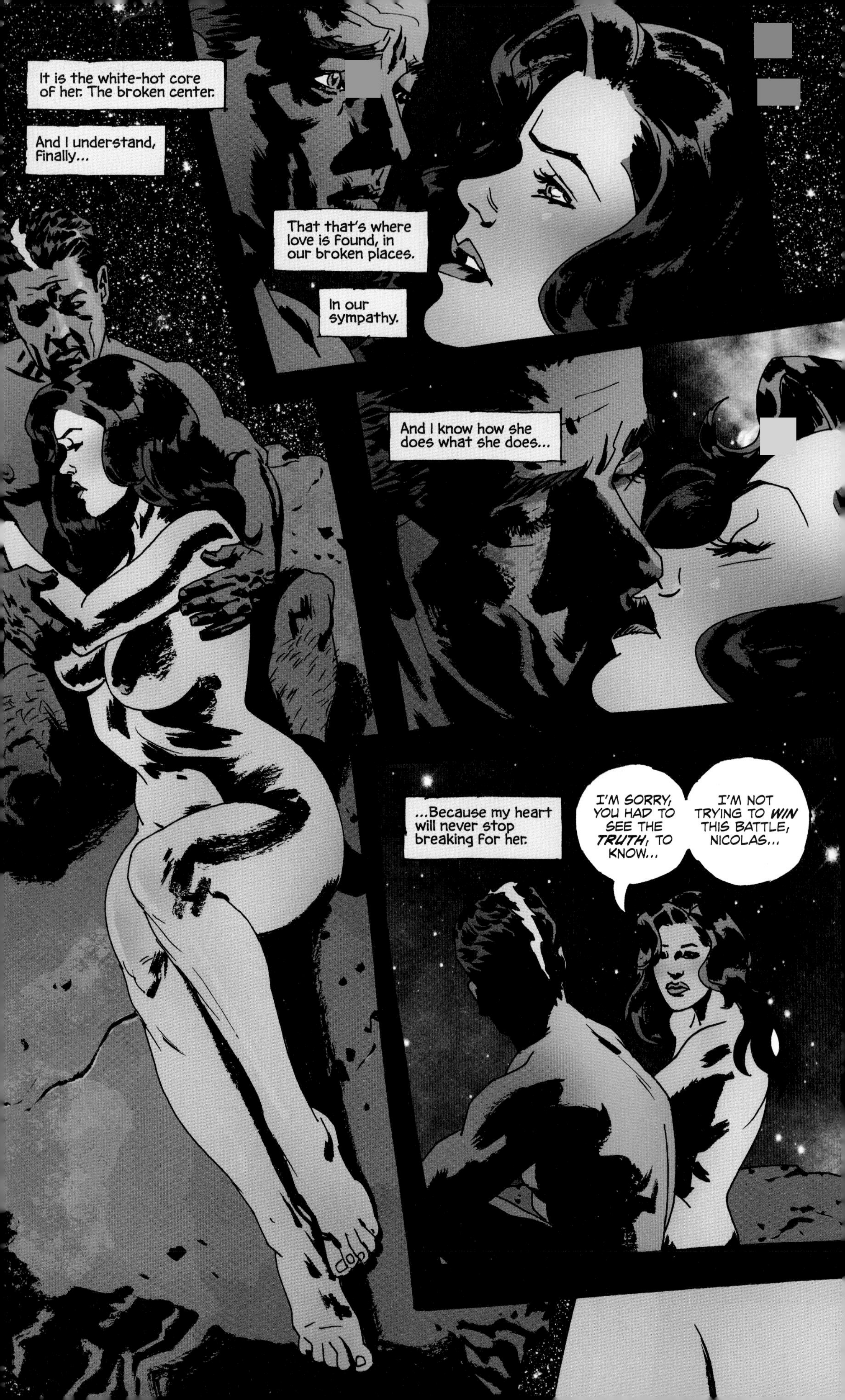
It is the white-hot core of her. The broken center.
And I understand, finally...
That that's where love is found, in our broken places.
In our sympathy.
And I know how she does what she does...
...Because my heart will never stop breaking for her.
I'M SORRY, YOU HAD TO SEE THE *TRUTH*, TO KNOW...
I'M NOT TRYING TO *WIN* THIS BATTLE, NICOLAS...

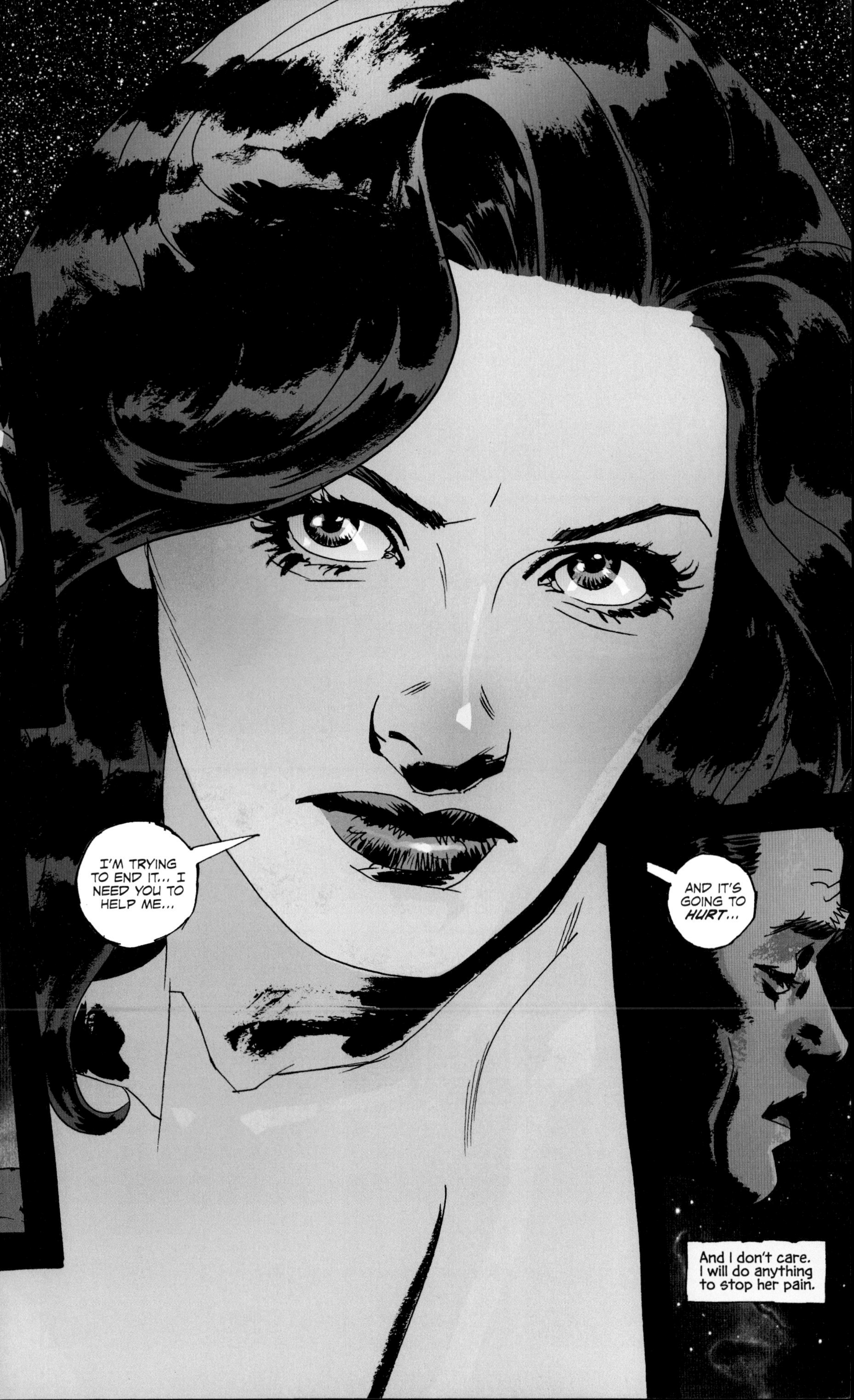
I'M TRYING TO END IT... I NEED YOU TO HELP ME...
AND IT'S GOING TO *HURT*...
And I don't care. I will do anything to stop her pain.

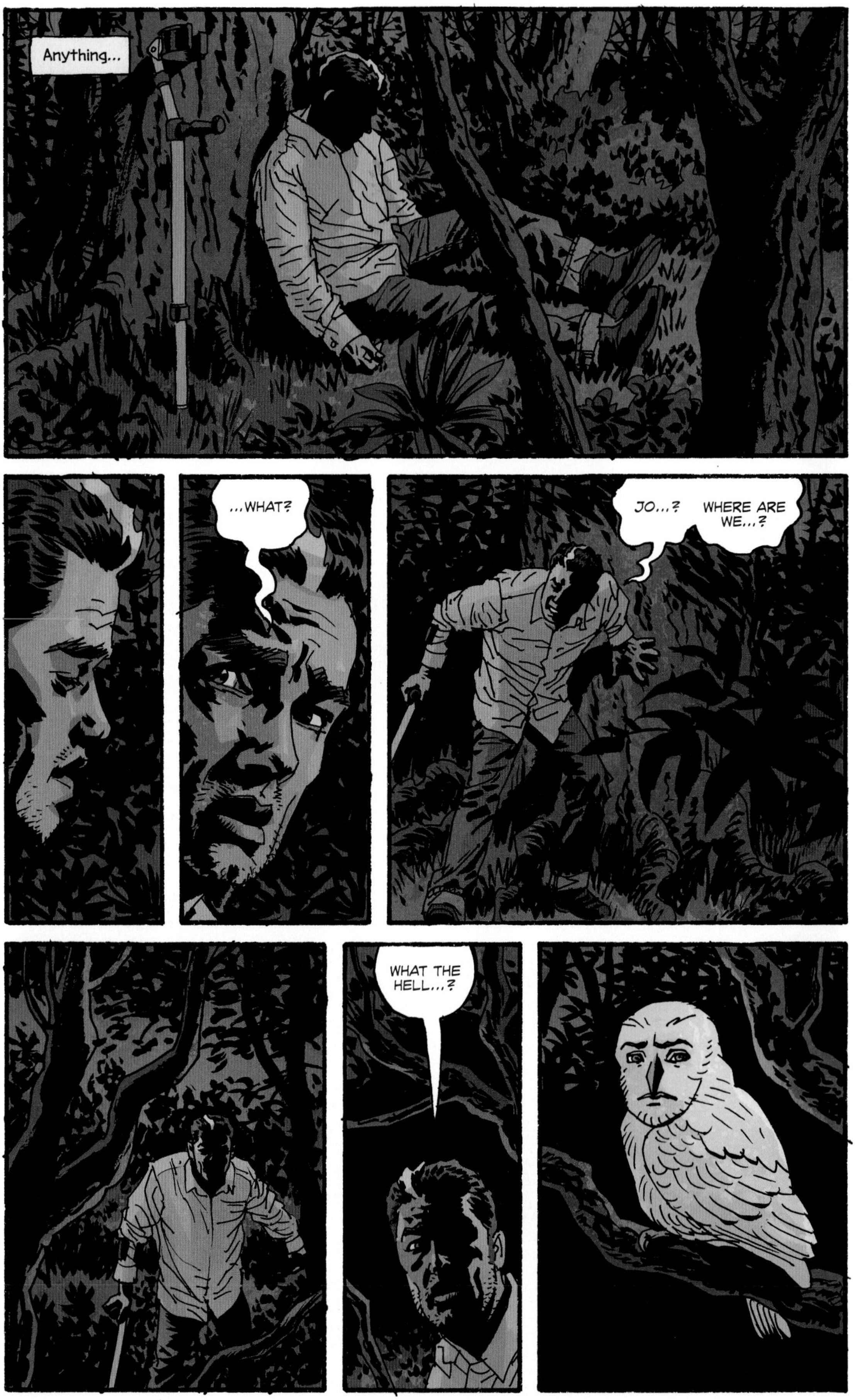
Anything...
...WHAT?
JO...?
WHERE ARE WE...?
WHAT THE HELL...?

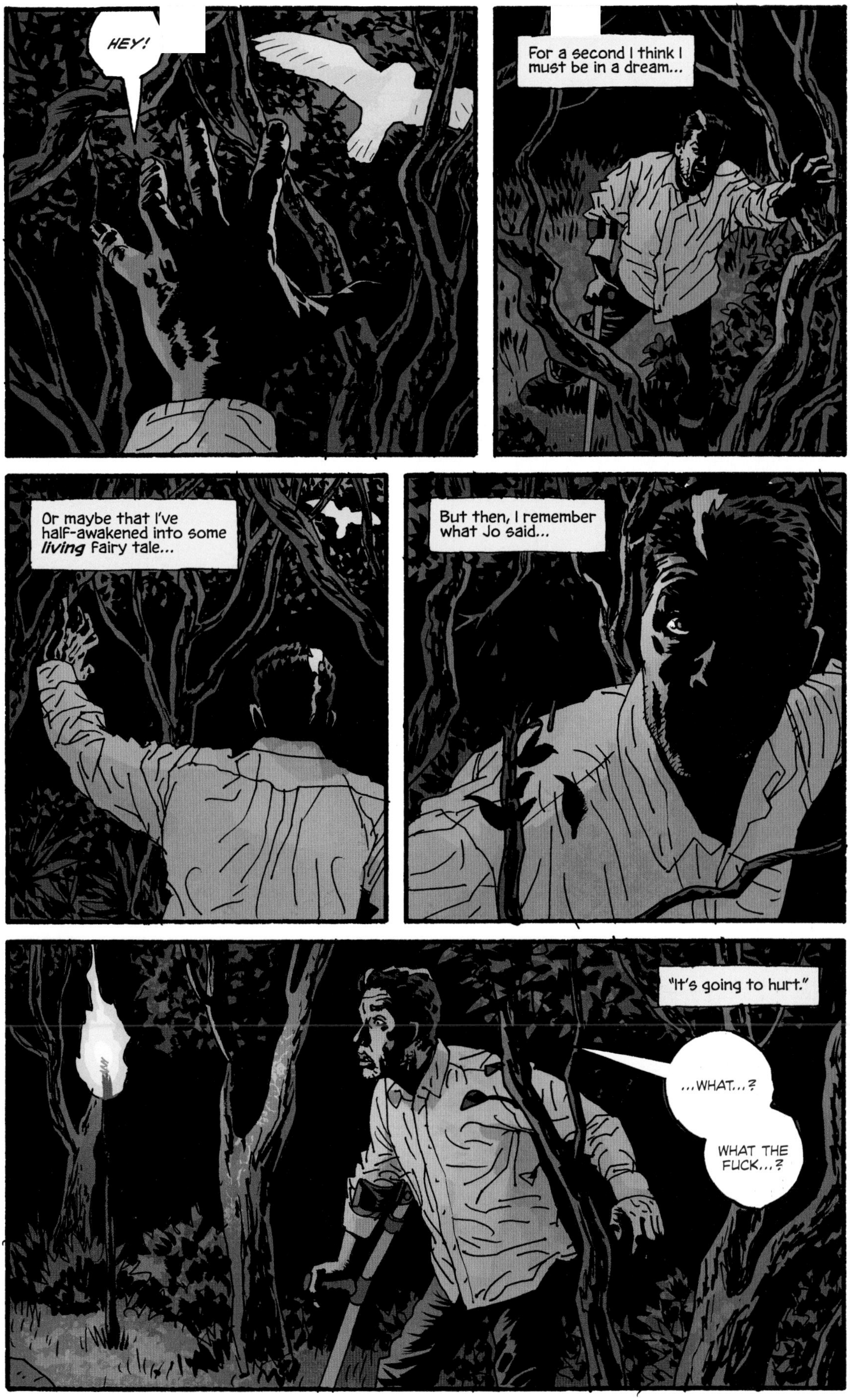
HEY!
For a second I think I must be in a dream...
Or maybe that I've half-awakened into some *living* fairy tale...
But then, I remember what Jo said...
"It's going to hurt."
...WHAT...?
WHAT THE FUCK...?

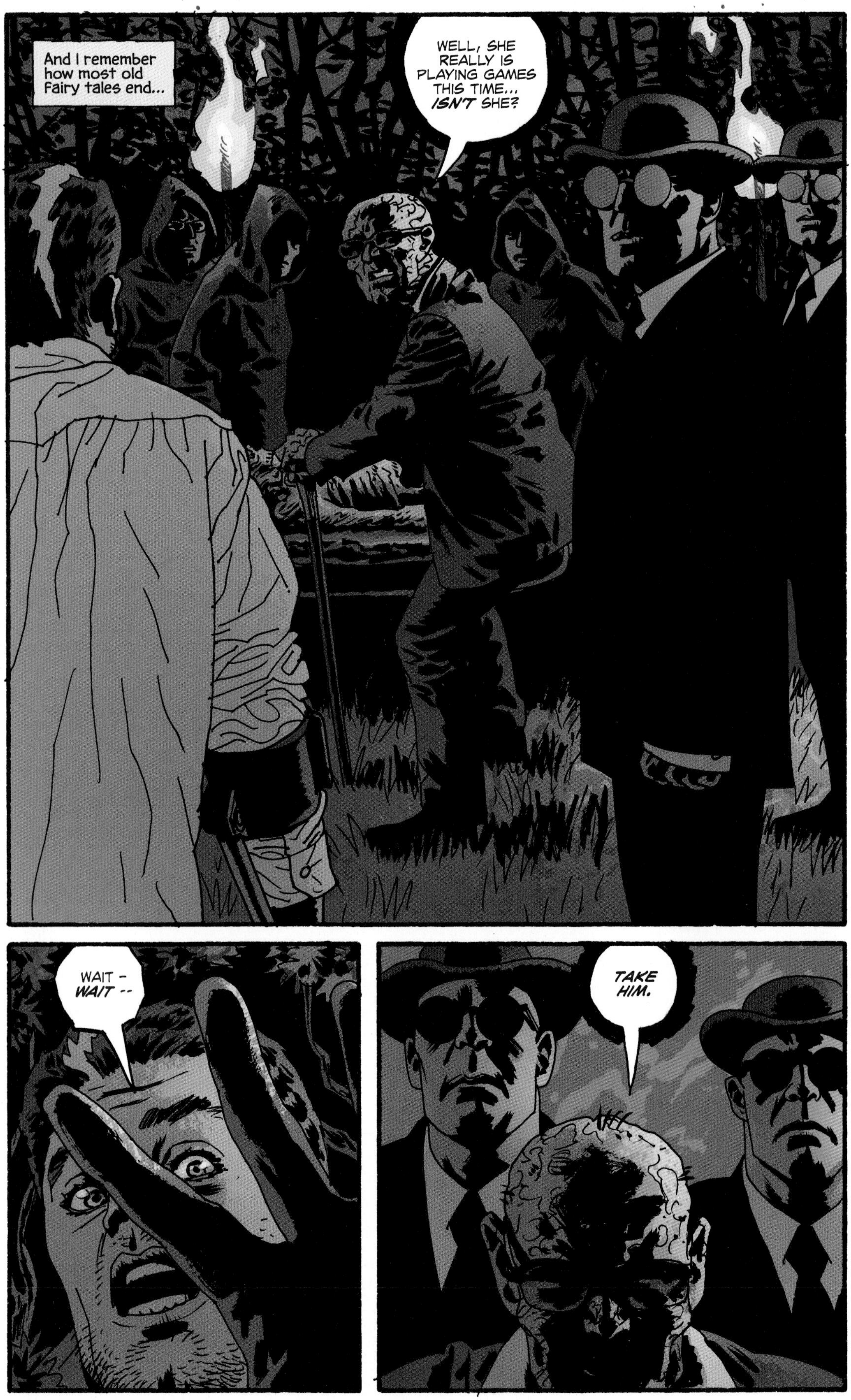
And I remember how most old fairy tales end...
WELL, SHE REALLY IS PLAYING GAMES THIS TIME... *ISN'T* SHE?
WAIT - *WAIT* --
TAKE HIM.

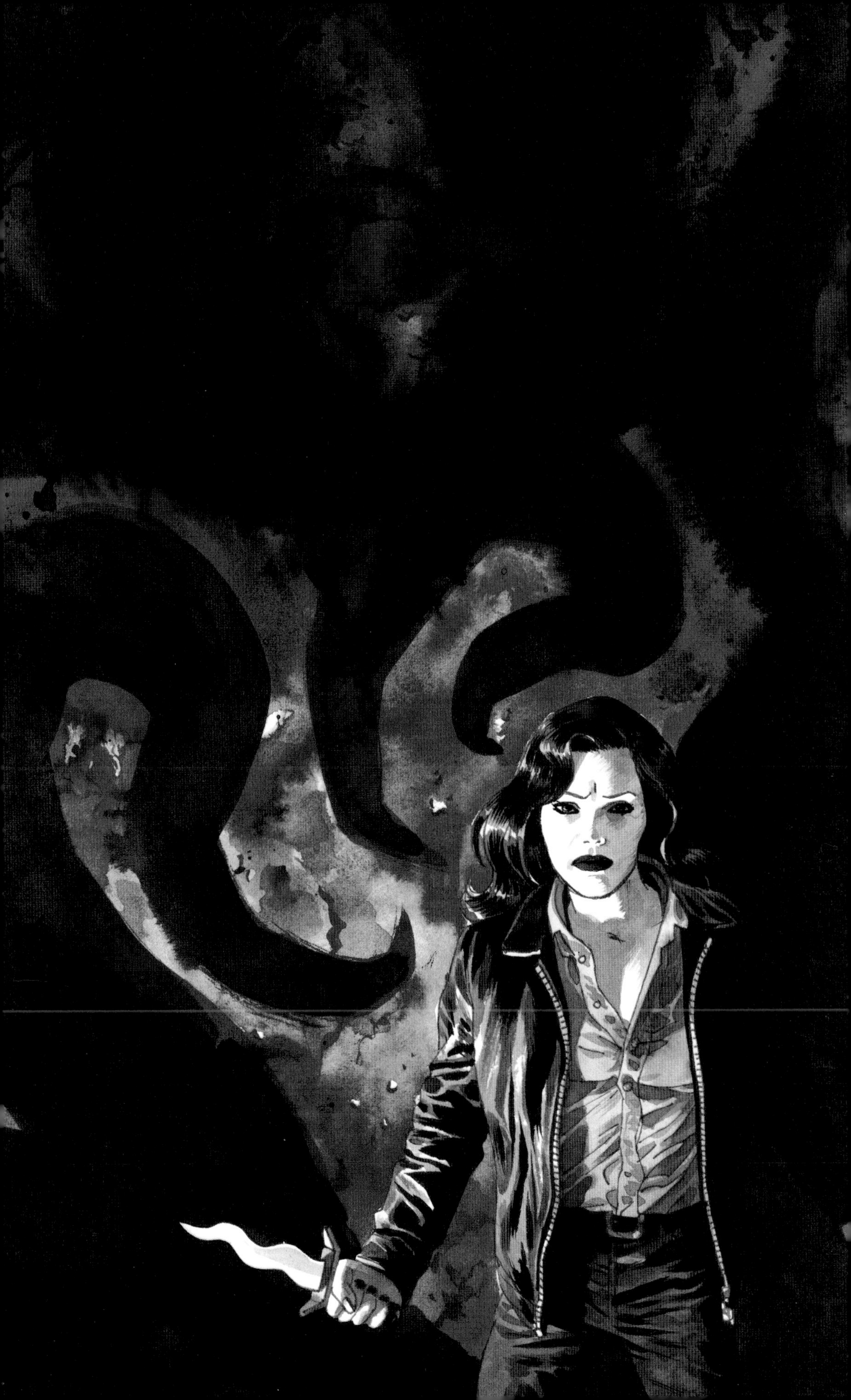

Chapter Five

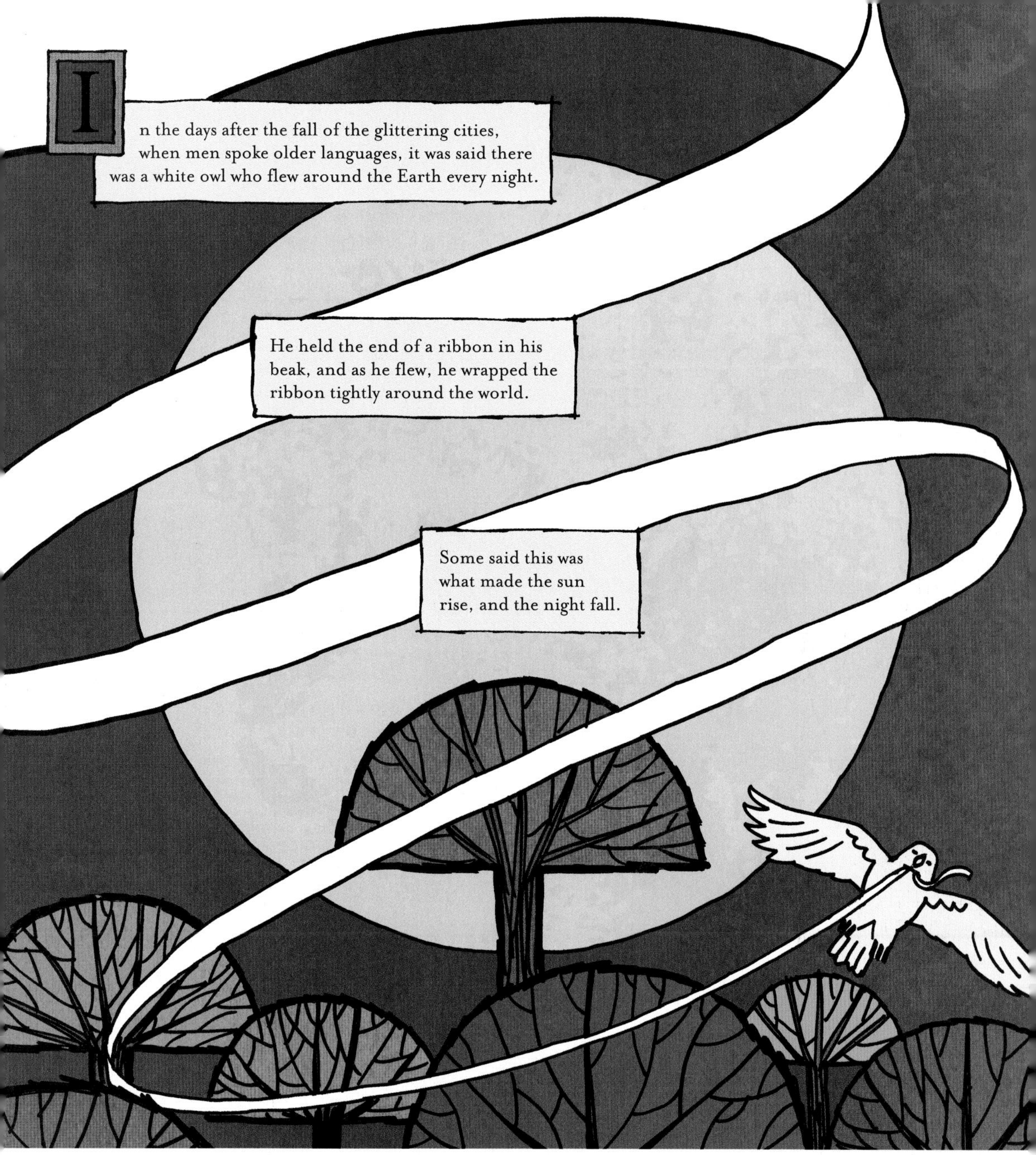
In the days after the fall of the glittering cities, when men spoke older languages, it was said there was a white owl who flew around the Earth every night.
He held the end of a ribbon in his beak, and as he flew, he wrapped the ribbon tightly around the world.
Some said this was what made the sun rise, and the night fall.

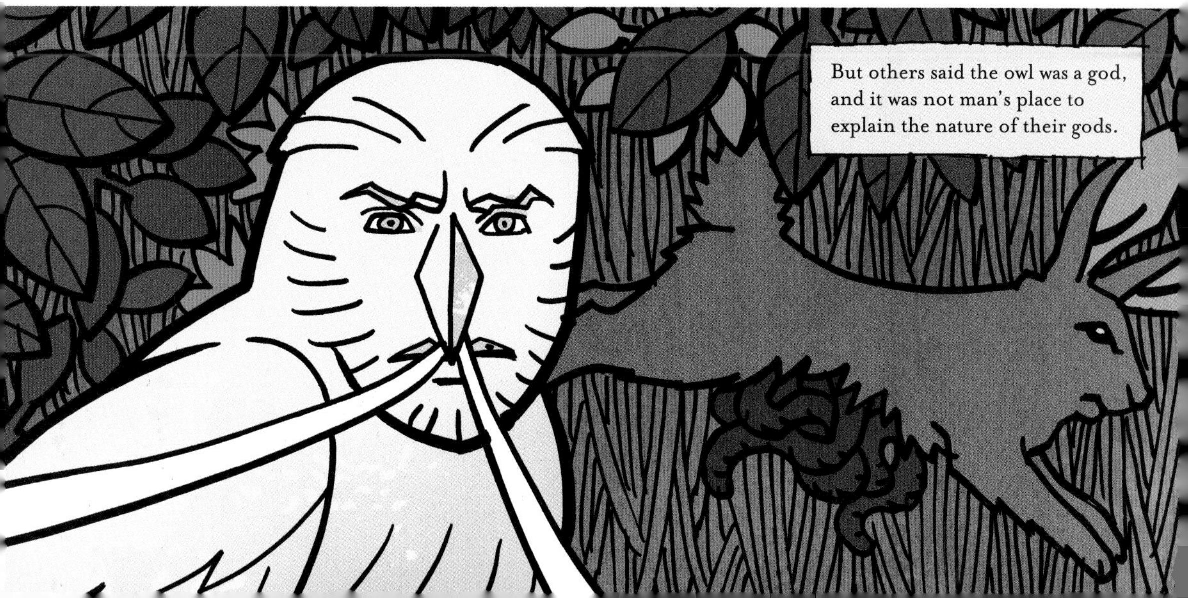
But others said the owl was a god, and it was not man's place to explain the nature of their gods.

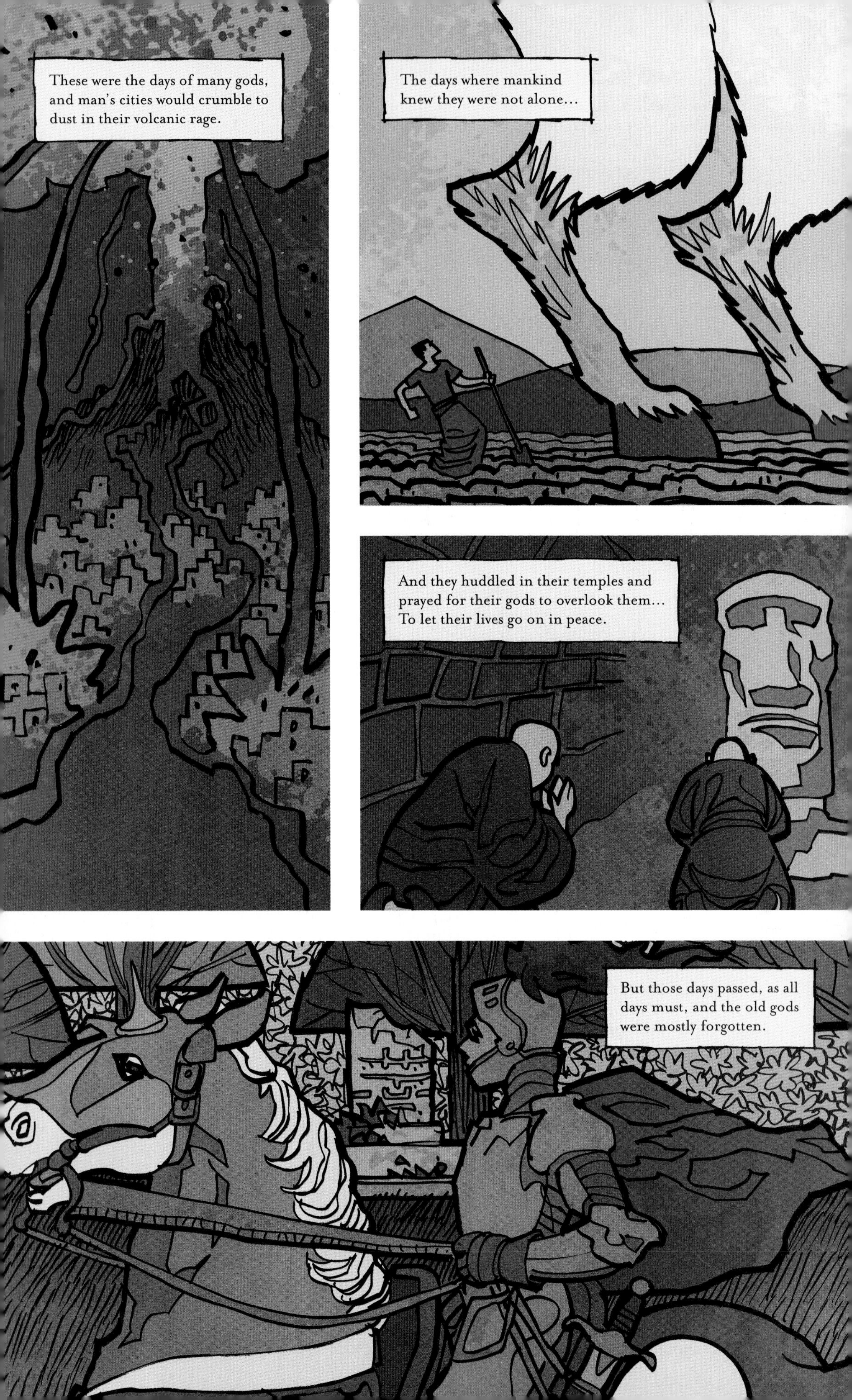
These were the days of many gods, and man's cities would crumble to dust in their volcanic rage.
The days where mankind knew they were not alone...
And they huddled in their temples and prayed for their gods to overlook them... To let their lives go on in peace.
But those days passed, as all days must, and the old gods were mostly forgotten.

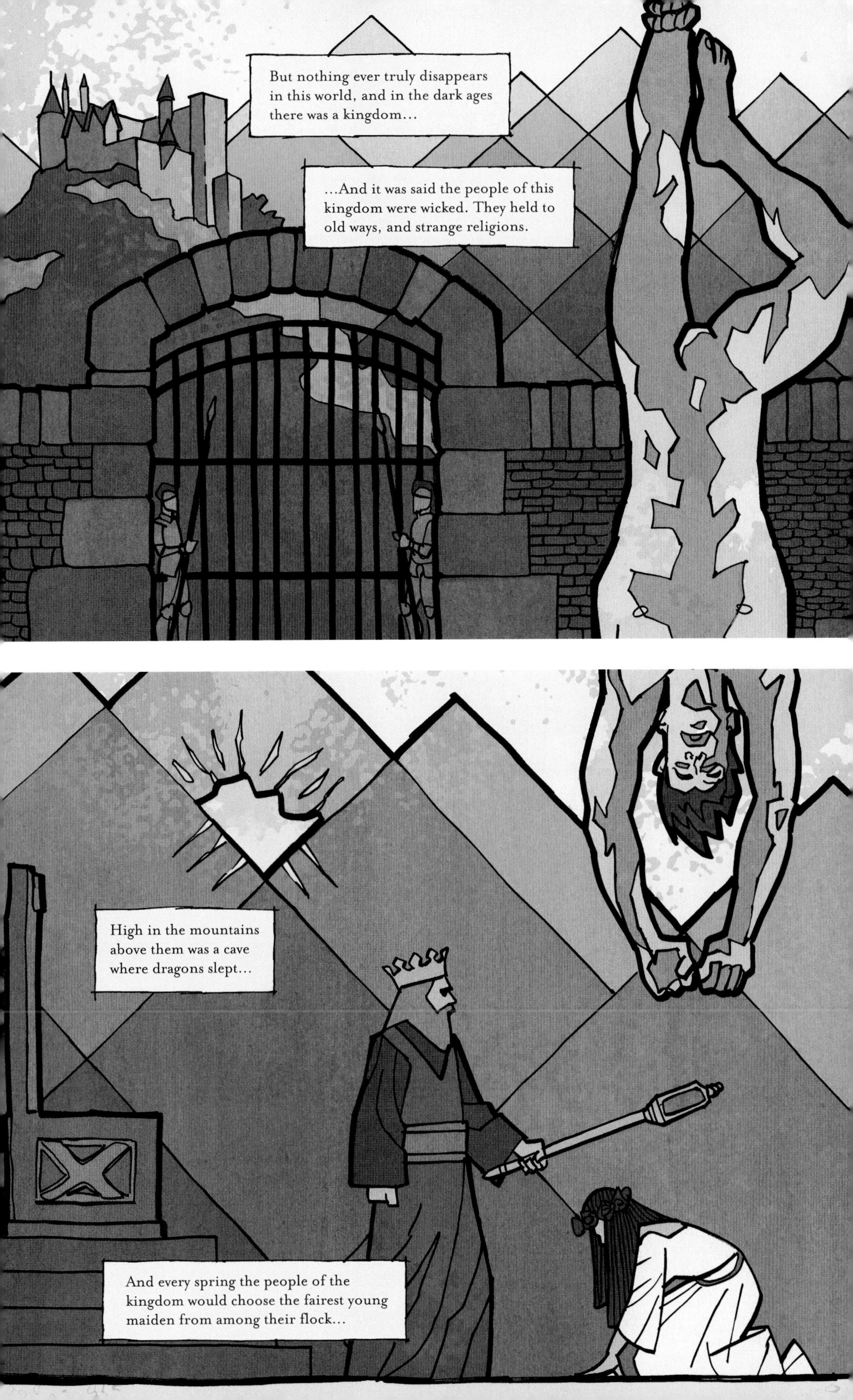

But nothing ever truly disappears in this world, and in the dark ages there was a kingdom...
...And it was said the people of this kingdom were wicked. They held to old ways, and strange religions.
High in the mountains above them was a cave where dragons slept...
And every spring the people of the kingdom would choose the fairest young maiden from among their flock...

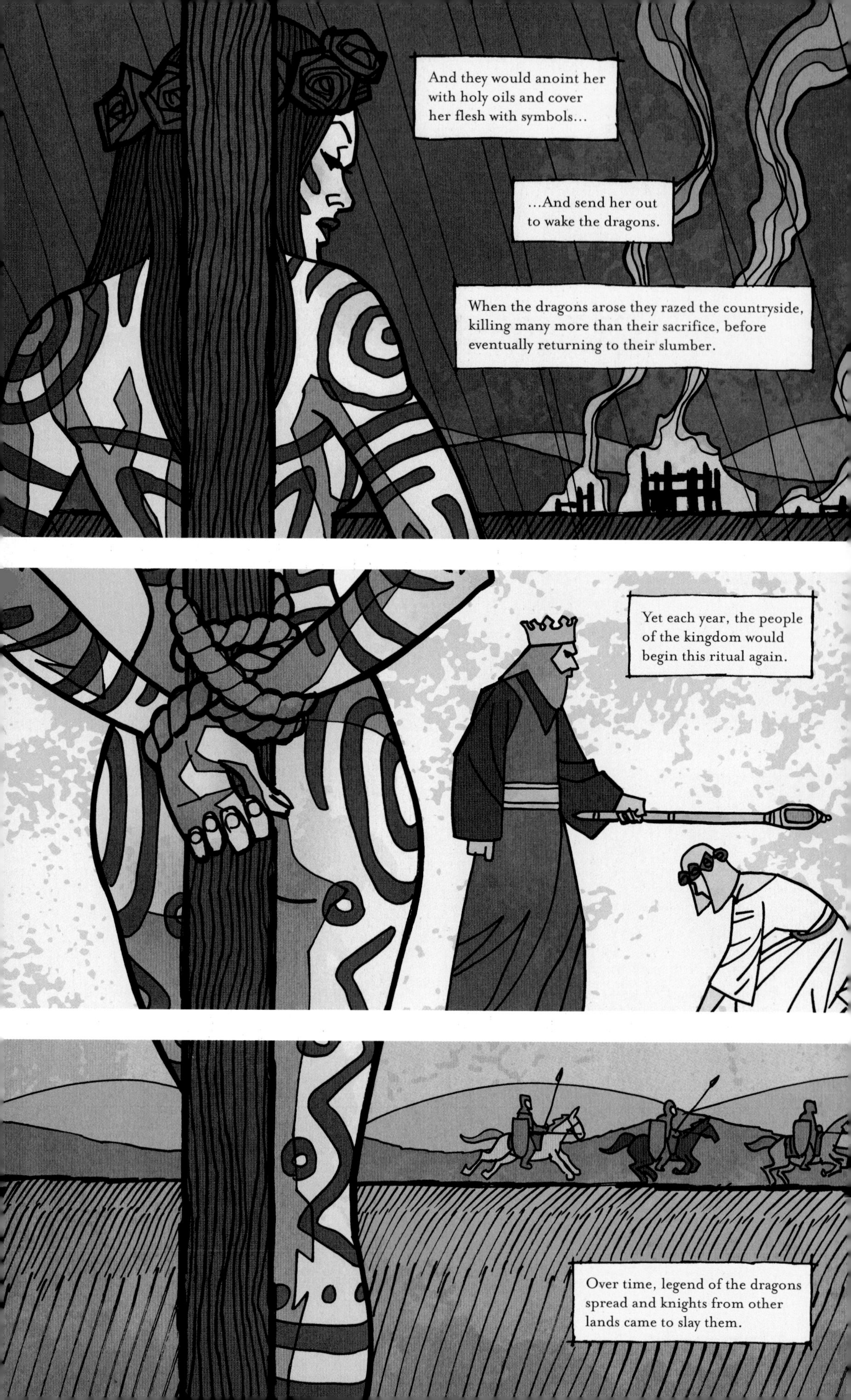
And they would anoint her with holy oils and cover her flesh with symbols...
...And send her out to wake the dragons.
When the dragons arose they razed the countryside, killing many more than their sacrifice, before eventually returning to their slumber.
Yet each year, the people of the kingdom would begin this ritual again.
Over time, legend of the dragons spread and knights from other lands came to slay them.

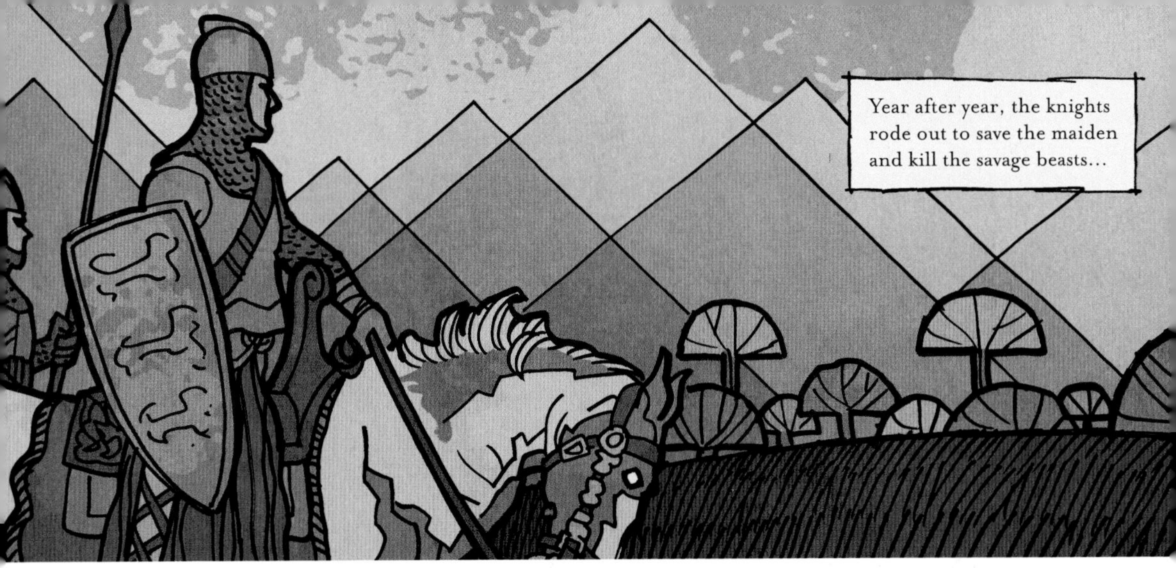
Year after year, the knights rode out to save the maiden and kill the savage beasts...

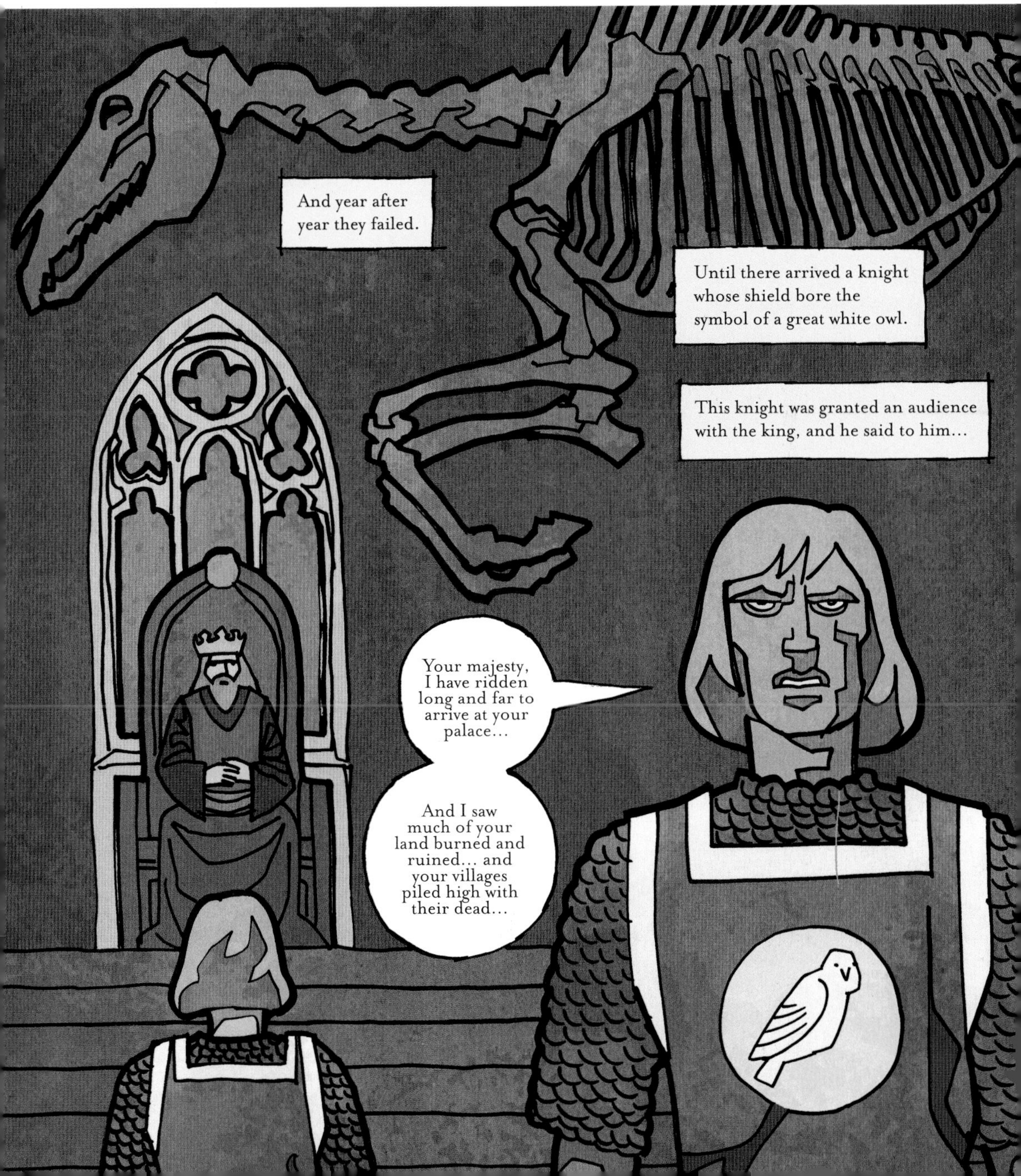
And year after year they failed.
Until there arrived a knight whose shield bore the symbol of a great white owl.
This knight was granted an audience with the king, and he said to him...
Your majesty, I have ridden long and far to arrive at your palace...
And I saw much of your land burned and ruined... and your villages piled high with their dead...

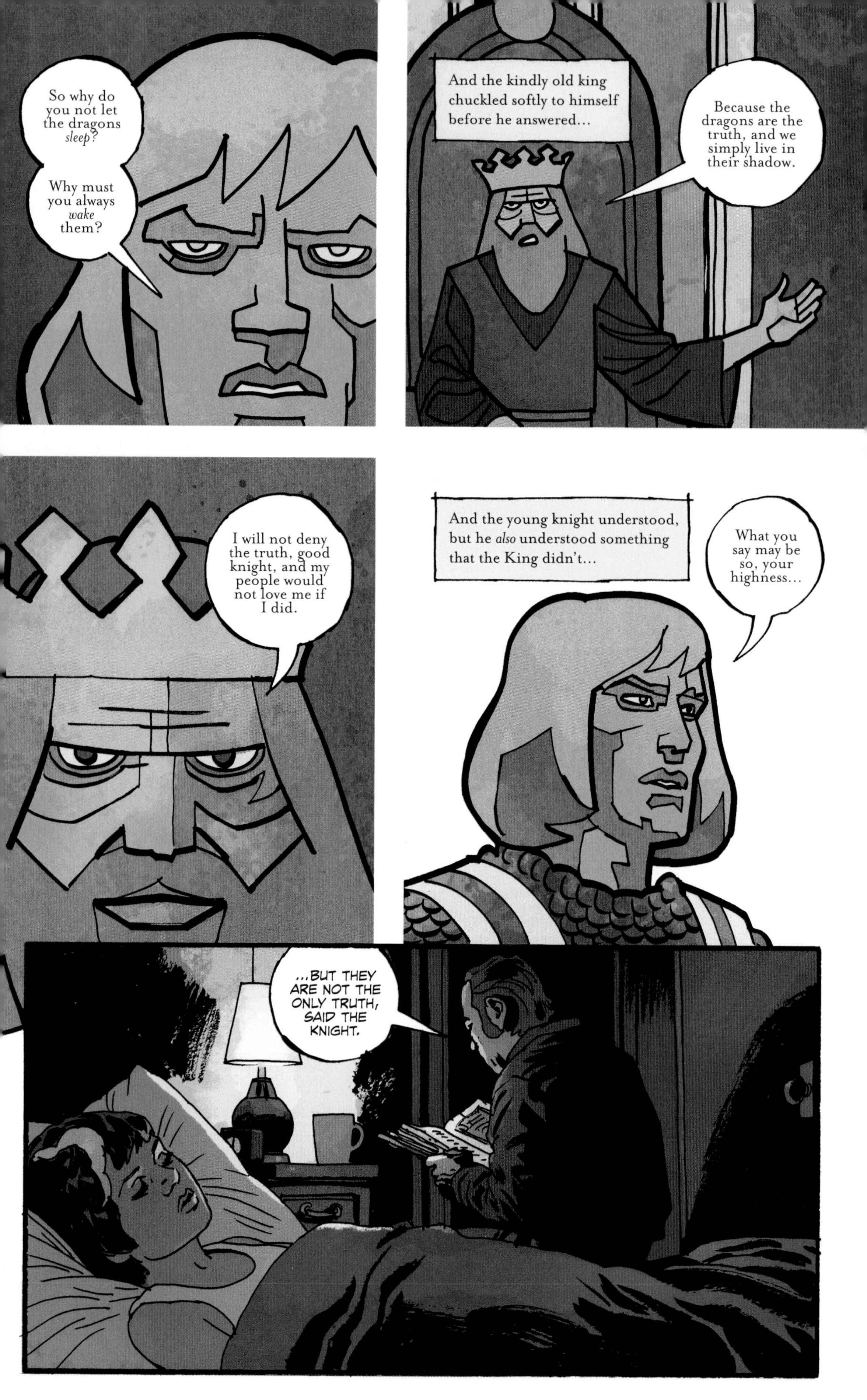

So why do you not let the dragons *sleep?*
Why must you always *wake* them?
And the kindly old king chuckled softly to himself before he answered...
Because the dragons are the truth, and we simply live in their shadow.
I will not deny the truth, good knight, and my people would not love me if I did.
And the young knight understood, but he *also* understood something that the King didn't...
What you say may be so, your highness...
...BUT THEY ARE NOT THE ONLY TRUTH, SAID THE KNIGHT.

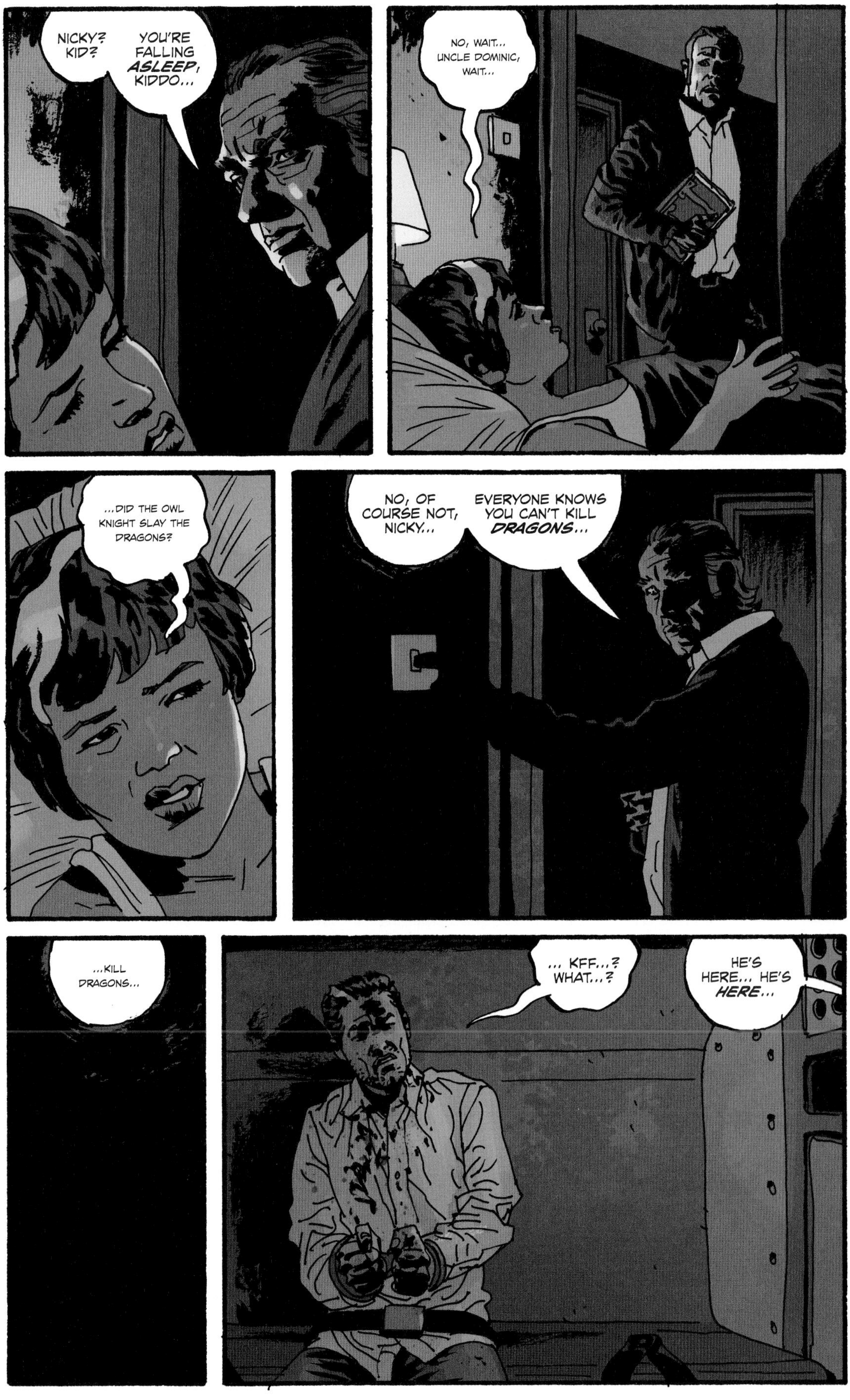
NICKY? KID?
YOU'RE FALLING *ASLEEP*, KIDDO...
NO, WAIT... UNCLE DOMINIC, WAIT...
...DID THE OWL KNIGHT SLAY THE DRAGONS?
NO, OF COURSE NOT, NICKY...
EVERYONE KNOWS YOU CAN'T KILL *DRAGONS*...
...KILL DRAGONS...
... KFF...? WHAT...?
HE'S HERE... HE'S *HERE*...

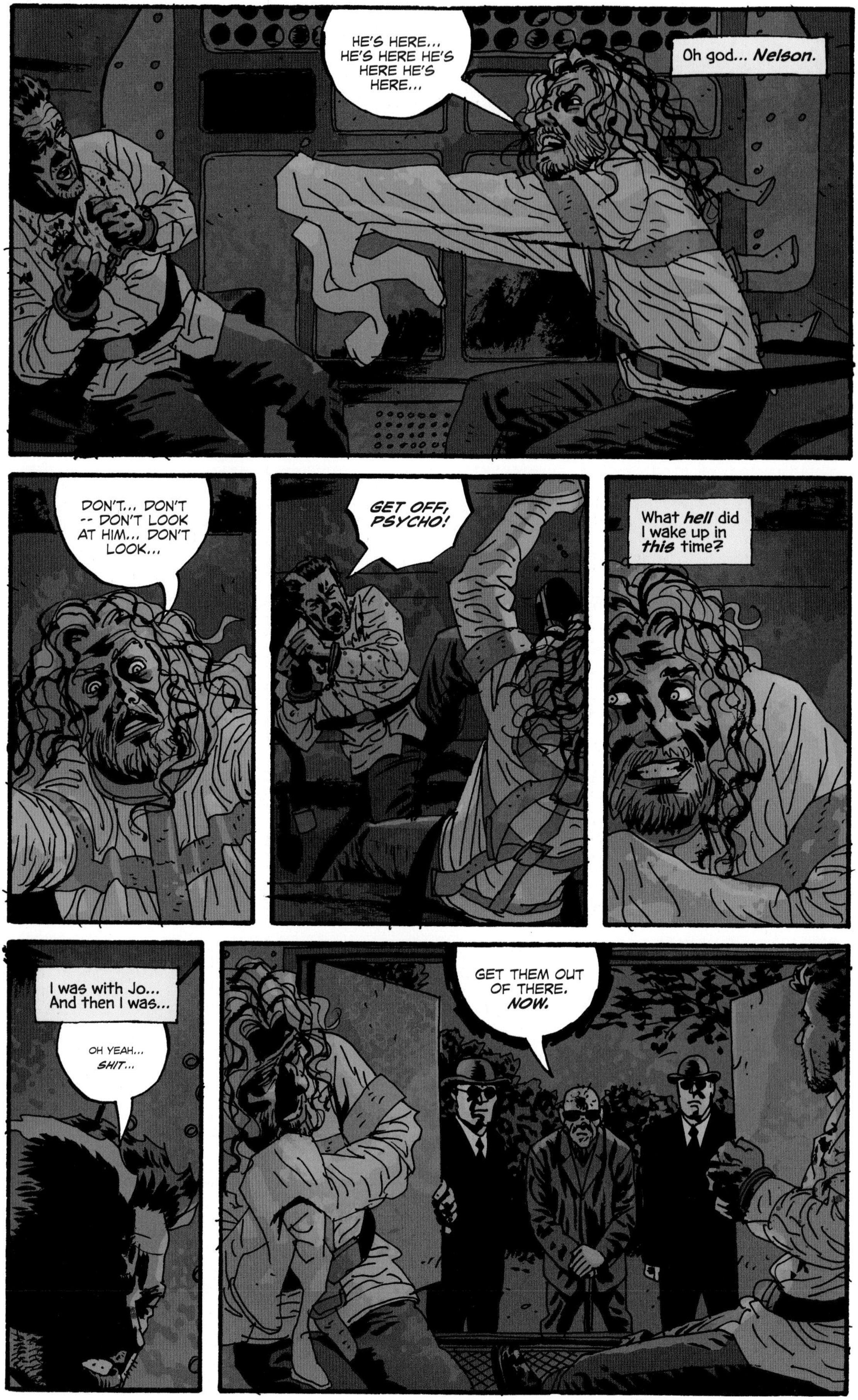
HE'S HERE... HE'S HERE HE'S HERE HE'S HERE...
Oh god... *Nelson*.
DON'T... DON'T -- DON'T LOOK AT HIM... DON'T LOOK...
GET OFF, PSYCHO!
What *hell* did I wake up in *this* time?
I was with Jo... And then I was...
OH YEAH... *SHIT*...
GET THEM OUT OF THERE. *NOW.*

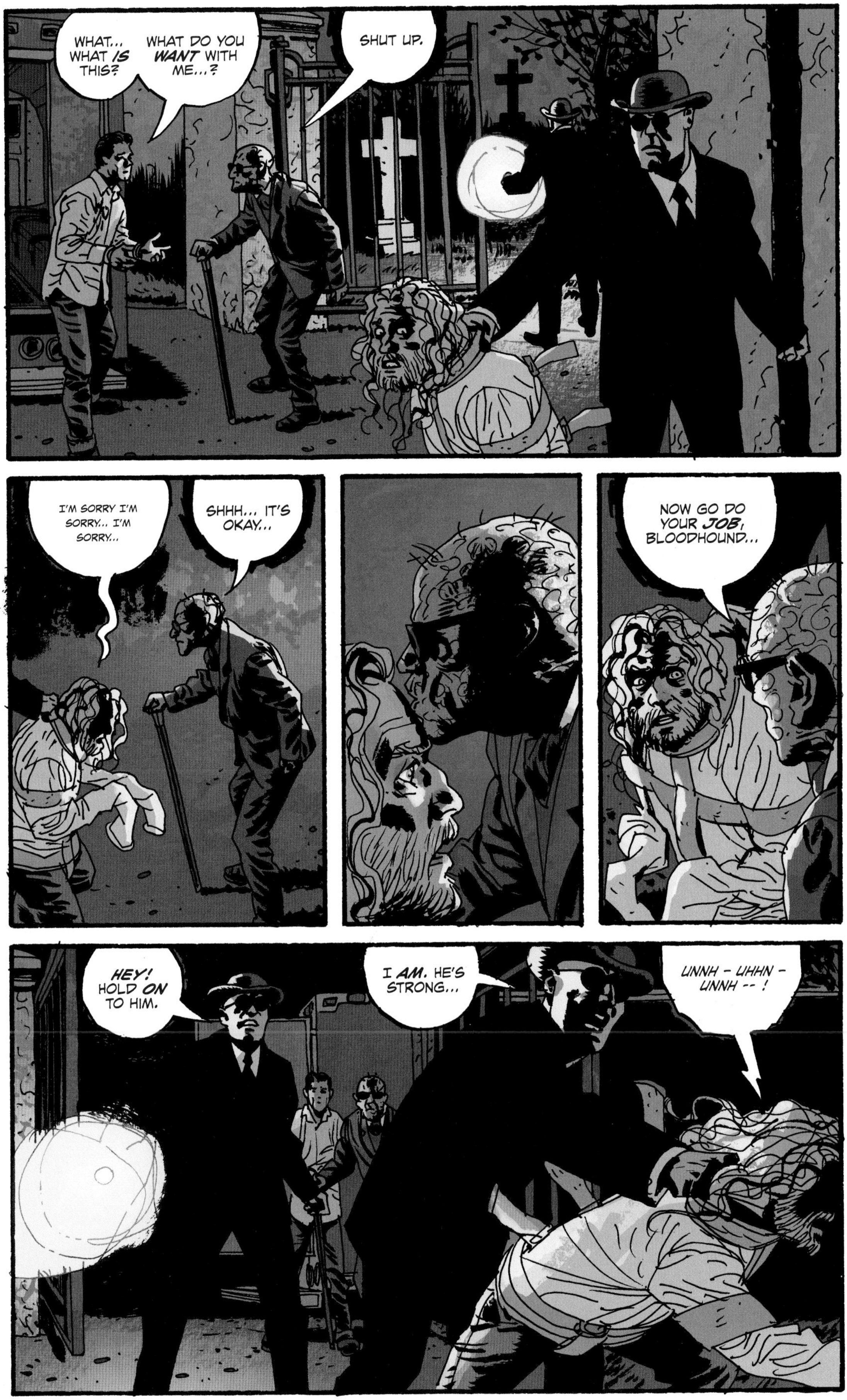
WHAT... WHAT *IS* THIS?
WHAT DO YOU *WANT* WITH ME...?
SHUT UP.
I'M SORRY I'M SORRY... I'M SORRY...
SHHH... IT'S OKAY...
NOW GO DO YOUR *JOB*, BLOODHOUND...
HEY! HOLD *ON* TO HIM.
I *AM*. HE'S STRONG...
UNNH - UHHN - UNNH -- !

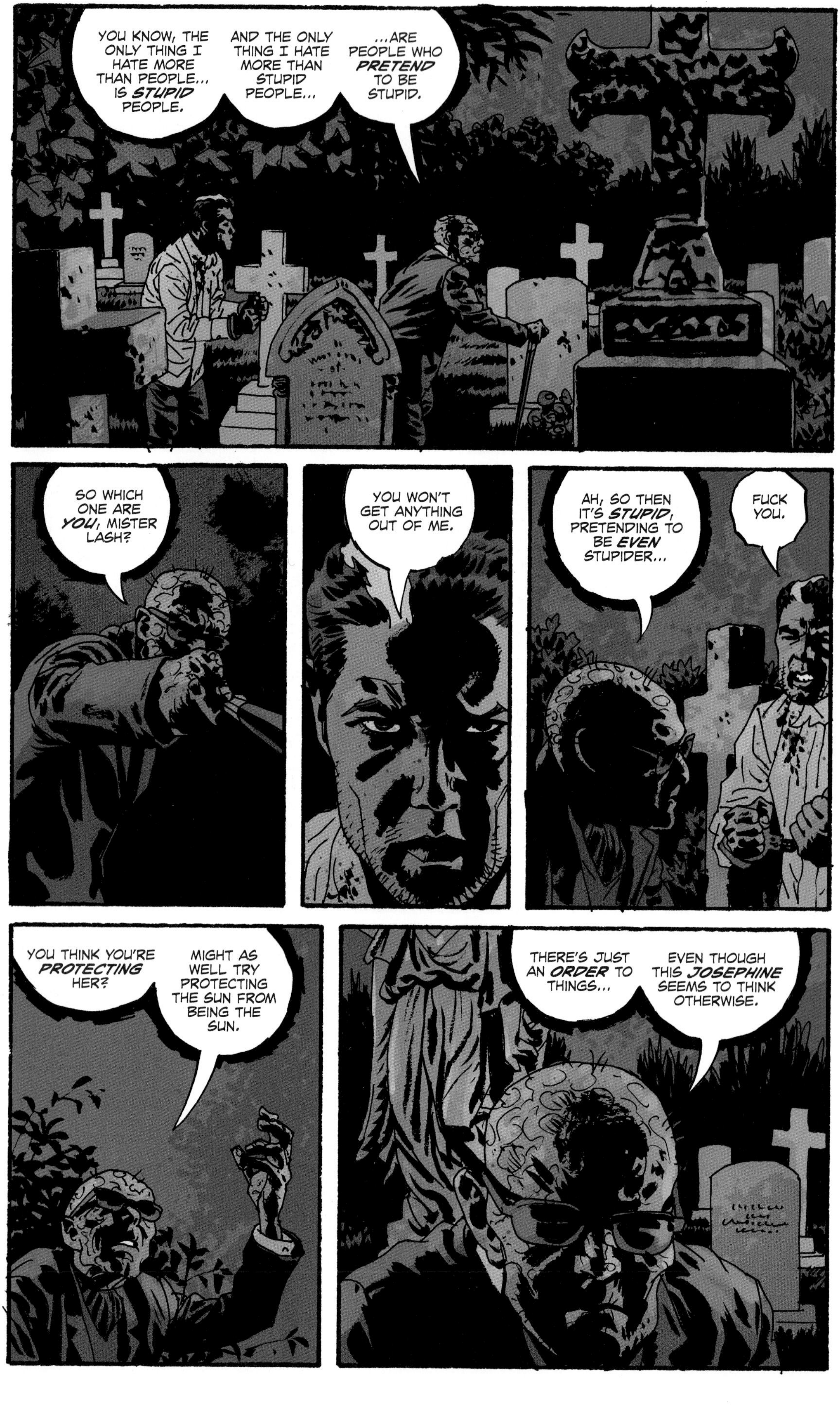
YOU KNOW, THE ONLY THING I HATE MORE THAN PEOPLE... IS STUPID PEOPLE.
AND THE ONLY THING I HATE MORE THAN STUPID PEOPLE...
...ARE PEOPLE WHO PRETEND TO BE STUPID.
SO WHICH ONE ARE YOU, MISTER LASH?
YOU WON'T GET ANYTHING OUT OF ME.
AH, SO THEN IT'S STUPID, PRETENDING TO BE EVEN STUPIDER...
FUCK YOU.
YOU THINK YOU'RE PROTECTING HER?
MIGHT AS WELL TRY PROTECTING THE SUN FROM BEING THE SUN.
THERE'S JUST AN ORDER TO THINGS...
EVEN THOUGH THIS JOSEPHINE SEEMS TO THINK OTHERWISE.

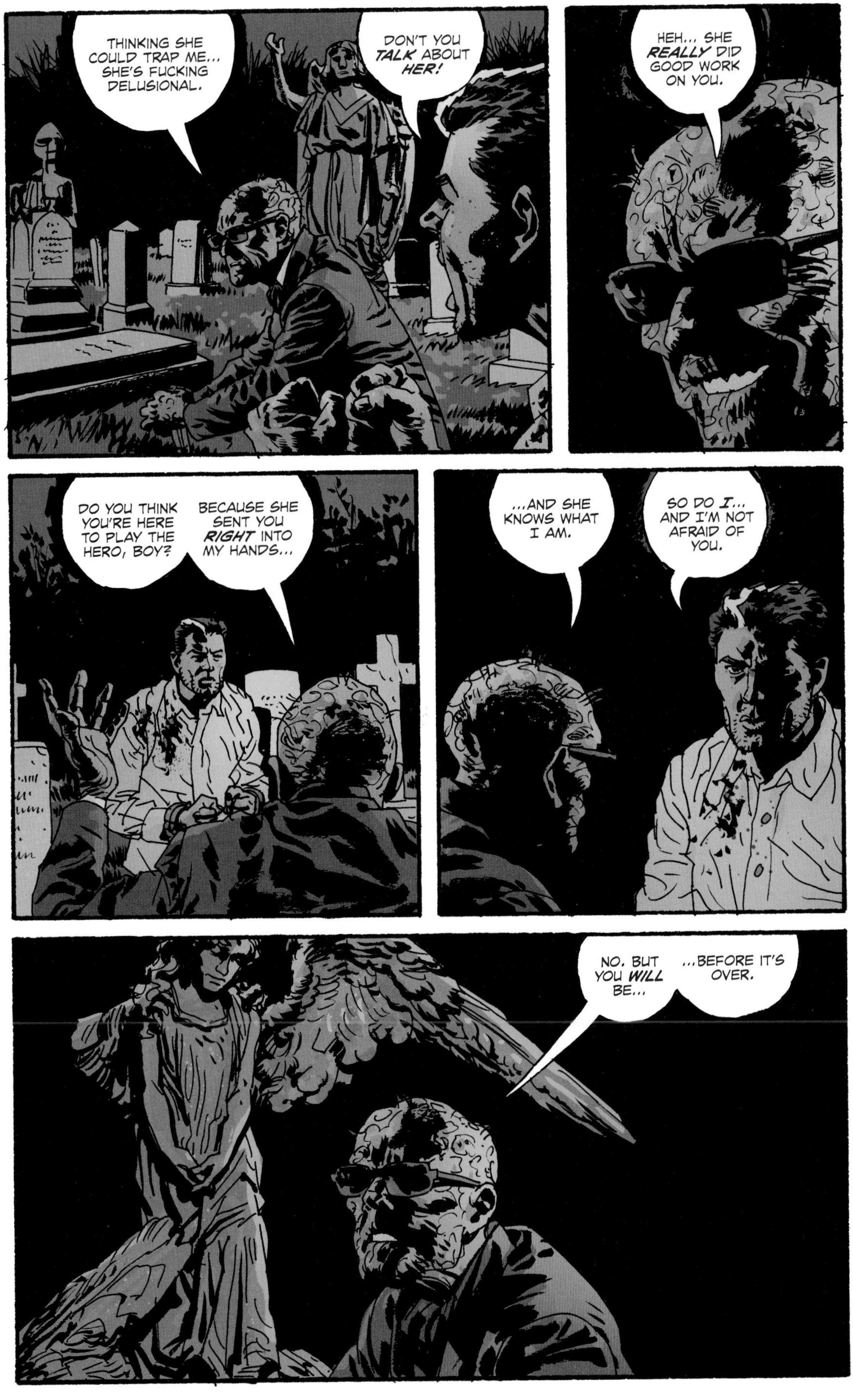
THINKING SHE COULD TRAP ME... SHE'S FUCKING DELUSIONAL.
DON'T YOU *TALK* ABOUT *HER!*
HEH... SHE *REALLY* DID GOOD WORK ON YOU.
DO YOU THINK YOU'RE HERE TO PLAY THE HERO, BOY?
BECAUSE SHE SENT YOU *RIGHT* INTO MY HANDS...
...AND SHE KNOWS WHAT I AM.
SO DO *I*... AND I'M NOT AFRAID OF YOU.
NO. BUT YOU *WILL* BE...
...BEFORE IT'S OVER.

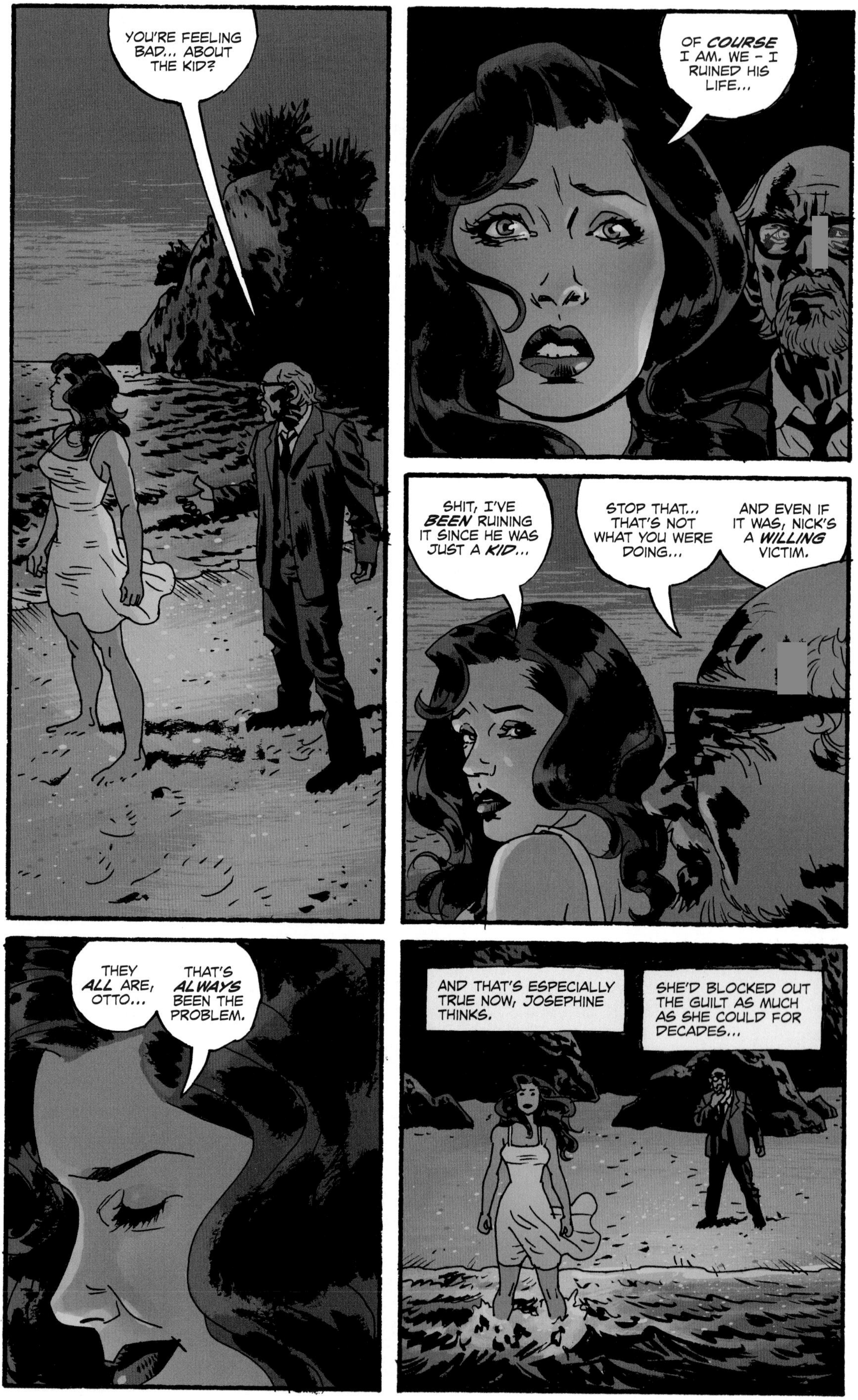
YOU'RE FEELING BAD... ABOUT THE KID?
OF COURSE I AM. WE - I RUINED HIS LIFE...
SHIT, I'VE BEEN RUINING IT SINCE HE WAS JUST A KID...
STOP THAT... THAT'S NOT WHAT YOU WERE DOING...
AND EVEN IF IT WAS, NICK'S A WILLING VICTIM.
THEY ALL ARE, OTTO...
THAT'S ALWAYS BEEN THE PROBLEM.
AND THAT'S ESPECIALLY TRUE NOW, JOSEPHINE THINKS.
SHE'D BLOCKED OUT THE GUILT AS MUCH AS SHE COULD FOR DECADES...

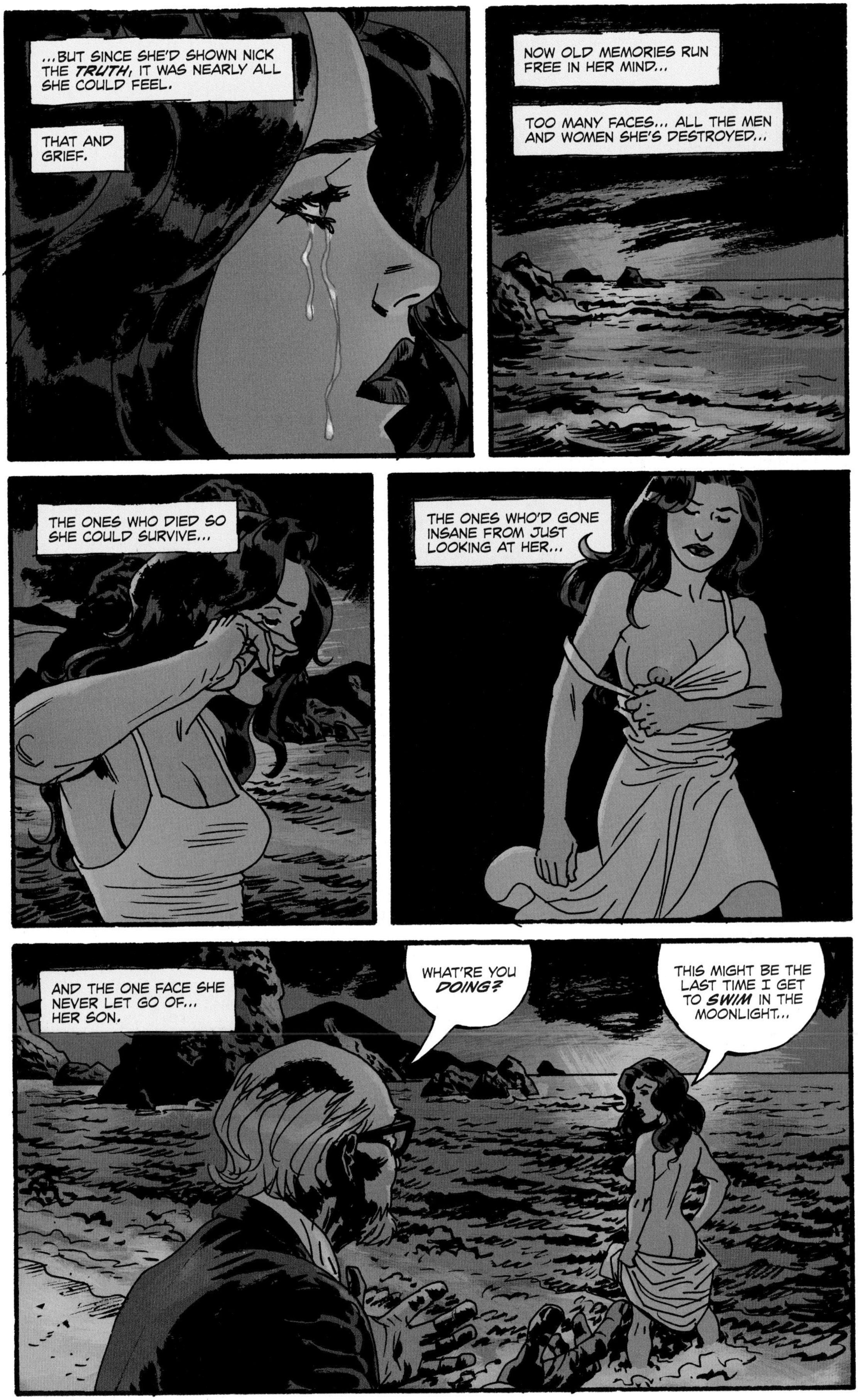
...BUT SINCE SHE'D SHOWN NICK THE *TRUTH*, IT WAS NEARLY ALL SHE COULD FEEL.
THAT AND GRIEF.
NOW OLD MEMORIES RUN FREE IN HER MIND...
TOO MANY FACES... ALL THE MEN AND WOMEN SHE'S DESTROYED...
THE ONES WHO DIED SO SHE COULD SURVIVE...
THE ONES WHO'D GONE INSANE FROM JUST LOOKING AT HER...
AND THE ONE FACE SHE NEVER LET GO OF... HER SON.
WHAT'RE YOU *DOING?*
THIS MIGHT BE THE LAST TIME I GET TO *SWIM* IN THE MOONLIGHT...

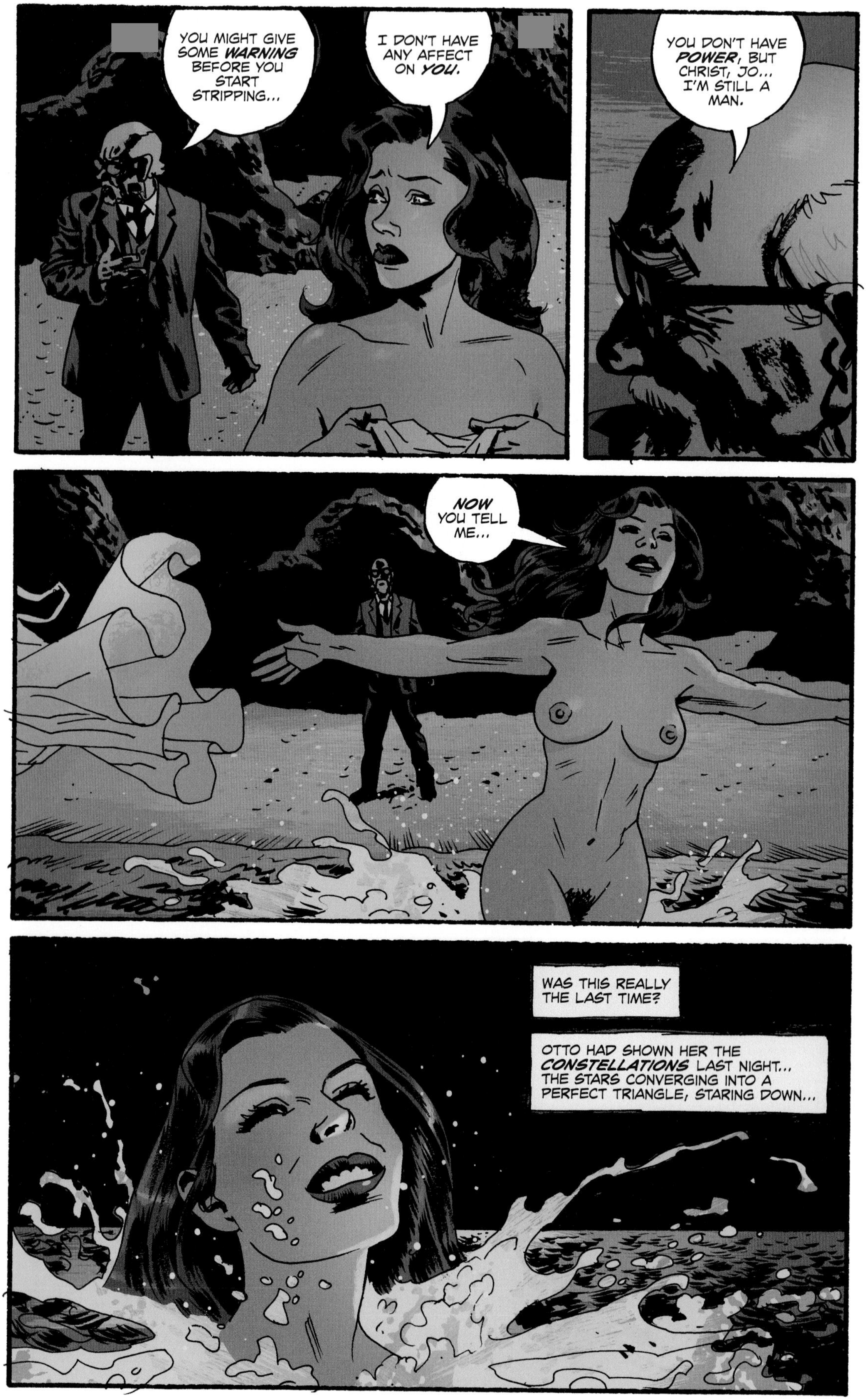
YOU MIGHT GIVE SOME WARNING BEFORE YOU START STRIPPING...
I DON'T HAVE ANY AFFECT ON YOU.
YOU DON'T HAVE POWER, BUT CHRIST, JO... I'M STILL A MAN.
NOW YOU TELL ME...
WAS THIS REALLY THE LAST TIME?
OTTO HAD SHOWN HER THE CONSTELLATIONS LAST NIGHT... THE STARS CONVERGING INTO A PERFECT TRIANGLE, STARING DOWN...

BUT NOW SHE COULDN'T SEE THEM.

STILL, SHE COULD FEEL IT IN HER PULSE...

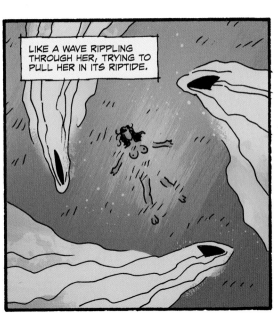

LIKE A WAVE RIPPLING THROUGH HER, TRYING TO PULL HER IN ITS RIPTIDE.

SHE REMEMBERS THE DAYS SHE RAN FROM THAT PULL.

HERE, COVER YOURSELF... YOU'LL CATCH YOUR DEATH.

IT'S FREEZING OUT HERE.

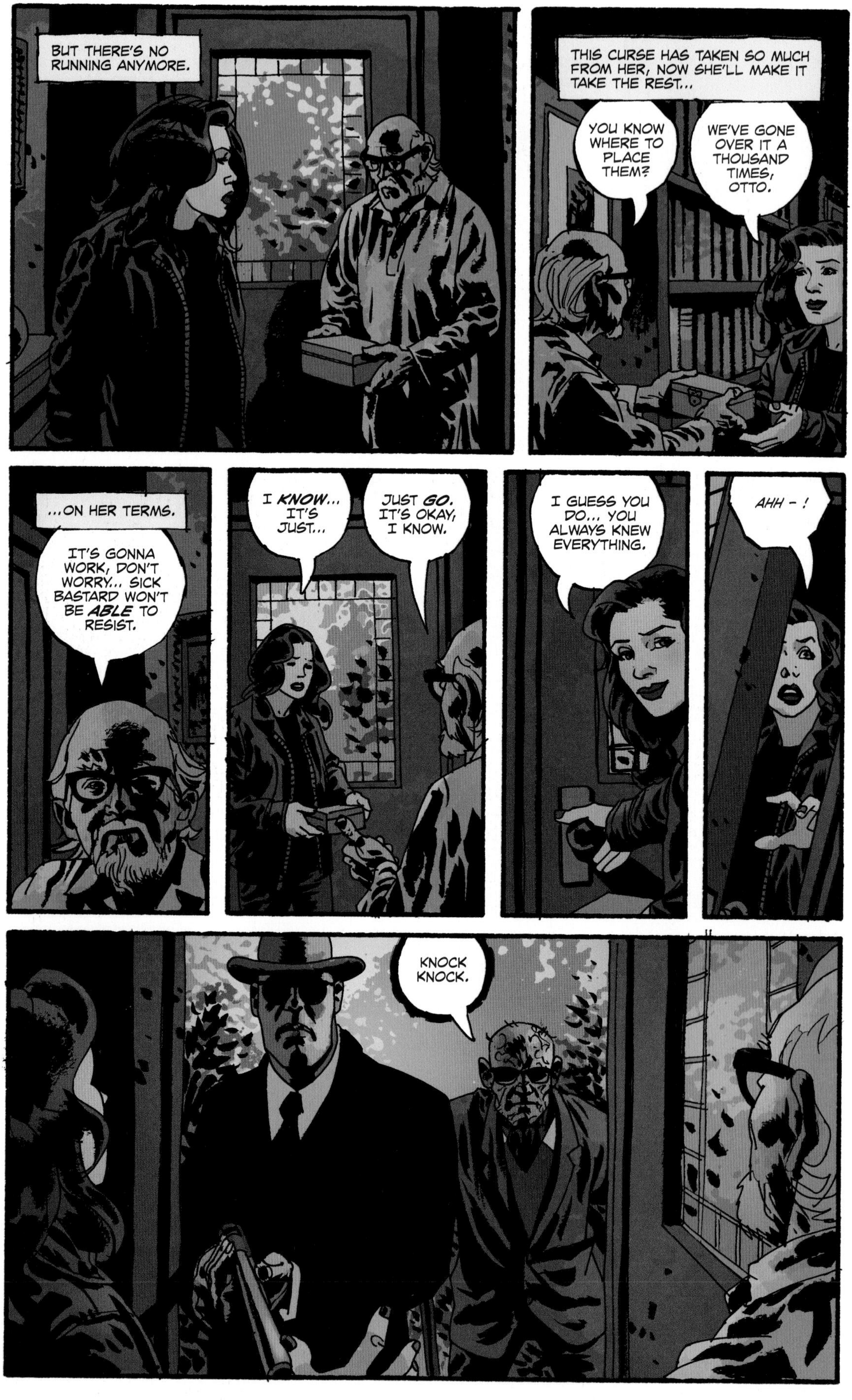
BUT THERE'S NO RUNNING ANYMORE.
THIS CURSE HAS TAKEN SO MUCH FROM HER, NOW SHE'LL MAKE IT TAKE THE REST...
YOU KNOW WHERE TO PLACE THEM?
WE'VE GONE OVER IT A THOUSAND TIMES, OTTO.
...ON HER TERMS.
IT'S GONNA WORK, DON'T WORRY... SICK BASTARD WON'T BE ABLE TO RESIST.
I KNOW... IT'S JUST...
JUST GO. IT'S OKAY, I KNOW.
I GUESS YOU DO... YOU ALWAYS KNEW EVERYTHING.
AHH – !
KNOCK KNOCK.

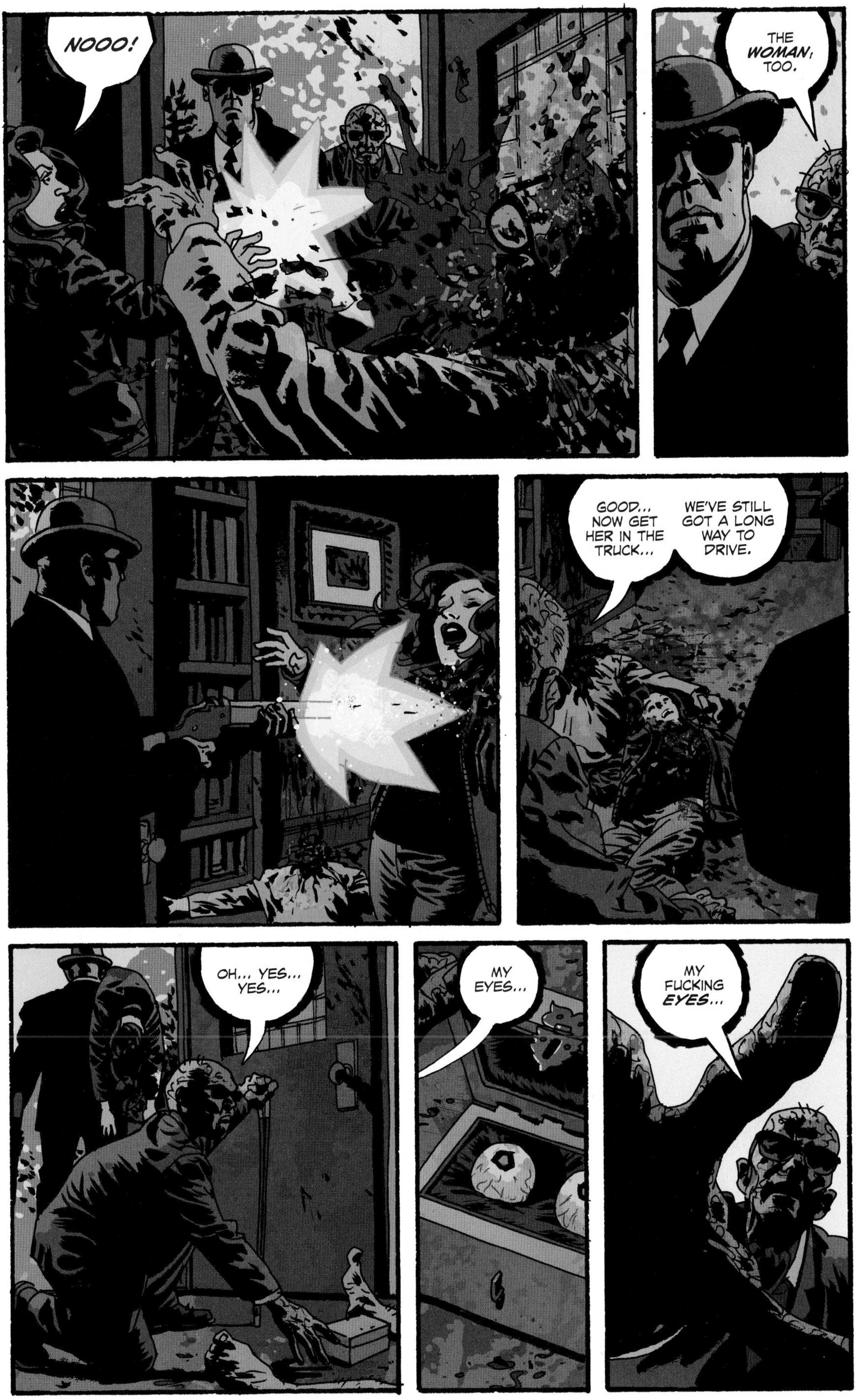
NOOO!
THE *WOMAN*, TOO.
GOOD... NOW GET HER IN THE TRUCK...
WE'VE STILL GOT A LONG WAY TO DRIVE.
OH... YES... YES...
MY EYES...
MY FUCKING *EYES*...

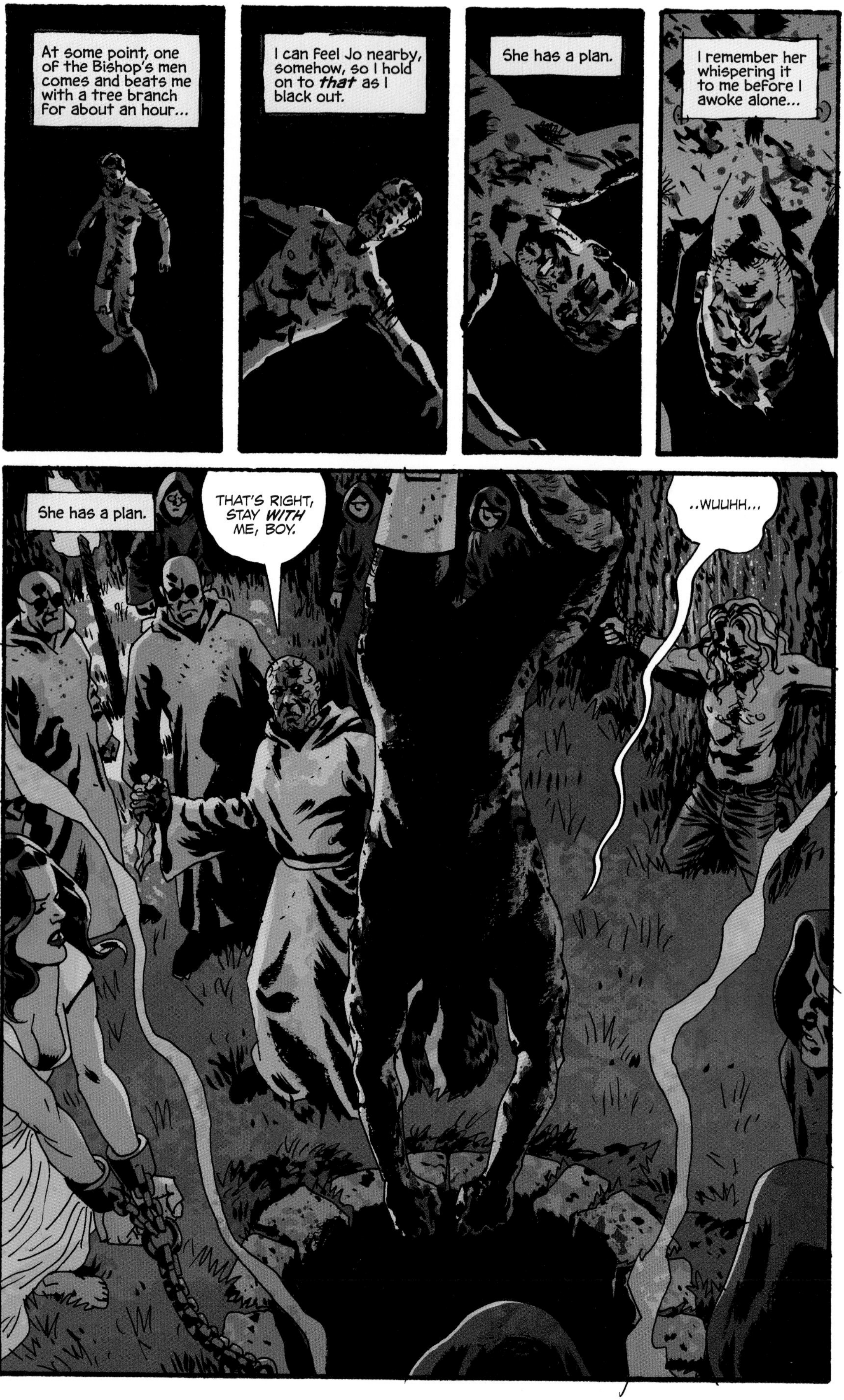
At some point, one of the Bishop's men comes and beats me with a tree branch for about an hour...
I can feel Jo nearby, somehow, so I hold on to *that* as I black out.
She has a plan.
I remember her whispering it to me before I awoke alone...
She has a plan.
THAT'S RIGHT, STAY *WITH* ME, BOY.
..WUUHH...

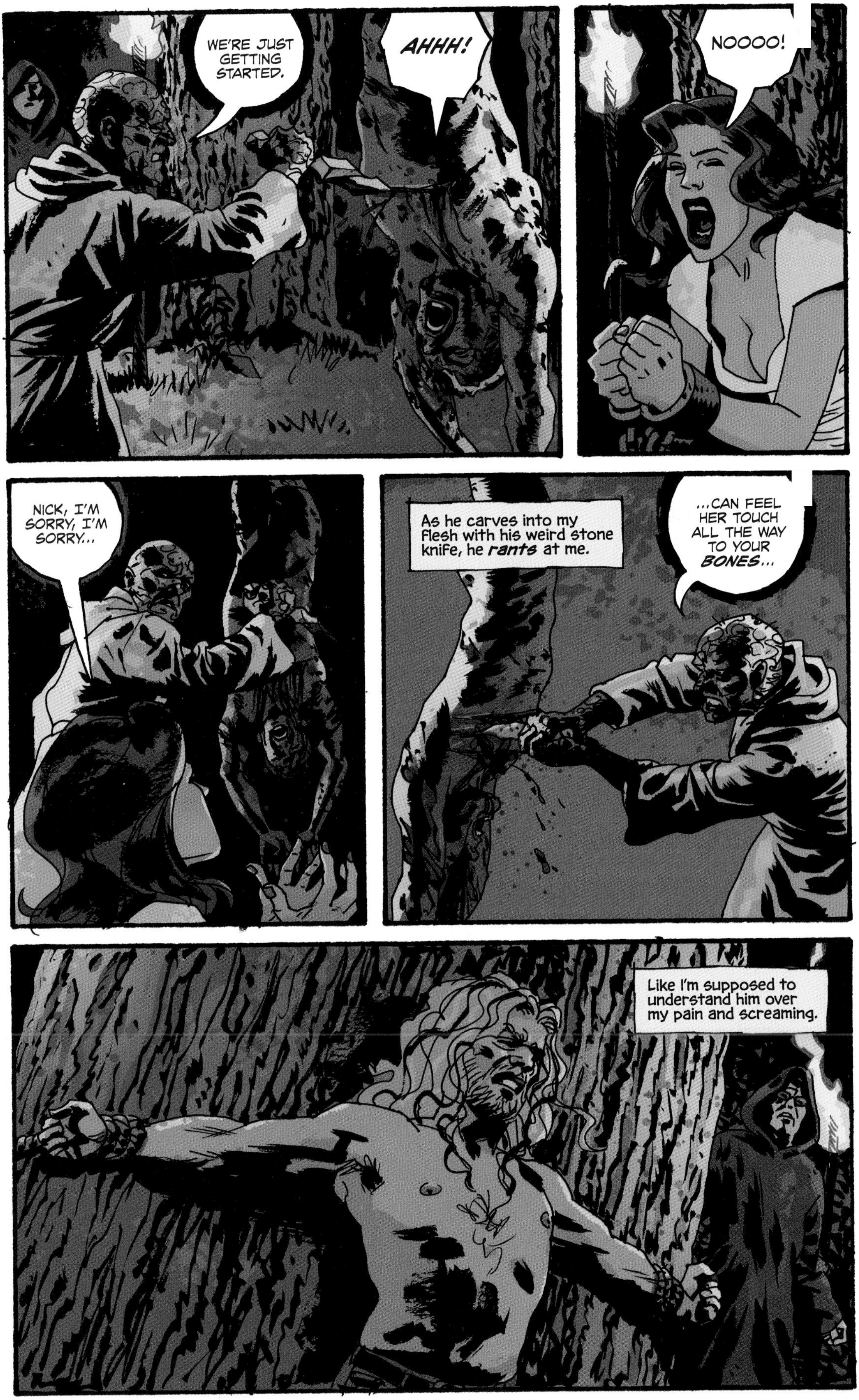
WE'RE JUST GETTING STARTED.
AHHH!
NOOOO!
NICK, I'M SORRY, I'M SORRY...
As he carves into my flesh with his weird stone knife, he rants at me.
...CAN FEEL HER TOUCH ALL THE WAY TO YOUR BONES...
Like I'm supposed to understand him over my pain and screaming.

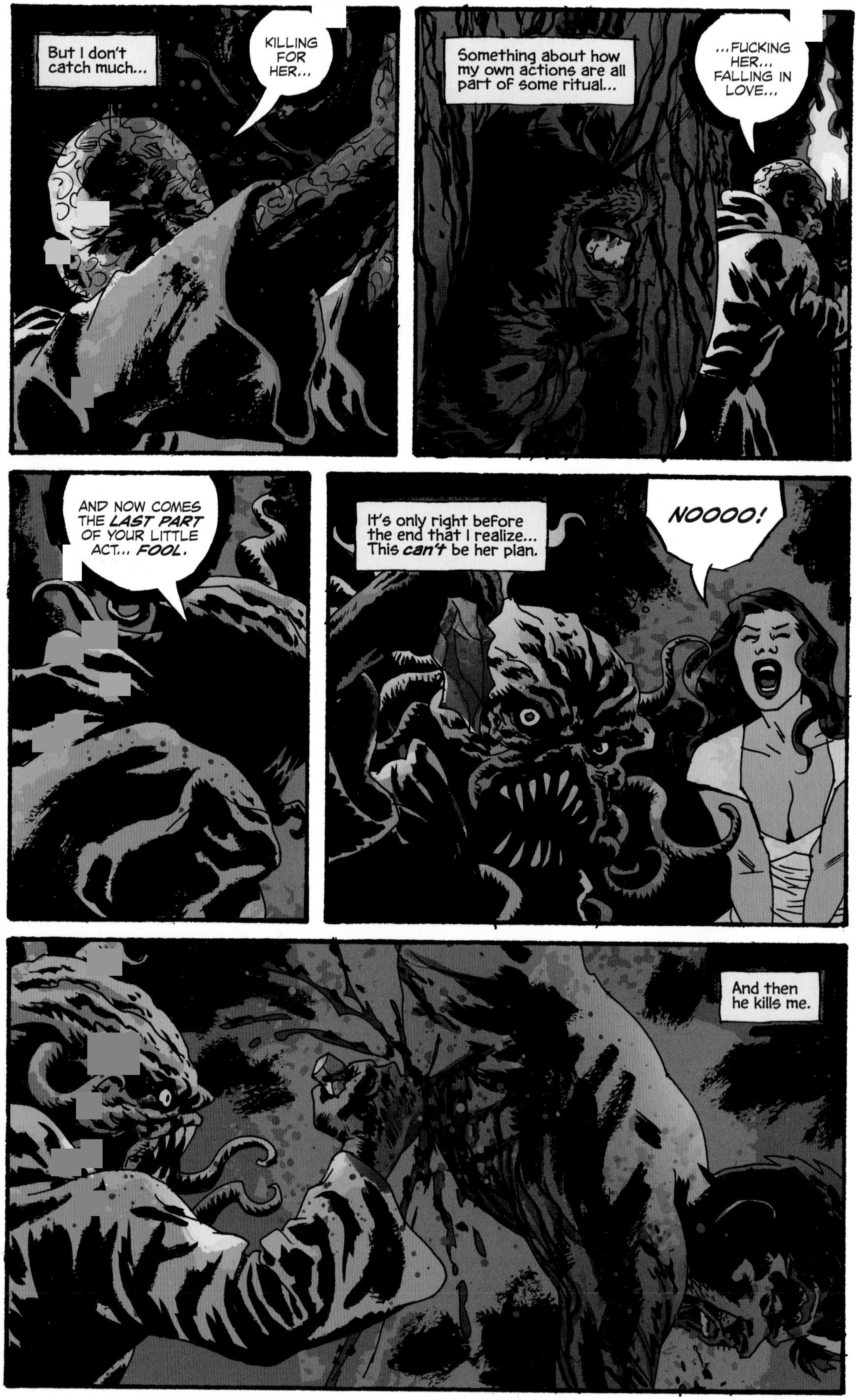
But I don't catch much...
KILLING FOR HER...
Something about how my own actions are all part of some ritual...
...FUCKING HER... FALLING IN LOVE...
AND NOW COMES THE LAST PART OF YOUR LITTLE ACT... FOOL.
It's only right before the end that I realize... This can't be her plan.
NOOOO!
And then he kills me.

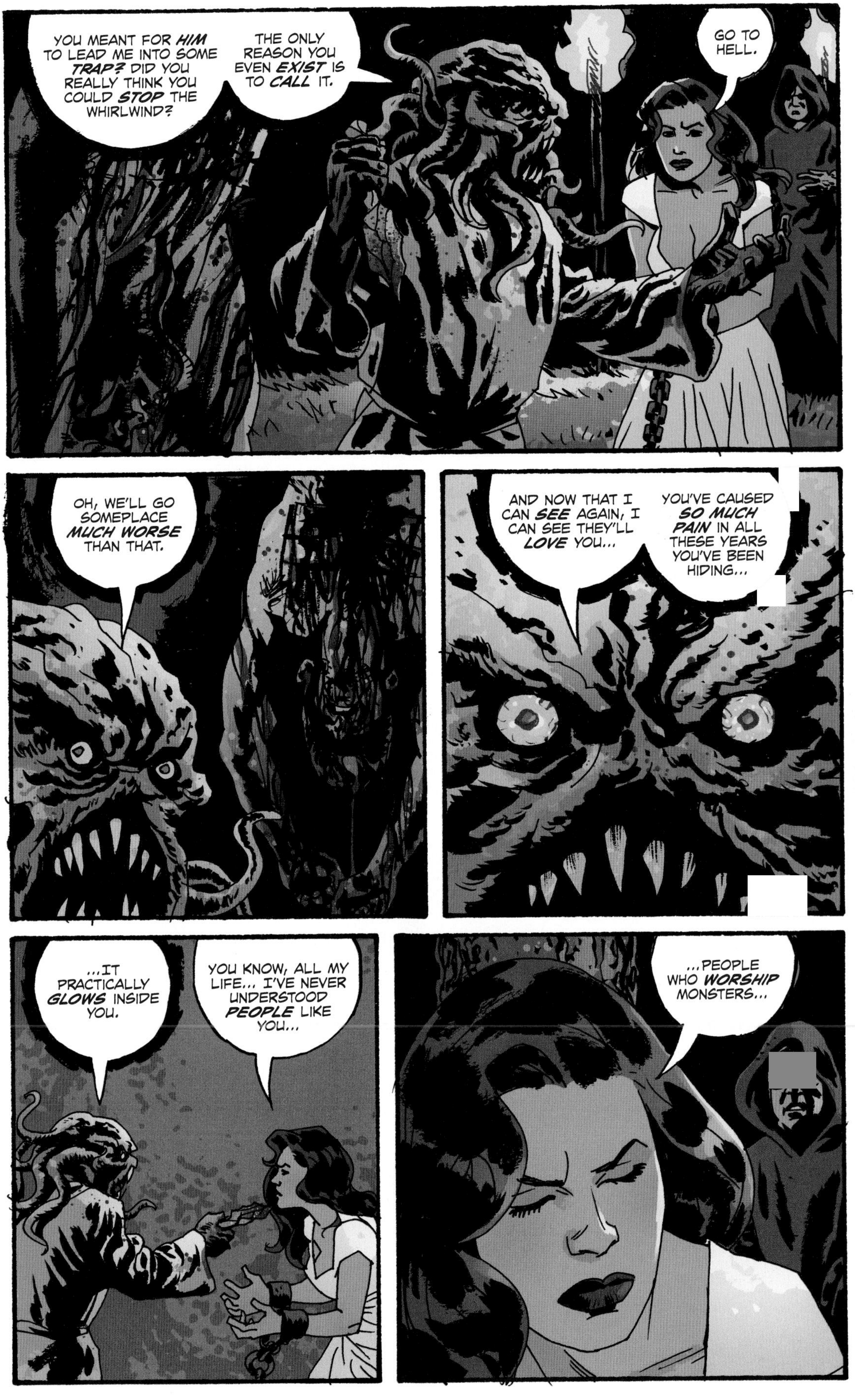
YOU MEANT FOR HIM TO LEAD ME INTO SOME TRAP? DID YOU REALLY THINK YOU COULD STOP THE WHIRLWIND?
THE ONLY REASON YOU EVEN EXIST IS TO CALL IT.
GO TO HELL.
OH, WE'LL GO SOMEPLACE MUCH WORSE THAN THAT.
AND NOW THAT I CAN SEE AGAIN, I CAN SEE THEY'LL LOVE YOU...
YOU'VE CAUSED SO MUCH PAIN IN ALL THESE YEARS YOU'VE BEEN HIDING...
...IT PRACTICALLY GLOWS INSIDE YOU.
YOU KNOW, ALL MY LIFE... I'VE NEVER UNDERSTOOD PEOPLE LIKE YOU...
...PEOPLE WHO WORSHIP MONSTERS...

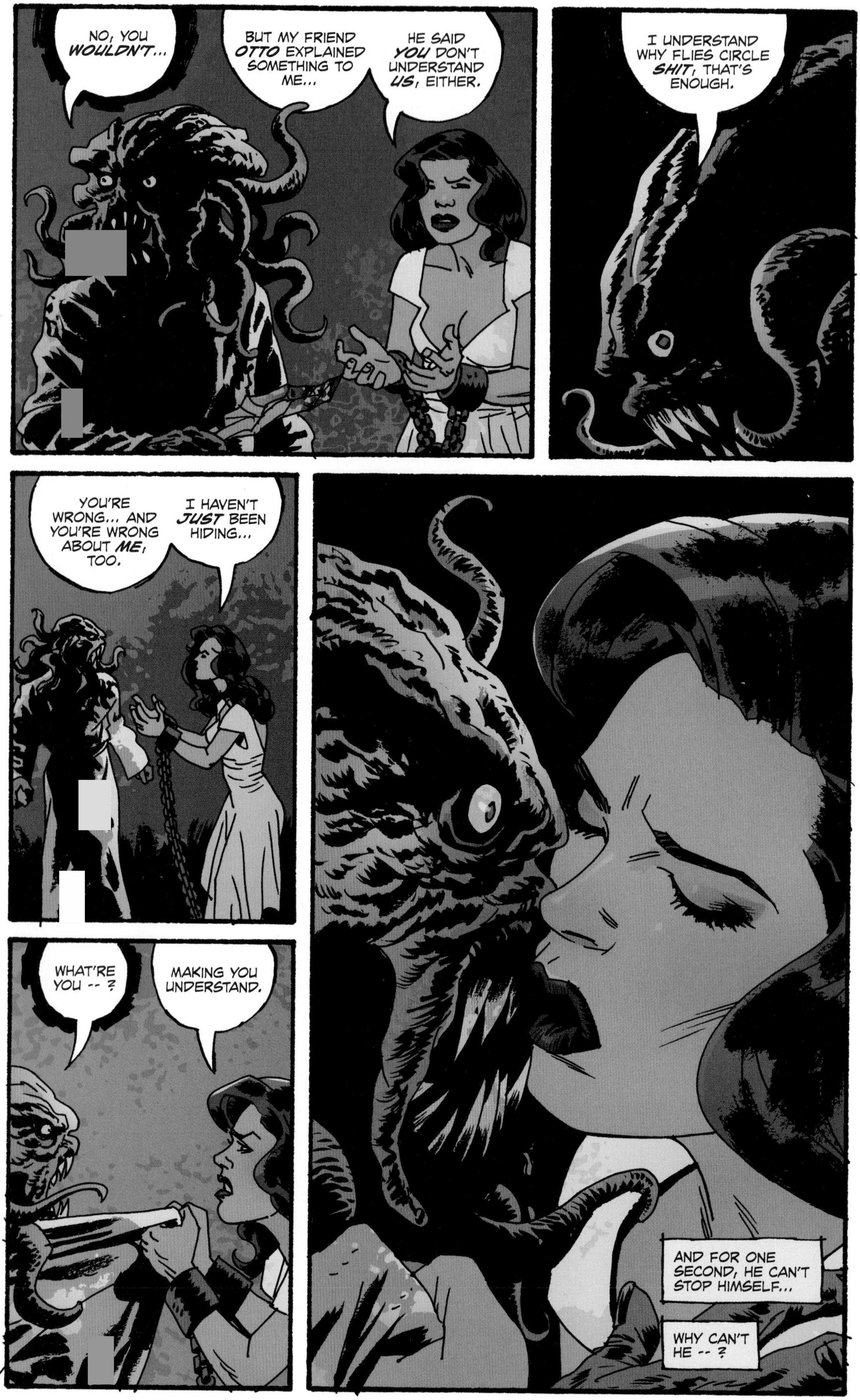
NO, YOU WOULDN'T...
BUT MY FRIEND OTTO EXPLAINED SOMETHING TO ME...
HE SAID YOU DON'T UNDERSTAND US, EITHER.
I UNDERSTAND WHY FLIES CIRCLE SHIT, THAT'S ENOUGH.
YOU'RE WRONG... AND YOU'RE WRONG ABOUT ME, TOO.
I HAVEN'T JUST BEEN HIDING...
WHAT'RE YOU -- ?
MAKING YOU UNDERSTAND.
AND FOR ONE SECOND, HE CAN'T STOP HIMSELF...
WHY CAN'T HE -- ?

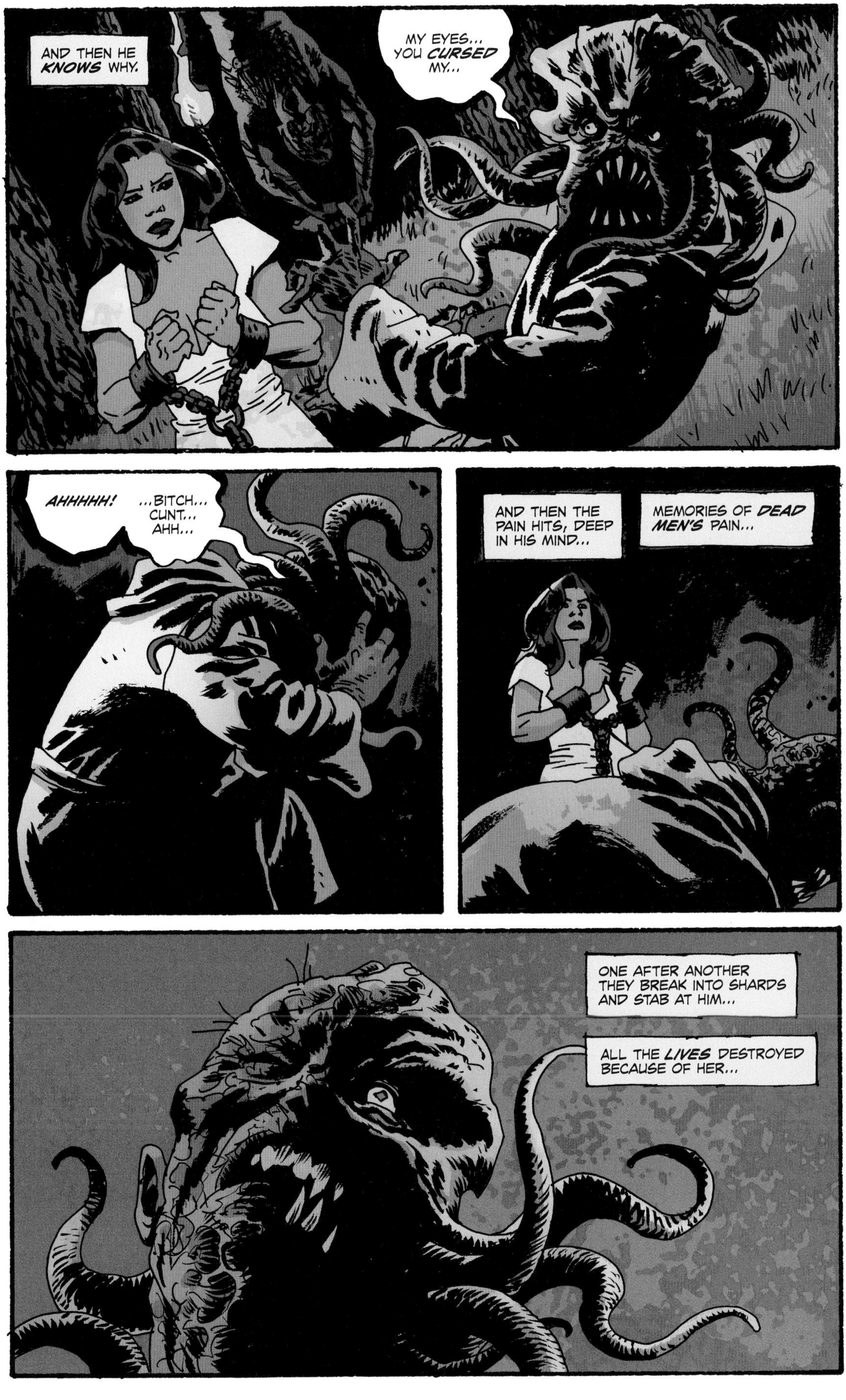
AND THEN HE *KNOWS* WHY.
MY EYES... YOU *CURSED* MY...
AHHHHH!
...BITCH... CUNT... AHH...
AND THEN THE PAIN HITS, DEEP IN HIS MIND...
MEMORIES OF *DEAD MEN'S* PAIN...
ONE AFTER ANOTHER THEY BREAK INTO SHARDS AND STAB AT HIM...
ALL THE *LIVES* DESTROYED BECAUSE OF HER...

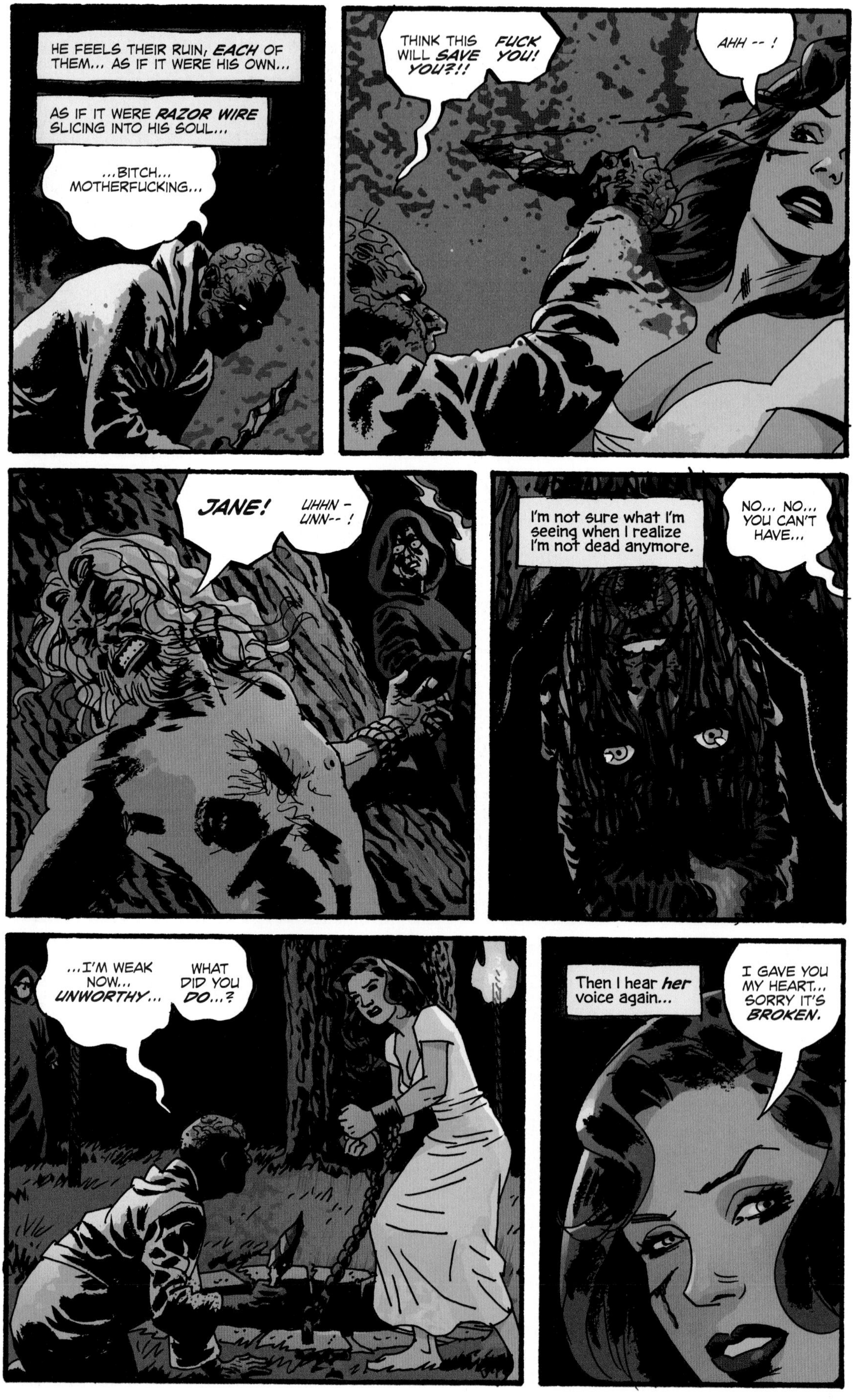
HE FEELS THEIR RUIN, EACH OF THEM... AS IF IT WERE HIS OWN...
AS IF IT WERE RAZOR WIRE SLICING INTO HIS SOUL...
...BITCH... MOTHERFUCKING...
THINK THIS WILL SAVE YOU?!!
FUCK YOU!
AHH -- !
JANE!
UHHN - UNN-- !
I'm not sure what I'm seeing when I realize I'm not dead anymore.
NO... NO... YOU CAN'T HAVE...
...I'M WEAK NOW... UNWORTHY...
WHAT DID YOU DO...?
Then I hear her voice again...
I GAVE YOU MY HEART... SORRY IT'S BROKEN.

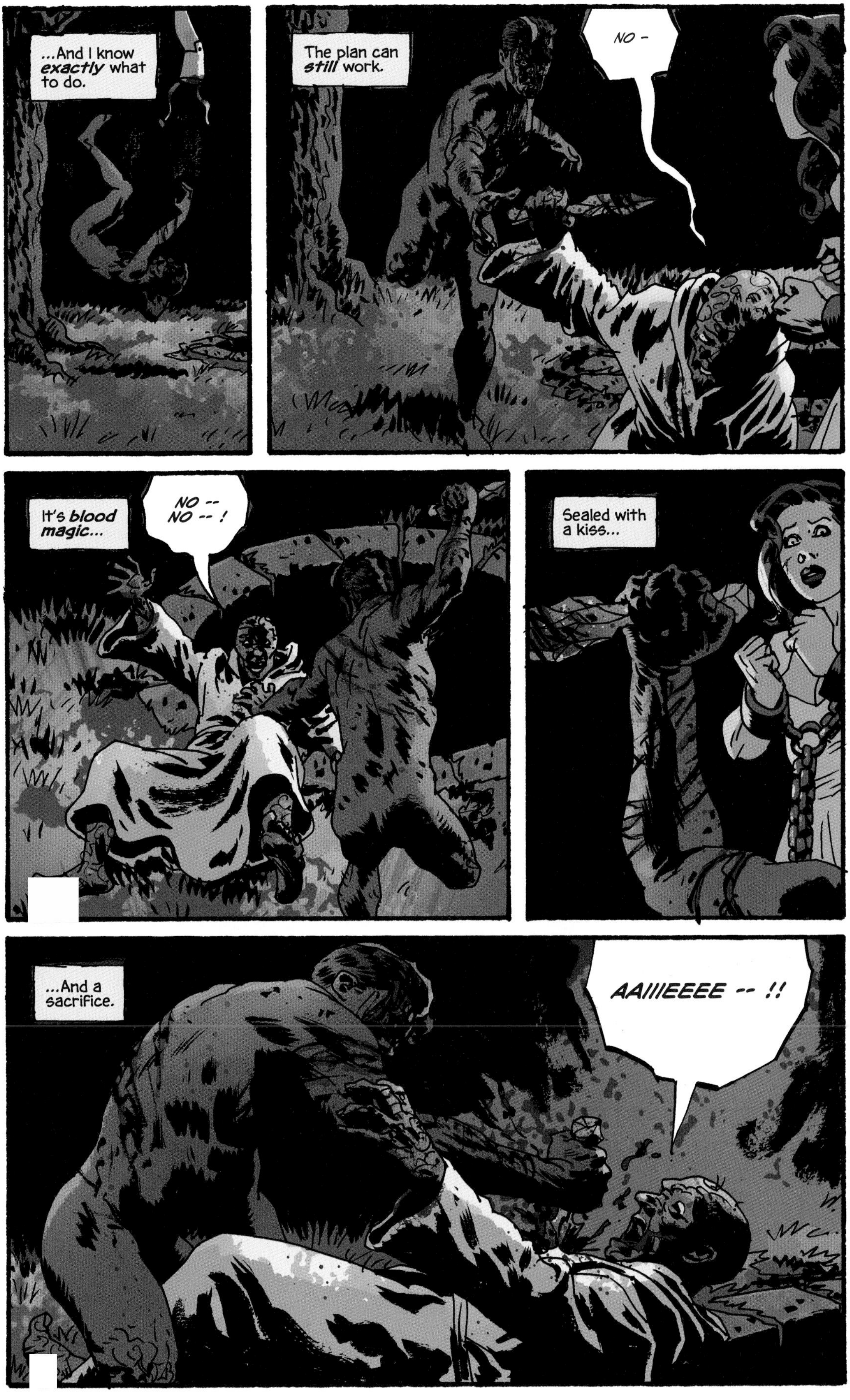

...And I know *exactly* what to do.
The plan can *still* work.
NO -
It's *blood magic*...
NO -- NO -- !
Sealed with a kiss...
...And a sacrifice.
AAIIIEEEE -- !!

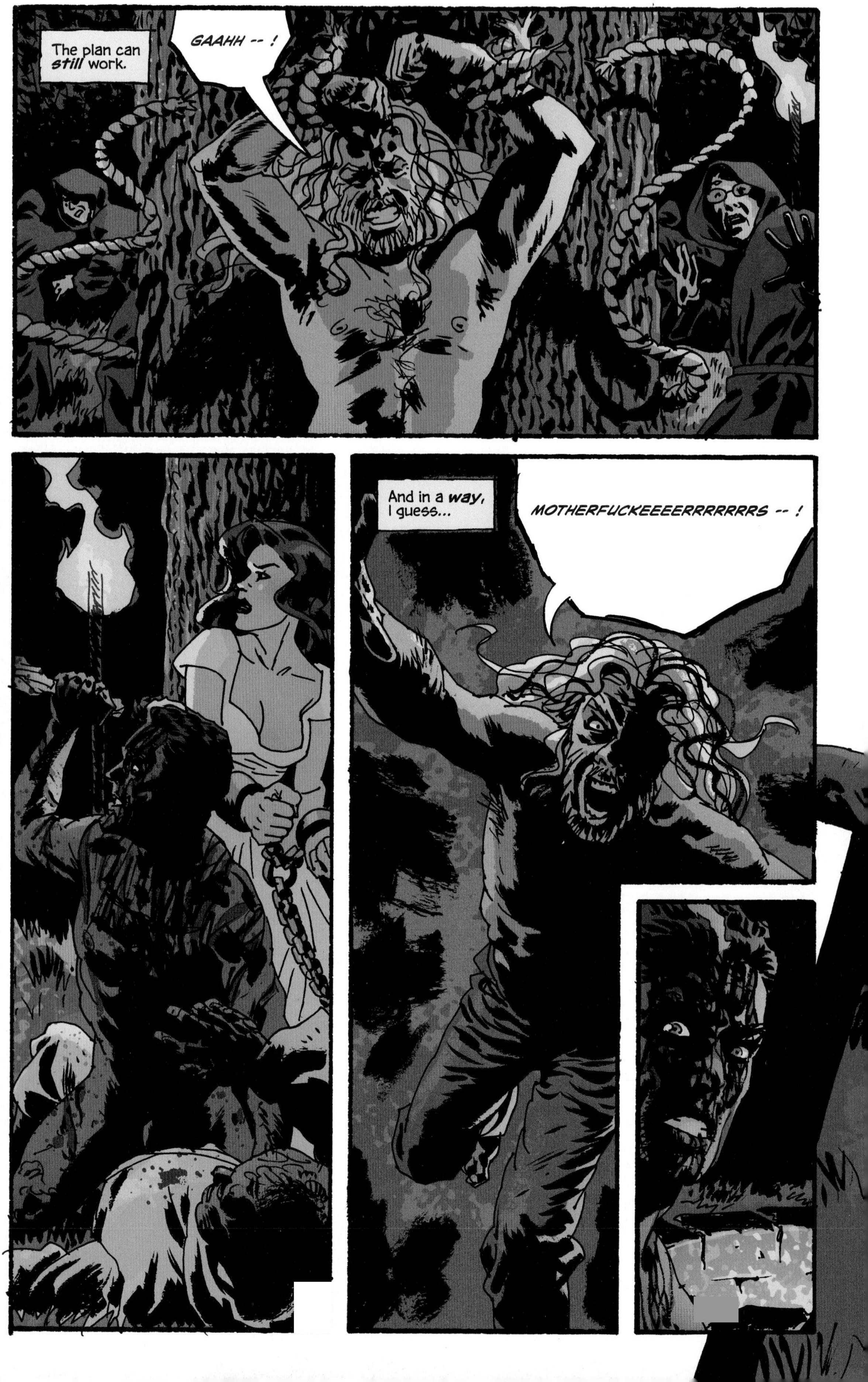

The plan can *still* work.
GAAHH -- !
And in a *way*, I guess...
MOTHERFUCKEEEERRRRRRRS -- !

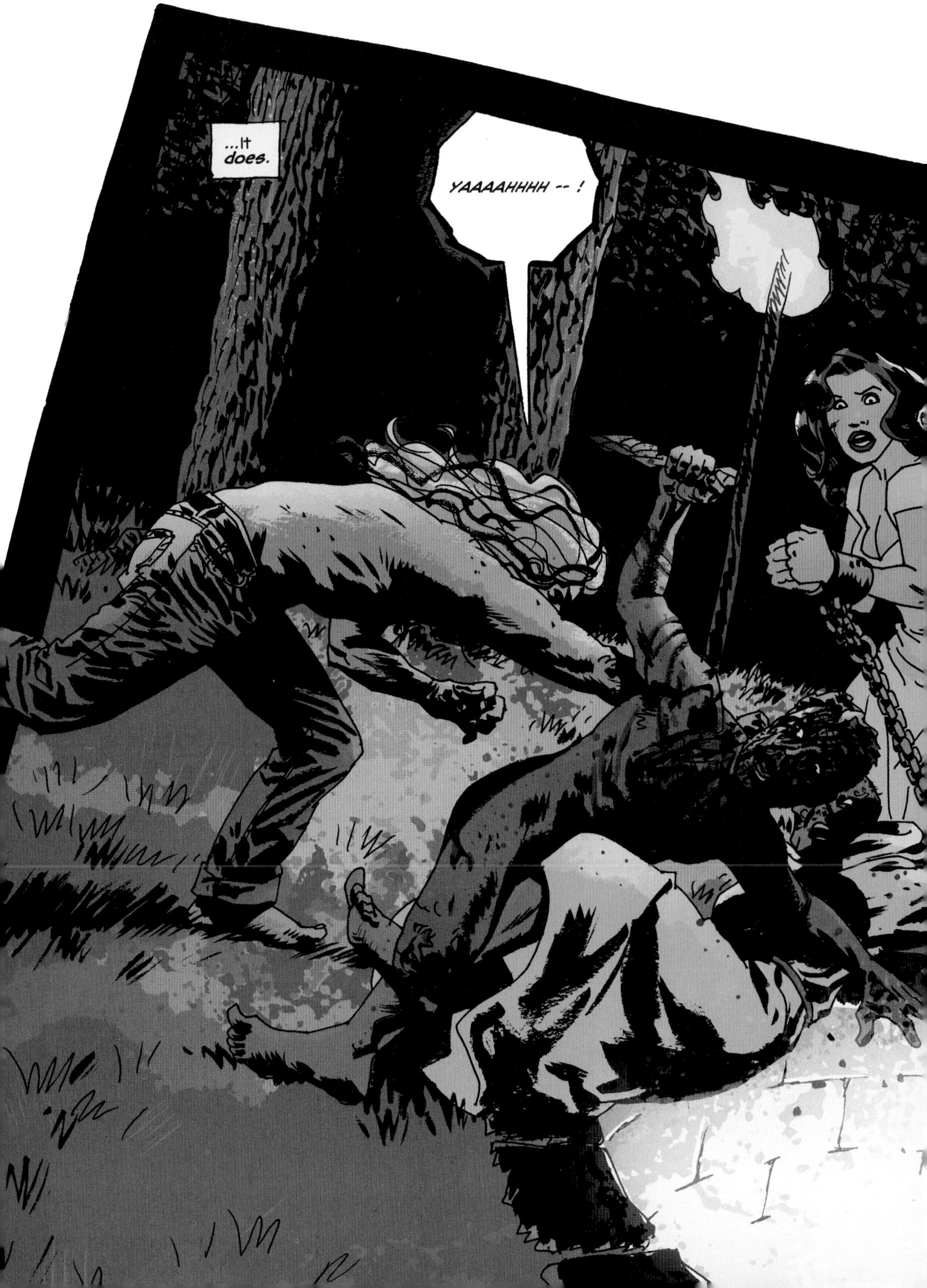
...It does.
YAAAAHHHH -- !

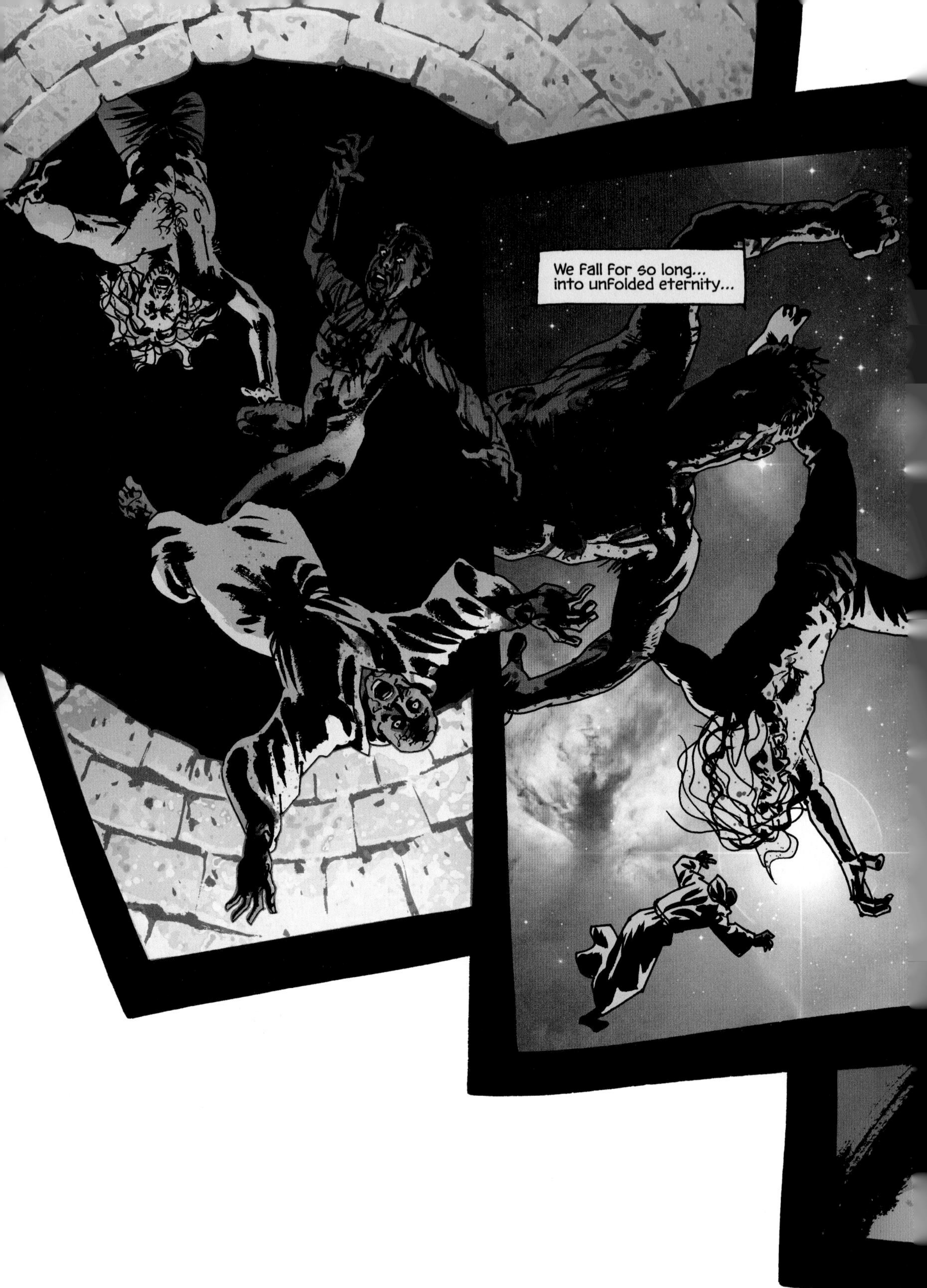
We fall for so long...
into unfolded eternity...

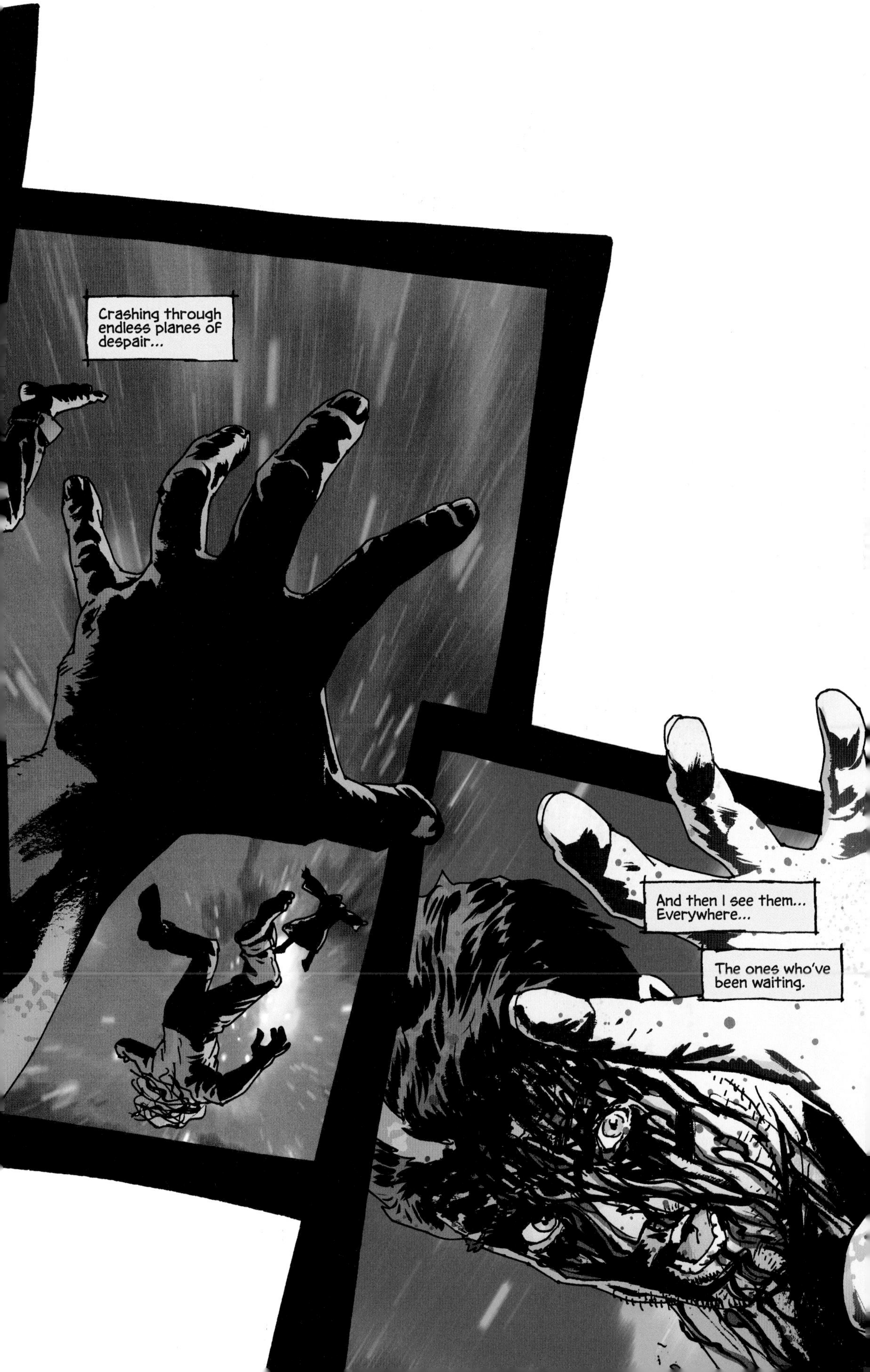
Crashing through endless planes of despair...
And then I see them... Everywhere...
The ones who've been waiting.

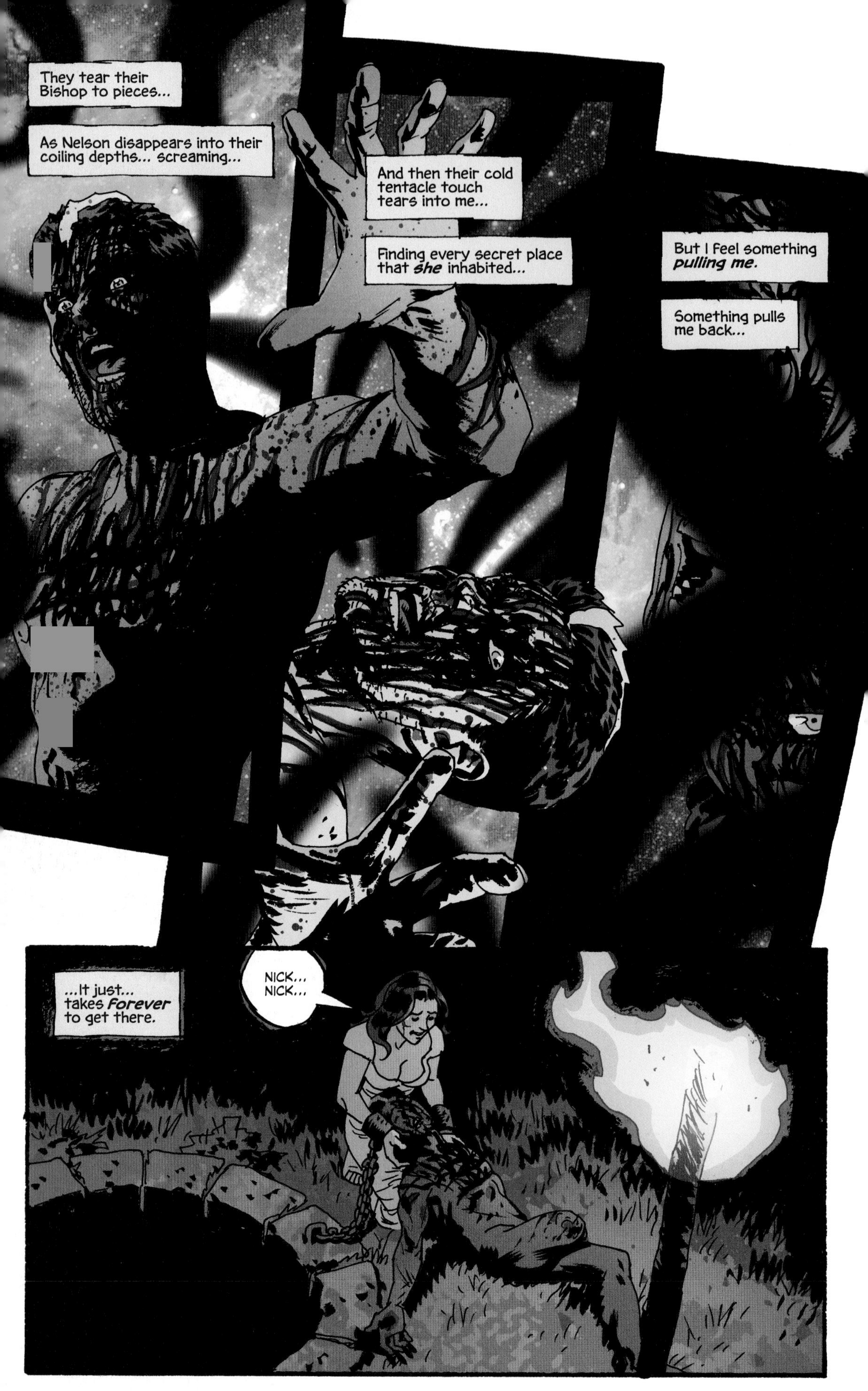
They tear their Bishop to pieces...
As Nelson disappears into their coiling depths... screaming...
And then their cold tentacle touch tears into me...
Finding every secret place that *she* inhabited...
But I feel something *pulling me.*
Something pulls me back...
...It just... takes *forever* to get there.
NICK... NICK...

One Year Later

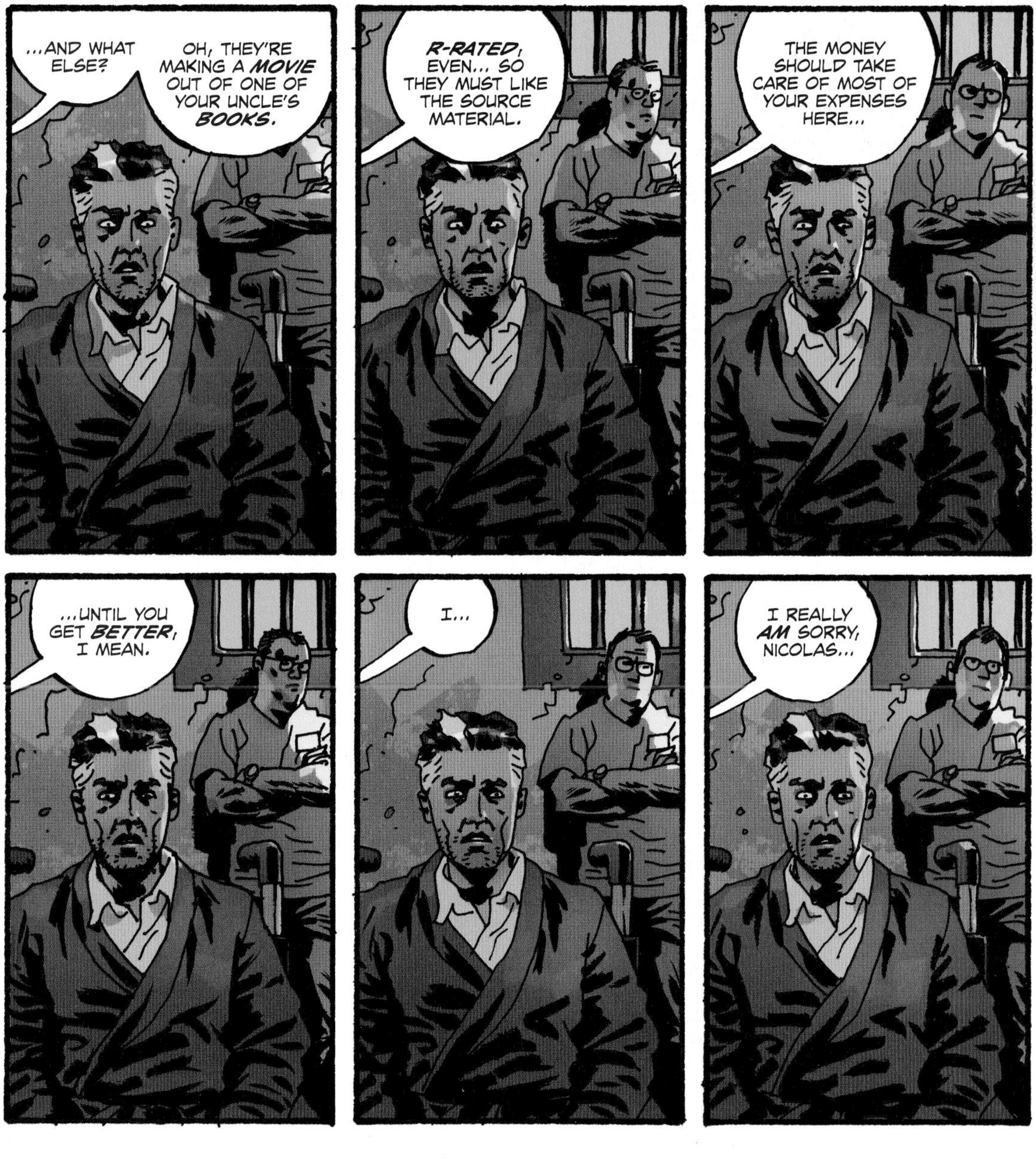
...AND WHAT ELSE?
OH, THEY'RE MAKING A MOVIE OUT OF ONE OF YOUR UNCLE'S BOOKS.
R-RATED, EVEN... SO THEY MUST LIKE THE SOURCE MATERIAL.
THE MONEY SHOULD TAKE CARE OF MOST OF YOUR EXPENSES HERE...
...UNTIL YOU GET BETTER, I MEAN.
I...
I REALLY AM SORRY, NICOLAS...

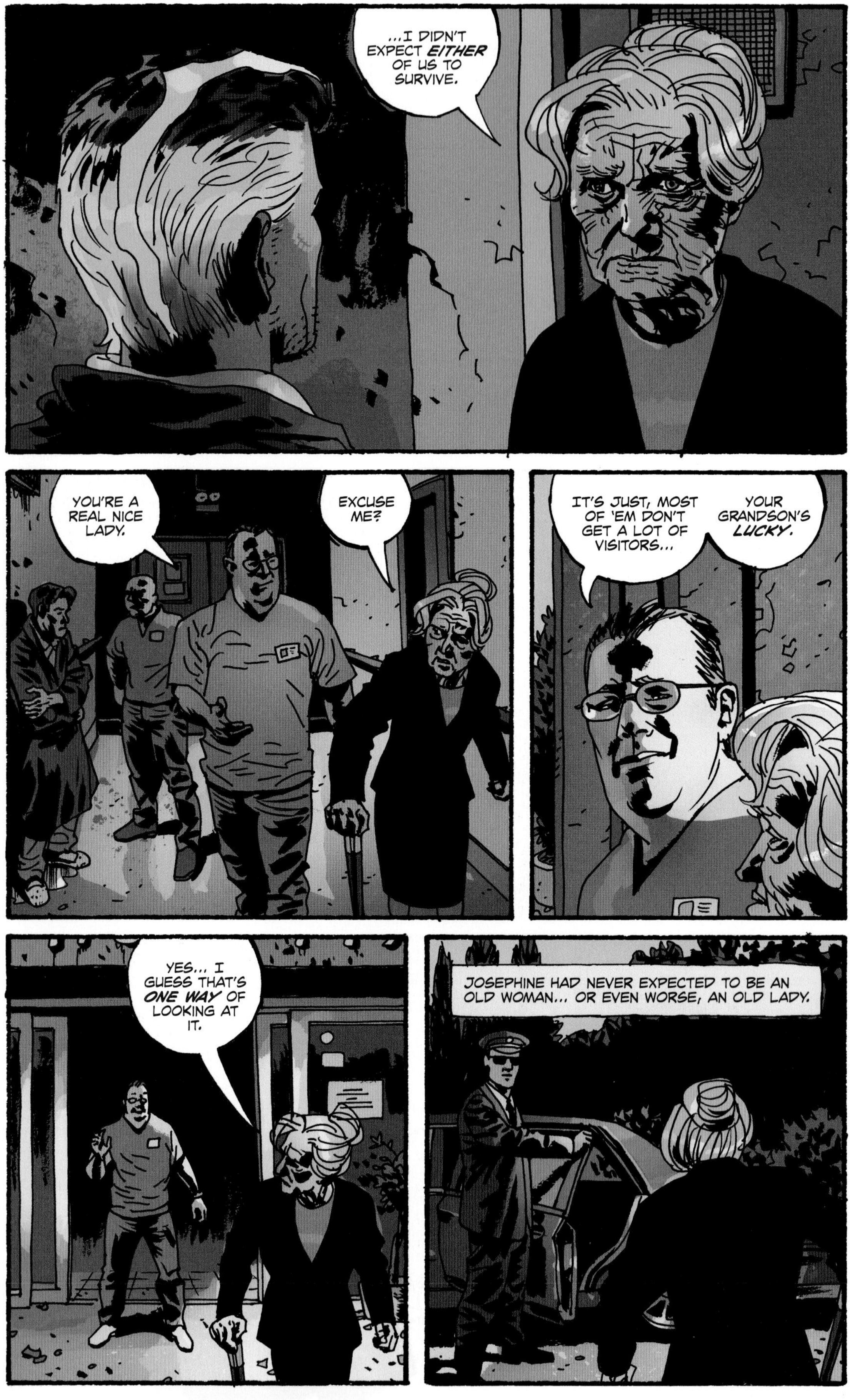
...I DIDN'T EXPECT *EITHER* OF US TO SURVIVE.
YOU'RE A REAL NICE LADY.
EXCUSE ME?
IT'S JUST, MOST OF 'EM DON'T GET A LOT OF VISITORS...
YOUR GRANDSON'S *LUCKY.*
YES... I GUESS THAT'S *ONE WAY* OF LOOKING AT IT.
JOSEPHINE HAD NEVER EXPECTED TO BE AN OLD WOMAN... OR EVEN WORSE, AN OLD LADY.

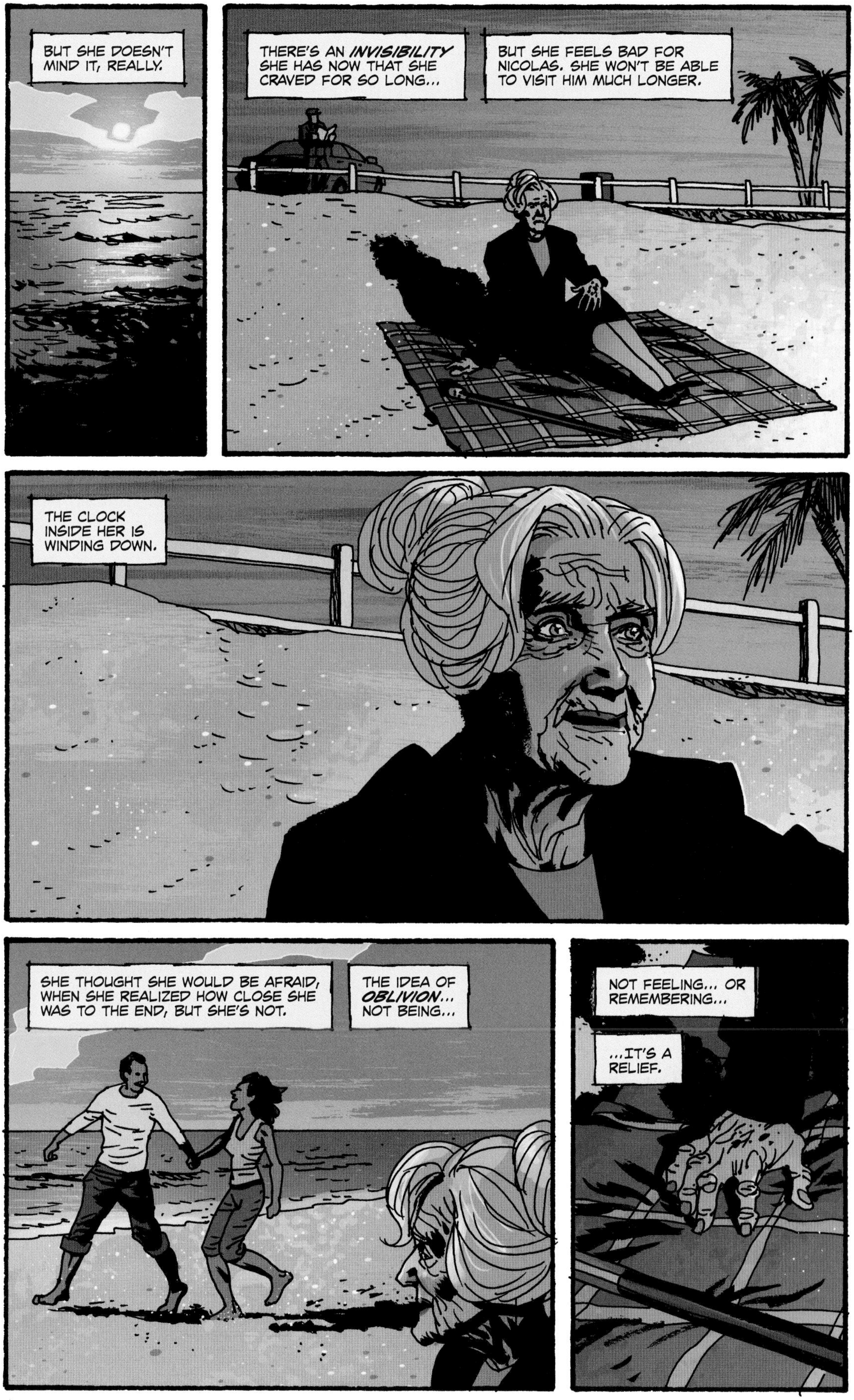
BUT SHE DOESN'T MIND IT, REALLY.
THERE'S AN *INVISIBILITY* SHE HAS NOW THAT SHE CRAVED FOR SO LONG...
BUT SHE FEELS BAD FOR NICOLAS. SHE WON'T BE ABLE TO VISIT HIM MUCH LONGER.
THE CLOCK INSIDE HER IS WINDING DOWN.
SHE THOUGHT SHE WOULD BE AFRAID, WHEN SHE REALIZED HOW CLOSE SHE WAS TO THE END, BUT SHE'S NOT.
THE IDEA OF *OBLIVION*... NOT BEING...
NOT FEELING... OR REMEMBERING...
...IT'S A RELIEF.

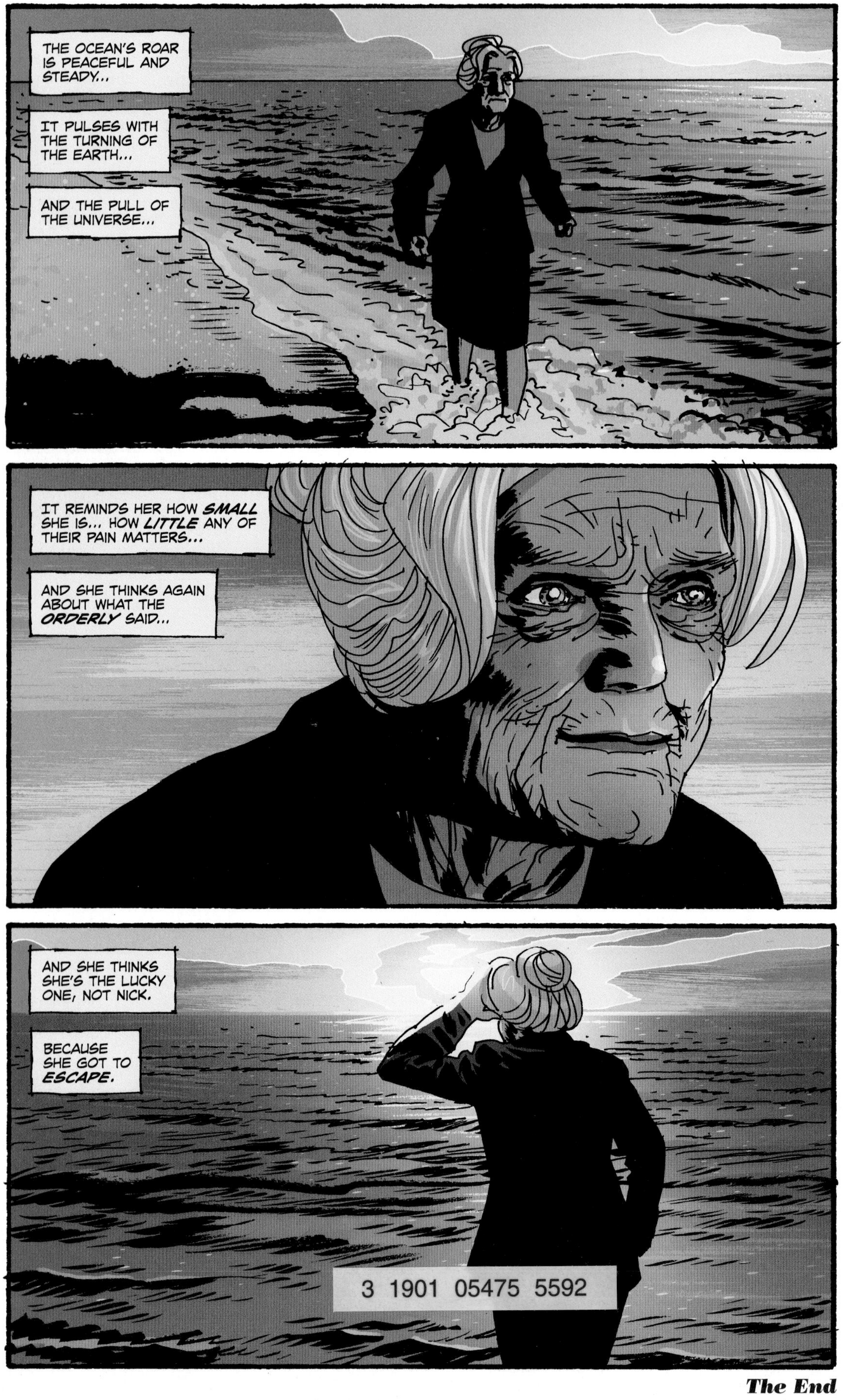
THE OCEAN'S ROAR IS PEACEFUL AND STEADY...
IT PULSES WITH THE TURNING OF THE EARTH...
AND THE PULL OF THE UNIVERSE...
IT REMINDS HER HOW *SMALL* SHE IS... HOW *LITTLE* ANY OF THEIR PAIN MATTERS...
AND SHE THINKS AGAIN ABOUT WHAT THE *ORDERLY* SAID...
AND SHE THINKS SHE'S THE LUCKY ONE, NOT NICK.
BECAUSE SHE GOT TO *ESCAPE.*

The End